High Hopes for

Vicki Beeby writes historical fiction about the friendships and loves of service women brought together by the Second World War.

Her first job was as a civil engineer on a sewage treatment project, so things could only improve from there. Since then, she has worked as a maths teacher and education consultant before turning freelance to give herself more time to write.

In her free time, when she can drag herself away from reading, she enjoys walking and travelling to far-off places by train. She lives in Shropshire in a house that doesn't contain nearly enough bookshelves.

Also by Vicki Beeby

The Women's Auxiliary Air Force

The Ops Room Girls
Christmas with the Ops Room Girls
Victory for the Ops Room Girls

The Wrens

A New Start for the Wrens
A Wrens' Wartime Christmas
Hopeful Hearts for the Wrens

Bomber Command Girls

The Girls of Bomber Command
A Wedding for the Bomber Girls
Christmas for the Bomber Girls
High Hopes for the Bomber Girls

VICKI BEEBY

High Hopes
for the
Bomber Girls

CANELO

First published in the United Kingdom in 2025 by

Canelo, an imprint of
Canelo Digital Publishing Limited,
20 Vauxhall Bridge Road,
London SW1V 2SA
United Kingdom

A Penguin Random House Company
The authorised representative in the EEA is Dorling Kindersley Verlag GmbH. Arnulfstr. 124,
80636 Munich, Germany

A CIP catalogue record for this book is available from the British Library.

Print ISBN 978 1 80436 915 9
Ebook ISBN 978 1 80436 917 3

Cover design by Becky Glibbery

Cover images © Alamy, Arcangel, Shutterstock

Printed and bound in Great Britain by Clays Ltd, Elcograf S.p.A.

Look for more great books at
www.canelo.co | www.dk.com

For my family:

Mum

Duncan, Jana & Emma

Chris, Katka & Elena

Chapter One

January 1945

The registrar beamed at the couple standing before him. 'It gives me great pleasure to declare you husband and wife.'

Jenny Hazleton heard a sniffle. Glancing at her friend Pearl, she saw her dabbing at her eyes with an already damp handkerchief. Jenny's chair creaked as she leaned across to hand her a fresh one, but Pearl's husband, Greg, got there first.

'I suppose it's not every day your grandmother marries your long-lost grandfather,' he observed, enfolding his wife's hand with his own.

Jenny's wistful smile broadened as she looked back at Deedee and Thomas, now Mr and Mrs Haughton. Thomas, a sprightly septuagenarian, beamed at his wife, his face glowing almost as much as Deedee's freshly hennaed hair. The couple's obvious joy at finally being united after years apart brought tears to Jenny's eyes.

Beside her, Pearl gave a hiccupping sob.

'Don't mind me,' she muttered. 'My emotions are all over the place at the moment.' She tugged Greg's hand to lie on her still-flat stomach.

Jenny's friend Thea, occupying the seat on the other side of her, laughed and clapped when the couple kissed. Jenny tried to catch her eye, but Thea turned to her boyfriend, smart in his RAF uniform, and whispered something in his ear. Then she leaned across Jenny to speak to her sister. 'Can't you leave your husband alone for five minutes, Pearl? Come on – they're signing the register.'

It was hard not to feel lonely, surrounded by happy couples. Although Jenny was delighted for them all, she couldn't help comparing her empty life with theirs. Pearl had not only met and married Greg, a pilot in the Royal Australian Air Force, in the time she had been in Lincolnshire, but she had also discovered that the wealthy man who had supported her ambitions in journalism was actually her grandfather. Thea, Pearl's younger sister, was very much in love with Fitz, the bomb aimer who had served on Greg's crew when they been at RAF Fenthorpe. Although they weren't officially engaged, Jenny had no doubt the pair would be married before long. As she watched the sisters sign the marriage register as witnesses, she wondered if they would still have time for her in their lives.

–

Once the formalities were over, Deedee and Thomas invited the girls back to the Gatehouse for a small celebration meal. 'Just the family,' Deedee said, with a squeeze of her new husband's arm.

'I suppose I should be getting back to the Waafery,' Jenny said, feeling awkward.

Deedee immediately pulled her to her side, weaving her free hand through Jenny's arm. 'Nonsense. You're family too.'

There was such warmth in Deedee's tone that Jenny didn't doubt she meant it, and she allowed the other woman to lead her out of the register office, feeling a little better.

A short bus ride later – Deedee and Thomas had wanted to keep the wedding simple – and the small party arrived at Fenthorpe Hall, Thomas's ancestral home. This had been requisitioned by the RAF and was now occupied by the officers of RAF Fenthorpe and their wives. However, Thomas had been able to move into the Gatehouse at the end of the long drive, and this was where the newlyweds would start their married life. As the group trooped up the steps to the Gatehouse's front door, Mrs Stockwell, Thomas's housekeeper, hurried inside straight away, removing her hat as she did so, saying she needed to put the meal in the oven.

Deedee made to follow her, but Thomas caught her hand and pulled her to his side. 'You're the bride,' he said. 'I'm supposed to carry you over the threshold.'

Deedee raised her eyebrows. 'I'd like to see you try. I'm hardly—' She broke off with a squeak as Thomas hoisted her into his arms and carried her into the hall without a stagger. It was Deedee who seemed to be breathless when he lowered her to the floor. 'You've been eating your spinach.'

'Nonsense. You're as light as a butterfly, and as colourful as one, too. I was too busy trying not to fluff my lines to say so before, but you look beautiful in that dress.'

'That dress' was a gorgeous creation Deedee had brought back from her home in Shrewsbury, a flowing drapery of silk that was printed in vivid blocks of teal, royal blue and orange. It would have looked ridiculous on any other woman yet on Deedee it was perfect.

The group gathered in the living room.

'I still can't believe you're going to be living here, Deedee,' Thea said, squeezing herself into an armchair next to Fitz. 'Just think of all the extra free time I'll get now I don't have to write to you. All we need now is for Fitz and Greg to get posted back to RAF Fenthorpe and I'll never have the bother of writing again.'

Jenny noticed Fitz exchange glances with Greg. Thea evidently did too, for she sat up and looked from one to the other. 'What is it? Have you got your posting yet?'

Greg shook his head. 'Not yet, but we've got a crew together and Fitz and I were the only ones with a preference for a posting, so we requested RAF Fenthorpe.'

This was evidently not news to Pearl, for she showed no surprise. 'I'm keeping my fingers crossed. Imagine – we might actually be able to live together at last!' She grinned at Thomas and Deedee. 'How would you feel about having us just at the top of the drive?' Despite her smile, Jenny thought she looked a little strained. This was hardly surprising. Pearl had already seen Greg through one tour flying bombers, and must now be mentally preparing herself to endure another thirty missions.

'Anyone else on the crew from *C-Charlie*?' Thea asked.

'Just Edwin,' Greg answered. Jenny felt a tremor run through her body. She gripped the arm of her chair and concentrated on keeping her expression impassive as Greg continued. 'After what happened in the Netherlands, he was as eager as me to return to operational flying.' He was referring to their crash-landing behind enemy lines before Christmas. The two friends had been missing for weeks, and, although Jenny didn't know what they had endured, she knew from their emaciated state when they had turned up at the Christmas dance that they hadn't had an easy time.

Jenny didn't know how she felt about seeing Edwin again, assuming they were posted to Fenthorpe. On the one hand she missed the friendship they had shared, but on the other she couldn't forget the humiliation of his rejection when she had tried to kiss him at the dance. Only a month had passed since then and they'd had no contact. She couldn't help but worry she had not only lost him as a potential sweetheart but had also ruined their friendship.

Greg was still speaking. 'I'm happy with the new crew, though. Everyone's already completed one tour, so it's an experienced bunch.'

He went on to list names unknown to Jenny, but she found she didn't want to hear any more. She sprang to her feet, muttering something about going to help Mrs Stockwell in the kitchen. She needed space to work out how she felt about the possibility of Edwin returning to Fenthorpe.

She was just returning from the kitchen, carrying a tray loaded with plates and Mr Haughton's finest silver cutlery, when she met Thea in the hall.

'I'll help,' Thea said, relieving her of the bone china plates. She followed Jenny back into the living room, to the dining table, which had already been draped with a crisp linen cloth and decorated with sprigs of holly and other evergreens.

'It would be wonderful to have Fitz back in Fenthorpe,' Thea said as she arranged the soup spoons.

'Yes, it would.'

Apparently her attempt at feigning enthusiasm failed miserably, for Thea gave Jenny a searching look. 'You know, in all the excitement of getting Greg and Edwin safely home and then Deedee's wedding, I never asked about your plan to manoeuvre Edwin under the mistletoe. What happened?'

'Well, it was all rather chaotic, what with Greg and Edwin appearing out of the blue and then Deedee announcing her engagement…' Jenny allowed her words to tail off, hoping to convey that she had never got the chance to speak to Edwin rather than having to tell an outright lie.

But Thea was not to be put off. She frowned. 'Now I come to think about it, you've been acting strange every time Edwin gets mentioned. Something happened. What was it?'

'Didn't Pearl tell you?'

Thea shook her head. 'You know Pearl, she wouldn't breathe a word of anything that she had been told in confidence.'

Jenny sighed and glanced across the room. Seeing the others still gathered around the fire, deep in conversation and clearly not paying any attention to her or Thea, she made up her mind. Pearl had seen what had happened with Edwin, but Jenny had done her best to appear unconcerned, not wanting to spoil her friend's joy at Greg's safe return. Now, however, after a whole month of keeping her heartache to herself, she could use a friend to confide in. 'It was awful,' she said. 'I felt such a fool. After the dance, I wanted to pretend nothing had happened.'

Thea's gaze sharpened. 'Why? What did he do?'

Jenny felt her cheeks burn with remembered humiliation as she explained. 'I did what I said I was going to do. I led him under the mistletoe and I kissed him.' Recalling the moment when she had thought he would return the kiss, only for him to gently disengage himself, she blinked away tears. 'I would never have done it if I didn't think he felt the same way, but he stopped me.'

'I don't believe it. Are you sure you didn't misunderstand?'

Thea's reaction only made it harder for Jenny to carry on. 'Positive. He was very kind but said he was sorry and couldn't do it.'

Indignation flared in Thea's eyes. 'He must be mad! You only have to look at him when he's with you to know he's been desperate to kiss you.'

'That's what I thought.' It was a huge relief to know Jenny hadn't been alone in thinking Edwin had harboured feelings for her. 'I would never have dreamed of kissing him if I hadn't believed he wanted to.'

'What else did he say?'

Jenny shrugged. 'Not much. Just something about still being friends, then Pearl arrived and sent him to the kitchen for food.'

'I don't understand him,' Thea said. 'He's been pining after you for as long as we've known him.'

'That can't be true, or he'd have kissed me back.'

Thea shook her head. 'No. There's something else going on. He's been showing all the signs of being completely besotted with you.'

'Do you really think so?'

'I know so. Listen.' Thea counted off each point on her fingers. 'Whenever we go out as a group, he always sits with you; he was always making up the most feeble of excuses to visit the Met Office whenever you were on duty; and don't forget the way he lights up like a searchlight beam whenever he sees you.'

Jenny couldn't disagree, having observed the same symptoms and reached the same conclusion. 'It doesn't change anything though,' she said, picking up the cutlery and returning to her task. 'He made it clear he didn't feel that way about me, and

now, if he ends up back in Fenthorpe, I'll have the embarrassment of having to see him again. I don't think I could bear
it.'

Thea placed the last of the napkins into a silver ring before
answering. 'You should go on a few dates with other men,' she
said finally. 'Show him you're not eating your heart out over
him. If that doesn't bring him to his senses, nothing will.'

'I don't know.' Jenny couldn't imagine going out with any
man apart from Edwin. 'Edwin was the only man I know who
appreciated my bookishness.'

'That's not true, I know plenty of men who would jump at
the chance of a date with you. I mean, look at you! With your
blonde hair and blue eyes, you'd just have to crook a finger and
half the men on the base would come running. I'd love to have
your colouring.'

Jenny eyed Thea's glossy auburn hair and dark eyebrows with
envy. 'You wouldn't say that if you had pale lashes and you
hadn't been able to get any new mascara for weeks. The way I
look at the moment, most of the men would be running in the
other direction. Not that I care,' she hurriedly added, 'because
I'm not interested in any of them.'

'You look lovely,' Thea told her. 'Anyway, I'm not saying
you've got to marry any of them. Just go out. Have some fun.'

'Maybe. I'll think about it.' Although she said that more to
get Thea off the subject than because she agreed.

Thea gave her a dubious look, but Jenny was saved from any
more attempts at persuasion by Mrs Stockwell, who announced
that the meal was ready. Everyone made a move to the table,
putting an end to their private conversation.

Jenny did her best to conceal her low spirits from the
others as they tucked into Mrs Stockwell's delicious carrot soup,
followed by fisherman's pie. It was, after all, a celebration, and
she was genuinely happy for Deedee and Thomas and didn't
want them to guess her disappointment. By common consent,
no one spoke of the war or Fitz and Greg's plans to return to

operational flying. Instead, they spoke of Deedee and Thomas's plans.

'I'll be moving here,' Deedee explained. 'It was a wrench packing up my cottage – I have so many happy memories of bringing up my girls there. But I can't live in the past, not when the only man I ever wanted is here in Lincolnshire.' She reached across the table and squeezed Thomas's hand. 'Anyway, we don't need the money, so I've been able to rent the cottage out at a peppercorn rent to a poor woman who's recently been widowed. It's good to know I can do some good with the place that I was never comfortable accepting.'

Jenny knew that she was referring to the way Thomas's father had persuaded Deedee to leave Thomas over fifty years ago after he'd intercepted a letter she had written to Thomas, telling him she was pregnant. Deedee, believing Thomas didn't love her, had moved into the cottage that old Mr Haughton had bought for her on the other side of the country, on condition that she never contacted Thomas again. Deedee had always felt guilty for accepting what had amounted to a bribe.

As they were scraping up the last crumbs of a rich fruit cake from their plates, Thomas rose. 'I want to thank you all for joining us on this happiest of days,' he said. 'I know it's usually traditional for the guests to give the bride and groom gifts, but, as you know, we asked you not to get us anything as we already have more than enough. Instead, we'd like to break with tradition and present each of you with a small gift, as a token of our gratitude for your support.'

Jenny was sure she wouldn't be included in this unexpected gift-giving and watched with no expectations of her own as the bride and groom handed gifts to Pearl, Thea, Fitz, Greg and Mrs Stockwell. Each present, although small, had clearly been carefully chosen and was generally something that had been precious to either Deedee or Thomas. Once Greg had opened his gift – a pair of gold and amber cufflinks – Jenny assumed there would be no more presents. However, she was taken aback when Thomas, his eyes twinkling, handed her a heavy parcel wrapped in newspaper. 'I know just what you like. You've already been through all the books I have on my shelves, so I made a special trip to Lincoln to find these for you.'

With trembling fingers, Jenny untied the ribbon and eased aside the paper to reveal a stack of books. It was an eclectic choice, with Vera Brittain's *Testament of Youth* at the top of the pile, followed by a book about Gertrude Bell's travels through Syria. There was also a Georgette Heyer novel and another by Agatha Christie, and Jenny itched to dive into them right away. It was with the greatest reluctance that she put them down. Only then did she remember to thank Thomas and Deedee properly.

Thomas chuckled. 'I knew you'd appreciate them, and we took a lot of care to choose books we thought you'd enjoy.'

'Oh, I will.' Jenny's gaze strayed to her precious books before she tore it away to smile at the happy couple.

Thea nudged her. 'There you go – Thomas likes your book-ishness,' she said in an undertone. 'And there will be plenty of young men at RAF Fenthorpe who feel the same way. Now, are you going to promise to get out more, or do I have to confiscate your books until you do?'

'You wouldn't!'

'Try me.'

Thea reached for the books, and Jenny's hand shot out to cover them. Although she knew Thea wouldn't really carry out her threat, she could see the concern in her eyes and knew she genuinely wanted to help. It was this, more than the ultimatum, that made up Jenny's mind. 'Fine. I'll make an effort to go out more.'

'And you won't turn down a date just because it's not with Edwin?' Thea seemed to be considering something. 'In fact, I can't leave it to you. Either you get yourself a date by the end of next week or I'll find a bloke for you. There's a very nice lad in the Instrument Repair Section who fancies you.'

Jenny knew Thea too well to doubt she would do it. 'I'll find someone myself, thank you very much.' She preferred the quiet, studious type and didn't think Thea would know any men who fitted that description. Except Edwin, of course, and he was off limits. 'But I need more time. One week isn't long enough. Give me until the end of next month.'

Thea rolled her eyes. 'I'm asking you to find a date, not a husband. You've got until the second week in February and no longer.'

Chapter Two

February arrived, and it was a good thing Jenny hadn't seen much of Thea since the wedding because she had done nothing about finding a date. The only change was the arrival of a howling wind that had the inhabitants of RAF Fenthorpe huddling in their greatcoats whenever they had to step outside. On this particular morning, it seemed to chase Jenny all the way from the outer door of the Watch Office and down the corridor to the far corner where the Meteorological Office was situated. Clutching the clipboard with that hour's readings to her chest, she opened the Met Office door, praying no senior officers would be present, because she could feel a lock of hair had come loose and was not just dangling over her collar but must be coiled on her shoulder.

Thankfully there was no one more senior than Corporal Helen Longford present, and she was inclined to be lenient. The corporal had been a meteorological assistant even longer than Jenny and knew how impossible it was to stick to the uniform regulations when forced to go outside to read the various weather instruments every hour without fail.

'Still breezy, then?' Helen asked, her eyes twinkling.

'Just a bit.' Jenny staggered to the plotting bench in the middle of the room and flung down her clipboard and pencil. She sank onto her stool and hastily repinned her hair, and only when she knew she was presentable did she peel off her greatcoat and hang it on the hooks by the door. Every inch of exposed skin felt as though it had been attacked by sandpaper, and she wasn't looking forward to her next hourly trip. While she wouldn't change her job for the world, on days like this she felt a twinge of envy towards the WAAFs who worked in warm offices all day. 'I can't imagine why they haven't scrubbed operations yet.'

'I think they're hoping it will ease up by the afternoon.'

'I doubt it.' Jenny picked up her pencil and began the task of coding the observations, ready to send through to Group headquarters. In her time at Fenthorpe she had developed a feel for the weather and from what she had seen, this wind was set to continue all day. It was frustrating that, as a mere Met assistant, she wasn't qualified to produce forecasts, although many of the navigators at RAF Fenthorpe had come to respect her judgement and would often seek her out on days they were flying to ask her opinion. Her heart gave a twist at the thought of one navigator in particular who had always taken her seriously.

On the verge of explaining her reasoning to Helen, she glanced at the clock and got a nasty shock. 'Golly, look at the time. I'll have HQ sending rude messages if they don't get these readings soon.'

She dashed to the teleprinter and hammered out the coded readings on the keyboard, praying that the temperamental machine was behaving. The message went through a fraction before the clock's minute hand clicked onto the hour, and she returned to her seat, breathing a sigh of relief.

'Don't relax yet,' Helen told her. 'The last of the weather reports came through from HQ just before you came in. They need plotting.'

Jenny didn't mind. Plotting synoptic charts was one of her favourite parts of the job, taking the raw data from all the weather stations in the country and marking it up on a chart of the British Isles. Although it was only her task to plot the data, not interpret it, as she worked she could visualise what the Met Officer on duty would do with the chart, joining up all points of equal barometric pressure and marking on lines showing approaching warm or cold fronts. She was endlessly fascinated by the science of meteorology and longed to learn more. A few months ago she had even approached her CO to enquire about the possibility of training, but her CO had put an end to her hopes. 'Not possible, I'm afraid, Hazleton,' she had said. 'There's no requirement for new Met Officers. If you're after a commission, your best bet would be General Duties.' But Jenny hadn't wanted to spend her days inspecting billets and disciplining WAAFs for uniform infringements, so she had opted to forgo promotion. She had comforted herself with the knowledge that advancement would inevitably involve being transferred to a different station, and she had no desire to leave Fenthorpe and be parted from her friends. Besides, she was used to teaching herself from books.

She was still bent over her work when one of the Met Officers, Flying Officer Unwin, arrived. 'Ah, Hazleton. Just the person I was looking for.'

Jenny straightened and put her pens down, taking care not to splash red and black ink on her chart. It was only when she rose to face Unwin that she noticed he was not alone but was accompanied by a young WAAF with a pretty, round face and grey eyes that shone with enthusiasm. Jenny immediately took in the buttons on her jacket, which didn't shine with the lustre of her own or Helen's; a sure sign that this girl hadn't been in uniform long, for it took months of frequent polishing to give brass buttons a really good shine.

Unwin ushered the girl forward. 'This is ACW2 Green, who's arrived to fill the gap left by Verity's departure.' Verity had been a married Met assistant who had left just after Christmas when she had confessed that she wasn't simply putting on weight but was, in fact, expecting a baby in three months. Although women could continue in the WAAF after marriage, pregnancy meant leaving, and so Verity had been discharged and returned to her family. Jenny couldn't help wondering how Pearl, who had recently discovered she was expecting, was faring. However, she didn't have long to wonder about her friend, for Unwin went on, 'Hazleton, I'd like you to take Green under your wing and show her the ropes.'

'Of course, sir, I'd be happy to.' A glance at the clock showed her that it was nearly time to take the next hourly readings. She addressed Green, who had removed her cap and hung it with her greatcoat on the pegs. 'You're going to need those. We'll start with the readings.'

Green perched her cap back on her head, and Jenny noted that she had dark brown hair rolled over a ribbon or band fastened around her hairline. It was a style adopted by many WAAFs, including herself, although the newcomer somehow managed to wear it like a film star. When she put on her greatcoat, it swamped her petite figure.

As they strolled down the corridor, Jenny said, 'You can call me Jenny, by the way. What's your first name?'

'Lily,' the girl replied. 'I'm so happy to be here. This is my first posting.'

This confirmed Jenny's suspicions, and her heart sank. Fenthorpe was a busy station, and they had now lost an experienced Met assistant only to have her replaced by a beginner. Remembering her own first few weeks at Fenthorpe, Jenny knew Lily would need a lot of support.

Still, it wasn't as if she had anything better to do with her time.

The moment they stepped outside, Lily hugged her arms to her chest. 'It's freezing.'

It was only then that Jenny took in the stockinged legs below the hem of Lily's greatcoat. 'I'm not surprised, in that skirt. Haven't you been issued your battledress yet?' This consisted of trousers and a short jacket that buttoned to the waistband of the trousers and was much more practical wear for those whose duties took them outside. At Lily's mournful shake of the head, Jenny offered to take her to stores, where she would be issued with the items she needed. Then she pointed at the white wooden box with its louvred doors, a short way up a cinder path. 'Here's the Stevenson screen. I suppose you know what to do?'

Lily brightened. 'This is where we read the maximum and minimum temperatures and the wet and dry bulb thermometers.' She described how to use all the instruments installed behind the door, and Jenny relaxed, reassured that Lily seemed to have paid attention to her training at any rate.

She handed her the clipboard. 'Go on, then.'

Jenny watched while Lily correctly read and reset the maximum and minimum thermometers and then checked the muslin cloth round the wet bulb thermometer to ensure it wasn't in danger of drying out. When she finished, Jenny ran her eye over the readings and said, 'Good. Now, what's your estimate for visibility?' She pointed across the airfield. 'If you look in this direction, you'll get the clearest view to the horizon.'

Lily hesitated, although this didn't surprise Jenny. It took experience to estimate distances. 'I'm not sure,' she said after squinting at the view for a few moments.

Jenny took pity on her and pointed out the landmarks she used as reference. 'See the windsock? That's about a thousand yards away. Then that barn you can see across the fields is two miles.'

'So there's no haze, then.'

'Exactly.'

And so the tour continued; next they estimated cloud cover, height and type and then went up to the roof to the anemometer to measure the wind speed. Climbing the steel staircase to the roof was not a pleasant experience in the circumstances but at least it wasn't icy. It was no surprise to Jenny to see that the wind had picked up since the last observation. Finally it was back to the office to read the barometer.

'I was thrilled to be posted to an operational station,' Lily said as they strode back round the building. Her eyes were shining, although that might have been nothing more than the wind making them water. 'It must be so exciting to meet the crews.'

Although Jenny had no wish to squash Lily's enthusiasm, she felt obliged to warn her of the downsides. 'They're a good bunch. It's tough when they don't return, though, so some of the girls are hesitant to get too close.' A pity Jenny hadn't thought of that when she had befriended Edwin. The agony she had suffered when he had gone missing before Christmas still gave her nightmares, and Edwin had been one of the lucky ones.

'Oh, I didn't think of that.' Lily turned horrified eyes on Jenny. 'That must be awful.'

However, Jenny wasn't sure how well the message had sunk in, for when they returned to the office they found two navigators there, asking about the forecast for that night, and Jenny found it hard to hide her amusement at Lily's starstruck expression.

Later, when they headed out to take the next hourly observations, she asked, 'Well, what do you think of RAF Fenthorpe so far?'

'I'm going to love it here.' There wasn't a shred of doubt in Lily's voice. 'I can't wait to go out and make friends. I overheard someone talking about the local pub – the Piebald Pony?' Her face screwed up. 'I don't think I heard that right. Doesn't sound like a pub name.'

Jenny laughed. 'Oh, it is. It's actually the White Horse, but the sign is so old, the paint's peeling and it's turned the poor old white horse piebald. I'm going there this evening, actually, to meet some friends. You can come along if you like.'

Lily agreed with enthusiasm, and Jenny hoped Pearl and Thea wouldn't mind.

Once the readings were all taken, Jenny told her, 'This time you can code them ready for the teleprinter.' She glanced at her watch. 'You'll have to hurry. You've only got ten minutes.'

She strode to the Watch Office, only to bump into a tall, lanky officer outside the door. 'Sorry, sir,' she gasped, making a hasty salute. Only then did she look at the man's face and take in the warm brown eyes and the light brown hair that she knew he could never get to lie flat. It was Edwin.

Heat flooded her cheeks, and she knew her face must be scarlet. 'Edwin!' she gasped. 'What are you doing here?'

'I've just been posted.'

'Here?'

'Yes, didn't you know?'

Jenny shook her head, not trusting herself to speak.

Edwin, too, was looking flustered. Probably trying to think of the best way of making his escape, considering the way she had flung herself at him the last time they had met. He rubbed his nose. 'I was sure Thea or Pearl would have told you. I'm back on Greg's crew. Fitz too.'

'I knew you were on the same crew but I didn't know for sure where you were going. Are you really back in Fenthorpe?' Jenny hardly knew what she was saying. It was obviously the case. Edwin would hardly be here if he'd been posted to a different station. Still, the reminder that he must have come for the latest forecast helped her gather her scattered thoughts, and she hastened to say, 'Anyway, you must be here for the latest weather. I'll leave you to speak to the duty officer.'

They trooped into the Met Office just in time to hear the duty officer announce, 'All ops are scrubbed.'

Jenny looked at Edwin. 'I suppose that lets you off for tonight.'

He shook his head. 'Oh, I've only just arrived. We weren't slated to fly tonight. I came to see you.'

Jenny didn't know what to say. Did that mean he did like her after all? Lost as she was in fantasies of him explaining away his rejection as a terrible mistake and declaring his undying love, it took her a moment to realise Lily was speaking.

'There's a group of us going to the pub later,' she was saying. 'You should come.' She stuck out her hand, and Edwin shook it. 'I'm Lily, by the way.'

'I suppose I could.' He looked at Jenny. 'If you don't mind me tagging along.'

The bubble of hope that had briefly expanded in Jenny's chest burst. If he wanted to see her that badly, he would sound more keen. Now she could kick herself for not taking Thea's advice and lining up a date so she could airily give that to Edwin as an excuse. The trouble was, if she didn't go, Lily certainly would. Nightmare scenarios flitted through her mind – of Lily turning up for duty tomorrow, full of her date with Edwin, of the pair becoming a serious item, of Lily blushingly announcing their engagement. 'I don't mind at all,' she blurted. 'I'm looking forward to it.'

Edwin left the Met Office feeling dazed. What had just happened? After all his good intentions, how was it that the first place he had visited upon his arrival had been the Met Office? He had promised himself he would stay away from Jenny, yet after only the briefest visit he seemed to have asked her to the pub. It was a good thing the other girl had taken it as a general invitation and invited herself along as well.

He should never have agreed to join Greg's crew again. It was inevitable that he and Fitz would request a posting at Fenthorpe. The trouble was, he knew and trusted both Greg and Fitz and couldn't think of anyone he would rather serve with. And trust between crew members was vital if you were to have a hope of surviving your tour.

Are you sure you only joined to serve with your friends again? Or was it because you knew it would bring you back in contact with Jenny? Fitz shook his head as though he could dislodge the intrusive thought.

However, his thoughts crowded in, clamouring for his attention, as he went to find the rest of his crew. Why had Jenny agreed to meet him? The last time he had seen her was on Christmas Day, when she had done her best to avoid him after the embarrassment of her kiss. Although at the time she had attempted to laugh away his rejection, saying it would have been bad luck to ignore the mistletoe, he knew her well enough to know she had been hurt and confused.

He hadn't been confused at all. He knew exactly what he wanted, and it had been to return the kiss and give vent to all his pent-up feelings. But it would have been wrong, and so he had gone against his instincts and disentangled himself. At the time, although the rest of his leave had been awkward, he had consoled himself with the knowledge that he would soon be returning to the operational training unit at Market Harborough and that after that he would stay away. He had thought friendship with her would be enough, but it clearly wasn't, so it was best if they didn't see one another again. Yet now he was back in Fenthorpe, he could no more stay away from Jenny than a compass needle could avoid magnetic north.

He had to clear the air between them if there was any chance of salvaging their friendship, and to do that he would have to tell her why they could never be together.

Chapter Three

The rest of Edwin's day was taken up with the usual admin that always surrounded a move to a new base, although he and the rest of his crew had managed a brief training flight in their new Lancaster, *J-Jackson*, during a lull in the weather. As it was getting late by the time he had finished, he headed straight for the White Horse.

His gaze fell on Jenny the moment he entered the snug, and his heart gave a little jolt. With her fair hair shining in the lamplight and her eyes sparkling with laughter at something Lily had just said, she was easily the most beautiful woman in the room. He had to remind himself all over again of the reasons why they couldn't be together.

Only when he tore his gaze from Jenny did he notice that Greg, Pearl, Fitz and Thea were also present. Greg, it seemed, had wasted no time in telephoning Pearl to let her know he had arrived and now they were sat in the corner, arms wrapped round each other, deep in conversation.

Thea was also thoroughly engrossed in Fitz's company, yet for some reason, when Lily waved him to the seat they had saved Thea directed a scowl at Jenny. She recovered herself enough to give Edwin a warm smile, though. 'Good to see you again, Edwin,' she said. 'I've been assigned to *J-Jackson*, so I'm the one you need to see if you have any problems with the navigation instruments. I didn't realise you were coming tonight, though.' This last was said with another glare at Jenny. 'When Jenny told me she'd arranged to meet someone here, I thought she meant someone else.'

Although she was still looking at Edwin, he had the feeling that her words were mainly directed at Jenny; she appeared displeased with her friend for some reason that he couldn't quite fathom. He seemed to have missed a chunk of conversation and it made him uncomfortable. Seeing that everyone else already had drinks, he muttered something about going to the bar and dashed off.

The discussion was still ongoing when he returned, for as he placed his pint on the table he was just in time to hear Thea hiss, 'This wasn't what I meant.' Then she noticed him, gave a little start and moved to make room for him, meaning she was placed between him and Jenny.

On the way here he had rehearsed what he would say when he got a chance to speak to Jenny alone, but now, at this crowded table, he couldn't see how he was ever going to manage it. He let the conversation wash over him while he looked around the snug, searching for other familiar faces. There were other aircrew present, although no one he recognised. That was hardly surprising considering it was nearly two years since he had last been here. He was appalled at how young many of them looked. Had he ever looked that fresh-faced? Probably. He knew his face had lines that hadn't been there at the start of his first tour, and, after the events following his crash landing in December, he felt he had changed beyond recognition.

It was thoughts of Jenny, of returning and being able to discuss whatever obscure subject she happened to be studying, that had helped him through the ordeal, and now he feared he had lost her friendship too. If there was any way he could salvage it, he knew he had to take it. Friends were too precious to lose, and Jenny was the best of them. If there was any way of getting her alone, he had to try.

Lily, sitting on his other side, was clearly bored with the conversation, which had moved on to discussing the where-abouts of Greg's former crew, the ones who had not wanted to join the new crew or had been unavailable.

'What about Jack?' Thea was asking. 'Last I heard he'd left hospital, but I lost touch with him after that. I hope he's still well.'

'More than well,' Fitz said with a grin. 'He's back on duty now.'

'Not flying ops?' Thea asked, looking worried. Edwin could understand her anxiety. Although he didn't know the full story, the stress of being a tail gunner had resulted in him being hospitalised for some months. He hoped Jack hadn't been forced to complete his tour.

Fitz shook his head. 'No, the medical staff made it clear he shouldn't do that. He's working in the armoury section at RAF Snaith now, and is very happy. But the best news is, he got married last month.'

During the exclamations of delight, Lily gave an obvious yawn.

'I'm sorry,' Edwin said to her. 'We've been very rude, discussing people you don't know.'

Lily shook her head. 'Don't mind me. It's only natural you'd want to speak about old times on your first day back.' She pushed her chair back from the table.

Jenny glanced across the table at her. 'Are you going? I'll come with you. You shouldn't walk back alone. Not in the dark.'

But Lily pointed at a group of WAAFs across the room who were busy chatting to a group of young men, all wearing brevets marking them as aircrew. 'Those girls are in my hut. I'm going to join them. Don't wait for me – I'll walk back with them.'

She dashed across the room, leaving nothing but a lingering scent of her rather cloying perfume, and was soon sitting between two young gunners looking very pleased with herself.

Thea pulled a face. 'I feel rotten now. We should have made her more welcome.'

Jenny chuckled. 'Don't feel too bad. She made it quite clear that her main aim in life was to chat up the lads and have fun. I think she'll be happier over there than she was with us.'

Greg glanced at his watch. 'We ought to be making tracks, anyway. If we're flying ops tomorrow, I want us all to be fresh.'

'I'll walk as far as Fenthorpe Hall with you,' Pearl said. 'I can catch the bus from there just as easily as from here.' For she was currently billeted in Lincoln, having been seconded to work full time on the newspaper she had set up during her time at RAF Fenthorpe.

'I'll walk you two back to the Waafery,' Fitz told Thea and Jenny. He glanced at Edwin. 'What about you?'

'Why not? I could do with the walk.' And it would give him a chance to speak with Jenny.

Sure enough, once they had parted company with Greg and Pearl Thea and Fitz soon dawdled and dropped back, evidently wanting to make the most of their time together, and were quickly swallowed up in the darkness.

The moment he knew they were out of earshot, he drew a deep breath. 'I'm sorry,' he said, only to have his words echoed by Jenny, speaking at the same time.

He stared at her in surprise, wishing he could make out her features, but he could see nothing but her silhouette, outlined against the starry sky. 'You've done nothing to be sorry for,' he said.

'You know that's not true.' Her voice was low and slightly husky, as though she had to force out each word. 'I... embarrassed you. At the dance.'

'No, you didn't.'

'Don't pretend. I made a complete fool of myself, because I thought...' Even with his ears muffled from the freezing air under his scarf, he heard her heartfelt sigh. 'It doesn't matter what I thought,' she said finally.

Edwin couldn't bear to hear her so despondent. 'It *does* matter what you think. I care about you a great deal and I feel awful for hurting you. You have nothing to apologise for, unlike me, who is entirely at fault.' He could sense rather than see her paying him avid attention. Maybe it was the slight catch

23

of her breath, but he knew she was drinking in every word, straining her ears not to miss a thing. He braced himself to say the words that he knew would destroy her hope. 'The thing is,' he continued, 'I enjoyed your company so much, I forgot myself, forgot what I owed to others. I haven't been entirely honest with you, you see.'

'What do you mean?' She spoke in the same tense, strained voice.

The kindest thing was to say it with no attempt to cushion the blow. 'I'm engaged to another woman. Have been since before I first came to Fenthorpe.'

Jenny's first reaction was shocked laughter. *How absurd!* 'Are you having me on?' She knew it couldn't be true because he'd never mentioned a fiancée in all the time she'd known him. But when there was no laugh in response, a cold fist closed round her heart.

She could just make out his form in the dim light, and saw him remove his cap and run a hand through his hair. 'No. It's true. I'm sorry.'

'But… I don't understand.' She was fighting back the tears now, willing herself not to crumble. But she needed to know how she could have persuaded herself to believe this man had been in love with her when he had been in love with another all along. And it wasn't just her. Thea had thought the same. She clung to that thought as she listened to his reply.

'I'm not trying to excuse myself,' he said. 'But I want you to know that I truly valued your friendship at a time when I was feeling very alone and frightened. I told myself that we were just friends and I was doing nothing to betray Mina.'

'Mina. Is she your fiancée?' Jenny hated herself for the flare of jealousy that seared her gut.

Edwin nodded.

'And you've been engaged to her the entire time we've known each other?'

'Yes.'

So far her emotions had ranged from confusion to hurt, but now anger crept into the mix. She was glad now that she couldn't see his face because the darkness bestowed a confidential air upon the conversation, making it easier to tell him exactly what was in her heart. 'Why did you never tell me? We were friends. You can't deny that, at least.'

'I never told anyone at Fenthorpe. You're the first to know.'

'Lucky me.' Mired as she was in a deep bitterness of spirit, the words burst out before she could stop herself.

'I know I was wrong. I wish I could explain but I can hardly explain it to myself.'

A pause followed in which there was no sound but the crunch of their footsteps on the gritty road. They had left the village behind now, and the hedgerows rose up on either side in impenetrable blackness, their jagged outlines visible against the midnight blue of the night sky. Jenny was forced to concentrate on the dim circle of light cast by her torch to ensure she didn't trip over an unseen obstacle. The dull ache in her chest that had been ever present since what she had come to describe as the 'mistletoe incident' flared to a sharper pain, stealing her breath.

'I think you should try to explain yourself. I might have been mistaken about any deeper feelings I thought you held for me, but you can't deny we were friends. Why would you hide something so important from me?'

'That's twice you've said we *were* friends. Has that changed?'

She wanted so badly to assure him that of course she was still his friend, but her deep sense of betrayal checked the impulse. 'I think that depends on you. If you can be honest with me now, then maybe we can salvage something. I need to know why you wouldn't tell a friend that you've been engaged for the whole time you've known us. As well as disrespecting me, it's an insult to your fiancée.'

'I know. All I can tell you is that I got engaged a few months before I came to Fenthorpe for the first time, when I was with my first crew.'

'You had a crew before you flew with Greg and Fitz?' It hadn't occurred to her before, but she should have remembered that Greg's former crew had been put together from survivors of other crews. She had only become friendly with Edwin a month or two after he had become Greg's navigator, and had never thought to ask about his earlier career in the RAF. When you were friends with someone who could be lost in action the next day, you tended to focus on the present.

In the pause that followed, the sound of Thea's laughter drifted through the night air, and the reminder that she alone of her friends was unloved brought tears to Jenny's eyes. She dashed them away with the back of her hand and forced herself to focus on Edwin's reply.

'They were all killed over Hamburg but I wasn't flying ops that night because I'd stupidly sprained my wrist a couple of days earlier, falling off my bike. I remember that I'd nearly walked to the pub that night and only decided to cycle at the last minute.' He gave a humourless chuckle. 'For weeks afterwards I started to second-guess every decision, wondering if this was the one that would result in me getting killed, until I thought I'd go mad. Gradually I learned to live in the moment, not let myself think of anything but the present. My old crew were the only ones that had known of my engagement, and I didn't mention Mina to anyone else, but not because I was hiding her existence.' He sighed, and they walked a few paces in silence. Even though she could hardly see him, Jenny could tell he was struggling to find the right words. 'I don't know,' he said finally. 'It's as though my past felt like a dream. Nothing felt real apart from the present moment, and the only way I could survive was to push every other thought from my mind. I'm sorry I misled you. The last thing I ever wanted to do was hurt you.'

There was nothing but sincerity in his voice, and Jenny felt some of her resentment fade, knowing how aircrew had to develop their own way of dealing with the constant threat of death. Yet she wasn't going to let him off that easily. 'But surely you write to your fiancée, and she to you? You must see her when you go on leave.'

'I do write, of course, but somehow I can distance myself from the life I knew with her because she's not here. And although we do meet when we can, she's in the WAAF too, so we don't get together as often as we'd like.'

'She's a WAAF? What does she do?' She had a sudden, horrible thought that this Mina might be transferred to Fenthorpe or a nearby station.

'I'm not sure exactly. She isn't allowed to say. Something mysterious at Bletchley Park. She was whisked off there as soon as she was out of basic training, and it didn't take long for her to be commissioned. Like me, she was at Cambridge – a maths scholar.'

Of course she was. A heavy weight settled in Jenny's chest. No wonder Edwin preferred Mina to her. Jenny had not even sat her School Certificate, let alone attended one of the most prestigious universities in the country. A man like Edwin, who had been working on a doctorate in astronomy, would never be able to love an uneducated girl like her. Mina was a WAAF officer, doing important work at Bletchley Park. How could Jenny compete with that?

She had a choice to make now. She could nurse her wounded heart and decide it was too painful to see Edwin any more, or accept his friendship. Part of her wanted to run away and try to forget him, forget that he could never return her love. But that would mean losing a friendship she treasured as much as her friendship with Pearl and Thea. And Pearl and Thea didn't appreciate her thirst for knowledge in the same way that Edwin did.

'What do you say, Jenny?' It was as though he was reading her mind. 'You've become important to me. I didn't deliberately deceive you – I just pushed my other life out of my mind to help me cope. I'm sorry I hurt you. Can you forgive me? I miss you.'

If Edwin had criticised Mina at all, Jenny would have refused. She had been around men long enough to take the hackneyed, 'my wife/fiancée/girlfriend doesn't understand me' line with a pinch of salt. Even now she would probably be doing herself a favour if she refused him. She knew exactly what Thea would say: *You need to let yourself get over him. Go out and meet other men.* In fact, she caught herself glancing over her shoulder to reassure herself that Thea and Fitz hadn't caught them up and she had only heard Thea in her imagination. Pearl would worry, too. *You're opening yourself up to hurt.* Yet while she knew both of her friends' imaginary voices were right, by cutting Edwin from her life she would cut herself off from the magical world of learning and knowledge that he had opened up. From the start, he had encouraged her in her quest to expand her mind, never making her feel small for having no qualifications but admiring her for her determination to make up for it. What other man would treat her like that? No one she also enjoyed simply being with, she was sure. She couldn't turn him away. She also couldn't deny the growing fear that had taken up residence in her mind now that he was returning to operational flying. He had already been shot down once. If anything should happen to him while they were estranged, she would never forgive herself.

She drew a breath. 'I've missed you too. I'll try to forgive you.' It was the best she could offer for now.

'Thank you.' The relief in his voice was so clear, most of Jenny's reservations fell away. Only one remained: she was as much in love with Edwin as ever and she would never get over him if she didn't let him go.

Chapter Four

Now Edwin, Greg and Fitz were back in the bomber crews, Jenny prayed more fervently than ever that the war would soon end. However, despite constant reassurances in the news that the Allies were making significant gains, peace couldn't come soon enough for her. And the inevitability of victory only seemed to have increased the bombing campaign. Operations didn't let up, and Greg's crew were only in Fenthorpe for three days before *J-Jackson* made her first bombing run. Jenny, Thea and Pearl were back to their pre-dawn vigils, waiting with the other volunteers, handing out tea to the returning crews.

Thankfully, in the three missions that followed all of the Lancasters returned safely, with only minor injuries sustained. *J-Jackson* made it through without a scratch, which pleased Thea no end, as she was responsible for keeping its instruments in working order. Everyone seemed to breathe a sigh of relief once those early missions were completed with ease, and they settled into their new routine, learning once again how to close their minds to the ever-present fear and take whatever happiness they could find in the present.

On a freezing day at the end of the first week in February, Thea and Jenny both had the day off. A trip to Lincoln beckoned, and so after breakfast they signed out at the guard room and caught the bus into the city centre. It being a bitterly cold day, once they had done a quick tour of the shops they climbed the hill and took refuge in the Bishop's Pal, the tearoom at the Bishop's Palace.

'What shall we do next?' Jenny asked, her chilled fingers wrapped around a steaming mug of cocoa. 'I'm too cold to wander with no purpose.'

'I suppose we could see if Pearl is free for lunch,' Thea replied. 'Then maybe we could see the matinée at the Regal.' She gave a sly grin. 'We might meet some nice chaps in the upstairs cafe. Find you a date.'

'Don't start that again. I promised to get out more, and I have. I was at the Piebald Pony the other day, wasn't I?'

'But you were with Edwin. The whole point of you going out more was to meet *other* blokes. How are you going to know you couldn't fall for anyone else if you don't try?'

Jenny sighed. This was so close to what she had imagined Thea would say, it was why she hadn't minded too much that this was the first time the two friends had spent much time together since that evening. She hadn't even had a chance to relate the conversation she'd had with Edwin on the walk back to RAF Fenthorpe. When they had parted company with the men at the gate, Thea had chatted nineteen to the dozen about her joy at once more being in the same place as Fitz. Then once they had reached Hut Three, they had been drawn into an impromptu game of cards around the stove, and had not had a private moment since.

'If you must know, I was so shocked when I saw Edwin that I hardly knew what I was saying. The next moment, Lily had invited him to the pub, and I couldn't back out because I hated the thought of them going alone.'

'You don't have anything to worry about on that score. He's clearly besotted with you, even if he can't admit it to himself. I think he just can't find the words to tell you.'

Jenny drew a deep breath, bracing for the inevitable outcry. 'Yet that didn't stop him asking another woman to marry him. They've been engaged for years.'

'What?' Thea's exclamation could have shattered glass a hundred yards away. A well-turned-out elderly woman at the next table turned an icy glare on Thea, who clapped a hand over her mouth. 'Oops. Sorry!' She leaned across the table and lowered her voice. 'But seriously, are we talking about the same person – Edwin, who's clearly besotted with you and is the last person you'd expect to have a woman on the side?'

Jenny nodded, not trusting herself to speak. In the days since the revelation, she'd had to keep her feelings bottled up, although she was longing to confide in her friends. Now all the bitter disappointment, hurt and anger threatened to burst out. She drew several deep breaths, then blew onto her cocoa to disguise her distress, desperate not to disgrace herself by crying in a public place. If the woman at the next table had objected to Thea's single-word exclamation, she doubted she'd approve of Jenny's uncontrollable wails and sobs.

Thea had no reservations about letting her feelings show. 'You've got to be kidding me. He's been engaged all this time?'

Another deep breath and Jenny felt able to speak. 'I know. And for your information, as he was engaged long before he met me, I'd rather you not talk about him having a woman on the side, because that would be me. Not that we got up to anything, I hasten to add.'

She might have known Thea would take this the wrong way. She raised her cocoa in a mock toast. 'Ah, Jenny. I'm so proud of how you've progressed. When I first knew you, you could hardly be dragged away from your latest book. Now you're someone's woman on the side.'

'Keep your voice down! And I'm not, nor have I ever been, Edwin's woman on the side. All that ever happened between us was a kiss for about one-millionth of a second before he stopped it.'

But Thea ignored her. 'I can see the headlines now – "Jenny Hazleton: the scarlet woman of Fenthorpe".'

Despite herself, this was so outrageous that Jenny couldn't hold back a giggle. 'You're impossible. If I'm a scarlet woman, I dread to think what that would make you.'

'But I'm a reformed character. Anyway, I made you laugh, and that's the important thing. If you can laugh about something, it can't be as bad as all that.' Then her expression sobered. 'Not that I'm making light of your feelings, of course. If you want to talk about it, I promise not to make fun of you. I know how much Edwin means to you, and I'm sure you must be feeling awful.'

Thea was right, though. Laughing had helped, releasing her from the maelstrom of pent-up emotions and freeing her enough to speak without bursting into tears. 'I would like to speak about it, if it wouldn't bore you.'

'Bore me? Jenny, you're my friend! You were there for me when I nearly lost Fitz, and I'm here for you if you need a shoulder to cry on. It's what friends do. Hang on, let me order some more drinks and then you can tell me everything.'

This was exactly what Jenny needed, and so, over yet more cocoa and a slab of rich fruit cake, she repeated word for word what Edwin had told her and exactly how that had made her feel.

'The worst of it is,' she said, when there was nothing left on her plate but crumbs and her mug was empty, 'that his fiancée, Mina, sounds like she's got the life I always wanted but could never have. *She* didn't have to leave school at fourteen. She was reading maths at Cambridge. I'm still a lowly LACW, but she's an officer, doing something terribly hush-hush and important at Bletchley Park.'

Thea pulled a face. 'Sounds like she had everything handed to her on a plate, if you ask me. I bet she comes from a wealthy family and was sent away to the very best boarding school.'

'Whatever her life was like, it was definitely nothing like mine.' Jenny, whose mother had died when she was born, had been brought up by her grandparents after her coal miner father had passed away from lung disease when she was ten. 'She probably had family who understood and encouraged her instead of expecting her to do nothing but marry and produce the next generation of miners. And I bet her weekends involved something more glamorous than checking her hair for nits.' She would never forget the shame of her first day at RAF Fenthorpe, when her medical had revealed she had headlice, most likely picked up from one of her brothers' children during a visit home. 'Mina probably had loads of friends, and they spent their free time visiting museums and galleries.' Jenny had only been able to dream of a life filled with such mind-improving activities, and living in her grandparents' smallholding in the Forest of Dean had made meeting old school friends difficult and something for special occasions only. It had been a lonely life, and she had jumped at the escape offered by the WAAF when she had turned eighteen. 'She must be so much more sophisticated,' she concluded sadly. 'No wonder Edwin prefers her to me.'

Thea shook her finger in Jenny's face. 'Now you listen to me. Maybe you didn't have the same start in life as this Mina, but that makes you all the more remarkable. You didn't sulk because you had to leave school at fourteen. No, you didn't give up, feeling sorry for yourself, you taught yourself from whatever books you could lay your hands on. And you're one of the most intelligent girls I know. As far as I'm concerned, that makes you ten times better than a girl who had her education handed to her on a plate. You put me to shame, that's for sure. Every time I see you poring over a book, I go all hot and cold all over when I remember how I moaned about Pearl forcing me to stay on for my higher cert. You've really made something of yourself, and if Edwin can't see that then it's his loss.'

Tears welled in Jenny's eyes. Unable to answer for a moment, she grasped Thea's hand and squeezed it. 'I bet Mina doesn't have friends as wonderful as you,' she said when she could speak.

'I'm sure she doesn't,' Thea replied with a grin. 'And I bet she's really ugly. Edwin's probably with her out of pity.'

Drying her eyes, Jenny giggled. 'We mustn't be nasty. However she looks, she must be a lovely person, or Edwin

33

would never have fallen in love with her.' But the thought of Edwin being in love with another woman brought a fresh surge of pain.

'Fine. If you're going to be so nice about it, I can't stop you, but whatever you say, I am angry with him for hurting you. He had no right to act like you were the only one for him when he was engaged to someone else. How did he explain it?'

Jenny frowned. 'He said something about focusing so much on the present that he didn't allow himself to think more than one day ahead. I thought it made sense at the time, but now I come to tell it to you, I still don't understand. You know what? I *am* angry. I really thought he was falling for me, and the only reason he didn't speak was because of the war. And now I feel such a fool.'

'You're not a fool and you're right to be angry. But it's all the more reason why you should go out with a few other men.'

'I don't know. Going out with a man I hardly know isn't my idea of fun.' That was what had attracted her to Edwin. He had enjoyed the same things as Jenny – books and talking about books and learning new things. Her feelings for him had developed over time, rooted in deep friendship. 'I'd rather be friends with someone and go from there. Going on a date seems so pressurised. I know that must sound strange to you.'

'No, not at all.' Then Thea gave a wry smile. 'Well, maybe a little. But we're two very different people, and I can see that your way has its merits.' She frowned into her cup. 'I still think you need to mix with other people, though. Give yourself a chance to get to know some other men. Leave it with me. I'll think of something.'

–

Jenny didn't have to wait long before Thea came up with a plan. She had just returned to her hut after a long night on duty, and had flung herself onto her bed, feeling too weary even to get changed, when Thea flew into the hut.

'You've got to see this. Come with me.'

Jenny groaned and buried her face in her pillow. 'Go away! I'm too tired.'

'It won't take long, and you have to see.'

With a put-upon sigh, Jenny rose, knowing Thea wouldn't give up until she'd had her way. 'What is it?' she asked as she stumbled, bleary-eyed, from the hut in Thea's wake. 'A toad in the ablutions block again?'

'Don't be silly. I wouldn't drag you out of bed for that.' She led the way into the recreation hut, or 'rec' as the WAAFs had taken to calling it.

In the evenings its stove was lit, and off-duty WAAFs could sit in the tatty but comfortable armchairs and read the supplied newspapers and magazines or choose from the selection of board games and jigsaws piled on one of the tables. This morning, however, the stove was unlit, and Jenny flung herself into an armchair, shivering. 'Come on, then. Tell me why you brought me here.'

'This.' Thea pointed at the large noticeboard covering most of the back wall, upon which was a mosaic of messages of all shapes and sizes. Some were official typed notices, while others were scrawled by hand on curled scraps of notepaper.

Jenny groaned again. 'Please just tell me. My eyes are all blurred after spending half the night reading instruments by the light of my very dim torch and the other half staring at synoptic charts.'

'Fine.' Thea pointed at one of the typed notices. 'This one is a list of the new classes they're starting this week, and there's one I thought you'd be interested in.'

'But I've tried doing one before, remember, and it didn't work because I'm not free to attend all the sessions.'

RAF Fenthorpe had started an extensive education programme for its personnel, putting on evening classes in subjects ranging from art to zoology. The teachers were either personnel with expert knowledge or teachers and lecturers from the local area. Every time a new schedule was posted, Jenny would read it with longing, wishing she could take all the classes. However, her watch rotation meant that she could never commit to attending class on the same night every week. The one class she had signed up to the previous year – intermediate inorganic chemistry – she'd had to abandon because she ended up missing so many sessions that it was pointless to carry on.

'This one's different, though. Listen.' Thea cleared her throat and read from the list outlining each class. '"Open lectures: a series of lectures given by RAF Fenthorpe personnel. Lecture slots are still available. If you want to share your expert knowledge in any subject and can present it in an hour-long lecture, please give your name to the education officer." There, you see,' she finished, 'the lectures won't be connected, so it doesn't matter about the ones you have to miss. And they're on twice a week, so the chances are you'll get to at least one of them. What do you think?'

Jenny joined Thea at the noticeboard and read the description for herself. 'I think it's a really good idea. Why this sudden interest in my education?'

'I said I would find a way to get you to meet new men, didn't I?' Thea's eyes were shining.

'This is actually not a bad idea. I was worried you were going to make an entry for me in a lonely hearts column.'

'I'd never do that to you, especially not after that business Deedee uncovered with the fake theatrical agent.' Thea shuddered, and Jenny knew she was remembering the man who, posing as an agent, had abducted several young women. 'But this is perfect,' Thea went on. 'You said you preferred being friends with a man before you went out on a date, so this way you can get to know them in the class first. What do you say – are you going to sign up?'

'Okay.' Besides being interested to hear the lectures Jenny knew that, if she refused, Thea would still insist on getting her to meet new men. This way she could attend a hopefully interesting lecture and Thea would never know if she had never spoken to any of the men present.

'Great.' Thea pulled a pencil from her pocket and wrote Jenny's name on the attendance list. Then, to Jenny's shock, she added her own. 'What? You didn't think I was going to let you go alone, did you?'

'I didn't think you were interested in' – Jenny peered at the list of lectures that had already been scheduled – 'the art of cheesemaking.'

'Why not? I love cheese.'

Jenny glared at her until she relented. 'Maybe you're right. But if I wasn't there, you would just go to the lecture, take notes and leave. I'm going to be there to make sure you make the most of the opportunity to befriend any nice men. You don't have much time left.'

'Until what?' Jenny stared at Thea, trying to look innocent. She knew exactly what Thea meant but had hoped she'd forgotten.

'You promised to get yourself a date by the middle of the month, remember?'

So much for Thea forgetting.

Her friend was giving her a stern look. 'You're not going to back out, are you? Just one date. If it's really awful I promise I won't make you go out with anyone else, but I want you to try. For your own good.'

Put like that, Jenny thought, she couldn't go back on her word.

Edwin collapsed into an armchair in the anteroom and closed his eyes. Thanks to the stubborn fog that had rolled in, ops had been scrubbed. It meant that he now had a whole evening of leisure after spending most of the day feeling keyed up in preparation for a mission.

Someone nudged his arm, and he looked up to see Fitz looming over him. 'Coming to the pub later?'

Edwin thought about it. There was a chance Jenny would be there and, while he hoped his apology had cleared the air between them, he didn't think it was a good idea to see her socially just yet. 'Not this time,' he replied. 'I think I'll have a quiet evening in.'

Once Fitz had gone, he settled back for his snooze, enjoying the heat from the fire on his face.

'There you are, Holland, I've been looking for you.'

Edwin opened his eyes to find the education officer standing where Fitz had been only moments earlier. His brow was furrowed, and he looked like the weight of the world rested on his shoulders. 'Why – is something wrong?'

'Everything's gone wrong. The person scheduled to give the cheese lecture tonight has gone down with a stomach bug.'

Edwin had to think about this for a moment before it dawned on him that *cheese lecture* wasn't some obscure mission codename but was literally a lecture about cheese. 'Oh, that's bad luck. Are you going to cancel?'

'I'll have to unless I can get someone to step in.' The education officer regarded Edwin with raised eyebrows, and it dawned on Edwin what he was after.

'I hope you don't want me to talk about cheese for an hour. I could probably describe the difference between Cheddar and Stilton, but that's my limit.'

'No, but I recall you saying you could give a talk on the night sky, and I wondered if you had something already prepared.'

Edwin silently said goodbye to his planned quiet evening with his books. Now he regretted being organised and preparing something well in advance. 'I suppose I could do it. What time?'

'Wonderful!' The frown lines disappeared from the man's face. 'It starts at eight.' He rattled off the details of the classroom where the lecture was scheduled to take place and the time when the next transport to the base was leaving.

Edwin, knowing he would get no more rest that evening, hurried to his room to read through his notes. He could only

38

hope the people hoping for a lecture on cheese wouldn't be too disappointed.

–

While Edwin was used to giving lectures, having been required to do so as a postgraduate student at Cambridge, he usually liked to be more prepared than he felt that evening. Therefore he was careful to arrive in time to draw some diagrams on the blackboard in advance, then he sat at the front desk and gave his notes another read-through. He didn't look up when the door opened and the first arrivals shuffled in, whispering and bringing the night chill with them.

Only when it was time to begin did he rise and look up with a smile. 'Good evening,' he said, his gaze sweeping the group. It was larger than he had expected, every table occupied by two if not three people. Just how many people at Fenthorpe were interested in cheese? 'I expect some of you are wondering why I have a diagram of the constellation Orion behind me when I'm supposed to be giving a talk about cheese. I'm sorry to tell you that the person due to give that talk has been taken ill, so, instead of cheese, you're going to get a lecture on the stars and constellations you can see in the February night sky. I'm afraid it has little to do with cheese unless—' Here he had intended to make a joke about the moon being made of green cheese, but at that moment his gaze fell on Jenny at the front of the room, and he stumbled over his words as his heart gave a lurch.

He should have known she would be here. He had never known anyone so determined to accumulate as much knowledge in as many subjects as possible. So much for trying to avoid her for a while.

He'd delivered enough lectures in his time to be able to recover from a distraction, so he only faltered briefly before picking up his thread again. However, throughout the lecture he was constantly aware of Jenny's presence even when he was looking elsewhere. In fact, he deliberately avoided looking directly at her; he was worried that seeing her face would cause him to lose track again. When speaking he was usually able to register the reactions of all listeners so he could decide if he had pitched his talk at the appropriate level; this time, he was so focused on Jenny that he had no idea how the other listeners were reacting to his descriptions of the stars forming Orion or how to use them to locate the neighbouring constellations. Even though he didn't look directly at her, he knew she would be drinking in every word and committing it to memory.

He only became aware of the rest of his audience when he happened to glance at his watch and saw that his hour was nearly up. 'That seems like an appropriate place to round this off,' he said, 'but when the fog clears, do take the time to look for the stars I pointed out. Any questions?'

Jenny's hand shot up. Of course it did. 'This is a bit off the subject,' she said, when he nodded at her to speak, 'but I've often wondered something about the moon.'

'Go on,' he prompted when she hesitated.

'Well, this might sound like a stupid question, but why is it that sometimes when there's a crescent moon I can see the dim shape of the rest of the moon? I mean, we can only see the part of the moon that's reflecting sunlight, so how come there's enough light to see the part that's not catching the sun?'

'That's not a stupid question, it's a very good one.' He was looking at her properly now, and saw her slightly worried expression relax in relief. 'You're quite right that there's no sunlight reflecting from the dark part of the moon disc, so the light to see that must be coming from another source, one that's not as bright as the sun. Can you think what that is?' Unconsciously he had slipped into the role of tutor, encouraging Jenny to reason out the answer for herself, and he was delighted when he saw understanding dawn in her expression.

'Oh!' she exclaimed. 'It's sunlight reflected from the Earth!'

'Exactly! We call it earthshine.'

'Earthshine,' Jenny repeated, her expression one of wonderment. 'What a beautiful name.'

'I think so too.' For a moment he forgot there was anyone else in the room, and he gazed at Jenny, taking pleasure in the sheer joy of learning radiating from her face. It was so bright, he could imagine it being seen thousands of light years away.

Then someone sneezed, bringing him back to awareness with an abrupt jolt. Seeing his hour was up, he thanked the class and sent them on their way.

Jenny lingered behind, and it was only now that he noticed she had been sitting with Thea. How had he not seen her before? He gathered up his notes but his fingers were suddenly clumsy, making him drop the papers onto the floor; they slid over the polished concrete, scattering wildly. Cursing under his breath, he dropped to his knees and scrabbled to collect them.

'Here, let me help.' Jenny crouched down beside him. 'That was a fascinating talk,' she told him. 'Are you going to do any more? I was really interested in what you said about Betelgeuse.' And suddenly they were chatting away exactly as they had done in past times, before the kiss. The next thing he knew, he had promised to speak to the education officer about giving more lectures, and had even suggested they should do a class outside while the nights were still long. By the time he had collected all his notes and was bidding goodbye to Jenny and Thea, he was starting to hope that maybe he hadn't completely ruined their friendship. Surely this proved that they could still enjoy companionship based on their mutual enjoyment of learning without him betraying Mina.

Chapter Five

'That wasn't exactly what I had in mind.' Jenny couldn't see Thea's face in the dark but, judging from her caustic tone, she was scowling. 'You were supposed to be meeting other men, not spending the lecture mooning over the man you're supposed to be getting over.'

'I wasn't mooning over him. He was giving the lecture. I couldn't exactly ignore him, could I?'

'No, but you should have seen your face when he was explaining about earthshine. You'd gone all misty-eyed. If it had been a movie, the film score would have cued soaring violins at that point.'

'Don't be ridiculous. I was interested in what he was saying, that's all.' But Jenny couldn't deny the way her chest had gone all fluttery when he had smiled at her. She wasn't going to tell that to Thea, though, because she didn't want Thea to stop her going to the lectures. The glimpse into a world of learning had been like the offer of water in the desert. She was sure she would have acted in the same way had they just been to a lecture about cheese. Pretty sure, anyway. Although not so sure that she didn't feel the need to deflect the conversation away from her. 'Anyway, you're the one who persuaded me to go.'

'I wouldn't if I'd known who was giving the lecture. I—' Thea broke off abruptly and, in the darkness slightly ahead of her, Jenny heard her friend stumble and mutter under her breath.

'Are you okay?'

'I'm fine, just wandered off the path and tripped over something. I can't see a thing in this blasted fog. Here, give me your hand.'

Jenny cast the light of her torch around until she saw where Thea was standing. She held her hand out and moved towards her until Thea's flailing hand caught hers.

'That's better,' Thea said. 'Now at least we'll get lost together.'

They walked on in silence for a minute or two, concentrating on where they were putting their feet. Jenny was grateful she wasn't on duty that night, although estimating visibility would have been easy, as it was zero.

When Thea spoke again, her voice was gentler. 'I'm sorry you're hurting over Edwin. You know, you don't have to go out with other men if you don't feel ready. I suppose I'm so happy with Fitz, I can't imagine you being happy unless you've got a boyfriend as wonderful as him. But if you'd prefer to be alone, that's fine, too. I mean, you'll never be alone because you've got me, Pearl and Deedee.'

'And my books,' Jenny said with a laugh.

'And your books.'

'I know you're right, though.' Jenny spoke in a low voice. 'I mean, I know I need to be open to accepting another man into my life, and that can't happen if I don't have any other male friends apart from Edwin. But tonight I realised that I enjoy Edwin's company so much, I couldn't bear to lose his friendship. I've never known anyone like him. So if friendship is all he can offer, that's still a wonderful gift. After the dance, I thought I could never get over the embarrassment, but now I think we can get past that. So I promise to carry on coming to these lectures and I will try and get to know a few other men, but I won't cut one of my best friends out of my life just because we had a stupid misunderstanding.'

'So you're still going to try to get a date by the middle of the month?'

Jenny sighed. 'If I do and it's a disaster, promise you'll never make me go on another?'

'Cross my heart.'

'All right, then. I'll try.'

—

Jenny was still worrying how she was going to find a date when she reported for duty the following day. With only a week until her deadline, she was going to have to make a real effort to mix with new people, and the prospect didn't fill her with joy. Still, a promise was a promise, and she was determined to show Thea she wasn't so hung up on Edwin that she couldn't bear to meet anyone else.

Lily arrived soon after her and greeted Jenny with a smile. 'What are we going to do today?'

'The same as every day but this time you're going to plot the synoptic charts.' At least she could forget her worries in the comfort of familiar routine.

A short while later, Jenny had the printout of the latest weather observations from around the country and had plotted the first set to show Lily what to do. 'You must be careful to use the correct colours, so the Met Officer can see at a glance whether he's looking at a temperature or dew point,' Jenny told her. 'Now it's your turn. Plot the next set yourself so I can see if you're ready to work unsupervised.'

'I think I am, although I really appreciate your help.' Lily bent over the chart to add the wet bulb temperature, and Jenny was pleased to see that she correctly chose to use the red ink pen.

'You're getting there,' Jenny said. 'I remember I spent hours every day studying my notebooks when I first arrived, but I quickly got used to it. How are you finding life in the camp?'

'Oh, it's wonderful. Everyone's so friendly. I went out to Lincoln last night with the girls from my hut and it was such fun. I never went on a night out until I joined the WAAF.'

'What, never?' Jenny stared at her, surprised. Going out with friends hadn't been easy for her, growing up as she had in a tiny village in the Forest of Dean, but she had managed the occasional trip to the Palace cinema in Cinderford and even a rare trip to Gloucester.

Lily shook her head, biting her lip. 'My parents are very strict and they didn't let me go out in the evenings unless it was with them.' Then she brightened. 'But I'm making up for it now. There's so much fun to be had in Lincoln, I'm so glad I was posted here. And I met a lovely chap the night we went to the pub. He's a gunner on *P-Peter*.'

'Oh? What's his name?' Jenny didn't think she knew any of *P-Peter*'s crew.

'Richie Evans. Do you know him?'

Jenny shook her head. 'What's he like?'

'He's ever so handsome, and he looks so dashing in his uniform. He's got lovely dark hair and these really soulful eyes, just like Tyrone Power. He's going to take me to the cinema on Saturday, as long as he's not flying ops.'

'That's nice.' Jenny bit back a smile at this description that was all about Richie's appearance and nothing about character. 'I hope he's kind, too.'

'Oh, he is. He said the cinema would be his treat. Actually, I wondered if you would come too.'

'On your date?' Jenny couldn't think of a more excruciating way to spend an evening.

'Well, a double date. Richie's got a friend – *P-Peter*'s wireless operator – and I said I'd bring a friend along for him.'

It was Jenny's first instinct to say no, as going out on Saturday would mean missing the rescheduled cheese lecture. But then she remembered Thea's challenge. If she turned this date down, she was unlikely to be able to arrange another in the short time left, so she might as well accept. 'Fine, I'll come along. What's this wireless operator's name?'

'Ben. I didn't catch his surname.'

'What's he like?'

'Oh, I don't know. He was there at the pub when I met Richie, but he was very quiet.'

This reassured Jenny. Quiet sounded more her type. Not that she expected to prefer Ben to Edwin, but she would at least be keeping her promise to Thea by going out. As the middle of the month was rapidly approaching, she was unlikely to secure a date in time by any other means, having failed miserably to do so until now.

There wasn't much opportunity to chat after that, for word went round that ops were on that night as the fog had cleared. The rush was on to gather all the information the Met Officer would need to present the weather briefing, and presently the various navigators popped into the office to glean what information they could about wind speeds.

Even though she was expecting to see him, Jenny's heart still gave a little lurch when Edwin walked into the Met Office. She was pleased to see him approach as it indicated that he, too, was serious about reclaiming their friendship.

'I heard you were flying tonight,' she said, doing her best to put on a cheerful face and not give a hint of the worry that would only increase until he landed safe and sound.

He nodded. 'What's your forecast?'

Jenny glanced at the chart. 'Well, it's hard to be certain, of course, because the weather's coming from the west, but I don't think the wind will pick up. It looks like you'll have a build-up of stratocumulus clouds above three thousand feet, and there will be a risk of icing until you're above them.'

'That's useful to know. Thanks.'

'I really enjoyed your talk last night. Are you going to do any more?'

'Would you like that?'

'Oh yes, I was fascinated, and you only covered Orion and its neighbouring constellations. There's so much more to learn about.'

'Well, maybe I will. I enjoyed it last night too. Are you going to the cheese lecture on Saturday? I thought I might drop in.'

Jenny's heart sank. 'Oh, I can't. I promised Lily I'd go to the cinema with her.' She couldn't bring herself to tell him she was going on a date. Ridiculous when Edwin was engaged to another woman.

She was absurdly pleased when his face fell. 'That's a shame. Maybe I'll give it a miss then.'

At his reaction, she couldn't help remembering what Thea had said about showing Edwin that she wasn't sitting around pining after him. Despite wanting to back out of her arrangement with Lily, she hardened her heart and said, 'You should go. I'd like to hear about it. Anyway, good luck tonight.'

Edwin released a breath of relief when the Lancaster's wheels touched down safely. Another successful mission crossed off, and apart from a few unpleasant minutes when the flak had been exploding around them at Karlsruhe the mission had been uneventful. There had been several technological advances since his last tour, including the use of 'window' – strips of tinfoil that they dropped from the aircraft at designated locations to confuse the enemy's tracking systems. Thanks to that, they hadn't been attacked by night fighters, something he had learned to dread on his previous tour.

He gathered up his charts and instruments and clambered out of the Lancaster after his crewmates. Now he had completed four missions, he felt more settled and decided he had made the right decision to volunteer for a second tour. While he would always suffer from nerves in the run up to each mission, he was confident they wouldn't get the better of him. And, importantly, now he'd had a chance to assess his other crewmates in action, he knew he could rely on them. He had known he could depend on Greg and Fitz, of course, but there was always a worry when forming a new crew that there would be a weak link. But everyone had performed well.

Fitz caught up with him on the way to the waiting bus and slapped his back. 'Another uneventful run. I could get used to this.'

Edwin grinned at him. 'Me too.'

A slight figure bundled in a greatcoat jogged up to them, and Edwin saw it was Thea. She had evidently been slated to meet the returning crew to make note of any necessary repairs. She launched herself at Fitz and gave him a swift kiss, much to the amusement of the rest of the crew. 'Don't tell any of the WAAF officers you saw that, or I'll probably get transferred to Orkney,' she said. 'Anyway, welcome back. Any instrument damage I should know about?'

'Nothing for me,' Edwin said, then moved to get on the bus and give Thea and Fitz some privacy, although not before he heard Fitz say, 'I don't think anything was damaged, but perhaps you should give everything a thorough going-over.'

Edwin snorted and shook his head as he took his seat. Although he couldn't help comparing the easy, comfortable relationship Fitz had with Thea to his with Mina. He enjoyed her company and always looked forward to spending time with her, but he would never dream of joking or making suggestive comments like Fitz and Thea. Inevitably his thoughts slid to Jenny. When she had kissed him, he had felt a heat flare that he had never experienced with Mina, and it suddenly struck him how much he would like to have with Jenny what Fitz had with Thea.

He tried to slam the door on that thought, painfully aware of how unfair he was being to Mina. For the first time he wondered if there was a way to extricate himself from his engagement without causing her hurt.

Then he remembered a letter that he had collected just before leaving for that night's mission. It had been from Mina, and he had left it in his locker to read on his return. She always wrote engaging letters, telling him her news but without, of course, giving away her occupation at Bletchley Park. He would read it carefully and try to work out what it revealed of her feelings for him. After all, they had been apart for longer than they had been together. Perhaps she had found someone else. *Like he had found Jenny.* But he suppressed that thought. It was wrong of him to think that way about Jenny while he was engaged to Mina.

Now he had made up his mind, he longed to study the letter. However, first he had to endure the debrief and then the bus ride back to the officers' mess at Fenthorpe Hall. The traditional post-mission breakfast of bacon and real eggs provided a brief distraction but, as soon as he could excuse himself, he sank into a cosy armchair in a quiet corner of the anteroom and opened the letter.

> *Dear Ed,*
>
> *I will keep this brief because I have to report back on duty soon and I need to put this into the post before I do, for reasons that will become clear.*
>
> *You see, I have finally arranged a whole week's leave! I know that as you have only just arrived in Lincolnshire you won't be able to take any leave yourself, but I have missed you so much that I have decided to take my leave in Fenthorpe. Remembering what you told me about the White Horse, I have already booked a room there, making it easy for us to meet whenever you are off duty. I will be arriving on Saturday and I will take whatever time you can spare me. I really can't wait to see you. It has been far too long. If nothing else I want to see for myself that you are in one piece after your experience in December. So be prepared to be spoiled!*
>
> *With all my love,*
>
> *Mina*

Edwin stared at the closing line: *With all my love.* It seemed Mina's feelings were unchanged. With a heavy heart, he reread the line about his experience in December. Although he knew she was referring to his crash behind enemy lines, his guilty conscience read it as being about Jenny's kiss. His body might be whole after the crash, but his heart was in tatters. Would Mina notice? He could never tell her. The sad fact that she had nowhere else to spend her leave was uppermost in Edwin's mind, and he felt partly responsible for that. Mina had no one else in the world, so he could never break their engagement if it meant leaving her all alone. He owed her that much.

It had only taken Jenny five minutes to realise that this double date was not going to be much fun. Jenny and Lily had taken the bus into Lincoln in the afternoon, as Jenny had agreed to show Lily the sights. Then an hour before the film at the Regal was due to start, they had gone to the cafe in the cinema, where they had arranged to meet their dates.

Jenny's first impression of Ben Newton was that he was, as Lily had said, quiet. The two men were already there when Jenny and Lily arrived, sitting side by side on one side of a table, so the girls slid into the opposite seats.

'This is Ben,' Lily said, pointing to an undeniably good-looking young man with light brown hair and intense blue eyes. Then she leaned across the table and took the hand of the man who must be Richie. Lily had not exaggerated his film-star good looks, although Jenny thought he had been over liberal with the Brylcreem, as his dark hair was slicked back so smoothly it looked like it had been painted on with varnish.

'I'm Jenny,' she said to Ben, deciding she had better introduce herself, because Lily was now too occupied gazing dreamily at her date.

Ben nodded at her but said nothing.

'Lily tells me you're a wireless operator.' This was a pointless remark, considering that his aircrew brevet with its embroidered

'S' for 'Signaller' announced his trade, but she couldn't think of anything else to say.

Ben just nodded again, and Jenny was starting to wonder if he would rather communicate in Morse. She glanced at Lily to see if she could enlist her help in getting the conversation going, only to see her leaning across the table, her lips locked with Richie's.

She plastered a smile onto her face and turned back to Ben. 'How long have you been at Fenthorpe?'

At that point the waitress arrived to take their order, sparing Ben the effort of replying. Richie disengaged himself from Lily and ordered lemonade for them without asking what anyone else might want, then returned his attentions to Lily.

Jenny sighed inwardly and thanked her lucky stars that she only had to sit through another fifty-five minutes of this before the film was due to start. At least then she wouldn't be expected to carry on a conversation. Once their lemonade arrived, she tried again.

'I've got a brother who's tacky-turn like you, so I don't mind, but you've got to try and say something or this is going to be a very long evening.'

'Taciturn.'

'What?' She had been so surprised to finally hear him speak that she hadn't registered what he'd said.

'You said "tacky-turn" but actually it's pronounced taciturn.'

'Oh.' Just her luck to make a slip like that on a first date. 'I'm always doing that. Mispronouncing words I've only ever read, I mean.' He could have corrected her in a kinder way, though. Still, she made an effort to smile and say, 'Thanks for telling me how to say it properly.' He probably hadn't meant to sound so patronising.

His lip curled. 'No problem. Of course, it's not something I've ever done, but you're not alone. The other day Richie here went to see *The Uninvited* at the cinema, and described it as mackerbree when he meant macabre.'

Deciding it was expected, Jenny gave a polite laugh, although she didn't like the way he made fun of his friend. When she had made similar howlers with Pearl and Thea, they had put her at her ease by telling her about mistakes *they'd* made, not other people.

Now Ben had started speaking, he didn't stop. He told her all about the vital work he did without once asking her about hers. 'No one seems to appreciate that being a wireless operator is one of the most difficult and demanding trades. Everyone goes on about how amazing the pilots are, but no one stops to think about the wireless operators. It requires a lot of intelligence to learn about how all the radio equipment works.'

'Yes, my friend Pearl was an R/T operator. I remember her studying electrical circuits and Morse and all sorts.'

Ben looked put out. 'Well, I expect the WAAFs only had to do a watered-down version of the course. Anyway, being a wireless operator's not only about radio equipment. We have to man a gun as well.' And he rambled on about the unlikely number of enemy fighters he had shot down, sounding very aggrieved that none of his crewmates had ever witnessed his kills so he couldn't claim them.

All in all, it was a relief when it was time to go into the auditorium.

They were gathering up their belongings when Jenny heard herself being hailed by a familiar voice that brought a blush to her cheeks. She spun around to see Edwin standing just behind her. 'I forgot you said you were coming tonight,' he said. His gaze drifted to Ben, standing beside her, so she introduced him, feeling rather flustered.

Then Edwin gestured to a tall blond woman standing beside him. Until that moment, she hadn't noticed her, having been entirely focused on Edwin. 'Jenny, this is my fiancée, Mina Allen.'

Jenny's heart sank to her dowdy regulation lace-ups. Despite what she had said to Thea, she had secretly harboured the wish that Edwin's fiancée would be plain, but this was not the case. Mina wouldn't have looked out of place on a *Vogue* cover; her willowy elegance lent an air of chic to her plain collared jersey and tweed skirt. Jenny had always taken pride in going out in her best blues, but she felt like a plain country bumpkin in comparison to Mina. While she had fair hair and blue eyes of a similar shade to Edwin's fiancée, there the resemblance ended. For Mina's hair was a smooth cascade of wavy silk falling to her shoulders, whereas, if Jenny ever unpinned her hair from its regulation above-the-collar roll, it had a tendency to form straggly rat's tails. She had never felt more unattractive. No wonder Edwin preferred Mina.

Yet if she had expected such a gorgeous creature to turn up her nose at Jenny, she was soon put right. Mina's face lit up and she seized Jenny's hand. 'Oh, I've heard so much about you. It's lovely to meet you at last.' Then she indicated Jenny's companions, who were making their way towards the door. 'But I see we're going in, so I won't hold you up. I'm staying in Fenthorpe for the week, so I expect I'll see you again.'

Jenny went to take her place beside Ben, her head in a whirl. She hadn't expected to like Mina, but even in that brief meeting she had instantly warmed to her. Why was she surprised, though? Edwin was a good judge of character, so it stood to reason that his fiancée would be someone Jenny would like. She also wondered what Mina had meant when she had said she had heard all about Jenny. There had been no trace of jealousy. It reinforced her reluctant acceptance that Edwin had never loved her, had only felt friendly feelings towards her, and she had totally misread his intentions.

The lights dimmed and the newsreel started, but Jenny couldn't take any of it in. Mina was staying in Fenthorpe for the week. She could only be staying at the White Horse, as there was nowhere else to stay in the village. That meant she would be bound to run into her again. She couldn't decide if this was a good thing or not. On the one hand she wished she could ignore her and pretend she didn't exist, but on the other she was curious to get to know the woman who had captured Edwin's heart.

A hand gripped her leg just above the knee, and she jumped violently. She was so shocked at first that she didn't know what to do, but, when the hand slid upwards, she pushed it away, shuddering at the contact with Ben's hot, sweaty palm. She shifted to move as far away from him as possible, which wasn't far considering the narrowness of the seats.

Ben leaned closer and breathed in her ear, 'Don't worry, darling, no one can see,' and his roving hand was back on her leg.

Jenny shot to her feet, shaking him off. 'Sorry,' she whispered to Lily, who was obliged to stand to let her out, 'I forgot I needed to pay a visit.'

She dashed down the side steps and into the ladies' lavatory, where she stared at her pale face in the peeling mirror while she washed her hands. First Edwin and Mina and now this. All in all, this was a night she wanted to forget.

Chapter Six

Jenny didn't get a chance to speak to Thea or Pearl about Mina until she met up with them at the White Horse the following evening. As there were no ops on that night, she walked into the snug expecting Edwin and Mina to already be there. She was relieved when she didn't see them, for she wanted to tell her friends about his fiancée before they saw her for themselves. However, Thea and Pearl had arrived and were settled in their usual corner seat. She gave them a wave and went to buy a half of shandy before joining them.

'Tell us all about your date, then,' Thea said when Jenny sat down.

Pearl brightened. 'You had a date? Who with?'

'A wireless operator called Ben Newton. I don't think you know him.' And Jenny wished she didn't know him, either. Just saying his name brought back memories that made her skin crawl.

Thea's brow furrowed. 'Wait. I think *I* know him.'

Pearl rolled her eyes. 'Are there any men you don't know?'

'Plenty. I've been a reformed character since I met Fitz. But I know Ben slightly because I worked on his Lanc for a while. What did you think of him, Jenny?'

Jenny wrinkled her nose. 'He was a bit full of himself.'

'I'm so glad you said that. I don't like him much either, and was really hoping you weren't going to say how wonderful he was.'

'Not likely.' Jenny explained about the 'tacky-turn' incident, finishing with, 'And then in the cinema, I spent the whole film shoving his hand off my leg.' She tried to make light of the incident, not wanting to think too much about how Ben had refused to accept that she wasn't playing hard to get. She had heard other women talk about men with octopus hands and now she knew what they meant.

'No second date then?'

'No way. Although do you know what he said at the end of the evening? He said, "There's a dance in the sergeants' mess next week. I bet the other WAAFs will be green with envy when they see you're with me."'

Her friends' cries of disbelief caused a few heads to turn, and it was only when the other customers in the snug returned to their own conversations that Pearl said, 'The nerve of the man! I hope you put him in his place.'

'I was so shocked I couldn't think of anything other than to say that I was on duty that night. Which was true, thank goodness.'

'Shame,' Thea remarked. 'If you could have stood being with him for another couple of dates it would make Edwin jealous.'

'Fat chance of that.'

'What do you mean?' Thea asked.

Jenny sighed. 'Because he was at the cinema last night. With his fiancée.' She described the meeting, ending with, 'Trust me, when you see her, you'll understand. Not only is she stunningly pretty, she's also really nice.'

Thea scowled. 'I hate her already.'

'Don't say that! Anyway, be careful. She's staying here, so she could walk in at any moment, and I don't want her to know we've been talking about her.'

She looked around the snug, fearing Mina might emerge from a dark corner. Then she frowned. 'Where are Greg and Fitz? I thought they'd be here.'

'They'll be along in a minute,' Pearl told her. 'Last I saw, they were in the public bar playing a game of darts.'

'How are you feeling, anyway, Pearl? I haven't seen you for a while. Is everything all right with' – she lowered her voice, unsure if Pearl would want anyone else to hear – 'with the baby?'

'I'm fine.' Pearl gave a beaming smile and pressed her hand to her flat stomach. 'It's hard to believe little Greg or Pearl is growing in here.'

'Have you told anyone else yet?' Jenny was relieved to have the spotlight on someone else for a while so she didn't have to think about Edwin with Mina.

Pearl shook her head. 'It's still early days yet, and I want to carry on working for as long as possible. I mean, I've seen a doctor, of course, and had it confirmed, but I don't want to make it official with my CO yet. I'll have to say something when I get too big for my uniform, but I'm hoping that won't be for a while.'

'And how's married life with Greg, now you're living together?' Thea asked. For Pearl had now made the move to married quarters at Fenthorpe Hall.

Pearl's answering smile stretched from ear to ear. 'It's wonderful. And we've actually made time to start discussing all the important stuff that we never got round to before.'

'As I recall, you hadn't discussed whether to start a family. Have you got round to talking about that yet?' Thea said, eyes twinkling.

Pearl quelled her with a look. 'No.' Then she grinned. 'I think the horse has well and truly bolted on that one. But anyway, I have news.'

'What?' Jenny sat up, glad the conversation appeared to have moved well away from Edwin and his fiancée.

'We've actually dared to discuss what we'd like to do after the war.' Pearl's expression sobered. 'I hope it's not tempting fate or anything, considering what Greg's doing now. I think having a baby on the way has finally freed him of the mental block that wouldn't let him think beyond the present. Anyway, he has a job waiting for him at the air company he worked for before the war, and I have to confess I'd love to see Sydney, so we're going to move to Australia.'

Thea's face fell. 'But that's on the other side of the world.'

Pearl bit her lip. 'I know. I'm sure I'll be dreadfully homesick, and I'll miss you, Deedee and Thomas horribly, but just think – you'd be able to visit. With Greg's aviation contacts he says he could arrange flights. Wouldn't that be exciting?'

'I suppose.' Thea didn't sound excited. 'It's just... well, I'm going to miss having you around, looking out for me.'

Pearl snorted. 'That's rich, considering you've always told me to stop interfering in your life.'

'I know. I can't help being contrary.'

'If you want, I'll write to you every week with unwanted advice.'

Thea brightened. 'Promise?'

'As long as you promise to write straight back telling me exactly where I can stick my advice. If you didn't, I'd worry that you were ill.'

The two women hugged, caught between laughter and tears. Jenny watched them, feeling wistful. This was partly due to the knowledge that she might not have her friends around for much longer, but there was also the worry over what she was going to do after the war. Her friends had both qualifications and men to provide for them. She had neither.

'Anyway,' Pearl said once she had extricated herself and wiped her eyes, 'We're not saying goodbye just yet. The war's not over.'

Thea opened her mouth to reply, but then her gaze latched on to something over Jenny's shoulder. 'Oh, my word, I think that must be Mina.'

Jenny craned her neck and saw Edwin at the bar with Mina at his side. Her gaze instantly fell on Mina's hand where it was tucked into the crook of Edwin's elbow, and something shrivelled inside her. She made to turn away, hoping neither of them would notice her, but before she could do so Mina looked her way, waved and said something to Edwin, pointing in her direction. Once they had their drinks, they carried them to the corner table.

'Mind if we join you?' Edwin asked.

' 'Course not,' Thea replied, shuffling her chair closer to the wall to make room for the extra chairs Edwin had gone to fetch. While he was doing that, Thea smiled at Mina. 'I'm guessing you're Mina. I'm Thea.'

When the introductions were over, Mina gazed around, clearly taking in every detail of the cosy, smoky room with its polished tables and horse brasses decorating the ceiling beams. 'It's wonderful to be here at last. I heard all about you and Fenthorpe last time Ed was based here, but… well, things were difficult for me just then and I could never get over here.' Jenny noticed that her hand gripped her glass so hard as she said this that her knuckles turned white, and couldn't help wondering what Mina meant. But then hardly anyone had lived through five years of war without experiencing hard times.

'Anyway,' Mina went on, 'I'm here now and it's wonderful to meet you all.'

'I heard you were in the WAAF,' Pearl said. 'What do you do?'

'Oh, I'm just a clerk.' Mina gave a negligent wave of the hand.

'She's a squadron officer.' Edwin gave her a fond look that curdled Jenny's stomach. 'If she was in uniform, we'd all have to salute her.'

Mina pulled a face. 'Then it's a good thing I'm on leave. I can't stand all that saluting business. But Ed always likes to tease me about outranking him.'

There it was again. It had niggled when Mina had called him Ed the first time. Jenny couldn't think of him as anything other than Edwin. Ed didn't sound like him at all, and it irritated her to hear Mina call him that. Or maybe it was just that it was a sharp reminder that Mina had known him before the war, knew the real Edwin. Maybe 'Ed' was his true self and 'Edwin' was just the person he'd become when he'd been forced to put his life on hold and join the RAF. It was becoming painfully clear that Mina was a part of his life in a way Jenny would never be.

She didn't trust herself to speak and could only pray that her expression didn't reveal her inner turmoil as she listened to the conversation. The trouble was, aside from her objection to Mina calling Edwin 'Ed', Jenny couldn't help warming to her. She had seemed genuinely embarrassed when Edwin had announced her rank, and she certainly didn't act like some WAAF officers Jenny had met, who treated the other ranks as though they were below them and not worthy of their attention. All in all, it was annoying that she couldn't find anything to dislike.

Thea and Pearl certainly seemed to have taken to her, and Jenny had faith in their ability to read people.

Her introspection came to an end when Mina addressed her directly and she was forced to reply. 'Ed tells me you work in meteorology. That must be fascinating. Do you enjoy it?'

'Oh, I love it.' Her enthusiasm in her subject overcame her reticence. 'I'm just a Met assistant though, so I don't make forecasts. I only take the readings and plot them on the chart.'

'Don't let her fool you,' Edwin said. 'There's a lot more to it than that, and all the navigators with any sense know to double-check the forecast with her.'

Warmth spread through her chest, and she shot him a grateful smile. Maybe she didn't have as long a history with Edwin as Mina, but his intervention was a reminder of their close friendship. Even though he didn't return her love, she was still special to him, and she would always treasure that knowledge.

'I've always admired people who understand the weather. I suppose I'm interested in it because as a mathematician I'd love to have a go at modelling weather systems. My studies were always highly theoretical but when I return to academia I think I'd like to do something with a more practical application.'

'How did the two of you meet?' Pearl asked.

'It was at Cambridge. I was an undergraduate and I went to a lecture by Arthur Eddington about the expeditions to view the solar eclipse. I found myself sitting next to a first-year postgraduate, and we got talking afterwards. We were still talking three hours later, and the rest is history.'

Jenny looked away as Mina gave Edwin's shoulder a loving squeeze. Mina's story was another painful reminder of the huge differences between them. Jenny would have given her eye teeth to be able to spend even one day in a centre of learning such as Cambridge, and here was Mina speaking of it as though attending lectures by eminent scientists was no amazing occurrence, let alone being there with Edwin.

'What about you, Jenny?' Mina asked. 'Is there anyone special in your life?'

Apart from Edwin, you mean? Jenny wanted to say; instead, she shook her head. 'It's not easy when I work such irregular hours.' This was a feeble excuse, considering working shifts had not prevented Pearl or Thea from starting relationships, and she hoped Mina would accept the statement without examining it too closely.

Mina's face clouded. 'I know what you mean. My work's rather like that, and of course it has to take priority. Put that together with Ed's duties, and we've scarcely seen each other in years. But I mustn't complain. Everyone's in the same boat. Anyway, back to you. Are you sure there's no one? What about the man I saw you with last night?'

'Oh, no. I was there as a favour for my friend. Lily.' Jenny added the name to emphasise that she hadn't been there for Ben's sake. While she couldn't bring herself to look at Edwin, she hoped he was listening. 'She needed to bring someone along for a double date. I'd never met Ben until last night and I'm sure I won't see him again.'

The conversation moved on, Mina turning to Pearl, eager to know more about the *Bombshell*, the newspaper for 5 Group personnel that Pearl edited. Pearl was more than happy to answer her questions, and Jenny drank the rest of her shandy, glad of the reprieve.

Finally, Mina turned to Jenny again. 'I don't suppose you could show me where the ladies is?'

Ah, so this was the moment where Mina would show her claws, warn Jenny off her fiancé. Jenny led the way to the chilly lean-to, bracing herself for an attack, but while they were in the white-tiled room Mina didn't say anything right away but produced a lipstick from her pocket and opened it, revealing that it was worn down to a tiny stub. She looked into the mirror and applied it before turning to Jenny, looking grave.

Here it comes, Jenny thought.

'You've probably guessed I asked you out here so I could speak to you alone.' When Jenny nodded, she went on. 'The thing is, I'm worried about Ed.'

'Really? Why?' Jenny hated herself for the jolt of anticipation she felt as her mind flew through the possibilities. Perhaps Mina was worried Edwin was poised to break off their engagement.

'I'm sure something happened when he and Greg were in the Netherlands.'

Jenny frowned. 'What do you mean? He looked awful when he got back but he's fine now.'

Mina shook her head. 'I know I haven't seen much of him recently, but he did come to see me in Bletchley after Christmas and he seemed… distracted. He tried to brush it off, saying it was shock from the crash and the effect of seeing how desperately hungry the family were who took them in, but I'm positive there was more to it than that. He insisted he was fine, though, and then clammed up. It's the reason I fought so hard to get leave now, to be honest. I'm going to make another attempt at getting him to confide in me.'

Jenny felt hot with shame. Here she was, through no reason but jealousy, thinking the worst of Mina, yet it was Mina who had pointed out that Edwin might still be struggling after his experiences. While she had noticed that he had been quieter than usual, she had put it down to embarrassment over the mistletoe incident. With hindsight she could see that Edwin's muted behaviour might be down to distress of some kind, and she was furious with herself for missing it. 'You're right,' she said. 'I think he has been subdued. I hope you can help him.'

'I'll certainly try, but that's why I wanted to get you alone. He might not want to confide in me. He can be... very protective of me and, knowing him, he's trying to hide his problems because he doesn't want to worry me. If I can't get him to speak, will you try? He trusts you, and if he can open up to anyone it might be you.'

There went Jenny's resolution to avoid Edwin, not that she had ever made it with a whole heart. No matter how much it might hurt knowing they could never be more than friends, she couldn't stay away from him if she thought he was suffering.

–

Shortly after they returned to their table, Greg and Fitz appeared, having finished their match. Now Jenny was the only one not in a couple, and she felt awkward and not a little lonely. Pulling on her coat, she rose. 'I'm feeling pretty tired and I've got an early start tomorrow, so I'd better go back.'

Thea gave her a sympathetic look. 'I'll come with you. I'd have to leave soon anyway, because I didn't get a late pass.' She grinned. 'And Fitz is taking me dancing tomorrow, so I don't want to use the back door and risk getting caught.' The back door was a hole in the fence behind the Waafery that allowed WAAFs to enter and leave the camp without signing in or out. It was an open secret, though, so, by unspoken agreement, no one used it too often in case the authorities decided to fix the hole. She then turned to say a loving goodbye to Fitz.

'I'll wait outside,' Jenny said quickly, not feeling up to watching any more happy couples that evening. Without waiting for a reply she said goodbye to the others, then pushed past the crowd at the bar and headed for the door.

In the narrow passageway running between the snug, the public bar and the main door, she was obliged to press herself against the wall to let a group go past. It took a little while, as they each had to manoeuvre past the heavy blackout curtain. While she waited, she happened to glance into the public bar, and did a double-take when she noticed Lily's boyfriend standing among a group watching a darts match. He appeared to be in deep conversation with a young woman who wasn't Lily. She was curvy and pretty, with copper-coloured hair styled in victory rolls. As Jenny watched, the woman whispered in Richie's ear, and he said something in reply. Although they weren't far from Jenny, she couldn't hear what he said above the hubbub of the crowded bar. Then he pulled an envelope from his pocket and pressed it into her hands. Jenny's senses prickled. There was something furtive about Richie's actions, and the way the woman thrust the packet into her pocket without examining it that made Jenny suspect there was something dodgy going on. She tried to crane her neck to get a better look at the woman, who was not in uniform, but someone closed the door to the public bar at that moment, blocking her view. She went to wait outside, trying to make sense of what she had seen. Should she mention it to Lily? In the end she decided to casually drop into conversation that she had seen Richie at the pub with another woman, but to say nothing of the exchange she had witnessed. After all, it could be perfectly innocent, just her dislike of Richie leading her to suspect him of underhand dealings. She would give him the benefit of the doubt.

'Sorry to keep you waiting,' Thea said a short while later, breezing out of the door, sounding thoroughly unrepentant. 'You know how it is.'

Jenny could only wish that she did. Not that she begrudged Thea time with Fitz, knowing as she did how quickly happiness could be shattered. She wove her arm through her friend's and they picked their way along the dark pavement, eyes firmly on the painted white kerb to keep them on course.

'So that's Edwin's fiancée,' Thea said, fiddling with her torch. A second later, it illuminated a pale circle ahead of their feet.

'You can say it,' Jenny said. 'You liked her. So did I.'

'I'm sorry. I wish I didn't. I really wanted her to be a complete cow.'

Jenny sighed. 'I did too, so don't feel bad about it. But really, it's better this way. Imagine how awful it would be to see Edwin engaged to a woman who couldn't make him happy.'

'But then he would break it all off with her and get together with you. Then *you* would be happy too.'

'There's no guarantee he would realise she wasn't right for him until it was too late. As much as I want to be with him, I couldn't bear to see him unhappy. At least this way I know he's with someone who cares for him.' If she said it enough times, she might start believing it.

'You're a far nicer person than me. I could never be so understanding if Fitz suddenly announced that he was in love with someone else.'

'I wouldn't expect you to. He's already told you he loves you, so for him to go off with someone else would be a betrayal. Edwin, on the other hand, has never been anything but a friend to me. My feelings are completely one-sided, as much as it pains me to admit it.'

And the fact that Mina had noticed Edwin's suffering when Jenny hadn't was proof that she was far more deserving of his love. Still, it hurt, and she didn't have to hide that hurt from Thea.

She jumped when Thea's arm wrapped around her shoulders. 'I still think you should try and stay away from him. It would be less painful.'

'How can I? Even if he didn't come to me every day for a weather forecast, I would see him at the pub with you and Pearl when we're with Greg's crew. Or are you suggesting I stop going out with you two as well?'

'I suppose you're right.' Thea heaved a sigh. 'I just don't understand why Pearl and I should be happy with the men of our dreams when you, who are far more deserving of happiness, should have to watch your dream man with another woman.'

Part of Jenny wanted to bury her face in Thea's shoulder and howl. Yet she had the sense that if she gave in, screamed at the unfairness of the world, she would sink so deep into despair that she might never break free. Besides, she still had plenty to be grateful for, especially at a time when so many people were suffering devastating losses. She needed to stay positive and be thankful for what she did have and not dwell too deeply on life's might-have-beens.

'You know, in most of the novels I read, the hero or heroine has to endure some kind of trial. Maybe this is just my trial, and I'm going to emerge from the other side a better person.'

'I like your thinking.' Jenny could hear the smile in Thea's voice. 'All right, then. If this is your story, and having to let go of Edwin is your trial, who are you going to walk off into the sunset with? Not Ben, I hope.'

'Who says I have to walk off into the sunset with a man to achieve a happy ending? What about the ending of *Casablanca*? Rick doesn't get his girl, but he does the right thing in letting her go and he walks off with Louis.' Jenny had sobbed over that ending when she'd seen the film, wishing Rick could have ended up with Ilsa, but now she was starting to understand Rick's reasoning.

'Well, I suppose that's a better ending than dying of consumption, which seems to be the ending heroines got in most of the books I was forced to read at school.'

'Oh, I read some books like that. Weren't they awful!' Jenny eagerly seized upon the change of subject. But even though the friends didn't return to the subject of Edwin, Jenny couldn't rid herself of the worry Mina had put into her mind. Why had his experiences after the crash affected him more deeply than Greg? She hoped that he would be persuaded to confide in Mina, because she had no idea how to tackle the subject if it fell to her. Yet if he needed help, she couldn't turn her back, no matter the hurt it would cause her to spend more time in close company with him. She loved him too dearly to walk away.

Chapter Seven

The following day, there were still no ops on, although Edwin got the sense that a big event was brewing. He tried not to dwell on it and did his best to devote his full concentration to the training flight Greg insisted upon. Yet all day there was the constant niggle in the back of his mind that their missions had been too easy up to now. No matter how much he tried to shake it off, he couldn't get away from the feeling. He didn't mention it to Greg or Fitz, knowing they both had their own way of dealing with the stresses associated with being aircrew and not wanting to disturb them.

His unease was probably exacerbated by the fact that, when he had gone to the Met Office for a forecast before their training flight, Jenny had not been there. She wasn't always there, of course. She might be off duty or out taking readings. But somehow it put him out of sorts for the rest of the day.

The test flight passed without a hitch, though, and once they were finally free to leave the base he headed into Fenthorpe to meet Mina.

She wasn't in the White Horse but, when he wandered up the high street to see if he could find her, he soon saw her walking down the opposite pavement. Her face lit up when he called to her, and she dashed across the road to meet him. She wore her uniform greatcoat, which covered her clothes apart from the occasional flash of tweed as her stride revealed her skirt. It hit him with a lurch of guilt that, although he was happy to see her, he didn't feel the same jolt of pleasure he always felt upon seeing Jenny.

'Let's go for a walk,' Mina said when she reached him, and wove her arm through his. 'There's still an hour or so of daylight left, and it would be a shame to waste it.'

'Why don't we go for a stroll through the grounds at Fenthorpe Hall?' Edwin said. 'The fields will be too muddy at this time of year, but I'm sure you must be dying to get out of the village for a bit if you've been here all day.'

'Sounds lovely.' Mina rested her head on his shoulder as they walked. 'Not that I'm complaining about the village. It's a pretty place, and I've had a lovely day.'

'Still, I'm sorry you had to spend so much of it alone when you came all this way to see me.'

'That's hardly your fault. Anyway, now we've got the whole evening together, which more than makes up for a day spent alone.'

So she had been lonely. Not for the first time, Edwin wondered why she had visited now instead of waiting for a time when they could both get leave at the same time. It was a sad reflection on all she had lost that she had no family to visit. And that was partly his fault too. It occurred to him then that she must have been terribly lonely when he had been reported missing. While she was not to tell him anything about the nature of her work, she had confided that she had found it difficult to make friends with the other women she worked with.

'Are you all right, Mina?' he asked. 'It's just occurred to me that you didn't have anyone to support you when I was missing. I'm afraid I never considered that until now.' He had thought of her, of course, and had hated the idea of her worrying about him, but he had thought more of Pearl and her fear for her missing husband. And Jenny. All his thoughts always seemed to lead him right back to Jenny. How had he got into this mess? Mina's lack of friends and family was precisely why he couldn't abandon her now.

Mina hugged his arm, turning her face to his with a sweet smile. 'It was a horrible time, but your mother was very kind, always being sure to keep me informed.'

And that was another reason for not ending the engagement. His mother thought the world of Mina, so breaking up with her would mean tearing his mother apart from someone she already regarded as a daughter.

'My parents told me you even went to see them,' he said. 'That was kind of you. I know your work keeps you busy.'

They had reached the end of the village by now, and they had to pause at the point where the pavement ended while a military truck trundled past, its wheels casting a fine spray from the puddles. He stepped in front of Mina to shield her from the worst of it.

She gave a rueful smile. 'You don't have to protect me from everything, you know.'

'Maybe not, but I wouldn't be much of a fiancé if I let you take the brunt of the spray.'

She opened her mouth, then shut it abruptly. Judging from her frown, she was debating whether to say something.

'What's the matter?'

'Funnily enough, that's what I wanted to ask you.' Now the road was free of traffic again, they continued their walk. She reached for his arm again but, instead of weaving her own arm through his, she took his hand. The frown was still on her face, and he had a sinking feeling he knew what she wanted to say.

'I'm perfectly fine,' he said, trying to keep the irritation from his voice.

'Then why won't you talk to me? Something happened to you in the Netherlands, and you haven't been quite right since.'

'I've told you all about it. If I'm not quite myself, can you blame me? We're supposed to be living in enlightened times, so how is it that children can be starving just a few miles across the sea?' It was true, he did feel that way about the emaciated children belonging to the family who had sheltered them, yet it wasn't the whole truth. But to tell her what was really bothering him would mean confessing the full horror of what he had done. It wasn't so much that he didn't want her to know, more that he couldn't bring himself to say it out loud. As much as possible, he kept the memory buried, and it only surfaced in his dreams. To tell someone else what he had done would make it real. Would make him a murderer.

This wasn't the first time Mina had tried to prise the truth from him, although before she had always accepted his explanation without comment and changed the subject. Now, however, Mina shook her head. 'I spoke to Greg last night, when I was waiting for you.'

He swallowed, his mouth suddenly dry. Surely Greg wouldn't have betrayed his confidence? 'What… what did he say?'

She turned on him, a flash of triumph in her eyes. 'So you admit there's something you're afraid he might tell me!'

Edwin shook his head. 'No.'

'Then why did you look so scared?'

'I've told you everything. Honestly.' He held his ground, even when she narrowed her eyes at him. He wondered all over again what exactly she did at Bletchley Park, because right now he wasn't at all sure that she wasn't an expert at interrogation techniques.

Finally she sighed and rested her head back on his shoulder. 'I'm sorry. I'm only trying to help. I wouldn't try getting you to confide in me if I didn't care so much for you because I can see how this is eating you up inside.'

'It… was a ghastly time,' he allowed himself to say. 'I don't like talking about it, because I don't like bringing the war into what little time we have together.'

'And as I've already told you, I don't need protecting. You can't shelter me from all the horrors of the war.'

'Maybe I'm trying to protect myself.' The words tumbled out almost before he thought them. 'Maybe I just want to survive long enough to see the end of the war. Can you blame me for that?'

The creases on her brow smoothed. 'No. Of course not. I'm sorry. Forget I mentioned it.'

If only he could forget what he had done.

The pain Jenny felt at seeing how well suited Mina and Edwin were was as sharp as ever the following day and wasn't helped by Lily's incessant chatter.

'Ben really likes you,' Lily said, buffing her hands in the cold wind while Jenny made a note of the wind speed. 'You should come out with me and Richie again.'

Ben really likes himself, Jenny wanted to say, but refrained. Instead, she simply remarked, 'He's not really my type.'

'What is your type, then?' Lily asked as they clattered down the metal staircase off the Watch Office roof.

Edwin. Edwin's my type. 'Golly, this wind is making my eyes water.' She wiped away the sudden tears that had welled in her eyes. Once they reached the foot of the stairs, she set out along the path to the Stevenson screen and gave Lily a bright smile, hoping her distress didn't show. 'Oh, you know, someone who's kind, likes reading, that sort of thing. Someone I can talk to easily.' *Like Edwin.*

Lily wrinkled her nose. 'How dull. I like Richie because he's exciting and *sooo* good-looking.' She pretended to swoon, the back of her hand pressed dramatically to her forehead. Then she practically skipped the final few paces to the Stevenson screen and flung open the door. 'When we're together I feel all jittery and breathless. I know it's early days, but I think I'm in love.'

These were all things that Jenny felt too. If she'd had the energy, she would have cautioned Lily to wait until the initial euphoria had subsided before declaring herself in love, but it was hard to bestir herself when she was feeling so heartsore. Instead she let Lily chatter on while they noted the remaining observations. However, when they returned to the Met Office, the heightened tension in the air sharpened her flagging concentration. It told her that ops were on that night even before the duty officer informed them. To Jenny's relief, Lily picked up on the sense of urgency and settled to her tasks, attentive and dedicated. While she might have had her head turned by Richie, it didn't seem to have affected her sense of duty.

If anything, the upcoming mission had made her thoughtful. When they went out for the next hourly readings she asked, 'Where do you think they're going?'

Jenny reset the minimum thermometer before replying. 'I don't know, but I prefer not to think about it.'

'You've got friends among the aircrews. How do you cope?'

Jenny gave her a sympathetic smile. 'By concentrating on my work and not letting my imagination get carried away with me. If it helps, remember that the crews are relying on you to play your part.'

'It doesn't feel very important, reading temperatures.'

'It is, though. If they didn't need us to do it, trust me, the WAAF would have assigned us elsewhere long ago. But it's vital. The navigators couldn't plot their routes without accurate data on wind speeds. And they need to know if there's a danger of icing. And don't forget the forecasters need as much accurate data as possible from all over the country if they're to be able to predict suitable weather for a mission and what the conditions will be like over the target. While the individual tasks we do might seem insignificant, they all make their contribution.'

Lily jotted down the final reading, then closed the door to the Stevenson screen, appearing to think about what Jenny had said. 'I suppose you've got a point. But how do you cope when you're not on duty?'

'Well, that's not so easy. But I still try to keep busy. I write letters to my family or go for walks. And I often volunteer to hand out tea when it's time for the crews to return. If you have trouble sleeping, you should join us.'

'I will. It's a good idea.'

They hadn't long returned to the warm Met Office, and Jenny was making a start plotting the latest readings on the chart, when Edwin walked in. With Mina's concerns uppermost in her mind, she studied him surreptitiously while he spoke to the duty officer. On the surface he seemed as confident as usual and as cheerful as anyone could be on the morning of a mission. Yet when he approached her afterwards for her version of the forecast, she thought she detected a shadow lurking behind his smile. What had happened in the Netherlands that he was still affected weeks later? She caught herself actually looking forward to seeing Mina again, because she wanted to ask if she'd had any success in worming the truth out of him.

'Target dead ahead, Skipper,' Edwin said. It was an unnecessary observation. There was no way anyone could miss the inferno. Everything glowed orange. It was no longer night, but the sun had fallen from the sky and engulfed Dresden. Immense flares belched from its surface, raking the skies. He could swear he felt the heat on his face, although that was surely impossible from this distance. With horror it dawned on him that the high winds that had sped them to their target must have also fanned the flames into an inextinguishable conflagration.

Dimly, he heard Greg's acknowledgement over the intercom, then his instruction to Fitz to commence the bombing run.

Bombing run? Edwin wanted to scream. *You want us to add to that?*

Then Fitz's voice sounded over the intercom, guiding the Lancaster to the position where they were to drop the bombs. It was hard to tell from the tinniness of his headset but Edwin thought he detected a shake in his voice. The Lancaster lurched and Edwin grabbed his dividers before they could slide off the table. How Greg could guide the aircraft when they were being thrown around in the violent air currents he couldn't imagine, but finally Fitz announced: 'Bombs away!' Edwin's stomach swooped as, released from the weight of the payload, *J-Jackson* surged upwards. 'Bombs gone,' Fitz announced a moment later.

'Hold steady, everyone,' Greg ordered. 'Waiting for the flash bomb.' Maybe it was his Australian accent, but Greg always sounded supremely relaxed, as though he was sunning himself on the beach instead of trying to keep a bucking, rolling Lancaster under control. It was this apparent confidence that helped Edwin get himself under control and, bracing himself against the fuselage, he hastily checked their course, ready to shout out the bearing of their return course. It took a moment to register that the drops splashing onto the paper were his own tears.

The crew were unusually subdued on the return trip. Even accounting for the fact that they had a particularly long distance to fly, Dresden being on the eastern side of Germany, almost into Czechoslovakia, there was none of the usual banter between the gunners as they kept a lookout for enemy fighters. Edwin could only imagine everyone was as shocked as him. They had been told they were taking the war to Germany – that was why they had volunteered for a second tour – and Edwin had never hesitated to do his duty, knowing that knocking out vital factories and supply routes was helping the troops on the ground as they attempted to break through the German lines. Every week came news of the latest parts of Europe that had been liberated, and he knew that Bomber Command's bombing campaign was a vital part of that advance.

Tonight, for the first time, Edwin questioned the purpose of bombing a particular target. Tonight there had been far more than a factory or railway line destroyed. The blaze that had lit the sky from horizon to horizon had been from a whole city ablaze. A city full of civilians no different from the people of Coventry, London or Liverpool. Edwin vividly remembered the pictures following the brutal attacks on Coventry. The people had declared it an act of evil. If that was the case, what did that make him? From what he had seen, Dresden had suffered worse than Coventry.

If he hadn't had to concentrate on their course he might have sat and wept, but the need to plot their progress and inform Greg of any corrections proved a welcome distraction, especially as they were now battling into a gale that threatened to throw them wildly off course if he didn't give his full concentration to the task. As the flight went on, he became aware of increasing exhaustion. At one point he even contemplated taking one of the 'wakey-wakey' pills issued to all aircrew. However, he had taken one on a previous mission, and it had given him the odd sensation of being both wide awake and exhausted, and his heart had been pounding for hours after the flight was over. He also hadn't been able to sleep afterwards, which had compounded his exhaustion. In the end he decided that, unless he feared he was in actual danger of falling asleep, he would leave the Benzedrine pill where it was.

Edwin was thankful that they didn't encounter any enemy fighters; he wasn't convinced the gunners had had their full minds on keeping a lookout. When he announced that they had crossed the English coast, there were sighs of relief from all the crew. Knowing they were only a short time from their destination revived him enough to have complete confidence that he wouldn't need any Benzedrine on this trip. This was one mission they would all be desperate to forget.

The landing passed by in a blur, and Edwin left *J-Jackson* in a daze. He was vaguely aware of reporting to a white-faced Thea that all his instruments were in fine working order, and then he was on the bus being transported the distance from the dispersal bays to the operations block.

As usual there were a handful of WAAFs waiting to welcome them back with mugs of hot strong tea. Edwin took the cup offered to him, suddenly aware that he was parched after the long flight.

'What happened? You look awful.'

It was only then that he realised that the WAAF who had given him his tea was Jenny. He forced a smile. 'Nothing. It was a routine mission, went like clockwork.' He became aware of his aching body, stiff and sore after hours of being hunched over the charts.

He took a sip of tea, not caring that it scalded his mouth, and it revived him. Glancing around at his crewmates, who had emerged from the bus with him, he saw everyone was haggard, bowed and stumbling like old men. No wonder Jenny was worried. She was still gazing at him doubtfully, so he made an effort to give a genuine smile.

'Honestly, we all made it through without a scratch. It was just a long flight.' And that was true. As far as he remembered it was the longest flight he had done, and certainly the one with the longest overland section, which always added to the stress of a mission. At least when they were over the sea they weren't facing anti-aircraft fire.

He must have been more convincing this time, for Jenny's features relaxed. 'Well, I'd better let you get on. Welcome back.' She hesitated as though debating whether to say something else. When she did speak, it was to say, 'I'm on night duty tonight, so I won't be able to come to the pub this evening. Give Mina my regards if you see her.' Although he was convinced that hadn't been what she had wanted to say.

He followed his crew into the locker room and, once he had shed his flying suit and returned his parachute and Mae West, he accompanied his crew to the briefing room, still clutching his tea. He answered the questions posed by the intelligence officer automatically, grateful that it was Fitz who responded to the one asking what they had witnessed over the target.

'It was an inferno,' he said in a strained voice that sounded most unlike himself. 'The whole city must have been destroyed.'

Greg chipped in. 'Dropping our bombs had as much point as throwing a match onto a blazing bonfire.'

'It's not your place to offer your opinion on your orders,' the intelligence officer replied. 'Just report what you saw, please.'

Usually the intelligence officers were gentle and tactful with the returning crews, who, after all, were usually on the brink of collapse from exhaustion by this time even if they had come through the night unscathed. Edwin stared at him in surprise and wondered if he also had his doubts about the purpose behind the all-out devastation they had caused.

It was only when he was on the transport laid on to return the officers to Fenthorpe Hall that he allowed himself to think about Jenny's words. Why had she asked him to give her regards to Mina? He had to admit being uncomfortable that the two women had met. He knew he had done wrong by Jenny and he wouldn't have blamed her if she had been cool towards his fiancée. However, she had proved herself the better person yet again by being nothing but warm and welcoming.

She was too good for him. Come to that, Mina was too good for him, but she depended on him and it would be cruel to end the engagement and leave her all alone. But now, after what he had witnessed tonight, he felt tainted. Or more tainted, considering what he had done after the crash. No, Jenny was better off without him.

Chapter Eight

If Jenny hadn't promised Mina to look out for Edwin, she would have stayed away from him after the Dresden mission. When she had spoken to him on his return, she had longed to wish him a happy Valentine's Day. Other WAAFs were kissing their sweethearts, making plans to celebrate the day later on, but after the mistletoe incident Jenny was unable to even mention it to him as a joke. It was another indication that, for the sake of her heart, she should take Thea's advice and go out with other people for a while, at least until she had recovered from her heartbreak, if such a thing was possible. However, Mina's concerns about Edwin had put that out of her head. All the crews had looked exhausted when they had tumbled out of the bus. And word had quickly got out about the horror that had been rained down upon Dresden that night, which explained why everyone had appeared grim, even the crew who had just completed their tour and should have been jubilant.

But Edwin had barely been able to look her in the eye. He reminded her of a faithful dog she had once had as a child who had cowered in the corner after chewing up her grancher's slippers. The way Silver had looked at her, as though he was undeserving of her love, was exactly how Edwin had appeared. She couldn't let him go. Not when he clearly needed a friend.

Yet it wasn't she who stayed away from Edwin but Edwin who stayed away from her over the next few days. At least, that was how it felt. He didn't seek her out in the Met Office, and, when she went to the White Horse on her next free evening, he wasn't there, even though the rest of his crew were present.

Mina wasn't there either, so she guessed they were spending the evening in Lincoln. It was a pity because she had wanted to engineer another opportunity to speak to Mina alone again and see if he had confided in her.

In the end she got an opportunity to see Mina on Friday, when she had a day off. She knew Edwin's fiancée must be due to return to Bletchley on Sunday, and so today would be her last chance to catch her alone as she wouldn't have a chance to get away the following day. Accordingly, she cycled into Fenthorpe after breakfast, determined to catch Mina before she went out anywhere.

As luck would have it, when she reached the village she saw Mina walking along the high street, which saved Jenny the bother of trying to get into the White Horse before it opened.

Mina greeted her like a long-lost friend. 'I'm so glad to see you,' she said once she had got off her bike and propped it against a wall, and kissed Jenny on the cheek. 'It's so trying having to wait in the village, never knowing when Edwin can get away. I don't suppose you know if they're flying ops today?'

'No. They don't usually announce anything until later. But Greg will probably want to take them on a training flight today, even if they're not.'

That seemed to make Mina's mind up. 'Are you free to come with me into Lincoln? I think I'll go mad if I have to hang around here all day.'

This suited Jenny and, as there was a bus leaving for Lincoln in ten minutes, while Mina hurried back to her room to fetch her coat Jenny secured her bike in the little yard behind the pub, having been given permission by the landlady.

The bus was packed with housewives clutching shopping baskets and men and women from RAF Fenthorpe eager to spend their day off in the city. Consequently, Jenny and Mina were forced to sit apart and didn't get a chance to speak. Jenny's situation was complicated when a finger tapped her on the shoulder from behind. She twisted around and saw a beaming Deedee.

'Fancy seeing you here. Have you got the day off?' Deedee asked.

Jenny nodded. 'I haven't seen you for ages. How are you settling in at the Gatehouse?'

'It's wonderful. At first I was afraid I would be homesick for Shrewsbury, but now I know that's impossible with Thomas and you three girls so close. It's lovely to have Pearl at the end of the drive, too.' She chattered on for a while about her excitement at welcoming her first great-grandchild into the world, then she sobered. 'And how are you, Jenny? Pearl tells me Edwin's engaged and his fiancée is here.'

Jenny felt her face flame. Mina was sitting a few rows further back, and Jenny could only pray she couldn't hear Deedee above the general chatter and the noisy engine. 'I'm fine,' she said, forcing a bright smile. 'I'm actually with Mina, Edwin's fiancée, today.'

'Is she on the bus?' Deedee craned her neck, examining the other passengers. 'Which one is she?' Then she seemed to pick up on Jenny's embarrassment, for she turned back abruptly and patted her shoulder. 'I'm sorry, dear,' she said, lowering her voice. 'I know how much he means to you. But things have a way of working themselves out, you know. Just look at me and Tom. Blissfully happy at last after all those years apart.'

This wasn't as comforting as Deedee must have intended, for Deedee and Thomas had been apart for over fifty years before finally finding each other again. Still, she nodded and said, 'It's lovely to see you and Thomas so happy together.'

'You'll be happy too, Jenny. I can feel it in my bones.' Deedee gave a twisted smile, 'And I daresay it won't take you another fifty years to get there. But really, getting friendly with his fiancée, are you sure that's wise?'

'Probably not. It's just sort of happened. The worst of it is, she's a lovely person. I can't help liking her.'

'You poor thing. It would have been so much easier if she'd been a complete cow.' Deedee sounded so much like Thea that Jenny laughed, and Deedee protested, 'Why? What did I say?'

'Nothing. I can just see where Thea gets it from.'

Deedee chuckled, 'Yes, much to Pearl's despair. But back to you – are you sure you'll be happy spending the day with the fiancée?'

'She has a name – she's called Mina. And yes, I'll be fine.' Jenny hesitated, wondering whether to confess their shared worries about Edwin, but decided not to break Mina's confidence. 'Honestly, you'd like her if you met her.'

'Perhaps I should. What are you doing tomorrow evening?'

'Not much. I'm on duty till eight.'

'But could you come to the Gatehouse for supper afterwards?'

'I could try to arrange a late pass.'

'Good. It's high time Tom and I had you young people round, and Mina must be lonely when Edwin can't get away. Introduce me to her when we get to the bus station, and I'll invite her too. Of course if Edwin, Greg and Fitz can make it, the more the merrier.'

The bus arrived in Lincoln soon after, and Jenny introduced Mina to Deedee.

'Oh, it's lovely to meet you! Ed told me all about your wedding,' Mina exclaimed. 'I thought it was so romantic.'

Jenny could see Deedee scrutinise Mina, and saw the moment she grudgingly accepted that she liked her. 'Thank you, dear. Now, how would you like to visit tomorrow evening?' She outlined her plans for supper, and Mina accepted with an enthusiasm that touched Jenny. The poor girl must have been terribly lonely for most of the week. Deedee took herself off to the shops soon after, having arranged to send Pearl to accompany Mina to the Gatehouse, and saying she would send invitations to Greg, Fitz and Edwin up to Fenthorpe Hall. Jenny had agreed to tell Thea.

'How lovely to meet her,' Mina said once Deedee had left. 'It will be a nice way to spend my last evening, too.' Her face clouded. 'I've tried speaking to Ed a few times now, but he insists there's nothing wrong. I think it will do us both good to be with others. I'd like to buy her a little thank-you gift. What would she like?'

Jenny thought about it. Gifts and trinkets were in short supply these days, as were flowers. 'Actually, she would probably like a book. She had to leave most of hers behind, and Thomas doesn't have many to her taste. She likes romances, the racier the better.'

'Oh, me too. I like Deedee more and more. Okay, then, lead me to a bookshop, one that sells the most shocking of romances. Maybe it's because I'm a mathematician,' she went on once they were heading for the high street, 'but whenever people buy me books, they always choose something terribly highbrow. But I'd much rather read a romance.'

Why did she have to be so nice? With an inward sigh, Jenny turned in to the next lane.

She took Mina to her favourite bookshop, one of those magical stores that looked tiny on the outside yet seemed to expand the further you wandered within. As they browsed the shelves, Mina quizzed Jenny on her reading preferences, and Jenny was obliged to explain about her upbringing. 'I grew up in the Forest of Dean,' she said. 'It was hard to get hold of new books, but occasionally I would find a book stall in a jumble sale or church fete, and I would buy whatever I could find. So my reading was dictated by the choices of the people donating them. It was fun, though. I read about some fascinating subjects that I would never have chosen if I'd had a wider selection. I used to enjoy romances too, but my granny never approved of those, so I stopped buying them.'

'What was it like growing up in a forest?' Mina looked impressed. 'I grew up in London. I can't imagine being surrounded by trees.'

'I suppose I took it for granted. It's strange living in Lincolnshire, though. I'm not used to being somewhere I can't hear the trees. The hut where I sleep is near the back of the

Waafery, not far from the hedgerow, and I always sleep better in the summer when it's breezy and I can hear the leaves.'

Mina replaced the book she'd been looking at and pulled out another. 'Oh, this one sounds good. A young woman in the clutches of a lonely, embittered duke.'

'Sounds perfect.' Jenny smiled. 'Although you should know I'm not being entirely selfless. Deedee always lets me read her books when she's finished them.'

'Excellent, so it saves me getting you something!'

Laughing, Mina went to pay, then she led the way outside. 'All this choosing books has left me parched. Where can we get a drink?'

'If you feel up to a steep uphill walk, we can go the Bishop's Pal. It's my favourite tearoom.'

After much puffing and panting, they climbed Steep Hill, then Jenny led them past the cathedral and to the Bishop's Pal.

'This is wonderful,' Mina said, looking around the room, and Jenny found herself taking in the cosy armchairs and vases of flowers as if for the first time. 'You're lucky living so close to Lincoln.'

Jenny opened her mouth to reply but was forced to wait at the ear-shattering noise of two or three Lancasters flying past, which set the cups and saucers around the room rattling.

'Or maybe not.' Mina had turned pale. 'I'm not sure I could cope, hearing planes flying past so often and wondering if someone you know is up there. Although' – she shrugged – 'Ed might find it easier to speak to me if he thought I had a better understanding of what he does.'

'Why – has he still not said anything?' Jenny looked at Mina, dismayed. She had serious doubts if she was the best person to get Edwin to open up, but neither could she refuse to help him.

Mina shook her head. 'I honestly think he's decided it would upset me too much to hear what he's been through. He's always been very protective of me.'

Jenny looked at Mina thoughtfully, nibbling the delicious treacly corner of her flapjack. 'You mentioned before about him being protective. Is there any particular reason? Sorry, that's really nosy. You don't have to answer.'

'It's fine. I don't mind. The thing is, I'm an orphan.'

'Oh, I'm sorry.'

'There's no need. I was very young, and I don't really remember my parents. And I wasn't left all alone. I had my younger brother, Daniel, and we were brought up by our uncle and aunt in London. The trouble was, they had their own children and, although they never neglected us, it was obvious they didn't love us. When I announced I wanted to read maths at Cambridge, they said they couldn't afford to support me through my degree, so I was forced to try and get a scholarship. When I met Ed, he seemed to take it upon himself to make up for all I had missed. He was shocked that I should have felt unloved as a child and he seemed to want to protect me from anything else bad ever happening to me again.'

There was a pause as Mina swallowed more tea. Jenny reflected that this sounded very much like Edwin. He did seem to want to solve the world's problems. She went cold as it occurred to her that that was why he had singled her out. Had he taken her on as a project? Detected a mind longing for learning and done what he could to help? It wasn't a comfortable thought. She had thought he had befriended her for her own sake.

'I can understand why he's protective of you,' Jenny said. 'I can see how it started – he does like to solve problems.'

'Yes, he's a problem-solver. That's exactly the right way to describe him.' Mina looked down at her plate, blinking. 'The thing is, it doesn't stop there, because—' She glanced up, and Jenny felt a lurch of shock when she saw Mina's eyes were swimming with tears.

Acting on impulse, Jenny reached across the table and clasped Mina's hand. 'I'm sorry, Mina. I didn't mean to bring up bad memories.'

Mina gave a little shake of her head. 'It's not you. This is something that's always hanging over me. Daniel was killed, you see. He joined up as soon as he was old enough and was killed three years ago.'

'That's awful,' Jenny whispered, feeling helpless. All she could do was say again, 'I'm so sorry.'

'Thank you. And I'm sorry for piling this on you when we hardly know each other.' Mina freed her hand from Jenny's, rummaged in her pocket and pulled out a hanky. She blotted away her tears and shot Jenny a determined smile. 'It's not as if I'm the only one to lose a loved one, and I can take comfort in my work, knowing I'm doing my bit to put an end to the war.'

'But it's made Edwin all the more protective of you.'

'Well, yes. He proposed not long after, and I've often wondered' – she gave a little shake of her head – 'but I'm being silly. It doesn't help, though, that we both get such limited leave. We hardly see each other, so most of our communication is done by letter and the occasional telephone call.'

Jenny nodded, remembering how hard it had been for Pearl and Greg before Greg's return to Fenthorpe. She couldn't help feeling guilty, remembering the times when Edwin had spent a forty-eight-hour leave in Fenthorpe, accompanying Greg or Fitz. She had presumed it was for her sake, but now she supposed it was because Mina had been unable to see him then. A little stab of pain accompanied that thought.

'I suppose if Edwin feels he has to look after you, it must be difficult for him to share what he's going through if he thinks you'd find it painful,' she said, determined not to let her upset affect Mina.

'Exactly. But whatever's bothering him, I can't bear to see him try to shoulder it alone. He can't go on like this.'

'No.' And although Jenny didn't say it, she was worried about how the burden was affecting his performance when he was on a mission.

Mina leaned forward, her eyes fixed on Jenny's. 'I can tell he's not going to open up to me on this visit. Whenever I approach the subject, he clams up all the more tightly. You know, at first when Deedee invited me to supper, I was disappointed because I thought tomorrow evening would be our last chance to talk, but now I think it's for the best, because he's more relaxed when he's got his friends around him.' She gave a wry twist of the mouth. 'Probably because he knows I can't start pestering him to talk. But anyway, I'd rather our last evening together be a happy occasion. If he doesn't voluntarily tell me what's on his mind, I'm not going to press him.'

'You're probably right.' Jenny could understand not wanting to part on bad terms. Especially when Edwin was doing such a dangerous job. There would always be the fear that they might never see one another again. 'I haven't forgotten what I promised. I won't stop being a friend to him, and, if I can persuade him to speak, I will. You never know, he might find it easier to speak to a friend.'

And one day she would finally stop hurting every time it hit her that that was all he felt for her.

Chapter Nine

Edwin always enjoyed visiting the Gatehouse. Quite apart from the wonderful food that Mrs Stockwell always seemed to magic out of thin air using minimal coupons, Thomas was good company, undemanding yet always seeming to know exactly how Edwin was feeling and always having the right thing to say. Now Deedee was there, it was as though the Gatehouse had come into full bloom. Even though Edwin had known nothing of Thomas's past, as soon as he crossed the threshold that evening he could tell that Deedee made Thomas complete. The living room was no longer a lone man's residence, comfortable as it had been. There were now touches that were unmistakably Deedee: a vivid turquoise and orange blanket over the back of the sofa; a stack of well-thumbed romances on one of the occasional tables; sprigs of greenery and snowdrops scattered in little vases about the room. And, of course, photographs of Pearl and Thea on the mantelpiece, Pearl and Greg's wedding photo taking pride of place next to an older, sepia-tinted photograph of a young bride who looked remarkably like Thea. He guessed this must be Pearl and Thea's mother. Elsewhere around the room there were also framed photographs of children, and it didn't take long to see that they were pictures of Pearl and Thea at various ages. Edwin guessed that Deedee was doing her best to include Thomas in his granddaughters' early lives, having kept his daughter from him in the mistaken belief that he hadn't wanted to know her.

Deedee bustled into the living room, carrying a full tea tray. Edwin hurried to take it from her.

She beamed at him. 'Thank you. Has Mina shown you what she bought me?' When Edwin shook his head, wondering if he should have bought a gift, Deedee reached into a large pocket in her pinafore skirt and pulled out a paperback book. 'I nearly hugged the life out of her when she presented me with this. I was looking at it in Lincoln only the other day, and it broke my heart to put it back on the shelf, but I really couldn't justify the extravagance of a new book when there are so many books here I haven't read.'

Thomas entered the room with Fitz and Greg at that point, and had clearly heard. 'I keep telling you I'll empty the shelves and fill them with romances if that's what you'd prefer.' And looking at his glowing face, Edwin could tell these weren't empty words. 'I'm sure Jenny could find a home for these.' He looked around the room. 'Where is Jenny, anyway? And Thea?'

'They can't get away until eight, so they'll be along as soon as they can. We'll hold supper for them, but Mrs Stockwell has provided snacks for those of us who can't wait that long.'

Mina entered the room at that point bearing a tray laden with a large carrot cake, plates and forks. 'We're having a backwards meal,' she announced. 'We're starting with cake, which I think is the best way to eat. Get the important food in first.'

Mina appeared more relaxed than she had been all week, and Edwin was relieved that she hadn't got him alone and subjected him to another interrogation. In fact, he was relieved not to be alone with her this evening. She would expect him to hold her hand, kiss her, and he couldn't seem to do that any more without thinking of Jenny. It was eating him up inside. It wasn't fair on either of them to continue with the engagement when his heart wasn't in it, yet how could he leave her when she had no one else? Especially when he had her brother's death on his conscience.

'Quite right too,' Deedee told her with a smile. 'A woman after my own heart.'

Edwin's conscience gave another vicious twist.

Deedee's gaze wandered over the bookshelves. 'I suppose we could get rid of the books by Dickens. I'm never going to read them, and then I could clear these off the table.' She indicated the stack of romances.

'That's easily dealt with.' Thomas swept the top shelf clear. 'These can go in my study for now, and I'll let Jenny take any she fancies.'

'That will be all of them,' Pearl said with a grin then went to help Deedee set her books in their place.

Edwin took his cake and found an empty seat next to Fitz. It happened to be beside the fire, and one look at the flames reaching up the chimney made him break out into a sweat. He turned slightly so he was facing into the room.

'You as well?' Fitz muttered in a voice meant for his ears only.

Edwin noticed his cake was untouched, and he looked sharply at his friend, only now noticing the shadow beneath his eyes and the lines of strain round his mouth. He had been so wrapped up in his own horror that he hadn't noticed anyone else's suffering. He checked to see they could not be overheard, and was reassured to see the others gathered around the bookshelves holding an animated discussion about which other books should make way for Deedee's romances. 'You really ought to read Heyer,' Deedee was saying. 'I know you'd enjoy her style.'

'I can't get Dresden out of my head,' he muttered. 'I can't stop thinking about all those fires.'

For a moment Fitz didn't respond; he simply nodded slowly, his eyes focused on nothing in particular. Or nothing Edwin could see outside his nightmares, at any rate. Edwin had just decided his friend wasn't going to speak and had opened his own mouth to make another comment when Fitz said, 'It was like looking into hell.'

Edwin recalled then that Fitz would have been viewing the scene through the bomb aimer's window below the cockpit. He would have been lying on his front, looking right down at the inferno. 'I don't think I'll ever forget it,' he went on.

'I don't want to forget it.' There was a peculiar vehemence to Fitz's tone. 'I owe the people of Dresden that much, at least.'

Edwin glanced across at Greg, who stood with his arm round Pearl, watching the book discussion without taking part. 'You know, you've got me thinking. Do you think the others feel the same way?' He meant the others in the crew. 'How's Greg taking it? I suppose I've been too busy with Mina this week to spend any time with him or the others, and I really should have done after an op like that.' As a newly promoted flight lieutenant, he was, after all, the senior officer in *J-Jackson*'s crew, outranking even the skipper. While he would always defer to Greg when they were in the air, he should make more effort to check on the men in between times.

Fitz's expression relaxed into a smile. 'Don't worry about Greg. I mean, he was as appalled as the rest of us, but he told me Pearl dragged the story out of him and refused to let him hold back, and he says that really helped. I would have told Thea, but I haven't had the chance yet.' He shot Edwin a curious glance. 'They can take it, you know. They're not fragile bone china that needs to be protected at all costs. They're WAAFs, after all. They know what we do.'

'But they're not the ones dropping the bombs.' He was the one who had guided *J-Jackson* to the target. Their bombs wouldn't have struck Dresden without his help.

Fitz ran a hand through his hair. 'You know, Thea said something the other day that made me think. She said she kept the instruments up to scratch, and we couldn't fly safely without them. So even though she didn't accompany us on each mission, she was as much a part of the crew as any of the men. And you could say the same about anyone on the base. We don't bear sole responsibility for our actions.'

'I suppose that's true.' Edwin thought of Jenny in the Met Office. He couldn't hope to plot an accurate route without factoring in the correct wind speed vectors. And he had no idea what Mina did, but he was sure that amount of secrecy wouldn't surround a job unless it was of the utmost importance.

'You should speak to Mina. I can see she wants to help you.'

Was it that obvious? 'Maybe,' he hedged. 'I'll think about it. I don't like to burden her when we hardly see each other.'

'It's funny,' Fitz said, 'but until Mina turned up I had no idea you were engaged. I always thought you carried a torch for Jenny.'

Edwin flinched, even though Fitz's tone had been conversational rather than accusatory. 'I'm not proud of keeping it secret. I tried explaining it to Jenny but I can hardly understand it myself, so I know I ended up sounding like the worst kind of liar.'

'Try me. Maybe I can help. I do understand that everyone has their own way of dealing with… well, what we face, without going mad.'

Edwin first impulse was to tell Fitz to mind his own business. After all, he was not proud of the way he had led Jenny on and he hated to even think of it, let alone explain to someone else. But then he recalled how understanding Fitz had been with Jack Knight, their rear gunner on *C-Charlie*, whose nerves had shattered under the relentless stress of their first tour.

'Well, I think I'd got into a state of mind where I had to completely separate my life in the RAF from everything else. I don't know why, but I thought that, if I sealed it up like a bubble, I could pretend whatever I'd done or seen wouldn't infect the rest of my life. That way, when I went home on leave, I didn't have to bring the war with me.' Edwin ran his fingers over the bands on his sleeve. 'I know I'm making a mess of explaining myself but in the end it was like the outside world didn't exist when I was here. Jenny was… an oasis in the midst of the madness. It didn't occur to me that I was doing anything wrong because I'd shut out the outside world and had practically forgotten Mina was in my life.'

'No, I think I understand. I suppose I did something similar. Only maybe it was easier for me to separate myself from my home life because I only had my mother to worry about at home. And it's not like I'll ever go back to my old life, because I knew when I joined up I was saying goodbye to dancing for good.'

It took a moment for Edwin to register that the chill draught on his neck was coming through the hall door, which had been flung open, and he jumped when Thea's voice said, 'You're too old, anyway. But I'll dance a tango with you any time.'

He twisted round in his chair just in time to see Thea lean over the back of Fitz's armchair and ruffle his hair. Jenny was just behind her, her face becomingly rosy from the cold night air. If she'd heard what he'd said about her, he would die of embarrassment.

She looked quite composed, however, and simply greeted him with a warm smile, so he guessed she hadn't.

Edwin thought she was an oasis! Jenny hugged that thought to herself all the way through the rest of the evening. Thea had flung open the door just as he had said it. She had shot Jenny a startled glance, then hastily spoken, to alert the men that they were no longer alone.

Mina, thankfully, had given no sign that she had heard, and somehow Jenny had managed to greet Edwin normally, as though she hadn't heard him admit how much she meant to him. She had always known in her heart that she was special to him, but it was good to hear him say it, even if it wasn't to her face.

When it was time for the party to break up, everyone replete with Mrs Stockwell's excellent lentil shepherd's pie, Mina ran up to Jenny and hugged her. 'I'm leaving first thing tomorrow, so I won't see you before I go.' She glanced around, and Jenny noticed her relax when her gaze fell on Edwin, standing on the far side of the room. Mina lowered her voice. 'Do what you can for him, please. I worry about him so, and he hasn't opened up at all.'

'Of course,' Jenny said, her head and heart too full of Edwin's praise to deny her anything. If anything, she felt sorry for Mina, knowing she didn't have Edwin's whole heart. Mina deserved to be loved completely.

Mina drew out a piece of notepaper from her pocket and thrust it into Jenny's hands. 'This is my address,' she said. 'Will you write and let me know how he is?'

'Of course.' Although honesty compelled her to add, 'but I can't break a confidence if Edwin tells me something he doesn't want shared.'

'I wouldn't ask you to. I just want to know that he's all right.'

–

'You know,' Thea said once she and Jenny were walking arm in arm back to the Waafery, 'if my grandchildren ask me one day how I spent the war, I'm going to have to tell them I spent most of it walking around in the dark.'

Jenny chuckled. 'There does seem to be an awful lot of that.'

'I've had a lot of conversations recently about what I'm going to do after the war.'

'Oh, me too. It's hard not to get excited now the end is well and truly in sight.' For the news had been full of the Russian advance from the east and the great advances led by Patton and Montgomery.

'Well, I've decided that the thing I'm really looking forward to is proper street lighting and torches that actually light up whatever they're pointing at.'

'Perhaps we should stop going out in the evenings if you hate walking in the dark so much.'

'What, and miss such gems of conversation as you being an oasis?'

'So you heard it too.'

'Yes, and I've been dying all night to hear what you think.'

Jenny sighed. 'It doesn't really matter what I think. He's still engaged to Mina. Nothing's changed.'

'Not yet, but it proves he loves you.'

'Does it?' Jenny cringed at how eager she sounded, and tried to tone it down. 'He could have meant anything.'

'Let me put it this way,' Thea said. 'If Fitz said to me, "Jenny's my oasis," I'd have some hard questions for the both of you.'

'But Edwin and I have always been good friends. He could just mean that I brightened his day.'

'That's not what an oasis is. It's a haven in the wilderness for exhausted, thirsty travellers. If that's not a declaration of love, I don't know what is.'

Jenny didn't respond at first. She gazed into the sky and picked out the constellation of Orion, standing sentinel above the horizon. Ever since hearing Edwin's lecture, she had looked for it on every clear night, and the sight of it comforted her, holding as it did such strong associations of him. Edwin was her oasis. She had never put it in those words before, but that was exactly what he had been to her. She had arrived in Fenthorpe, lonely, a little nervous and thirsty for the education that had long been denied her. Her WAAF training had filled some of that gap, and she had drunk in every scrap of information she had been given, but all that had done was reveal even more gaps in her knowledge. Where other trainee Met assistants had placidly accepted what they were told and followed instructions without question, she had wanted to know the whys and hows of the job. Why was it important to know the maximum and minimum temperatures in any hour? Why was the current temperature not enough? How was it possible to calculate the dew point from the dry and wet bulb temperatures? Her tutors had become impatient, having a substantial course to cover in a short time, so she had looked it up for herself.

Pearl and Thea had more than put an end to her loneliness. She knew they would be her true friends for life, however scattered they became after the war. But Edwin had been the only one who had been able to answer so many of her questions. He had seemed to delight in her thirst for knowledge and had encouraged her in her learning. Now she tried to put her feelings into words. 'Edwin's my Rigel.'

Thea laughed. 'It's a good thing I was at the same lecture, or I would have struggled to follow your train of thought. Edwin's the brightest star in the constellation of Orion?'

Jenny nodded, before realising that Thea wouldn't be able to see her. 'Yes. I think my circle of friends is like a constellation – each one a bright spot in my life and each bringing their own characteristics and personality to the mix. You and Pearl are also two of the most important stars, of course, but I've had to accept that now Pearl's married with a baby on the way, and you're with Fitz, you can't spend so much time with me any more.'

'I'm sorry. I hope you haven't been lonely.'

'Not at all. I don't blame you. I suppose I've thought about it more these past few weeks now Greg and Fitz are back here. But I'm not complaining, because Edwin's here too, and at least I get to spend time with him again even though I know we can never be together in the way I'd like.'

'You should tell him how you feel,' Thea said.

'I tried, didn't I? That didn't end well.' She still cringed every time she remembered the mistletoe incident. 'Anyway, I didn't know about Mina then. She's lovely and I could never come between them.'

She heard Thea's sigh even over the sudden rustle of wind in the nearby hedgerow. 'I wish things could be easier for you. I feel bad that Pearl and I are so happy in love while you have to watch the man of your dreams with another woman.'

'Don't feel bad. Honestly, I'd rather you and Pearl be happy than have us all three miserable together. Anyway, this way I get all the attention and sympathy.'

'I'm not so sure about that.' Jenny could hear the grin in Thea's voice. 'It won't be long before Pearl's waddling around like a hippo on duck's legs, and we'll all have to rally around her.'

'It's hard to imagine one of us with a baby,' Jenny said, grateful for the change of subject. 'Just think, in another six months or so she and Greg will have a baby and they'll be a real family.' She hoped she didn't sound as wistful as she felt.

Thea hugged the arm she had woven through hers. 'You'll love it. You'll be Auntie Jenny, and I predict you'll be so devoted to Little Pearl you won't have time for anyone else.

Jenny glanced up at Orion again and didn't think that would be possible.

Chapter Ten

Days flowed into weeks, and Jenny did her best to forget what she had overheard. She had meant what she'd said to Thea when she'd declared she wouldn't come between Edwin and Mina. Especially having heard that Mina was far more alone in life than her. Jenny was lucky. She had wonderful friends, and her family loved her in their own way even if they couldn't comprehend her desire for learning. She threw herself into her work, rejoicing that every day the Allies were making real progress and the end of the war was becoming more and more certain. Knowing that she might never have as good an opportunity again for learning, she also attended all the evening lectures she could, drinking in every scrap of knowledge she could. All around, nature reflected the rising optimism, and the hedges and trees first produced swollen buds that then burst, tinting the landscape with a pale green mist. As March gave way to April, she enjoyed walking outside, feeling the warmth of the sun on her face.

'Things are getting quite serious with Richie,' Lily told her happily one day when they were in the snug at the White Horse. It was the first Saturday in April, and Jenny only had another six days to go before she was going home on a week's leave. Neither Pearl nor Thea had been able to get away that night, and Jenny had at first decided to stay in the rec with one of her new books from Thomas. Lily, however, had had other ideas and persuaded her to come to the pub.

'Why aren't you out with him tonight?' Jenny asked now. Richie's crew wasn't flying ops that night. 'If things are that serious, I'd have thought you'd be out together.'

'He's busy. Said he had to help out a friend, but he'd make it up to me the next night off we get together.' Lily's irritation at being stood up for a friend showed in her expression, and Jenny could see she was very much Lily's second choice of companion.

'Anyway, what about you?' Lily asked, making a clear attempt to regain her humour. 'You should go out with Ben again. He was asking after you the last time I saw him.'

'I already told you he's not my type.' This was a polite way of saying she wouldn't go out with him again if he was the last man on Earth. He had asked her out several times since the awful cinema trip, seemingly unable to comprehend that Jenny had no desire to see him again. Each time she had refused him gently but firmly and she hoped he had now got the message.

'You need to get your act together. At this rate the war will be over and you'll be the only one without a fellow at the end of it all.'

Jenny gazed at Lily, mystified. She made the war sound like nothing more than a game of musical chairs. Perhaps it was because RAF Fenthorpe hadn't suffered any major casualties since Lily's arrival, but Jenny couldn't help feeling that she didn't take the war as seriously as she should. She could only hope the girl was taking her duties more seriously. Now that Lily was a fully fledged Met assistant, it was no longer Jenny's responsibility to keep an eye on her work. 'I'm happy as I am,' she said.

'Oh, you don't fool me.' Lily shot Jenny an arch look. 'We all know you'd be only too happy to dance the night away if you were asked by a certain navigator.'

Jenny's face went hot. 'If you're talking about Edwin, we're just friends. And I'm friends with his fiancée too.' Had she made her feelings that obvious? She'd hate to think the whole of Fenthorpe was associating her with Edwin.

'All right, keep your hair on. I was just teasing. But you're a pretty girl. You should be out having fun.'

It was on the tip of Jenny's tongue to ask if plain girls were allowed to have fun too, but she didn't get the chance because Lily had changed the subject back to her own love life. 'Anyway, talk of having fun, I've got a forty-eight-hour pass coming up, and Richie's managed to wangle one at the same time. We're going up to York together.'

Jenny looked at Lily, unsure what to say. It wasn't unusual for unmarried couples to go away together, and guesthouses tended to have rigid rules that insisted single women stayed in separate rooms, if not on separate floors. Jenny knew of several women who had taken trips together entirely innocently. Yet something about the way Lily had announced her trip suggested that the pair weren't intending to do much sightseeing. 'You will be careful, won't you?'

Lily tossed her hair. 'You sound like my mum. I wouldn't have come out with you if I'd known you were such a stick-in-the-mud.'

'I'm just looking out for you. I wouldn't be a good friend if I didn't. You haven't known Richie that long. How well do you really know him?' Jenny suddenly remembered seeing him hand a mysterious package to the unknown woman. 'I'm still not happy with what I saw him doing with that woman in the public bar.'

She had described it to Lily at the time, but she had dismissed it. Now Lily gave a toss of the head. 'I'm sure it was nothing. He's promised me I'm the only one he loves and that's enough for me, so it's no good trying to talk me out of it.'

Jenny sighed inwardly, wishing she had stayed in the rec with her book. Books were so much less complicated than people. 'I wouldn't dream of talking you out of it. I hope you have a good time. But don't let him persuade you to do anything you're not ready for.' She wondered if she should say more, recalling what Lily had said about her strict upbringing. If Lily hadn't been allowed a social life before, she was certainly making up for it now, but her lack of experience with men might make her vulnerable. On the other hand, Lily wasn't showing any sign of wanting to hear Jenny's advice, so she decided to leave it for now. It was clear Lily would do whatever she wanted and had no intention of listening to advice. Jenny would only cause friction between them if she persisted.

When it was time to leave, Jenny glanced into the public bar as they passed, and felt a prickle of unease when she saw the same woman she had seen with Richie that time standing at the bar. She gave her head an impatient shake. The woman must be a local, and it was hardly unusual to be out on a Saturday night.

But when they wandered out into the twilight, she idly glanced at a group of uniformed men, only to stop when she recognised the man in the centre. He was trying to persuade the others to return to the bar.

'No fear,' one of the others said. 'It'll be more'n my life's worth if I don't have the cash to treat my girl to the cinema next Tuesday. Anyway, I thought you were off to York next weekend. You should be saving for that.'

'Oh, don't worry about me. I've been saving for a while. Nothing to keep me from one last pint. What do you say?'

But the others weren't keen, and the group moved away.

Jenny nudged Lily. 'I thought you said Richie had to stay in camp this evening. That's him there, isn't it?'

Lily, who had been fumbling with her coat buttons, looked in the direction Jenny was pointing. The next moment she was running towards the men. 'Oi, Richie. I thought you weren't coming out tonight?'

The other men shook their heads in mock disapproval. 'You're in for it now, my lad,' one of them said.

Richie shifted from foot to foot, then, when Lily caught him up, put an arm round her shoulders. 'I thought I couldn't and by the time I found out I was free it was too late to ask you out. But now we're here, why don't we pop back inside for a quick drink?'

'Oh, but I can't leave Jenny.'

Jenny, not wishing to find herself playing gooseberry, looked around until she saw another group of WAAFs who were clearly heading back to the Waafery. She knew them vaguely as they lived in the hut next door to hers. 'It's all right. I'll walk back with the Hut Two girls.'

'Ben's still inside,' Richie told her with a grin. 'I know he'd like to see you again.'

'Not this time,' she replied. 'I'm quite tired.' Then to Lily, 'Have fun. Don't forget you don't have a late pass.'

'I won't, Mum,' came the cheeky reply.

As Jenny went to join the girls from Hut Two, she distinctly heard one of Richie's friends mutter as he walked away, 'He must be the son of a millionaire. I don't know where he gets all his money from.' And she remembered the envelope he had handed to the unknown woman in the pub when Mina had been there. Had the woman paid for whatever it contained?

–

Three days later, Jenny met up with Pearl and Thea for the first time since her evening in the pub. She and Thea had spent the afternoon in Lincoln and then met Pearl after work, and all three had returned for an evening with Deedee and Thomas. Over a very tasty corned beef hash, Jenny explained her misgivings about Richie, including the incident a few weeks ago when she had seen him hand a package to the unknown woman.

'Lily's head over heels in love with him, but I can't help thinking there's something not quite right about him,' she concluded. 'I've tried to put Lily on her guard, but she won't hear it.'

'Did you tell her what you saw in the pub?' Pearl asked.

'I did but the trouble is, I'm not clear exactly what I saw. Lily's sure it was something innocent and that I'm making mountains out of molehills.'

'But *you* don't think it was innocent,' Pearl stated.

'No. I can't explain it, but there was something about their body language that made me suspicious. But I can't go around accusing people of getting up to no good simply because they were looking a bit shifty.'

'Maybe it was black-market cigarettes or something like that,' Thea said. 'Not exactly above board, but not major criminal activity either.'

'That would explain the extra money he seems to have,' Jenny said. Her fears eased. While black-market activity was, strictly speaking, illegal, enough people were involved in it for most to turn a blind eye. After years of rationing, shortages were really starting to bite, and last time Jenny had gone home she had seen enough evidence to suspect her grandmother of buying some stores on the black market. As long as Richie didn't involve Lily, Jenny could see no reason to try to persuade her to stop seeing him.

'Still,' Pearl said, 'there's no harm in keeping your eyes peeled in case it's more serious. I could do with another big story before I have to stop work.'

Jenny laughed, the last of her misgivings fading away. 'Then let's hope we discover Richie is the kingpin in a major black-market ring so you can end on a high note.'

'Have you been told when you'll be finishing?' Thea asked.

'Nothing's certain yet, but probably the end of May if I can persuade the powers that be to let me stay that long,' Pearl said. 'I'm hopeful they will, because I'm not working on an RAF base.'

'How do you feel about leaving the WAAF?' Jenny asked.

'I'm going to miss it, I can't deny it. Still, I'm starting to get excited about seeing this little one.' Pearl put a hand on her midriff, which was no longer as flat as it had been. 'Anyway, at the rate I'm starting to grow, I won't be able to fit into my uniform for much longer. I've already had to let the seams out, and it used to be too big. And forget about doing up the buttons on my tunic.'

'Count yourself lucky you don't have to wear battledress,' Thea said. Both Jenny and Thea wore battledress when on duty and, although Jenny loved the extra warmth and freedom, she could see that trying to button trousers over a pregnancy bulge would be difficult, and they would be more of a problem to let out.

'I always used to be envious of you two, in your trousers,' Pearl said, 'but I don't think I could do them up now. I'm already finding Steep Hill more of a struggle. I've had to cut back on my visits to the Bishop's Pal, because I can't face the climb any more. Still, I think I'm going to be bored after I finish work. At least Deedee's nearby, so I can visit her. I wouldn't know what to do with myself otherwise.'

As the conversation turned to ideas for how Pearl could spend her free time, Jenny thought over what had been said about Richie. She had wondered whether to make another attempt to share her misgivings with Lily, but now she decided to hold her tongue. She could only hope that, if Richie was involved in the black market, Lily would have the sense to stay out of it. And she also hoped that she wouldn't do anything stupid in York. She couldn't think of a delicate way to ask if Lily intended on staying in her room each night and not creeping into Richie's bed. But however sure Lily was that she loved Richie, Jenny hadn't seen evidence of the same strength of feeling on Richie's side.

Edwin arranged his charts on the navigator's table, then swung out his chair so he could sit down and strap himself in ready for take-off. Once he was secured, he placed his scale, pencils, compasses and dividers by his left hand where they would not easily be knocked to the ground. Once everything was arranged to his satisfaction he studied his chart, blinking as he tried to bring the lines into focus. A shadow fell across the table and he glanced up to see Fitz squeezing past on the way to his position, trying not to knock Edwin's instruments off the table with his bulky parachute.

Fitz met his eyes and smiled, then his gaze sharpened. 'Are you all right, Edwin? You look a bit peaky.'

'I'm fine. I didn't sleep well last night, that's all.'

Or the night before that. Or any night since Dresden. While the rest of his crew seemed to have recovered from the horror of that night – outwardly, at least – Edwin couldn't shake it off. Maybe it was because he was still haunted by his experience in the Netherlands. Whatever the reason, it followed him into his dreams night after night, and he would wake up in a sweat. Last night had been particularly bad and he had woken with a pounding headache. It was a good thing they weren't flying ops today; he couldn't wait for this training flight to be over so he could return to his room and put his head down.

'Coming through! Move over, Fitz, I need to speak to Edwin before we take off.'

Fitz shifted and now Thea stood in his place. 'I didn't know you were joining us,' he said. Although they often took ground crew on training flights, and there were women on the ground crew, they weren't often permitted to fly.

Thea grinned. 'I twisted my sergeant's arm. I don't see why the men should have all the fun.' She pointed to the navigation instrument panel. 'I had to fix your DF indicator needle yesterday, so I'm here to check it's working properly.' She caught the wireless operator's eye as she continued, 'Once we're up in the air, Wilf, set the DF loop to the homing beacon' – she nodded up to the ceiling-mounted direction finder loop – 'and then Edwin and I can check his indicator.'

Edwin was finding it hard to concentrate on this stream of instructions on top of his own preparations for flight, and it was a relief when Thea went to strap herself in for take-off. He shut his eyes as the aircraft taxied to the top of the runway, wishing his head would stop pounding.

Once they were aloft, however, the need to concentrate helped him shake off his stupor, and although his head still ached he was able to plot their course without difficulty. At least, he hoped he wasn't making any mistakes. If they found themselves in the middle of Italy, he'd know he'd gone wrong somewhere.

Presently Greg gave permission to test the direction finder, and Wilf Ryan got out of his seat and reached up to set the DF loop. Once that was done, Thea hovered over the navigation table while Edwin read the bearing of the homing beacon from his DF indicator, checking with Greg that the corresponding indicator on his instrument panel gave the same reading. When they didn't end up in Italy but back above RAF Fenthorpe, they repeated the procedure twice more until Thea was happy the instrument was fully operational.

She grinned at Edwin. 'I didn't think there would be a problem, but I was longing to get back in the air for a while.'

Edwin tried to grin back, but his headache was worse again and, judging by Thea's suddenly worried expression, he hadn't managed a convincing smile. She frowned and called to Greg, 'Edwin's not well. I think we should land.'

Edwin was too relieved that they were returning to be embarrassed. Thankfully they were already on the circuit above Fenthorpe, so it was only a short while before they were on the ground. Once they had returned to their dispersal point, the others scrambled out but Edwin remained in his seat, wishing the aircraft didn't feel like it was still moving.

A hand squeezed his arm, and he looked up to see Greg's concerned face. 'There's an ambulance waiting to take you to sick quarters,' he said. 'Come on, I'll give you a hand.'

Edwin felt so shaky, he was ashamed to find he needed Greg's steadying arm to help him out of the Lancaster. The airfield swam around him as they walked the few steps to the waiting ambulance. When Greg handed him over to the ambulance crew, he said, 'Take good care of him.' But before he left to join the rest of the crew, his grip tightened on Edwin's arm and he spoke in a low voice meant for Edwin's ears only. 'And if you ever endanger my crew again by flying when you're not fit, I'll finish you off myself.'

The threat was still ringing in his ears when he was put to bed in sick quarters. The MO had declared him run-down to the point of exhaustion and said that in his weakened state he had probably picked up a viral infection that had caused a high temperature. He doused Edwin with aspirin and told him to get some sleep. And sleep Edwin did, a mercifully dreamless sleep, and he didn't wake until early evening. The MO came and had another word, then pronounced himself satisfied that Edwin's temperature had dropped. Finally he said, 'I'll be keeping you here for two or three days, until I can be sure your temperature won't spike again. After that you're on sick leave for at least a week.'

'I can't leave my crew without a navigator.'

'You're no good to them in this state.' The MO gave him a sympathetic smile. 'Enjoy some home comforts for a week, take some walks in the fresh air. Then when you come back you should be fighting fit.' The last thing he said before he left was, 'You've got a visitor, by the way. I'll send her in.'

Considering Thea had been the first to notice how ill he was feeling, he expected she would be his visitor. However, when the door opened it was not Thea who walked in but Jenny, her brow creased with anxiety.

'How are you?' she asked, sitting in the chair the MO had just vacated. 'I was so worried when Thea told me you'd been taken ill, but they wouldn't let me see you until now.'

Of course Thea would have gone straight to Jenny. He couldn't be cross, though, because he was genuinely glad to see her. He was sure his crew would be along later, assuming Greg would still be speaking to him after flying when unfit, but it was Jenny whose presence he craved.

'I feel much better now,' he told her. 'The MO thinks I picked up a virus.' He decided he didn't want her to know about the being run-down part. It made him sound weak when the rest of his crew were unaffected. 'It's amazing what an aspirin and sleep can do.'

'How long do you have to stay here?'

'Two or three days.' He grimaced. 'Then I'm being packed off on sick leave for a week.'

'Quite right too,' Jenny declared. 'You need a rest. Will you go home?'

Edwin thought about it. 'I don't know.' He pulled a face. 'Home's not that restful.'

Jenny looked mystified. 'But you're always telling me how pretty your home is.' He'd often told her about the Surrey village where he'd grown up and how stargazing from his back garden had inspired his love of astronomy.

'It is, but my parents are… well, they were pretty rattled by me being reported missing last year.'

'That's understandable. We all were.'

'I know, but when I went home on leave when I got back, they were treating me like I might suddenly explode. And then when I told them I was volunteering for another tour, they were really upset.' It was why he had escaped early and gone to Bletchley instead, even though Mina hadn't been on leave. 'The MO told me to get some rest, but I'd be spending the week walking on eggshells if I was with them.'

'Where will you go, then?'

He shrugged. Not Bletchley this time. He didn't have the energy to face the guilt that always came with seeing Mina. 'I've got a couple of days to think about it. Somewhere like Snowdonia might be nice and peaceful, even though I won't be up to climbing mountains.'

'How about a forest?' Jenny leaned forward, her gaze locked with his. 'If it's peace you're after, you can't beat trees. My leave starts in three days. You should come to the Forest of Dean with me.'

Edwin gazed at Jenny in silence for an agonising length of time. At least, it felt that way to Jenny. What had she been thinking, inviting him to spend his leave with her? But she couldn't deny a thrill at the prospect of a whole week in his company with no one to come between them. Apart from her granny, grancher and all her brothers, of course. She really hadn't thought this through.

He still hadn't answered, which compelled her to fill the silence. 'Gosh, I don't mean staying with me, what must you think? My grandparents' cottage is hardly big enough for me and them, let alone a visitor.' She couldn't seem to control her gabbling. 'But Newnham on Severn isn't far, and you could find a place to stay there. Or maybe even at the Speech House. I can't remember if they're still letting out rooms.'

Why didn't he answer? This was getting embarrassing now. Almost as embarrassing as the moment when she had kissed him and he had gently and oh-so-kindly stopped her.

'Do you really mean that?' he finally asked.

Jenny studied him before replying. He didn't look displeased. If anything, he looked keen. 'Yes, I'd love to have a friend nearby, and I know my grandparents would love to meet any friend of mine.'

He smiled. 'It would be fun to visit the Forest of Dean, and it would be nice to have your company.'

But of course he didn't mean anything more by his remark than friendship. She mustn't get carried away and let herself believe he had taken up the offer thinking anything would happen. Jenny's offer had slipped out, but on reflection she could see that getting Edwin away from Fenthorpe might be a good way to help him open up and confide in her. She hadn't forgotten Mina's request. And she mustn't let herself forget that it was Mina, not Jenny herself, who Edwin loved.

Chapter Eleven

Edwin made a swift recovery, and to Jenny's delight he was ready to travel down to the Forest of Dean on the same day as her. They took their bikes and, armed with railway warrants, temporary ration coupons and their luggage, they travelled by train to Westbury-on-Severn, as the station at Newnham was temporarily closed. After reclaiming their bicycles from the guard's van, they cycled the remaining distance – a gentle two-and-a-half-mile ride – into Newnham, where Edwin had booked a room.

'So this is the Forest of Dean,' Edwin commented as they wheeled their bicycles up the broad high street. 'Funny, I would have expected more trees.'

'Well, the people have to live somewhere,' Jenny retorted. 'We don't live in treehouses, you know. I promise you'll have seen more than enough trees by the end of your stay.'

'I was only teasing.' He looked around, appearing to take in the buildings lining the street with their elegant Georgian facades. 'I like it already. Which way to the Raven?' This was the inn where he would be staying.

Jenny led the way to the side street and the half-timbered Raven Inn and only left when he was settled in. She still had the uphill bicycle ride to her grandparents' cottage, and she wanted to get it over before she was too tired. She promised to come back the next day and show him some trees and they arranged to meet after breakfast.

Even though there weren't so many hills around RAF Fenthorpe, her work kept her active, and Jenny was pleased to find she could still cycle the two-mile uphill ride without difficulty. The cottage was on the edge of Oakdean – a cluster of cottages at the top of a hill. Trees formed a protective arc to the west while, to the east, fields dropped away steeply, giving the residents a fine view of the River Severn winding in a silvery horseshoe bend far below.

Of all the times to come home, mid-April was the one Jenny would have chosen. The signs of spring were all around, in the pale bronze-green of unfurling leaves and the blue mist of bluebells glimpsed between the tree trunks. She breathed in the loamy scent of damp earth mingled with the fresh, soapy scent of bluebells as she pushed her bicycle through the garden gate.

Her granny was in the garden feeding the hens, and didn't immediately notice her, so Jenny stood and watched while the hens made dashes for the food, clucking and squawking as they fought for the best scraps. Her granny looked no different from when Jenny had last seen her six months ago, wiry and strong as ever, her hair still so blond Jenny would have sworn she must dye it if she didn't know of her grandmother's strong feelings about women who wore make-up and coloured their hair. She wore a striped apron over a high-necked blouse and long grey skirt that looked like it had gone out of fashion at the start of the last war. All her clothes were faded and patched yet meticulously clean.

Eventually her granny straightened and caught sight of Jenny. 'You took your time,' she said. 'I've been expecting you these past two hours.'

'The train from Gloucester was delayed, and then I had to stop in Newnham to show my friend to his hotel.'

Her granny's gaze sharpened. '*His?* You've brought a man with you? You've not been getting into mischief, have you?'

'He's just a friend,' Jenny said. 'I did write and tell you about him.'

'Last letter from you was three weeks ago.'

'I posted it three days ago. It must have been delayed. I'm sorry.' She didn't know why she was apologising for something beyond her control, but her granny always made her feel that way.

'Well, you're here now, and you can make yourself useful. When you've put your things away come and give me a hand with the veg. Your grancher caught four rabbits this morning and I'm making a stew.'

'Who's eating with us this evening?'

'It's just us. But your brothers will be along later with Sarah, Kate and the children. It's the only day they'll able to see you.'

Jenny braced herself for a busy night. Although she loved her four brothers and their families, they were a boisterous lot and she had hoped for a quiet evening after her long journey. Jenny's brothers were all older than her and, when her father had died, their grandparents had brought them all to their smallholding. It had been a squeeze, with her brothers having to share the attic while Jenny had been relegated to a tiny box room. It had been a relief when her brothers had got married and moved out one by one, allowing Jenny to move into the vacated attic. She had stayed in the Oakdean cottage until she had joined the WAAF.

After putting her bike in the shed and leaving her kit bag in her bedroom, she went downstairs to the large kitchen. Her granny was alone, standing at the range, stirring the contents of a large pot. 'There are still some carrots and potatoes left in the root cellar,' she said without turning her head. 'Go and fetch some. Oh, and a swede, too.'

As a girl, Jenny had hated trips to the root cellar. It was built into sloping ground at the back of the shed, and she had always imagined the dark lime-washed room to be the haunt of ghosts. It was certainly the haunt of spiders, and she had hated the feeling of cobwebs brushing her head. Even now, as she reached to the back of a shelf, she was fearful that a spider would scurry up her arm. Still, after years of having to take weather readings at all hours, the root cellar didn't hold the same fears as before and she soon returned and started work scrubbing and peeling the vegetables.

'Tell me about this young man of yours,' Granny said as Jenny chopped the swede.

'He's not my young man, just a friend. I'm sure I've told you about him in my letters. His name's Edwin Holland. He's a navigator.'

'Very fancy. You must think you're too good for the likes of us after mixing with the Brylcreem boys.' This was a term for aircrew, referring to the popular perception of them slicking back their hair with Brylcreem and considering themselves a class above lesser mortals.

Jenny thought this was a bit rich, considering she had set to work without a complaint, but held her tongue.

'I don't know why you felt it necessary to join the WAAF when there's so much work to be done here.'

This was an all-too-familiar complaint. Jenny had long given up protesting that all women her age had to do war work. All she could do was attack the swede with fresh vigour and say, 'Well, I'm here now.'

'But for how long? A week, that's all. Your grancher and I aren't getting any younger. I don't know how long we'll be able to keep up the rent on this place, to be honest. Now if you'd married Tommy Harper like I'd wanted, you could have moved in here and taken it over. It breaks my heart to think of it lying empty when we're gone. Your brothers can't manage it on top of their work in the mines.'

But apparently Jenny would have been able to work the smallholding single-handed, considering Tommy Harper was also a miner, although how he coped was a mystery to her because he'd never lifted a finger to do a scrap of work when she'd known him at school. 'I'd have been miserable with Tommy. I hated him.'

'But he was sweet on you. He was always coming round here.'

'Because he was bullying me to do his homework.'

'What he needs is a good woman to sort him out.'

What he needed was a kick up the backside. She might have said so too, had not her grancher chosen that moment to arrive, bringing with him the smell of tobacco.

He kissed her cheek. 'Hello, poppet,' he said, using the pet name he had bestowed upon Jenny when she was a child. 'I was hoping you'd have arrived.' He went to kiss his wife. 'Now don't be scolding the girl, Florrie. She's got to live her own life.'

Jenny felt her tension ebb away. While she and Granny had never agreed on how she should live her life, Grancher had always supported her. 'It's lovely to see you, Grancher,' she said and, after tipping the prepared vegetables into the stew, she made them some tea.

Thanks to her granny's excellent cooking, the rabbit stew was delicious. Her grandmother seemed to mellow with the arrival of first Grancher and then her father, and Jenny was able to relate her news without any complaint that she had abandoned her family or any further statements that it was high time she married. But when her brothers arrived, Granny insisted she entertain the children while their mothers took a well-earned rest. By the time she retired to her bed in the attic she was exhausted and couldn't wait for her day out with Edwin. She was grateful she had him as an excuse to get out of the house or she knew her week's holiday would be spent doing nothing but chores.

When Jenny came to meet him after breakfast, Edwin was shocked to see how tired she looked. 'Don't tell me your family kept you up all night talking.'

Jenny laughed. 'Not quite, but I had to get up early to wash the supper dishes. There wasn't time to do them last night.'

'What do you fancy doing? We can stay here in Newnham if you're feeling too tired to go out and about.'

Jenny shook her head. 'That's my line. I thought you were supposed to be the convalescent.'

'I feel right as rain. Must be the wholesome Gloucester-shire air.' And he wasn't exaggerating. He had slept soundly for the first time in ages, helped, he was sure, by the complete lack of Lancaster engines disturbing his sleep. For even on the nights there was no flying from Fenthorpe, unless everyone was grounded by the weather there were often flights from one of the other nearby bases.

'That's good. If you feel up to cycling up a few hills, we could go out past the Speech House. We'll have to be a bit careful because there's a lot of forestry work going on, but we should be able to find a quiet spot for a picnic.' Jenny pointed at the cloth bag in her bicycle basket. 'I packed some food. Another reason why I had to get up so early. I needed to collect some eggs for egg sandwiches without Granny noticing.'

'Egg sandwiches!' The very thought set Edwin's mouth watering, even though he had not long finished a very satisfying breakfast. He couldn't remember the last time he'd had those. 'I'd cycle up Ben Nevis if I thought there was a chance of a decent egg sandwich at the top.'

'Come on then.' Jenny pushed her bike onto the road and set off. Edwin followed, then pulled alongside her so they could talk as they rode. He soon discovered that cycling in the Forest of Dean was much more strenuous than pottering along the lanes around Fenthorpe, which were mostly flat. The only hill he could think of near Fenthorpe was the one in Lincoln and he never cycled up there. At the top of the first gradient he realised his legs were still shaky after his illness, and he begged for a rest. There was a stile beside the road, and they perched on it, admiring the view down the sloping fields and out across the Severn.

There wasn't much space on the stile, and they had to sit so close together their thighs touched. Jenny was wearing a thin cotton dress with just a cardigan, and she shivered slightly when a breeze whisked around them.

'Here,' he said, taking off his jacket and wrapping it round her shoulders. 'You must be cold now we've stopped.'

Jenny gave him a smile that he felt as a physical jolt to the stomach. 'Thanks. It would have been sensible to have worn my uniform but it's so sunny I thought I could get away with a summer dress. And I did want to wear something else for a change.' She hugged the jacket around herself and moved closer.

Edwin didn't trust himself to speak for a moment. All he could do was nod and smile like an idiot. He had never felt this way around Mina. With her it had been all about their shared interests, and they had never run out of things to say to one another. With Jenny they had the same shared love of the world around them, but there was more. He had never been as intensely aware of Mina's physical presence in the way he was with Jenny, and even months later he couldn't stop thinking about the blissful moment when she had kissed him. He'd had to be firm, because if he'd given in to his instincts he would have kissed her back with enthusiasm. He had to fight that urge now as she leaned against him for warmth.

He sprang to his feet, feeling his forbearance wear thin. 'We should carry on. I feel rested now, and you'll feel warmer once we're moving.'

Jenny looked surprised but didn't argue. She returned his jacket, then pushed her bike back onto the road and set off. Edwin followed suit, and now he wasn't sure if his legs trembled from weariness or from the aftermath of having her pressed against him. He soon got into his stride and drew level with her again, so he guessed it had been the latter.

A short distance later, Jenny pointed to a lane that climbed to the left. 'That's the way up to Oakdean.'

'Where you live?'

She seemed to think about it, then shrugged. 'Where my grandparents live. It doesn't feel like home any more. It's funny, but I realised last night that Fenthorpe feels more like home even though I only have a bed in a hut there. I suppose it's because that's where all my friends are.'

'But your family are all here. And you must have old school friends.'

'Not really. I mean, my family still live around here but I had to get a job when I was fourteen, and after a while I lost touch with my school friends.'

Edwin gazed up at the hillside in the direction Jenny had indicated. There were a few houses beside the road but beyond them was the first sign of proper woodland, and the lane was soon blocked from his view behind oak trees showing the pale growth of new leaves. Even though he'd grown up in a village himself, it had been well linked to nearby towns and not all that far from London. He found it hard to imagine what it must have been like to grow up in a place like this. He would have asked Jenny now, but the road was rising again and he needed all his breath to keep up with her.

As they carried on his legs grew accustomed to the exercise, and he didn't feel the need for another rest. Another mile or so later the trees thinned again and they came into Cinderford. He had expected the small town to be as picturesque as the surrounding countryside, but he found it shabby and bleak and was glad when they reached the other side and the houses petered out. Soon they were cycling through what he would term real forest, and were surrounded by mature oaks. Like Jenny, he had worried about running into tree felling or army exercises, but that must be happening in a different part of the forest, for the only sounds he could hear over the whir of his bicycle chain and the wind in his ears were birdsong, the gentle rattle of leaves and the distant tap-tap-tap of woodpeckers. Finally, just when his legs were starting to feel tired again, he saw a stately stone building looming. As they approached, he saw that it sat at the side of a road junction. Jenny carried on past a little way, then steered into a lay-by.

'That's the Speech House,' she said, pointing at the building. 'It's where the Verderer's Court is held. It's a hotel nowadays, but they still hold the court there. I'm not suggesting we go in.' She glanced down at her dress. 'It's a bit posh, and I'm not really dressed for it, but it seemed like a good spot for our first trip. We can walk into the woods a way and have a picnic.'

This sounded like a good plan, so they propped their bikes behind a tree, took the cloth bag containing the picnic from Jenny's basket and then followed a path for a few minutes until they were out of sight of the road. Jenny unpacked the picnic, producing a greaseproof paper package holding the much-anticipated egg sandwiches, two bottles of lemonade and another bundle of greaseproof paper that she said wrapped two slices of the best fruit cake in the world.

The sandwiches were wonderful, made from thick slices of nutty brown bread and a generous egg and cress filling.

'This beats the awful grey bread we get in the officers' mess,' Edwin said between mouthfuls. 'It's so good it's probably a crime.'

'Wait till you taste the cake,' Jenny told him. 'My granny might not show her love in many ways, but I think that's because she pours it all into her cooking.'

'That's a funny way of putting it.' Edwin studied Jenny's face. 'Isn't your granny a loving person?'

Jenny sighed. 'I'm probably being unfair. She did bring me up, after all.'

'But?' Edwin prompted, sensing she was holding back.

'Well, she doesn't have any problem showing affection to my brothers. She just never has a kind word for me.'

Edwin couldn't believe anyone not wanting to lavish Jenny with affection. 'How can she be so heartless?'

Jenny's lips quivered, and she pressed them tightly for a moment before saying, 'I don't think she's being heartless. I think she genuinely believes she's doing me good.' Then she added in a lower voice, 'I do love her, and I know she loves me deep down. I can't help envying Pearl and Thea, though. Sometimes I wish Deedee was my grandmother too.'

'I've heard her often enough telling you you're family. You might not be related, but I think she regards you as her grand-daughter all the same.'

She smiled then. 'That's nice. Maybe that's why Granny hurt me more than usual this time. I was comparing her to Deedee.'

'What about your other grandmother? Is she still around?'

'No. My mother's parents both died before I was born.'

'Then it's easy. Deedee is just your other grandmother. Everyone has two.'

Jenny's answering smile was like the sun coming out after rain. 'I like the way you think. You always make me feel better.'

He couldn't speak for a moment. The breeze picked up a lock of blond hair and it trailed across her eyes. He saw her flinch and acted without thinking. With a gentle finger he reached out and brushed it away. She shivered at his touch yet didn't move away. He couldn't drag his gaze from her lovely face, and his vision tunnelled until it was the only thing he could see. He had never been so aware of another human being in his life. Although he had drawn back his hand, his fingers tingled as though they still touched her warm flesh. He could see the pulse point quivering in her throat and he was overcome with a sudden urge to place his lips upon it.

Had not the breeze returned to ruffle their hair, he didn't think he could have controlled himself. But then a drift of last year's dry leaves blew over them and they both rose, shaking out their clothes and hair. Edwin laughed, and the moment was gone.

Jenny gave a shaky laugh, which convinced Edwin that she had also felt the tension between them – nothing short of a magnetic pull. 'Let's finish the food before it gets ruined,' she said, handing him a bottle of lemonade and a slice of cake.

While the cake might well have been the best he had ever eaten, it was wasted on him, for his lips still burned from their imagined kiss.

Chapter Twelve

Had Edwin been about to kiss her? Jenny didn't know whether to be relieved or disappointed at the sudden gust that had stopped… well, whatever had been about to happen. Although they quickly returned to their easy conversation, she kept reliving the moment when Edwin had swept the hair from her face, his fingers lightly skimming her cheek, and she had been transfixed by the intensity of his gaze. Much as she thrilled to be in his company, it was almost a relief when their day came to an end and they parted ways above Newnham. She needed time to think. Perhaps then the tingling warmth of his touch would fade from her cheek.

She pedalled slowly up the hill, putting off the moment when she would have to face her grandmother again. She didn't want to see her until she had her emotions in check.

Did Edwin have feelings for her after all? It had certainly felt that way. Thea had always insisted that Edwin loved her, and Jenny had thought so too at first, or she would never have dared to kiss him. Then she had found out about Mina and had realised that Edwin could never love her when he was engaged to a woman who was everything she was not. Jenny, with her lack of education, couldn't hope to compete with Mina and her maths degree from Cambridge. She was so far above Jenny it made her dizzy to even contemplate it. She had been foolish to think Edwin could have loved her.

That was how she had felt until today. But that moment in the woods when time had seemed to stop made her rethink. Surely he wouldn't have looked at her like that unless he truly did have feelings for her? She felt as though everything had changed, yet in one way – the most important way – nothing was different. Edwin was still engaged to Mina, and Mina was her friend.

Shoving the *if onlys* to the deepest recesses of her mind, she returned home.

'Decided to join us, have you?' was her granny's greeting when Jenny entered the kitchen.

Jenny swallowed, determined not to get upset after the lovely day. 'I told you I was going for a cycle ride with Edwin.' She held out the bottles she had bought from Littledean on the return journey. 'I bought some extra lemonade to make up for the ones I took with me.'

'You didn't have to do that.' Granny's voice was surprisingly gruff. 'You're the only one that drinks the stuff. I bought it for you.'

'Oh. Thank you. We enjoyed it.' Jenny pulled on an apron and collected the dirty dishes, intending to wash up. 'Edwin enjoyed your cake, too. He said it was the best he'd ever tasted.'

'He was probably only saying it.'

'No, he really meant it.' She thought about it for a moment. 'I don't think I've ever heard him say something he didn't mean.' Had he ever said he was in love with Mina? She tried to recall everything he had told her, before realising what she was doing and ruthlessly squashing those thoughts. Mina was her friend! She refused to come between them.

'Sounds like a fellow worth knowing, then. He's certainly put a bloom into your cheeks.'

'Granny! I told you we're just friends.'

'Yes, I remember.' Her granny dropped the rolled pastry onto the pie dish and cut vents, muttering something Jenny couldn't quite catch but it might have been, 'Could have fooled me.'

Jenny decided to ignore it, and poured hot water from the kettle into the sink.

'When are you going to bring him up here to meet us, then?'

Jenny spun round and stared at her grandmother, heedless of the water dripping from her hands. 'What? Honestly, we really are just friends. You don't have to check up on him.'

'So you keep saying, but I'd like to meet him, all the same. If you're spending all that time together, it's only fair that you bring him up here so we can at least see you while he's here.'

On the face of it, the request was perfectly reasonable, yet the thought of her grandparents meeting Edwin made her cringe. He would be bound to mention Mina and that would give Granny a whole new reason to disapprove of her. 'I'll ask him. What day?'

'Wednesday. And you won't so much ask him as tell him. I think me and your grancher should meet this man.'

And Jenny mentally prepared herself for a series of lectures on the futility of eating her heart out over a man she could never have.

–

Edwin, looking surprised and pleased, had accepted the invitation without hesitation. 'You've told me so much about your home, it will be good to see it at last,' he'd said. 'I look forward to it.' So it was only Jenny who dreaded the visit, worried as she was about her granny's opinion and what she might say to him.

In the meantime there were still three days to go until then, and Jenny spent each day with Edwin, unable to prevent herself from seeing him even if she thought it was a bad idea. Besides, she hadn't forgotten Mina's request that she persuade Edwin to confide in her, and what better time to get him to talk than now when he was visibly more relaxed? In fact, the gradual lifting of his tension showed her just how troubled his state of mind had been. But although they cycled all over the Forest of Dean and spoke of a wide range of subjects, she could never find the right opening to encourage him to speak of his experiences in the Netherlands. Neither was there a repeat of the intimate moment on the stile. She didn't know whether to be relieved or disappointed about that.

Wednesday arrived and, with a flutter of nervous anticipation, Jenny cycled down to Newnham to fetch Edwin.

'You won't mind anything my granny says?' she said as they began the return journey. 'Only she can get some funny ideas sometimes and tends to speak what's on her mind.' What if she asked Edwin if he was in love with her granddaughter? Jenny shrivelled with embarrassment at the mere idea.

'You make her sound like Deedee,' Edwin panted as he put on a burst of effort to reach the top of the hill. In the few days since they had arrived, he had regained his strength enough to tackle most hills without the need to pause for a rest.

'If only. Deedee's outspoken but she's not rude. I don't think Granny means to be rude, to be fair to her, but she never seems to stop to consider if what she says might be hurtful.'

'Look, don't worry about it. I won't let anything she says bother me. I just want to enjoy seeing your home and taste more of your granny's wonderful food.'

'Oh, you'll get that all right. She's been preparing ever since she invited you. I think she feels her honour will be at stake if she so much as singes the pie crust.'

'Pie crust? I like the sound of that.'

'You should. She's making chicken pie.' Nervous though she was, Jenny had been looking forward to this ever since Granny had announced it was time to sacrifice a hen that had stopped laying. 'She doesn't make that for just anyone, you know.'

'Then I'm honoured.'

Edwin would have liked to reassure Jenny that nothing her granny could say would make him think badly of her or her home. She seemed so nervous about this meeting. But by this time they had turned off the main road from Newnham and onto the lane she had pointed out on their first trip. It climbed steeply uphill, and he didn't have the puff to speak as well as cycle. He stood up on his pedals, determined not to have to ask for a rest when Jenny seemed to be sailing up the hill with no effort. Although he was concentrating on the road and so didn't look out at the view, he could sense that the trees were closing in. Finally, when his lungs had reached bursting point, the road levelled. He freewheeled for a moment, drawing deep, gasping breaths and giving his burning leg muscles a chance to recover. After a moment he was able to take in his surroundings, and saw they had reached a cluster of cottages on the edge of the wood.

Jenny pointed at a small cottage at the far edge of the group and called over her shoulder, 'We're nearly there!'

He looked at the house with more interest now he knew it was her home. Its whitewashed walls made it stand out against the dark trees. It had a higgledy-piggledy roof, as though it had been built in stages over the years, and small leaded windowpanes. It sat in a large yard, surrounded by a well-maintained fence, and beyond he could see an orchard in full bloom.

'Welcome to my home,' Jenny said, holding the gate open for him while simultaneously shooing away a curious chicken.

Wheeling his bike through, Edwin could now see that, apart from a small area directly beside the house where a washing line was hung and the hens were pecking, most of the garden was dug into vegetable plots. Another gate at the far end led to the orchard. He pointed at the blossoming trees. 'This is exactly how I would expect a Gloucestershire cottage to look.'

Jenny's nervous expression relaxed into a grin. 'We can't do without our cider. Although I should warn you that if Grancher offers you any, drink it with caution or you'll end up in no fit state to cycle back to Newnham.'

'I'll consider myself forewarned.' He followed Jenny and propped his bike in the shed beside hers. It was only when he walked back outside that he noticed the view. They were on top of a hill, looking down at the silvery ribbon of the Severn.

'No wonder I got out of breath,' he said. 'I had no idea how high we'd climbed.'

He would have liked to have taken more time to admire the scenery but from Jenny's increasing agitation he knew that she must be anxious for him to get the introductions to her grandparents over. He took a moment to straighten his uniform, then followed her inside.

A man and a woman who looked to be in their late seventies were sitting at the kitchen table, drinking tea. They rose when Jenny and Edwin walked in, and Edwin saw that, although they were older than Deedee and Thomas, the pair looked spry and in good health. The Gloucestershire air must be good for them.

'This is Edwin,' Jenny said to them, twisting her hands as she spoke.

Edwin held out his hand to each in turn. 'It's lovely to meet you, Mr and Mrs Hazleton.'

Mr Hazleton, who had twinkling blue eyes beneath a mop of snow-white hair, shook Edwin's hand. 'Call me Harry,' he said. 'Any friend of Jenny's is a friend of ours.'

Mrs Hazleton swept him with a shrewd gaze before shaking his hand and returning his greeting. Edwin had the uncomfortable feeling she was taking in every detail, from the navigator's brevet on his jacket to the slight scuff on his left shoe, and was left unimpressed.

Grasping for anything to say to break the ice, he added, 'Jenny always says you're the best cook she knows, but I didn't believe her until I tried your bread and fruit cake the other day. They really were delicious.'

'And why wouldn't you believe her? I didn't bring her up to tell lies.'

'No, of course not. I just—'

Harry saved the day by clapping him on the shoulder and saying to his wife, 'You will have your little joke, won't you, Florrie.' Then to Edwin, 'Now sit down and have some tea. You must be thirsty after riding up that hill.'

Edwin folded onto his chair, his legs more shaky from his first encounter with Jenny's granny than from climbing the hill. Mrs Hazleton was definitely nothing like Deedee.

Mrs Hazleton pointedly didn't invite Edwin to call her Florrie, yet she unwound enough over tea to ask him about his life in the RAF and what he had done before the war. Although when he told her about his research into astronomy she sniffed as though he'd announced he was a rag-and-bone man.

'Still, you're polite for a Brylcreem boy,' she announced when the last of the tea had been drained. 'I suppose Jenny could have done worse.' She addressed her granddaughter for the first time. 'Dinner won't be until half past one. Why don't you take your young man for a walk? I think he could do with some fresh air. He looks rather peaky.'

Jenny, her face flaming, led Edwin outside. 'I'm sorry about that,' she said. 'I keep telling her you're not my young man, but I can't seem to get through to her.'

Edwin grinned, relieved to be away from the formidable Mrs Hazleton for a time. 'You mean she didn't believe you? Shocking!'

Jenny giggled. 'I nearly passed out when she said that. I think she was deliberately trying to scare you.'

'It worked,' he said with feeling. 'Anyway, where are we going?'

'I thought I'd take you through the orchard, then we can take a path into the woods from there.'

It was a welcome relief to be alone with Jenny after the awkward encounter, and for a while they walked in comfortable silence. Edwin enjoyed the warm sun on his face and allowed the birdsong to soothe his ruffled feelings. Overhead a pair of russet squirrels chased each other through the branches. He could see the walk was having a similar effect on Jenny and was glad to see the tension gradually ease from her shoulders.

Finally the path turned out of the woods and they found themselves once again gazing across the wide Severn Valley. A bench stood beside the path in the perfect spot to enjoy the sight, so it felt natural to sit and drink it all in.

'I always think this would be the perfect spot for a gaze bow,' Jenny said after a moment of appreciative silence.

Edwin stared at her, wondering if this was some strange term in the local dialect or perhaps something to do with archery. But when he noticed her downcast eyes, he belatedly remembered her knack of mispronouncing words she'd only ever read.

'I said it wrong, didn't I?'

He hastened to reassure her. 'No. Well, yes, it's pronounced gazebo, but gaze bow makes more sense.'

She perked up. 'Exactly! It's a place where you gaze from a set of bow windows.'

'I'm calling it a gaze bow from now on,' he promised her, and he was pleased to see her laugh and free herself of the last lingering remains of anxiety.

He turned back to the view. 'It almost feels like I'm flying.'

'I'd love to see the world from the air,' Jenny said. 'I wish they would let more women fly. I'm always jealous when Thea says she's been up.'

'I'm jolly glad you can't.' It was bad enough having to do it himself without having to worry about Jenny facing the same danger.

Jenny twisted in her seat to look at him, her gaze concerned. 'Is it really that bad?'

'It is, but probably not in the way you think. I'm too busy when we're on a mission to be scared. Most of the time, anyway. But waiting to take off, wondering if you'll ever see Fenthorpe again, that really takes it out of me. And' – he paused to rub his forehead, noticing that his hand had started to shake – 'whenever I hear about a crew that didn't get back I can't help thinking how easily that could have been us. How if we'd been assigned a different take-off time or if I plotted a slightly different route, the night fighters or flak that got them might have got us instead.'

Jenny hardly dared to breathe as Edwin spoke. Perhaps now was the right time to persuade him to speak of what was haunting him. 'Yet you did crash that time and you and Greg both survived.' With each word she feared Edwin would leap up and refuse to even think of the crash. However, he remained where he was, his gaze fixed on the view.

'Would you believe me if I said I wasn't afraid when we were going down?'

'Honestly? I'd have been scared out of my wits.'

'I always thought so too,' he replied. 'I've seen enough planes go down to imagine what it must be like, knowing you're going to crash. But actually there was too much to think about to have time to be scared. Greg and I knew we had to stay aloft long enough for the rest of the crew to bale out and then for us to avoid hitting any houses. Greg couldn't manage the controls alone – he needed my help to haul back the control column and stop us from slipping into a dive.'

Jenny, intently studying his face as he spoke, saw his eyes focus on the distance and knew he was reliving the moment. She couldn't imagine going through that without feeling utter terror, but, although Edwin's expression was taut, she thought it looked more like concentration than remembered fear. She didn't speak, hardly dared to breathe, in case she disturbed him and broke his train of thought. Now he was finally talking, she would do nothing to break the spell.

'I still don't know how we did it,' Edwin continued, 'but somehow we skimmed over the rooftops and made it as far as a patch of woodland before we knew we couldn't keep the Lanc in the air any more. Even so, Greg managed to keep us from going into a dive and pancaked onto the trees.' He shook his head. 'I'll never forget the noise of tearing branches and grinding metal. The trees broke our fall, though, and we fell to the ground in stages. I was flung across the cockpit and everything became a bit of a blur for a while. When I came to my senses, Greg was shaking me and yelling at me to move.'

His mouth tightened. 'That's when I became frightened. I knew we'd come down in enemy territory, and we'd heard rumours that German troops were in chaos and shooting downed airmen on sight because they couldn't deal with prisoners. Since we'd crashed close to a built-up area, we were sure there must be men out looking for us, and it could only be a matter of time before we were found. While Greg grabbed our emergency rations, I set fire to my charts and gathered up our logbooks. There was a strong smell of fuel, and I was starting to worry the plane would catch light before we could get out.'

Jenny could imagine the nightmare. While she might never have flown herself, she had been long enough in an airbase to know that fire was the aircrews' greatest fear. To the extent that she had heard more than one crew member swear they would rather jump without a parachute than be trapped in a burning plane. It was one of the thoughts that kept her awake at night, terrified for her friends who might have to face that choice in reality.

Of course, the main reason for her wakeful nights was the lingering trauma of those terrible days when Edwin and Greg had been missing. She hoped never again to suffer the same anguish she'd felt on hearing that the burnt-out remains of their aircraft had been found. With a body inside.

'But who was the dead man?' she blurted, only belatedly remembering her resolution not to interrupt his train of thought.

From the bleak look Edwin turned on her, she knew she had unwittingly stumbled on the reason for the shadow that had weighed upon him in recent months. Suddenly she wasn't sure she wanted to know, but she steeled herself, telling herself that, if it would relieve Edwin's burden to speak, she would listen for his sake.

She placed a comforting hand on his arm. 'It might help to talk about it.'

'Why, would it bring that man back to life?'

She knew then without a doubt that, whoever it had been, Edwin was responsible for his death. She had to choose her next words very carefully if she didn't want to push him even deeper into darkness. 'If you killed him,' she said finally, 'I know you must have had a very good reason. I know you well enough to be certain you wouldn't take another life unless you had no other choice.'

'But that's just it,' he cried, shaking off her hand and leaping to his feet with a suddenness that made her jump. 'I've always thought that if I ever found myself in a dangerous situation, my actions would be based on reason. But when it came to the crunch, I didn't think at all.' He dropped back onto the seat and buried his head in his hands. 'I killed a man without a thought. What does that make me?'

Jenny touched his shoulder gently, half expecting him to shake her off again. When he didn't, she turned the action into a hesitant caress. 'Why don't you tell me exactly what happened? I can't answer your question until I know what you did.'

Edwin drew a shuddering breath and raised his head, fixing his gaze on the view. 'I can't believe you still want to speak to me. I don't think you'll ever be able to look at me again if you know the truth, and I don't think I could bear that.'

'Edwin, I already know you killed someone and I don't think badly of you. There's nothing you can say that will change that.'

He shot her a sideways glance. 'How do you know?'

'Because I know you. I know how fascinated you are about the workings of the world and the universe, so much that you want to devote your life to their study. I know you want to make the world a better place, and that has always guided your actions. I don't think you could do anything that was inherently evil.'

He drew a shuddering breath. 'I always thought that about myself too. When I joined the RAF it was because I didn't think I could kill another human being, and there was useful work I could do in the RAF that didn't involve killing. Not face to face, anyway. I briefly considered becoming a conscientious objector, but I decided not to because I knew we had gone beyond the point of diplomacy, and the only way to stop Hitler was to fight him. I didn't even want to carry a revolver because I didn't think I could use one, but Greg persuaded me that, if I ever had to bale out over enemy territory, I might regret not having a gun. So I took one to keep him quiet, and attended the training, although I never thought I could actually use it on a person.'

He sounded so despondent and disgusted with himself that Jenny thought he might stop, so she prompted him. 'I believe you. So what happened in Holland?'

'We had just managed to retrieve everything of any use and had climbed out. Greg was sitting on the ground, strapping up his knee, which he'd twisted. We were deciding how best to burn the wreckage to stop the Germans getting hold of our equipment when a German soldier arrived. He didn't see me at first because I was screened by a tree. He aimed his rifle at Greg's back, and I didn't even think. I pulled my revolver and shot him. I didn't shout a warning, I just shot him, and hit him right in the chest.'

Chapter Thirteen

Edwin waited for Jenny to avert her gaze. He was sure she wouldn't be able to look at him now she knew the truth. However, to his disbelief she maintained eye contact, and he could see no sign of disgust in her expression. 'You made the right choice,' she said, her voice steady. 'He would have killed Greg. You were defending him.'

He needed to be sure she understood exactly what he had done. 'But what if he wasn't going to shoot? He might have meant to take him prisoner.'

'You thought he was going to shoot, though, didn't you?'

Edwin closed his eyes, picturing the moment again. It was so clear it was like the backs of his eyelids had become a cinema screen. He saw the German soldier stumble through the thicket and turn his gaze from the wrecked Lancaster to Greg, and he distinctly remembered his expression turning from surprise to rage and hatred.

'I remember now.' Edwin opened his eyes, wondering how he could have forgotten, and found Jenny's gaze still fixed intently on his face. The tight coil of tension in his chest relaxed fractionally. 'I don't know how I could have forgotten that part. When the soldier saw Greg, his face twisted in hatred. That was when he raised his rifle, and I was convinced he was going to shoot in cold blood.' He paused, unable to let himself off so easily. 'But I could have shouted a warning. I didn't have to kill him.'

'Edwin, listen to yourself. You had a split second to take action. You could only react based on what you had observed.

131

You saw his hatred and were sure he was going to shoot. If you hadn't shot first, he would have killed Greg. Pearl would be a widow now if it hadn't been for you, and her baby would have to grow up without a father. Imagine how you would have felt if you'd returned having failed to save Greg. Imagine how you would have felt the first time you saw Pearl.'

He stared at her, studying her for any sign of disdain or revulsion at what he had done, but he saw nothing but concern. It was impossible for him to give up months of self-recrimination, yet he could think of nothing to say in the face of her certainty.

Jenny went on, her voice gentler. 'I know you, and I know you're still asking yourself if you did the right thing. You can never be one hundred per cent sure the soldier would have killed Greg, but you have to trust in your instincts, believe that you made a split-second judgement – the correct one – based on your observations. I think the reason you'd forgotten about that man's expression until now is because you were in shock, and you've been reliving the worst moment – the moment you shot him – without trying to piece together the incidents that led you to that point.'

As Edwin had described his experience, he had lost awareness of his surroundings, being too sunk in his memory of that dark day. Now, it was as though his vision and hearing had suddenly returned, and the air exploded with sunshine and birdsong. He took in his surroundings with sharpened senses, and it seemed as though the sun shone that bit brighter and the birds sang with even greater joy. Far below, the Severn weaved its sinuous path through the landscape sparkling with diamond brilliance.

Then he looked back at Jenny, whose lovely face could more than compete with the view. He swallowed to combat the tightness in his throat, stunned that she could unravel his thought processes so easily. 'I think you must have read several books on psychology since I saw you last,' he said finally.

Jenny's lips twitched. 'Maybe one or two. I found them in a Christmas bazaar.' She raised her eyebrows. 'Am I right, though?'

'I don't know. I mean, I want to believe you, but it's all too much to take in. I'll need to think about it.'

'As long as you don't put yourself into a spin again.'

His chest swelled with gratitude. It wasn't everyone who could claim to have a friend as true as her, who knew him so well she had been able to cut to the heart of his problem.

The trouble was, he wished she could be more than a friend. He wished he could preserve this moment and forget about the many barriers keeping them apart, Mina most of all.

The sudden stab of guilt propelled him to his feet. 'Perhaps we should be getting back, before your grandparents wonder where we've got to.'

He offered her his arm and they retraced their steps through the woods. Jenny didn't say much, beyond the occasional exclamation to point out a pretty view or to laugh at the antics of a squirrel as it leapt from branch to branch. Yet she didn't press him to say more about his experience, and he was grateful. She had given him a lot to think about, and he needed to let it all sink in. Perhaps that was one of the reasons he had taken shooting the man so badly, he mused. He was used to acting after having time to carefully consider all options. Not that he was a slow thinker – he could usually reach a considered conclusion in less time than it would take to speak the problem, and working as a navigator had only honed his ability to think fast. Yet this act, one of the most momentous he had ever undertaken, he had had the merest lightning flicker of space to think about, and he had done so without really being aware of it. It was only now that he had forced himself to relive the experience that he could remember all that had led to his taking the fateful shot.

It was only when he saw they were nearly at the orchard, and he knew that this would be their last chance to speak privately that day, that he burst out, 'You know, if you hadn't forced me to think it through, I might have gone through my whole life thinking I shot that man in cold blood.'

Jenny paused, her hand on the gate. 'How do you feel now?'

'I'm not saying I've forgiven myself. It'll probably haunt my dreams for the rest of my life. But I'm starting to see that in a way, whatever I chose to do, I would have blamed myself. It was an impossible situation. But I do feel clearer in my mind that the soldier did mean to shoot Greg, and I could never have forgiven myself if I'd done nothing and watched Greg die.'

'I think you're right.' Jenny leaned back against the gate with a sigh. 'I hate this war. I hate what it's forcing you and all the crews to do. Why is it that it's always the ordinary people who pay the price in war, and the leaders who made us fight don't seem to suffer?'

Edwin smiled at her, unable to comprehend why this fierce, earnest young woman would still want him as a friend, one who she was prepared to do battle for despite the way he had rejected her. He knew he didn't deserve her, yet also knew he couldn't bear to lose her. Because he loved her more completely than he had ever loved Mina.

Was that why he hadn't told Jenny's granny of his engagement? When he'd been facing her interrogation, he'd had every opportunity to mention a fiancée but had held back. At the time he'd told himself that it was to protect Jenny from awkward questions about why she was going around with another woman's fiancé, but now he wondered if there was another reason. Was it possible that he hadn't given up hope of extricating himself from his engagement without hurting Mina? It was a question he felt unable to answer. If it was true, it would explain why he had felt able to confide in Jenny, difficult though it had been, when he had not spoken to Mina despite her persistence. Could it be that he was picturing a life with Jenny, one in which they shared all their thoughts and kept no secrets from each other?

It was a day that Jenny knew would remain golden in her memory for years to come. Years after Edwin had married Mina and Jenny was nothing more to them than a memory of a quaint, bookish forest girl who'd had ideas above her station. Her granny had remained surprisingly civil for the rest of Edwin's visit and had outdone herself with the most delicious meal Jenny could remember. The chicken pie was cooked to perfection, the last of the stored vegetables had been either roasted or mashed and it had all been served with a rich gravy. Jenny couldn't remember the last time she had felt so satisfied after a meal, and was pleased to see Edwin tucking in. Now that half her leave was over, she was happy to see that he looked much improved from his illness. The peace of the forest had worked its magic, and she was sure he would be passed fit for duty at the end of his week of sick leave. She was also confident that, having finally unburdened himself, his mind was well on the way to healing.

Overall, she was much easier about him when she waved him off that evening.

'Your young man's a pleasant enough sort,' her granny said when she came back into the cottage. 'For all that he's stuffed your head full of nonsense.'

'What nonsense?' she asked. 'Anyway, as I keep saying, he's not *my* young man.' Although she was very relieved Edwin hadn't mentioned Mina.

Her granny waved a hand at the stack of books Jenny had brought down to show Edwin after the meal. Now he had seen how far she had grown up from a bookshop or library, he had wanted to see for himself the eclectic selection she'd been able to find. 'If he had any idea of what's good for you, he wouldn't have encouraged you to read things like this.' She picked up a green hardback that had lost its dust jacket long before Jenny had picked it up at a church fete.

'Why?' Jenny retrieved the book – *Shipwrecks of the Welsh Coast* – and replaced it on the pile with a loving pat. 'What's wrong with wanting to learn things?'

'It's *what* you're learning that bothers me. I don't understand you. You spend all your free time with your nose in a book when all the sensible girls your age are finding themselves a husband. Then when you do meet a man who puts a bit of colour in your cheeks, you do nothing but talk about books with him. I'm starting to think you're telling the truth and you're really not interested in him.'

Jenny gazed at her granny in dismay. 'I'm perfectly happy as I am.' Admittedly she had to cross her fingers behind her back before replying. 'And I want to learn as much as I can.'

'But don't you see that most men don't want a wife who knows more than they do? They want one who cooks for them and looks after them.'

'I couldn't bear to live like that,' Jenny cried. 'I'd feel like a prisoner. I want to do something worthwhile with my life.'

'Are you saying my life isn't worthwhile? Is that what you think – that I wasted my life, bringing up my children and grandchildren? Taking care of *you*?' Were those tears welling in Granny's eyes? She turned away too swiftly for Jenny to be sure. Granny picked up the pail of kitchen scraps and flung open the door, saying, 'I can't talk of this now. I need to feed the hens.' She slammed the door so hard the crockery on the dresser rattled.

Jenny stood in stunned silence while around her the cottage seemed to settle as though recovering from a shock. Then the door opened again and she tensed, expecting her granny to storm back in with another volley of accusations, but she relaxed when Grancher entered instead, carrying a bucket filled with coal.

'Did I hear raised voices?' he asked in a mild voice.

Jenny could only nod, not trusting herself to speak.

Grancher crossed the room and pulled her into a hug. 'You mustn't mind your granny, poppet.'

'It's hard not to when she keeps telling me I'm good for nothing but being an unpaid housekeeper.' Jenny pulled back from the hug, blinking tears from her eyes. 'This was such a lovely day, too.'

'You have to understand that she found it hard bringing up a girl. Until you came along, we've had nothing but boys in the house.'

'What difference does that make?'

Grancher rubbed a hand over his forehead, leaving a streak of black grime behind. 'Your granny had always wanted a daughter but never had one. Then when the grandchildren started arriving, she hoped for a granddaughter, but for a long time there were still only boys, until you came along just when we thought there would be no more.'

'But I still don't understand.'

'She wanted someone more like her. Someone she could relate to in a household full of boys and men who were full of talk about the mines and football. Yet when you arrived, instead of being interested in what she considered to be feminine occupations, you spent every moment you could reading and wishing you could stay on at school.'

Jenny bit her lip, remembering her tears and arguments when she had been told she was to leave school and find work when she turned fourteen. At the time she couldn't comprehend why she hadn't been allowed to stay on at least long enough to take her School Certificate. Now, however, she knew it was because her grandparents had needed the income. 'I'm sorry I made such a fuss,' she said. 'I do understand why it wasn't possible then. But I can't fathom why she's so against me doing all I can to educate myself now.'

'Because while the outside world has moved on, in the forest it's much the same as it's ever been. She's worried about you.'

'But why? I'm fine. I love what I'm doing.'

'She's worried you'll never be happy here. Worried you'll never come home.'

'Oh.' Jenny swallowed. What could she say to that? The truth was that, from the first day she had started her Met assistant training and the world had expanded before her eyes, she had known in her heart that she wouldn't want to return home permanently, and she had never changed her mind.

Grancher raised his hand before she could say anything. 'It's all right,' he said. 'Much as I'll miss you, I can see how happy you are now, and how much more fulfilled you are since you've started doing work you love. I wouldn't want you to come back home and be unhappy. And your granny feels the same way, deep down. But you need to give her time to accept that from now on you'll only be home for occasional visits.'

In a flash of understanding, Jenny knew Grancher was right. 'I never looked at it that way before,' she said. 'I suppose I never really tried to see things from her perspective. I'm sorry.'

That was why Granny had been so hard on her – she had been afraid. First she had been afraid that Jenny would never settle to a life that her granny had considered was inevitable for a woman, and later afraid that she would never come back. It was a pity that life in the Forest of Dean was so narrow for people of her class. For generations, the only work had been the mines or leaving to go into service. There was no hope of betterment for anyone who chose to remain in the forest.

She gave a wry smile, remembering Edwin's reaction to the books she had shown him. He'd been impressed that her dedication to learning had even extended to wading through tomes such as *The Steam Engine: Its History and Mechanism*.

'Well, it's good to see you smiling at any rate,' Grancher said. 'You look like you're thinking of something happier. Someone whose name begins with "E" by any chance?' His eyes twinkled.

'Not you as well. No, well, I was thinking of him but just something he said.'

She carried the dirty crockery to the sink and made a start with the washing up, leaving Grancher to go and clean his grimy hands. As she worked, her irritation faded at her grandparents' assumption about her relationship with Edwin. After all, they weren't wrong about her feelings and it was only natural to assume that a young man she had brought to her home must be her sweetheart. She was also sorry she had upset her granny and knew it was up to her to put things right.

Accordingly, when Granny returned a while later, she immediately said, 'I *am* grateful for all you've done for me. Of course I don't think you wasted your life.' Then, not wanting to start another argument but needing to be clear, she added, 'I just meant that what was right for you isn't right for me.'

Granny sighed. 'So your grancher keeps reminding me. I suppose the day you left to join the WAAF, I knew you wouldn't be coming back here to live. The forest won't be good enough for you now you've seen the outside world.'

'I love the forest,' Jenny cried, stung. 'If there was work, I'd move back like a shot. I don't think there's anywhere in the world I'll love as much, and I'll come back as often as I can. Anyway, I've no idea what I'm going to do once I'm released from the WAAF, and there will be loads of people all with more qualifications than me looking for work, so I'll be at the bottom of the pile.'

Granny patted her hand a little awkwardly. 'You've got more gumption than any of them,' she declared. 'You'll go a long way, you mark my words. And if anyone tries to hold you back they'll have me to answer to.'

Jenny went to bed that night reflecting that, although she might never understand her granny, life with her was never dull.

The rest of the holiday passed too quickly for Edwin's liking. Every day spent with Jenny was healing in itself and, by the morning after his visit to her home, he felt fitter than he had in a long time. Their frequent cycle rides were clearly doing him good, and he resolved to cycle more on his return to Lincolnshire. Not that there would be so many hills to maintain his fitness.

Being with Jenny was both a pleasure and a pain because, although he knew he was more in love with her than ever, he could never tell her. Never let Mina down. The wish he'd secretly acknowledged could never be fulfilled, because he couldn't imagine any way of breaking his engagement without hurting Mina. However, thanks to Jenny's wise words, he was starting to accept that his actions in shooting the German soldier had not been because he was a cold-blooded killer but had been a necessary act of defence. He would never be comfortable with what he had done but neither could he have stood by and let Greg be murdered.

The trouble was that, as his guilt over the shooting receded, his horror over the Dresden bombing grew. More reports about the devastation in the city had filtered back to Britain, and people who remembered Coventry couldn't understand how the men of Bomber Command could do the same, if not worse, to civilians in Germany who were every bit as innocent as the citizens of Coventry had been. The men of Bomber Command were no longer heroes in public opinion.

The matter was painfully brought to his attention on their final day of their holiday. They had decided to celebrate Edwin's return to full health with a cycle ride right through the forest to Symonds Yat – a high rocky outcrop overlooking the River Wye. It was a beautiful day: glorious sunshine with just enough breeze to stop it from becoming too hot. While at the start of the week he would have been obliged to push his bike up the longer hills, now he managed them all without getting puffed out, and he couldn't resist singing for joy when swooping along the downhill sections. When they eventually reached the start of the footpath, they were rosy-cheeked and giggling like schoolchildren. Edwin couldn't remember when he had last enjoyed himself so much.

They left their bicycles propped against trees and followed the well-marked trail. Their way led through woodland until they reached the final rocky scramble to the top of Symonds Yat Rock. They had nearly reached the top when they came face to face with a middle-aged man who looked Edwin up and down.

Edwin saw the moment when he took in the aircrew brevet – his face contorted as if from rage. 'You should be ashamed of yourself after what you did to Dresden!' He pushed past, shoving Jenny aside, his elbow painfully jabbing Edwin's upper arm. He was out of sight before Edwin's reeling brain could catch up with what had happened.

He put a steadying hand on Jenny's arm. 'Are you all right?'

'I'm fine.' But her eyes blazed with indignation. 'What about you? How dare he speak to you like that!'

'No harm done. Come on. Let's get to the top.'

But the magic of the place had been ruined. When he reached the viewpoint, he leaned against the wall, taking deep breaths, trying to steady his rattled nerves. It took him a moment to take in his surroundings, and when he did he needed to clutch the gritty stone for dear life. The wall was the only thing that stood between him and a sheer drop that fell for hundreds of feet to the green valley below.

Jenny came to stand beside him and propped her elbows on the top of the wall. 'You know what I think? I think that man was just jealous. He probably applied for the RAF and failed to get in.'

He dragged his gaze from the dizzying view and smiled to see her fury on his behalf. With the breeze ruffling her hair like that, he could imagine her in the role of a Celtic warrior queen. 'Perhaps you're right.' Then he sobered. 'But he only said what plenty of people feel. What *I* feel.' He struggled for a moment to put his feelings into words. 'I think Dresden affected most of us. I can never describe the horror of it. Adding our bombs to the inferno seemed cruel and pointless, but at the time we thought we had our orders, so we did it. But now I'm not so sure that saying we were following orders can justify what we did.'

As had happened when he had finally spoken about the shooting, putting into words some of what he had felt since Dresden helped lift the burden.

Jenny was looking at him with solemn eyes. 'Do you regret volunteering for a second tour?'

He shook his head. 'No. I agreed with Greg. We'd seen first-hand the starvation in the Netherlands and knew we had to do what we could to liberate the occupied territories, and we've done that.' He shivered, remembering the children's emaciated bodies. 'I only hope they've got food now.'

Chapter Fourteen

The hopeful news coming in from Europe was what sustained him through the return to Fenthorpe and the prospect of resuming active duty. The end of the war with Germany seemed imminent but, if he had to drop more bombs, he would do it for the people who still suffered Nazi rule.

On his first morning back, he took the transport to Fenthorpe with the familiar tightening in his chest, wondering if he would be flying ops that day.

Soon the word was out – ops were indeed on that day. Edwin made his way with the others to the operations block and studied the list of aircraft and their crews slated to take part. He quickly found the list for *J-Jackson* and saw his name just below Greg's. A hand tapped him on the shoulder and he turned to see Fitz just behind him.

'I can't see the board. Are we down?'

Edwin swiftly checked that Fitz was also on the list and then nodded. 'A daylight mission. That's new.' While they were becoming more common now they weren't facing anti-aircraft attacks from the liberated areas, he hadn't yet taken part in one, and he wondered how it would feel to fly without the protection of darkness.

Fitz was frowning. 'Maybe we're going to Berlin, and they want us to make an early start.'

That made sense, and Edwin's tension increased as the time for the briefing approached. He didn't want a repeat of the Dresden attack. By the time he filed into the briefing hut with the rest of the squadron, he was starting to wonder if he could even go through with another bombing raid. With all the news of an impending ceasefire, he had hoped he had done his last raid. He took his seat, eying the curtain covering the map board, anxiety gnawing at his gut.

When the senior officers arrived and took their seats at the front, they looked oddly cheerful. Edwin wondered if his eyes were playing up; he had only ever seen them look grave in the moments before a mission was announced. The murmur of voices fell to an expectant hush when their CO rose and approached the curtain.

'Good morning, gentlemen. Today's operation is not a bombing run but a mercy mission. We have been chosen to take part in Operation Manna.' He pulled the cord that opened the curtain, revealing the map of Europe and the red trail that marked today's course. A murmur of surprise rippled around the room as, one by one, the men tracked the route and saw that it ended over the Netherlands. He exchanged glances with Fitz and saw his own confusion mirrored on his friend's face.

The CO continued. 'As you know, the Dutch people are enduring a severe famine, and the situation is acute in the areas still under occupation. Operation Manna is a food drop, delivering supplies to areas of greatest need.' He went on to explain that, after negotiation with the German commanders, participating aircraft would not be fired upon, on the provision that they stuck to defined air corridors.

This announcement was followed by another rumble of voices. Usually the announcement of a target was followed by a groan if a target was in a particularly notorious area, such as the Ruhr Valley. At best the reaction was a cautiously optimistic shrug when the target was closer to home. This time, Edwin felt a grin threaten to split his face from ear to ear.

Fitz elbowed him hard, and Edwin turned to see his friend beaming in delight, his eyes suspiciously bright. 'What do you reckon – is this the end of bombing missions?'

Edwin caught his breath. 'I hope so.' He felt as though he were emerging from a very long, dark tunnel.

He had to force himself to concentrate through the rest of the briefing, taking more thorough notes than usual in the navigator's briefing, determined that they would drop their supplies over the exact location and knowing how vital it was not to stray from their given route.

Greg caught his arm when the group were dismissed. 'About time,' he said. 'I hope the Brinkmans see some of this.' The Brinkmans were the Dutch family who had helped them after the crash.

The time leading up to take-off flew by in a series of last-minute tests and briefings. No one wanted anything going wrong on this most important of missions.

At the earliest opportunity Edwin raced to the Met Office, and was delighted to see Jenny there, leaning over a chart. Of all the people on the base, she would be the one who understood how important this mission would be to him, and there was no one he would rather share the news with. Not even Mina, he thought with a stab of guilt.

'Have you heard?'

'Heard what?'

'We're doing a food drop over the Netherlands.' He was surprised at how breathless he sounded.

Her eyes opened wide. 'That's wonderful. So that's why it's a daytime mission. I was surprised when I heard. Have they stopped the bombing, then?'

'I hope so.'

Jenny squeezed his arm, and Edwin felt the same jolt of awareness he had experienced that first day in the Forest of Dean. 'I hope so too.' Her eyes were misty. Then she cleared her throat. 'Well, you'll be pleased to know you'll have clear weather for your flight, with no strong winds and a low chance of icing.'

On the point of leaving, Edwin hesitated, suddenly realising that, assuming the flight went to plan, he and the crew would have the night off. 'Are you free to come out with the lads tonight? I think it'll be a night to remember.'

'You bet! I can't wait to hear all about it.'

By the time the crews were getting kitted out and collecting parachutes and Mae Wests, there was an almost festival atmosphere. Edwin was surprised, considering their flight would be much shorter than usual, to be handed a Benzedrine pill. In the end, he gave it to a man from another crew who said he had dropped his. This was one flight during which he would have no trouble staying awake.

Soon the crew had boarded and *J-Jackson* was taxiing to the head of the runway. Unlike on other flights, the crew were cracking jokes and doing imitations of the senior officers. When they lined up behind another Lancaster, Greg called over the intercom, 'I hear there's a dance at the Albion Hotel tonight. Who's with me?' To the enthusiastic cheers, he said, 'Right then. Give me your full concentration, because I want to enjoy tonight with all my limbs intact.'

For Greg to suggest this when he always refused to jinx a flight by planning ahead, Edwin knew he must also be giddy with excitement.

Taking Greg's admonition to heart, the moment the wheels left the ground Edwin checked and rechecked their bearing, and refused to let his focus slide. Flying in daylight was a welcome change, and, when they reached the point on the coast where they were supposed to rendezvous with the lights from other stations, he drew in his breath at the sight of all the aircraft in the sky. Flying at night with no navigation lights, great care had to be taken not to hit another aircraft. Now, Edwin could marvel at the sight – squadron after squadron, carrying food instead of bombs. He didn't allow himself long to take in the scene before he returned to his charts, ever conscious of the need to deliver their load to the correct destination. The Brinkmans and countless other families were relying on him.

Soon they were crossing the coast over the Netherlands, and Edwin gave the last course correction. He tensed as he followed their route on the chart, frequently checking for the correct landmarks through the ground periscope to be doubly certain their course wasn't drifting. Finally they were approaching Waalhaven airfield in the south of Rotterdam. Even when he saw other Lancasters release their loads, he still double-checked their position, wanting to be absolutely certain they had reached the correct location.

'Target dead ahead,' he told Greg, and the pilot followed the other Lancasters in, swooping low.

'Makes a change from dodging searchlights and flak,' Greg said.

'Makes a change from dropping bombs,' came Fitz's reply. Then, a moment later, 'Bombs away! Well, food away. You know what I mean.'

As Greg banked, steering on the return bearing Edwin had provided, Edwin gazed out of his window and saw figures, growing smaller as they climbed, running towards the bulky parcels. Several waved up at them, and Edwin felt a lump in his throat, feeling that he had finally done what he could for the Brinkman family. While he knew he would always be haunted by Dresden, at the same time he knew he could now start to let go of the crippling guilt.

Jenny was cycling to the Waafery beside Thea when the first roar of Merlin engines made her look up. One by one the Lancasters were returning, filling the air with an ear-splitting din as they circled the field, waiting for their turn to land.

Thea's hand shot up, making her bike wobble as she pointed at the aircraft flying low overhead. 'There's *J-Jackson*!'

Jenny craned her neck, picking out the familiar number on the fuselage, and her heart sped up. 'It's funny seeing them come back in the daylight.'

'It certainly beats the endless pre-dawn vigils,' Thea said, picking up speed again. She shot Jenny a grin over her shoulder. 'Not that I'll be getting much sleep tonight, because I intend to dance the night away.' Then as she was pulling ahead, she yelled, 'Race you to the guard room!'

147

Luckily for Jenny her week of cycling up steep hills had stood her in good stead, and despite Thea's head start they were neck and neck by the time they had rounded the final corner. With a crow of triumph, Jenny pulled ahead, and reached the WAAF guard room a full five yards ahead of Thea.

'Not fair!' Thea climbed off her bike, her cap askew, her cheeks bright pink. 'I think my gears must have rusted up.'

They signed in, then hurried to Hut Three, Thea still protesting that she would have won had her bicycle been in better condition.

The strains of 'Moonlight Serenade' drifted from the hut, and they opened the door to find preparations for the dance that night already under way. One of the other girls had an ancient wind-up gramophone and a large record collection, and they put on their make-up and dressed in their best uniforms to a selection of swing music.

Thea glided around the hut, dancing a waltz with an imaginary partner, her eyes dreamy. 'I'm going to dance every dance with Fitz tonight.' Then she raised her eyebrows at Jenny. 'What about you? Will you be dancing with Edwin? I'm still waiting to hear how your week-long date in the Forest of Dean went.'

'Don't be an idiot.' Jenny felt a blush heat her cheeks. 'You know he's just a friend.'

Thea's face fell. 'Still?' She dropped onto her bed and patted the space beside her. 'Come and tell Auntie Thea all about it.'

The other girls had finished getting ready by this time and had gathered in the rec until it was time to catch the bus. The gramophone needle reached the end of the latest record and the only sound emanating from the speaker was a scratchy hiss. Feeling suddenly flat, Jenny removed the needle from the record and then sat beside Thea. She tried to organise her thoughts, desperate to unburden her heart but knowing she would have to pick her words carefully so she didn't break Edwin's confidence.

'Come on, what happened?' Thea asked. 'I'm sorry if it sounded like I was making fun of you. I know it's not a laughing matter. But when he agreed to go with you, I hoped he might have decided to admit his feelings.'

'I suppose I did, too, deep down,' Jenny admitted. 'But it wouldn't have been right, not with Mina still in the picture.'

'I suppose not. So go on, what did happen?'

'We had a lovely time. We went on cycle rides every day. I enjoyed having a friend to show the sights to.'

'That's what you write on a postcard to your grandparents. Now tell me what really happened.'

Jenny sighed. 'Fine. We had… a moment.'

'A moment? What's that supposed to mean?'

'I don't know! That's why I didn't say anything before, because I can't work out what it means. It was our first day in the forest, and we stopped for a picnic.' Jenny described the moment when he had brushed hair from her face, reliving the delicious tingle that had spread from his fingertips right through her flesh. 'I thought he was going to kiss me, but either I was mistaken or he thought better of it.'

'I'm sure you weren't mistaken,' Thea said with all the authority of someone who had been over a hundred miles away at the time. 'What happened next?'

'Well, nothing really. We were a bit awkward for a day or two but after he came to see my grandparents, he—'

'Wait. He met your grandparents?'

'Well, yes. Granny got the wrong idea and thought he was my sweetheart and insisted on inviting him for a meal.'

'And what did she think after seeing the two of you together?'

Jenny was forced to admit, 'She still thinks he's sweet on me.'

'Ha! I told you. If even your granny thinks he's got feelings for you it must be true.'

'But it doesn't change a thing.' Jenny's voice was close to a wail. 'I'm sure he does have feelings for me. But he's clearly determined to stay with Mina, so there's nothing I can do about it.'

Thea's shoulders slumped. 'I suppose not.' She leapt to her feet and pulled Jenny up after her. 'Come on, or we'll miss the bus. With luck we'll find you a handsome pilot tonight who'll make you forget all about Edwin.'

–

But of course there was no one there who could hold a candle to Edwin, Jenny reflected some time later when the dance was in full swing. Over a sea of bobbing heads she could see Thea and Fitz dancing an energetic Lindy Hop. Pearl and Greg were sitting at her table, yet they had their heads together discussing baby names and Jenny didn't feel like joining in. Edwin had gone to fetch drinks and, judging by the crowd around the bar, he would be there for a while.

Letting her gaze drift over the dancers, she frowned when she saw a red-haired woman wandering through the crowd as though looking for someone. Although she was sure she had seen her before, Jenny couldn't work out where. She wasn't in uniform, so perhaps she was from the village. As she watched, the woman tapped a WAAF on the shoulder, asked a question Jenny couldn't hear and then, when she received a shake of the head in reply, moved on.

She leaned across the table to speak to Pearl and Greg. 'Do either of you recognise that woman in the green dress?' she asked. 'She looks familiar.'

Pearl eyed the woman with narrowed eyes for a moment before shaking her head. 'Doesn't ring any bells. She doesn't look well, though.'

It was true. Now she was closer, Jenny could see the woman had dark rings around her eyes and seemed agitated. At that moment she glanced in their direction and recognition kindled in her eyes. She forced her way through the crowd and approached Jenny. 'I've seen you with him. Where is he? He said he'd meet me here.'

Jenny exchanged a mystified glance with Pearl before saying, 'I'm sorry, who are you talking about?'

'Richie Evans. Where is he?'

The mention of Richie's name jogged her memory. Now she remembered seeing the woman in the White Horse at Fenthorpe. She had been with Richie, receiving a mysterious package. 'I'm sorry. I haven't seen him. He's probably here somewhere though.' As a matter of fact, Lily had proudly announced they were going together, but she wasn't sure if it was a good idea to tell this woman that he had a date.

'If you see him, tell him Rita's looking for him.' She wandered away, swaying, and Jenny wondered if she was drunk.

'What was all that about?' Pearl asked. 'How do you know her?'

'I don't. But I saw her with Richie Evans in the White Horse a few months ago. Do you remember me telling you about seeing Richie handing something to a strange woman? That was her.'

Pearl seemed to produce a notebook and pencil from thin air. 'I remember now. We thought it might be something to do with the black market. What else have you discovered? I still need that spectacular final story.'

'Why? Have you got a definite leaving date?'

Pearl nodded, her eyes mournful. 'The end of May.' She sighed. 'It's probably for the best. I've let out my uniform about as far as it can go, and I haven't been able to fasten my jacket for over a fortnight.'

Jenny grinned. 'It's a good thing you're not expected to go on parade. You won't have to stop writing, though, will you? I'm sure Thomas would carry on printing your articles.'

'He's already offered. But doesn't it feel too much like nepotism?'

Jenny thought about this. 'Not really. When you first met him you didn't know you were related, so his interest in you was entirely down to your talent.'

Pearl's face cleared. 'Do you really think so? I do want to carry on writing, although I'm going to have to fit it round caring for this little one.' She rubbed her bump.

Edwin finally arrived at their table, carrying drinks. 'Lemonade all round,' he said. 'We're probably doing another run to the Netherlands tomorrow and I want to be wide awake if we do.'

Jenny's heart swelled to see him looking so happy. 'Now there's a good article for the *Bombshell*, Pearl.'

Edwin sat up straight. 'I'd love to write a piece about Operation Manna if you let me,' he said to Pearl.

'Excellent. It's nice to have someone want to write an article instead of me having to threaten all sorts of dire retribution if something doesn't get written.' She scribbled a note in her book. 'Right. I've got you down for five hundred words by this time next week, so I hope you mean it, because I don't want to have to set Greg on you.'

'Oh, I mean it. For the first time ever, I actually hope we are flying ops tomorrow.'

Greg raised his bottle. 'I hear you. Here's to a successful Operation Manna.' They clinked bottles.

Chapter Fifteen

A little later, Jenny excused herself to visit the ladies. To get there she had to go through the hotel foyer, and she reached it just as Richie and Lily arrived. Lily waved at her, although without her usual enthusiasm, and Jenny wondered if they'd had an argument.

'You're missing all the fun,' she told them.

'I know,' Lily said. 'It's all my fault. I had the day off and I thought I'd lie down to rest for five minutes this afternoon, and the next thing I knew I'd missed the bus.'

'That's the trouble with working shifts,' Jenny said in sympathy. 'I never feel like I get quite enough sleep these days. I'm glad you got here in the end.'

'Richie was a sweetie and waited for me.' Lily squeezed his arm, although the grimace he bestowed on her in return didn't look entirely loving. 'We had to walk into Fenthorpe and catch the regular bus service into Lincoln.'

'At least you can catch the transport back to base with the rest of us,' Jenny told them, referring to the bus RAF Fenthorpe had put on to take personnel into Lincoln that night. 'Anyway, I must dash. I'll see you in there. Oh,' she added, glancing at Richie, 'I nearly forgot. Someone called Rita was asking after you earlier. I think she's left now, though.'

Lily released her hold on Richie's arm and asked him, 'Who's Rita?'

Richie scowled. 'Someone who'll leave me alone if she knows what's good for her.' He grasped Lily's elbow. 'Come on. We're late enough already.' He tugged her in the direction of the ballroom, and Jenny watched them go. She couldn't regret mentioning Rita in front of Lily. Lily hadn't looked at all happy and, if she saw sense and realised Richie was not treating her well, maybe she would finally break it off with him.

When she returned to the dance, however, she saw the pair huddled in a dark corner, deep in earnest discussion, so she could only assume that Lily had accepted whatever explanation Richie had given her. Thea and Fitz were back on the dance floor, and as she watched Fitz swung Thea high into the air, both laughing in delight. Thea's hair, which had unravelled from its sophisticated victory rolls, now fanned around her face in a gleaming auburn halo.

The wistful feeling had returned by the time she sat back down at her table. Possibly her feelings showed, for Edwin said, 'Would you like to dance?'

She shook her head. 'I think I might dislocate something if I had to try that.' She indicated Thea and Fitz, who now appeared to be experiencing some kind of synchronised electric shock.

As if the band had heard, the music wound down from the highly energetic number and eased into a slower melody. Greg rose and held out his hand to Pearl. 'You did promise me a dance tonight. How about this one?'

Pearl took his hand. 'I suppose we should make the most of it before my bump gets too big.' They headed for the dance floor, leaving Jenny alone with Edwin.

Edwin smiled. 'How about it? Is this number sedate enough for you?'

Deciding it would be more awkward to sit out the dance, she took his hand and let him lead her onto the floor. She realised her mistake as soon as he took her in his arms. A slow dance was too intimate. If they had danced to a lively song, they could have had a laugh, spinning and dipping. Now, however, Jenny was acutely aware of Edwin's hand resting on her back and his breath against her cheek. She racked her brains for something to say. Anything to break the tension that was building up between them until she half expected the air between them to sizzle with lightning. *Have you heard from Mina recently?* No, too crass. *Can you help me with this vector geometry problem I was trying out the other day?* But he probably would and, much as she was fascinated by vectors, she didn't really want to stop dancing. For all she knew, this could be the last chance she had to dance with him, and she wanted to make a memory that she could hold in her heart.

Finally she opted for, 'It's good to see you and the others so proud of what you achieved today.'

The smile that lit his face was another beautiful memory she would hold on to for the rest of her life. 'I *am* proud. You can't imagine how it feels to have done some real good today.'

'Seeing your face right now gives me a pretty good idea.'

'It sounds like we'll be doing this for some days, and I can only hope we spend the rest of the war dropping food instead of bombs.'

Their progress had taken them to the far end of the dance floor, near the table where Lily sat with Richie. Jenny couldn't help noticing that Lily's face was streaked with tears, and she was trying to decide if she should intervene when Richie leapt to his feet.

With a face twisted in anger, he snarled, 'You're just trying to trap me! Well, it won't work. You can't prove it's mine. From what I hear, it could be anyone's.'

He swung back his arm, and Jenny gasped. She turned to Edwin to ask him to put a stop to it, but Edwin had already released her and was marching towards the couple. He grabbed Richie's wrist before he could strike and then seized him by the collar.

'You don't want to do that. Come on,' he said and marched the seething man out of the door. Jenny turned to locate her friends, only to see Greg and Fitz already hurrying to Edwin's aid.

Jenny dashed to Lily's side. She put an arm round the sobbing girl and helped her to her feet. 'Come on,' she said.

Then Thea and Pearl arrived and between them they escorted Lily to a quiet lounge. It took a cup of tea fetched by Thea and the loan of Pearl's clean hanky before Lily's sobs had subsided enough to speak.

'Why don't you tell us what's wrong?' Jenny invited her, although she feared she had already worked it out.

Lily dabbed her blotchy face again before replying. 'I suppose there's no point trying to keep it secret. The whole camp will be discussing it after that scene.' Her shoulders heaved with further sobs and there was another pause while she visibly fought to get herself under control. Finally, she said, 'I'm expecting, you see.' She couldn't meet anyone's gaze.

Jenny put her arm around Lily's shoulders. 'I thought so,' she said. 'I'm guessing that little scene with Richie means he's shirking all responsibility.'

Lily's face crumpled, and Jenny had trouble making out her next words, which came between sobs. 'He said such mean things. Like how did I know the baby was his. And I thought we were going to get married.' Her words ended on a wail, and Jenny exchanged worried glances with her friends, feeling helpless.

Pearl took charge. 'I think the best thing is to get you back to base. There's a bus leaving for Fenthorpe in a few minutes, and that will save you having to face Richie and the rest of the camp on the transport. I'm afraid you won't be able to keep this secret, so you ought to see Section Officer Blatchford first thing tomorrow.'

'I'll go with you,' Jenny offered. 'I'm not on duty until the afternoon.'

That decided, they escorted Lily from the hotel. Edwin and Greg came with them.

'I left Evans with a flea in his ear,' Edwin told them. Evidently as senior officer he had taken the discipline upon himself. 'I know his skipper, and I'll see what pressure we can apply to see that he takes responsibility,' he added with a glance at Lily.

Jenny thought he meant to persuade Richie to marry Lily, and couldn't decide if that would make things better or worse for the poor girl. She couldn't imagine married life with a man who had threatened to hit her would be any better than the disgrace of being an unwed mother. But then another thought struck. 'You don't think he'll be on the same bus, do you? Perhaps we should wait for the next one.'

But Greg shook his head. 'I followed him a little way to make sure he didn't try to come back. Last I saw of him he was going into the Cardinal's Hat.'

As it turned out, although Richie wasn't on the bus, Jenny caught sight of Rita sitting right at the back. She firmly steered Lily to a seat near the front, doing her best to ensure the women didn't meet. What could Rita have wanted with Richie? Remembering Rita's distress and pale face, she could only hope Richie hadn't got her in the family way as well.

Edwin refused to let the unpleasantness at the end of the evening spoil his pleasure the next day when he learned they would be delivering more supplies to the Netherlands. He had a word with Richie's skipper over breakfast and hoped that would be an end to it. Sadly, however, he witnessed Flying Officer Palmer accost his gunner when they arrived at RAF Fenthorpe, and the encounter was not pleasant.

'You're going to have to take responsibility and marry the girl,' Palmer told Richie. 'It's the decent thing to do.'

'Yeah, well, I'd have to divorce my wife first, so that's not going to happen. If the stupid bitch wants a ring on her finger, she's going to have to find some other bloke to do the honours. Why did she have to ruin everything by getting knocked up?' Richie laughed at his skipper's incredulous expression. 'Come on, you're a married man too. Don't tell me you've never had a bit of fun on the side.'

'I most certainly have not. I love and respect my wife.'

'More fool you.' Richie stalked off, and Edwin watched him go, shaking with fury.

'Did you have no clue he was married?' he asked Palmer.

The pilot shook his head. 'I've never heard him mention a wife before. I think I'll do some digging to make sure.'

It was only after their flight that Edwin saw Palmer again. He was just leaving the locker room when he met Palmer coming the other way. Palmer grasped his arm and pulled him across to his locker.

'I had a word with a chap in the Accounts Section,' Palmer said. 'It's true. Richie's been sending a proportion of his pay home to his wife ever since he joined up. How am I ever going to tell that poor girl? Richie's made it perfectly clear he has no intention of speaking to her again, and I don't feel like forcing him to confess to her because frankly I think she's suffered enough.'

'I'll tell her,' Edwin offered. 'A friend of mine works with her, and I think I can enlist her help.'

He didn't see Jenny until they were in the pub that evening. He was relieved to see her because, knowing she was on duty that night, he had feared she wouldn't turn up.

'I can't stay long,' Jenny said when she greeted him, 'but I wanted to hear how the mission went today and whether Richie's skipper managed to speak to him.'

'Do you want the good news or the bad news?'

Jenny's face fell. 'I'm guessing this is about Richie? You'd better tell me.'

'It turns out he's already married.'

Thea, who had been walking past, evidently heard. 'What? The bastard!'

Jenny wouldn't have expressed it quite that way, but she completely agreed.

'Does Lily know yet?'

'I don't think so. I said I'd tell her but I was hoping you could be there for support as well.'

'Of course.'

'How did it go with Blatchford this morning?' Thea asked.

'She was actually very understanding and sympathetic,' Jenny said. 'She said Lily would have to leave but not right away, so she will get some time to decide what to do. I think she was relieved she wouldn't have to go back home straight away, because she's dreading telling her parents.'

'We ought to tell her about Richie as soon as possible.' It wasn't going to be a pleasant talk, and Edwin wanted to get it over with. 'Do you know where she is?'

Jenny grimaced. 'She's on duty. I'll only see her when it's time for me to relieve her, so I won't be able to tell her then. I don't know how I'm going to face her, knowing what I do. I think I'm going to have to catch her first thing in the morning.'

Edwin agreed to meet her when she came off duty. That decided, Jenny announced that she should return to the Waafery and have a nap for an hour or two before it was time for her night watch.

'No, don't leave, Edwin,' she added, when he rose and picked up his cap. 'Stay and enjoy yourself. It's still light, so I'll be fine walking back alone.'

But Edwin shook his head. 'I only came to tell you about Richie. I wasn't planning to make a night of it.'

In the event, Thea said she would return too, and Edwin found himself waiting outside the pub with Jenny while Thea paid a quick visit to the ladies. Standing in the golden evening light, Edwin was painfully aware of other courting couples walking hand in hand along the high street or giggling in shadowy corners as they indulged in a quick kiss and cuddle. After the closeness they had shared in the Forest of Dean, it was harder than ever to remember he could never be more than friends with Jenny.

He racked his brains for something to break the awkward silence, then they both spoke at once.

'What are you—?'

'Have you heard from—?'

They both stopped and laughed.

'You go first,' he offered.

'No, it's fine. I was only—'

Jenny broke off when they both heard a woman's voice nearby, wailing, 'But you promised!' Edwin wouldn't have paid much attention if he hadn't detected a note of desperation.

Jenny looked worried and twisted around, clearly looking for the woman who had spoken. It was hard to tell, but Edwin thought the voice had come from the narrow alley that led into the yard behind the pub.

Then a man, who sounded familiar, snarled a reply. 'I never promised you anything, and you know it.'

Jenny frowned. 'That sounds like Richie.'

Before he could stop her she stepped round the corner, just as the woman's voice said, 'I bet there are people who would be interested to hear what you've been getting up to.'

'You wouldn't dare.'

The man's voice dripped with menace. Edwin dashed after Jenny and saw Richie with the red-haired woman he remembered from the dance. Richie had her backed against the wall, and his fists were clenched. But when he saw Jenny and Edwin he stepped back and straightened. The woman pushed past and hurried onto the high street. Despite her keeping her face averted from Edwin and Jenny, Edwin caught a glimpse of tears streaming down her cheeks.

He glared at Richie. 'What was all that about?'

'None of your business.'

Edwin had never pulled rank before, but the man's insolence couldn't be tolerated. 'You'll address me as sir. And considering recent events, I'd advise you to stay out of trouble. You certainly shouldn't be mixing with even more women.'

Richie pulled himself into an exaggerated salute. 'Yes *sir*.'

'Get out of here.' Edwin jerked a thumb over his shoulder, then followed Richie out of the lane, watching him leave, making sure he didn't follow the woman.

'What was all that about?' Thea had arrived, only Edwin had been too occupied in watching Richie to notice.

'It sounds like Lily isn't the only woman Richie's got into trouble,' he told her.

Thea gazed up the high street, shading her eyes against the low sun. 'Is that the woman who was asking after Richie at the dance?'

Jenny nodded. 'It's awful. I've never liked Richie but I never imagined he could be so vile.' Her face creased in sympathy. 'Poor woman. And poor Lily. I don't know how I'm going to tell her he's married.'

Chapter Sixteen

If anything, the reality was even worse than Jenny had feared. She and Edwin took Lily into one of the classrooms, which at that time in the morning was deserted. It had been used the previous evening for a poetry class, and Jenny found herself having to explain the situation with Richie while sitting beside a blackboard with one of Shakespeare's love sonnets chalked up on it.

Lily cried all the way through, and, when Jenny said that Richie was already married, she sobbed, 'But he said he loved me. There has to be a mistake.'

'I'm sorry, but it's true,' Edwin said. 'Flying Officer Palmer has it on good authority that he's been sending pay home to his wife.'

After more tears, Jenny patted Lily's hand. 'What are you going to do?'

'I'll have to go home. My parents are going to be so angry.' Lily drew several deep breaths as she tried to control her sobs. Eventually, she said, 'Maybe I should write. That way I won't have to see their faces when they learn the news.'

'That's probably a good idea. Why don't you do it now and get it over with? I can take it to the post.'

Jenny took Lily back to her hut and let her use some of her precious writing paper. While Lily laboured over her letter, Jenny kept her promise to Mina and wrote to tell her that Edwin had finally revealed the full story of what had happened after the crash. Although she didn't go into details, she assured Mina that

Edwin now seemed much better and would hopefully be able to tell her everything the next time they met.

The reminder that Mina had a prior claim to Edwin's heart cost Jenny a fair amount of pain, but once she had finished and addressed the envelope, she did her best to forget her hurt and give Lily the encouragement she needed to complete her altogether more difficult letter. Two drenched handkerchiefs later it was done, and Jenny took both letters to the post, trying to imagine her granny's reaction if she had to go home and announce she was going to be an unmarried mother. She reached the conclusion that her granny would take it in her stride, preferring Jenny to do something plenty of other women in the Forest of Dean had experienced rather than trying to get an education.

–

In the days that followed, Lily became quiet and withdrawn as she awaited a reply. Jenny offered what support she could, never letting Lily's fate slip her mind even though the whole of Fenthorpe was awash with the momentous news of Hitler's suicide. The end of the war in Europe was now just about the only topic of conversation. Bombing raids from the base had stopped and, after their first few flights for Operation Manna, their Lancasters were used for another humanitarian mission – flights to Brussels for the repatriation of former prisoners of war. In this atmosphere of hope, Jenny felt torn in two, not only eager to celebrate but also wanting to be there for poor Lily who was in no mood for fun.

From then on, the news went from reports of battles to reports of meetings between leaders and generals. Jenny found it hard to take in that the end of the war, in Europe at least, was a foregone conclusion. With the danger of enemy bombs over, blackout regulations were lifted and the street lights were switched back on.

Finally the big day came. Jenny and Thea, who were off duty at the time, had gathered with Greg, Fitz and Edwin at the Gatehouse, where they played cards while keeping half an ear on the radio, which Thomas had left playing in the background. Then came an interruption to the scheduled broadcast and everyone immediately put down their cards. Deedee and Thomas clasped hands, and the other couples also clung together. Jenny hugged her arms to her chest, wishing she could hold Edwin. Churchill's voice came across the airwaves. When the announcement came of Germany's unconditional surrender, Pearl gave an audible sob, and Jenny was surprised to find tears were pouring down her cheeks.

'I can't believe it,' Thea said, hugging Fitz. 'It's finally over.'

Edwin was gazing blankly at the radio. 'We'll never have to drop another bomb.'

–

'I know I should be happy,' Jenny said to Thea later when they were walking back to the Waafery, 'but it hasn't sunk in yet.'

'Same here,' Thea said. 'I joined the WAAF not long after the start of the war. I don't know what else I'm going to do with my life.'

'Marry Fitz?'

Thea gave her a mysterious smile but said nothing.

Jenny was intrigued. 'Come on, you can't leave it like that.'

'Oh, all right.' Thea was practically dancing. 'He asked me just now when we were getting ready to leave, and I said yes!'

'What! Why didn't you tell us?' Then Jenny recollected herself. 'Congratulations, though. That's wonderful news.'

'It is, isn't it. We'll tell everyone tomorrow when we've got time to celebrate properly, but I wanted to tell someone. I'm so excited.'

'I'm really happy for you both. And not at all surprised. It's about time.'

'That's what I said to Fitz.'

'And I wouldn't worry about deciding what to do. We're still at war with Japan, so they won't be sending any of us home just yet.'

'That's true. At the risk of sounding selfish, I hope none of our lads gets sent to the east.'

'Have you any idea what Fitz wants to do?'

'We've talked about it quite a lot recently. He's hoping to stay with the RAF if they'll have him. He doesn't have any qualifications for anything else, so I think he'd struggle to get a decent job in civilian life.'

They arrived at the Waafery, still discussing the future, Thea full of ideas about her wedding. They felt too excited to turn in, so they headed for the rec, hoping to continue their celebrations. Although before they went in, Thea made Jenny promise not to breathe a word about her engagement until she'd shared the news with Pearl and her grandparents.

However, wherever the celebrations were happening, it wasn't at the rec. The only person there was Lily, holding a crumpled letter, tears pouring down her cheeks.

'Lily, what's happened?' Jenny asked.

Lily held up her letter. 'I just heard from my parents.'

Jenny sat beside her. 'Well at least they know now. They'll get over it.'

' 'Course they will,' Thea put in. 'By the time your baby arrives they'll be too overjoyed with their new granddaughter or grandson to—' She stopped when Lily broke into fresh wails. 'Why, what have I said?'

'You don't understand. My parents have told me they want nothing to do with me. I'll have to go into an institution.'

'There must be some kind of mistake,' Jenny said. She couldn't imagine any parent disowning their child.

Lily thrust the letter into her hands. 'Read it for yourself.'

The letter was short and to the point. Jenny read it, feeling sick. There was no concern for Lily's wellbeing or the fact that they were abandoning their grandchild. The letter was written by Lily's father, who told her in stiff, formal language that she was a disgrace and should no longer consider herself a part of the family. 'To let you into our home would be condoning your sin,' he wrote.

'I don't believe it,' Thea raged. 'I've a good mind to write and tell him his version of the Bible must have left out the bit about the Prodigal Son.'

But raging was no good. Jenny and Thea did their best to comfort Lily but they knew that, if she had no family to take her in when she left the WAAF, she would have no choice but to go to a home for unmarried mothers.

–

'I couldn't have chosen a better day for a day off if I'd planned it,' Jenny said, climbing down from the packed bus the following afternoon. It seemed like everyone for miles around had converged upon Lincoln to celebrate the end of the war in Europe. Even Pearl had joined them, saying it would be impossible to get any work done in the office and she might as well write a first-hand account of the celebrations later.

Everyone who could be spared had been given the day off, and, as there was to be no flying, that included the crews. Special transports had been laid on to take the men and women of RAF Fenthorpe into Lincoln, and, seeing the crowds flocking to the centre, Jenny thought this was a good thing, as the regular bus service must have been packed.

Thea grabbed Jenny's arm and pointed to a small knot of people in blue uniform standing by the bridge. 'There they are!' She jumped up and down, waving madly.

Jenny studied the group more carefully and saw it was Pearl, Greg, Fitz and Edwin. They pushed through the crowd to reach their friends, Jenny's heart all aflutter at the prospect of spending the celebrations with Edwin. And it was only natural to walk by his side when the others paired off. She took his arm, although she told herself it was to prevent them from being separated in the crush.

'Everyone's heading for the Stonebow,' Pearl told them, having to shout to make herself heard. 'They've rigged up speakers on the Guildhall, so everyone's going there to hear Churchill's speech.'

Pearl's announcement had hardly been necessary for, looking up the high street, Jenny could see the crowds converging on the stone arch across it a little further up, where the beautiful old Guildhall crossed the street. The stone gleamed gold in the afternoon sunlight. She could already hear the music, sounding tinny through the speakers, and while some people stood still, clearly waiting for the speech to begin, others waved flags and danced. The exterior of the Guildhall had been decorated with Union Jacks and the huge illuminated letters 'VE' stood in the windows above the archway.

They found a spot at the edge of the crowd, all mindful that Pearl needed to be protected from the crush. Even so, that didn't stop some of the more enthusiastic young women from dashing up to the men, kissing them and thanking them for all they had done.

'We were there too, you know,' Thea yelled after one girl who had left Fitz rubbing a smear of crimson lipstick from his cheek. 'The Lancs wouldn't have got in the air without us, but I notice you're not thanking us.'

What the girl might have said in reply they would never know, for the music died away and an expectant hush fell on the crowd, broken only by mothers shushing their overexcited children. Then Churchill's voice rang out through the speakers and Jenny was struck by the strange feeling that the stone walls that had absorbed centuries of history were now adding this moment to their long memory. As she heard the prime minister announcing their victory in Europe, a lump came to her throat and she thought back to all that had happened since her arrival in Lincolnshire three years ago. Images of the aircrews who

167

had served at Fenthorpe flashed before her eyes. Many of them had been lost, and she thought of all those who had been her friends. She was determined that their contribution would also be remembered on this day, for this was their victory as well, not just a victory for those who had survived.

When Churchill's address ended, Lincoln's mayor also said a few words, thanking the people of the city for their service and commiserating with those who had lost loved ones.

With the speeches over, the music started again, and the people showed no sign of dispersing. Not that Jenny wanted to leave. A ring of dancers formed right in front of them, and a moment later one of the dancers reached out and grabbed her hand, sweeping her into the dance. She soon saw Thea, Fitz and Edwin pulled into the circle too, like leaves in a whirlwind. Looking around the ring, she saw many of the dancers were also in uniform and she thought that, while the speeches had been to commemorate their victory, the dancing that followed was more like wild celebration that the war was over and they had survived.

Presently the ring broke up and, panting, Jenny went to join Pearl and Greg, who had remained standing in the same place. The others soon reached them.

'Pearl and I are going back to the newspaper offices,' Greg told them. 'We'll watch the rest of the celebrations from Thomas's flat.' For Thomas kept an apartment on the top floor of the Haughton Newspaper Group building, where he sometimes slept when required to work late.

Pearl rubbed her bump with a rueful smile. 'My bladder can't cope with being away from the loo for long. But Deedee and Thomas have extended their invitation to all of you too, although I expect you'll want to stay here and celebrate.'

'Tell them we'll come later,' Thea said. 'It's not every day we celebrate the end of a war, and I want to make the most of it.'

The others agreed and, after waving Pearl and Greg off, they rejoined the dancing. Two hours later, however, when Jenny had sung herself hoarse, they were all starting to flag, so they decided to take a break and visit the flat. Deedee greeted them effusively. 'To think this day is here at last,' she said, kissing each of them in turn. 'You can't believe how grateful I am to see all of you here and whole. Especially you two,' she added, addressing Greg and Edwin. 'After the scare you gave us at Christmas, I thought our family would see a repeat of the losses that we suffered in the last war.' For Pearl and Thea's father had been killed in the last weeks of the Great War.

As ever, when Jenny found herself included in Deedee's family, she felt a warm glow as though she'd been enveloped in a hug. This time, however, she spared a thought for her granny and grancher. Perhaps Granny hadn't lavished her with the support and praise she would have wished for but she loved her in her own way and had done her best for her. She reminded herself to write to her grandparents later so she could share this day of victory with them as well.

Deedee had made a rich carrot cake for the occasion, and she was soon doling out generous slices to everyone. 'Fuelling you up for the celebrations yet to come,' she said.

'You'd better count me out,' Pearl said, 'but whoever goes, I'm expecting a full report for the *Bombshell*. There's going to be a bonfire up on South Common, and they're broadcasting the king's speech from there. I want to hear all about it.'

'I'll write it for you,' Jenny offered.

Thea looked relieved. 'That's good, because I fully intend to dance the night away.' She glanced at Fitz. 'We've got news, actually.'

'You've finally got engaged!' Pearl cried. 'About time!'

Jenny, relieved that there was now no risk of her inadvertently blurting out the news, joined in the congratulations.

'Another wedding to plan,' Deedee said, beaming. 'Although for the sake of my heart, I hope you're not going to spring a surprise on me as shocking as the last one.' She squeezed Thomas's hand as she said this, for Thomas, who had

169

given Pearl away at her wedding, had been the shock Deedee was referring to.

'Why? Have you got any more former lovers we should be aware of?' Thea asked. 'Grandpa, you should watch out.'

'I'm not worried,' Thomas said, laughing. 'I've married her now, so she can't get away.'

There followed a spate of questions aimed at Thea and Fitz, with everyone wanting to know the couple's plans.

Finally Thea raised her hands to get everyone quiet. 'We haven't set a date yet because we want to know where we'll be living and what jobs we'll be doing first. Unlike my sister' – she shot a wicked grin at Pearl – 'we want to make plans *before* we get married. Fitz is going to apply to stay on in the RAF, so we're going to sort that out before setting a date. But as soon as we know, you can expect to receive invitations.'

The VE Day celebrations turned into an engagement party, and it was much later when Jenny, Edwin, Thea and Fitz set out to join the throngs making their way to the hill at the south of the city. A huge stack of pallets and wooden crates awaited them. At nine o'clock, the noise fell to a respectful hum while the king's speech was broadcast.

Yet again, Jenny found herself moved to tears as the king paid tribute to those who had died. Many of those around her were also wiping their eyes, and Jenny knew that most of them would have lost friends or family members as a result of the war. But when the king went on to say, 'Much hard work awaits us, both in the restoration of our own country after the ravages of war and in helping to restore peace and sanity to a shattered world,' she drank in every word, her nerves quivering. She felt as though he was addressing her personally. She had seen friends die, she had heard of the starvation in Holland and seen other friends suffer from shattered nerves as a result of the danger they had endured.

As she made mental notes for her promised report it was as though a switch had been flipped in her mind. Instead of writing a simple factual report, outlining the events of the evening, why not tie it in with the sacrifices made by the RAF personnel, explaining that they had willingly endured what they had in order to achieve the peace they were now celebrating? Wouldn't that be the best way of making it clear that they must do all in their power to ensure war never happened again? If she had learned anything over the years, it was that the written word held power.

And then her imagination took flight and she remembered all the times she had felt helpless in the face of injustice. Only she wasn't powerless if she could write about it.

Her mind buzzing, she watched as the bonfire was lit, spreading light into the dusk, a defiant beacon of hope after years of darkness. Then there was more music and the dancing started again.

Jenny's heart was too full of her new purpose to want to dance just yet. She turned to the person next to her, who happened to be Edwin. 'I know what I want to do,' she said. 'I want to be like Pearl and be a journalist. It's something I can do to highlight injustice and fight to make the world a better place.'

Then, she didn't know how it happened, but she was in Edwin's arms, kissing him. She clung to him, forgetting all the reasons why she shouldn't be doing this. Instead she let herself be controlled by the years of yearning. In that moment, there was no bonfire, no revellers and no music apart from the rapid beat of her heart. The only reality was Edwin's mouth on hers and his arms pulling her close.

She was jerked back to reality when someone bumped into them. 'Oops, sorry!'

She stood there, gasping for breath, staring at Edwin. In her peripheral vision she was vaguely aware of the continued revelry, but she couldn't tear her gaze from Edwin, who wore the same half dazed, half shocked expression she was sure must also be on her face. What had just happened? How could she have forgotten all her common sense? How could she have forgotten Mina?

Chapter Seventeen

Even after the dancer had bumped into him, breaking the kiss, Edwin couldn't corral his scattered wits. He gazed at Jenny, his lips burning, his arms aching with the need to hold her again.

'I'm so sorry,' Jenny gasped. 'I shouldn't have done that.'

Was it Jenny who had started it? Edwin couldn't remember. One moment she had been gazing at him, eyes shining, telling him she wanted to make the world a better place. The next moment they had been kissing. He couldn't for the life of him remember how it had started. He stared at her, unable to form a coherent thought, let alone speak.

Jenny, though, didn't seem to share his problem. 'It must have been the excitement of the celebrations,' she said. 'It made me act without thinking, but we can't let it happen again. I won't do that to Mina.'

Mina! He felt a rush of shame. For a few glorious moments he had completely forgotten her, forgotten that he mustn't do anything to hurt her. It was this thought that finally unfroze his brain.

'You're right. I'm sorry. I got carried away.' However it had happened, he wasn't about to let Jenny shoulder the blame. Anyway, if anyone should bear the greatest guilt it was him. He was the one engaged to another.

Gradually he became aware of the other revellers. Some still danced around them, although more were drifting off back into the city centre. He was racking his brains for something wise and comforting to say. Something to reassure Jenny that he wouldn't repeat his transgression. However, he still couldn't seem to think clearly and all he could think to say was, 'We won't let this spoil our friendship, will we?' Because nothing said, 'just good friends' like a passionate clinch by twilight.

He cleared his throat, thinking he should say something else, only he had no idea what. Thankfully he was saved by Thea and Fitz, who chose that moment to bound up to them.

'It looks like everyone's heading back to Lincoln. What do you both want to do?'

Edwin hesitated. He didn't think it would be a good idea for him and Jenny to be alone again, yet he couldn't expect Fitz and Thea to chaperone them. He glanced at Jenny and thought he could see her wrestling with the same thoughts.

'I don't really feel like fighting through the crowds any more,' he said. 'You three go on. I'll head back to Fenthorpe.'

'Don't be an idiot. We should stick together,' Fitz said.

'I don't mind going back,' Thea said. 'What do you think, Jenny?'

Jenny, who had been looking at her feet, gave a start. 'What? Sorry, I wasn't listening.' When Thea repeated her question, she said, 'If you don't mind, I'd like to go back.'

Thea frowned at her. 'Are you feeling all right?'

'Yes, I'm fine. Just tired. The crowd and the noise are getting a bit much, that's all.'

Thea glanced at her watch. 'It's only half past nine. The transport won't be leaving for another hour.'

Jenny looked as desperate to get away as Edwin felt. 'Why don't we walk? It's only two or three miles back to Fenthorpe from here. We'd be there in under an hour.'

'I'm up for it if you are,' Thea said. 'But I thought you were tired.'

'Only tired of the crowd. Not too tired to walk.'

Edwin had expected an uncomfortable walk in Jenny's company while Thea walked with Fitz. However, no sooner had they set out than Jenny took Thea's arm. 'You haven't said much about your wedding plans yet. I want to hear all about it.'

So Edwin found himself walking with Fitz. Before they started walking down the slope leading away from the city, the sound of cheering made them turn back.

'Look!' Jenny cried, pointing towards Lincoln. The cathedral, high on its hill, stood in a blaze of light. For a moment Edwin thought it must be bathed in moonlight, until he remembered that the moon was no more than a thin crescent. Then two circles of light played up and down the towers and understanding dawned. 'It's searchlights,' he said.

Beside him, Fitz gave a soft chuckle. 'The cathedral's been coned.'

'It's beautiful,' Thea said, her voice full of awe.

'It's hard to believe,' Jenny said. 'Only a few weeks ago, Thea and I were staggering around in the pitch dark walking home from the Gatehouse, because it was too dangerous to use anything but the dimmest of torchlight. And now here we are with the whole of Lincoln lit up like a Christmas tree and we don't have to be scared ever again.'

When they resumed their walk, it was in a reflective silence. Eventually Fitz broke it. 'Never thought I'd enjoy seeing searchlights.' And finally it properly sank in that the war was really over. That illuminations could be beautiful again and that they could start enjoying the simple things in life again and plan more than one day ahead.

But even while he joined in with the conversation, random thoughts and impressions bombarded Edwin from all directions. He couldn't forget how it had felt to hold Jenny in his arms and how soft her lips had felt against his. He was profoundly relieved that Fitz and Thea apparently hadn't seen them kiss, for Fitz would be bound to subject him to an inquisition if he had, and he had no idea what he would say. To explain that it had been an impulsive act brought on by high spirits didn't adequately describe the profound experience, yet what else could he say? For Mina's sake it could never happen again, yet that realisation was accompanied by a wave of desolation. And he also wondered if he should be honest and make a confession to Mina. But wouldn't that just hurt her? If he was determined not to let it happen again, wouldn't it be kinder to say nothing?

He was still tangled in indecision when they reached the turning to RAF Fenthorpe, with the way to Fenthorpe Hall straight ahead.

'You two should go on,' Jenny said to Fitz and Edwin. 'Thea and I have walked this way enough times on our own.'

'Absolutely not,' Fitz protested. 'There have always been other WAAFs going the same way before, but most of them are in Lincoln tonight. Quite apart from anything else, Deedee would have my guts for garters if she heard I'd let you walk back alone on a night like tonight.'

'Personally, I'm more afraid of Pearl,' Edwin added. He couldn't help wondering if Jenny had suggested parting ways because she was too embarrassed to stay in his company. But he agreed with Fitz and wouldn't be able to forgive himself if anything happened to the women alone in the dark.

They walked on, and Thea started singing 'Pack up Your Troubles' as a marching song. Soon they were all marching in unison, using their torches like searchlights, chasing each other's beams along the verge. Even Edwin managed to follow the advice of the song and put aside his worries as they sang.

'Pack up your troubles in your old kit bag, and smile, smile, smile,' he sang out, ignoring his throat, which was still scratchy from all the cheering earlier.

Then his torch beam fell on a hand lying by the roadside and he broke off with a yelp. He grabbed Fitz's arm, pulling him to a stop. Jenny and Thea, who had been walking behind, bumped into them.

'What's the matter?' Fitz asked.

Edwin didn't answer for a moment but shone his light across the verge, trying to find the hand again. But surely his eyes had been playing tricks.

Then his beam found a tangle of hair, and his mouth went dry.

'Oh, my God,' Fitz said in a strangled voice. 'Is that a woman?' He started forward and knelt beside the body. After a moment, Edwin forced his frozen limbs to move.

'Careful!' Fitz said. 'She's half lying in a ditch.'

When Edwin got closer he could see for himself. Only the woman's head and one arm lay out of the ditch. Her forehead rested against the bank as though she had settled down for a nap. He knelt beside Fitz, who had his fingers on the woman's wrist. 'Is she drunk?'

'I don't think so. I can't find a pulse. Help me turn her over.'

Taking care not to slide into the ditch, Edwin managed to grasp her under the arms and heave her onto her back. He let go with a gasp and staggered back when the woman's head flopped back onto the ground, and in the dim torchlight he saw open eyes gazing sightlessly at the sky.

Thea gave a low moan. 'She's dead, isn't she.'

It was pointless denying it.

Jenny felt sick. She edged forward, not wanting to see the body but needing answers. 'Who is it? How did she die?'

'I don't know. She's not from RAF Fenthorpe.'

Jenny caught a glimpse of the woman's face over Edwin's shoulder just as Fitz turned the beam of his torch to show her features. She flinched when she saw the sightless eyes, and clutched Edwin's shoulder. She closed her eyes, fighting nausea. Only then did the knowledge filter into her consciousness that she recognised her.

'It's Rita. You know, the woman who was asking after Richie at the dance.'

'You're right.' Edwin's body was quivering with tension; Jenny could feel the stiff muscles. 'I didn't recognise her at first.'

'How did she die?' Thea asked. 'Do you think she fell into the ditch?'

Fitz shone his light over the body. 'I can't see any obvious wounds, and her neck isn't broken.' He directed the light back onto the woman's face. Jenny averted her gaze, not wanting to see those dead eyes. She was sure she would be haunted by them for the rest of her life. 'Her face looks a bit bruised, but I can't see any injury severe enough to kill her.'

Edwin rose to his feet. 'Perhaps she was ill and fainted. Or… I don't know. But she didn't look well at the dance, did she? Anyway, we need to call the police. Where's the nearest telephone?'

Fitz also rose. 'Probably RAF Fenthorpe. I'll run ahead and raise the alert. You three wait here. It doesn't feel right to leave her lying there alone.' He didn't wait for an answer but ran off down the lane and soon disappeared into the gloom.

Still feeling sick, Jenny hugged her arms to her chest and paced up and down.

Edwin removed his jacket. 'Here. Take this.' He draped it across her shoulders. 'You're shivering.'

Jenny hadn't even noticed until Edwin had pointed it out. She felt a chill deep in the pit of her stomach, and she couldn't seem to control the shaking that made her whole frame quiver. How could an evening that had started so joyfully end in this way? The kiss seemed a minor event now.

'What about you, Thea?' Edwin asked. 'Are you cold?'

'I'm okay, I think.' Thea too was pacing. 'I just can't understand what Rita was doing out here all alone, especially if she wasn't well.'

But Jenny couldn't forget the last time she had seen Rita and the callous way Richie had pushed her aside. 'Maybe she wasn't alone. Did anyone see Richie in Lincoln?'

'Well, no,' Thea said, 'but that doesn't mean anything. It was so crowded I didn't really pick out any individual faces.' After a pause she asked, 'Why – you don't think he did her in, do you?'

Jenny pulled Edwin's jacket closer round her body. 'No. Forget I said it. I don't know what I'm thinking, to be honest.'

It felt like an age before Fitz returned. 'The police are on their way. They've asked us to wait. They're going to want to question us.'

'As long as it's someone more senior than the idiot who was no help at all when Georgie went missing,' Thea muttered, referring to an adventure Deedee had had at Christmas.

Fitz shook his head. 'I rang the Lincoln police.'

It wasn't long before they heard the sound of an approaching vehicle, and then the roadside was lit with dazzling headlights as a large black car arrived. Fitz waved to catch the driver's attention, and the car parked on the other side of the road.

A man emerged first from the passenger side and called, 'Which one of you is Flying Officer Fitzgerald?'

Fitz stepped forward. 'That's me. The body's here.' He pointed with his torch to the place where Rita's body lay.

The policeman said, 'I'm Inspector Farley, and this' – he indicated the man who had got out from the driver's side – 'is Sergeant Moles. If you wouldn't mind waiting while we examine the body, I'll have questions for you all.'

Jenny moved aside to stand by the car and was soon joined by her friends. She handed back Edwin's jacket with a smile. 'I'm not so cold now. Thank you.' Her head was in a whirl, though. One moment she had been kissing Edwin, her heart singing, the next they had stumbled across this dreadful sight. She stood in silence, unable to comprehend what had happened.

Presently Inspector Farley joined them. 'There's no sign of foul play,' he said, 'although we've called out the police surgeon, and he'll want to see the body before we move the poor woman to the mortuary. Now, could one of you please tell me exactly when you found the body. Did any of you move her?'

'I'm afraid I didn't think to check the time.' Fitz glanced around the group and they all shook their heads. 'It must have been about ten minutes before I phoned the police. I had to use the telephone at RAF Fenthorpe.'

'I see.' Farley jotted something in his notebook. 'And did you move her?'

'Yes,' Edwin said. 'She was lying face down when we found her. We thought she was asleep. You know, fallen down drunk, or something. It was only when we turned her over that we realised she was dead.' He gave a little shudder.

'Do any of you know her?'

'I don't know her,' Jenny said, glad her voice sounded stronger than she felt, 'but I recognise her. Her name's Rita, although I don't know her surname. We've seen her in the White Horse in Fenthorpe a few times, and at a dance at the Albion Hotel just over a week ago.'

'I see. And was that the last time you saw her?'

'No, I saw her outside the White Horse the day after the dance.' She turned to Edwin, feeling sick as she remembered the circumstances. 'She and Richie were arguing. Remember?'

'I do.' Edwin's face was grim. He addressed the inspector. 'She seemed to be begging him for something – I didn't hear what – but Richie looked like he was about to hit her, only he saw us and stopped.'

By this time Jenny had remembered more of the conversation she had overheard. 'Rita said something else before Richie went for her. She said something about people being interested to hear what he had been getting up to. It sounded like she was threatening to report him.' She looked at the inspector. 'I thought he'd got Rita into trouble and she was threatening to tell his wife.' Would he kill to stop her? She couldn't forget the fury in his eyes, and she also couldn't forget the cruel way he had treated Lily. But she didn't voice her suspicion, knowing as she did that her dislike of the man had biased her against him.

'You leave the investigation to us,' Farley said. 'I'll need all of you to give a statement, and it does sound like we should interview this Richie. But you need to trust us to do our jobs. If she was the kind of girl to get herself into trouble, then she might have had too much to drink and taken a tumble into the ditch. It was foolish of her to be out alone.'

Jenny stared at him, unable to believe what she had heard. 'How do you know she was out alone? Just because she was alone when we found her doesn't mean she was alone when she died.'

Farley drew himself up to his full height and shook his finger at her. 'Now look here, young lady—'

But before he could say more, another set of bright headlights lit up the scene and a second car rolled up. Farley went to speak to the newcomers, leaving Jenny shaking with anger.

Thea patted her shoulder. 'Well done for speaking up. I was about to give him a piece of my mind, but you got there before me.'

'I wish I hadn't said anything about Richie getting her into trouble now,' Jenny said bitterly. 'I said it because I thought it could be a motive for Richie to kill her, if she was threatening to tell his wife, but Farley seems to have taken it as a sign that this is all her fault.'

Edwin spoke up. 'Mina told me about a friend of hers who was attacked in London. She was furious because when the police heard the poor woman had been walking alone at night they implied the attack was all her fault for going out alone.'

'That's awful,' Jenny said. 'Why is it always a woman's fault? And it's like poor Lily being blamed for getting herself pregnant when Richie can get away scot-free.'

'I promise I'll keep an eye on Richie,' Edwin said. 'If he's involved in any way, I'll make sure he pays.'

Chapter Eighteen

The news of Rita's death sent shockwaves through Fenthorpe. Even though she hadn't been a part of RAF Fenthorpe, the fact that she had been found dead so close to its boundary was a huge blow to morale. The personnel were no strangers to death, but while they were used to losing aircrew, they hadn't expected a civilian from the village to meet their end in suspicious circumstances, and it put a dampener on their celebrations.

The day after they had found Rita's body, Edwin took the transport to the station as usual. He wasn't surprised to learn there were no operations on. It was a relief, too, for more than one of the crew looked bleary-eyed and in no condition to fly. Once they were released for the day, several of them returned to their billets or went to Lincoln for the day, but Edwin was in no mood for that. Anyway, Farley had informed him that he would visit the station that day to take their statements, so he needed to stay put. Therefore, although officers didn't usually go there, he and Fitz went to wait in the NAAFI, hoping to see Thea and Jenny. They found them already there, clearly having had the same idea. What he hadn't expected was to see Richie, chatting with a group of gunners and looking very pleased with himself.

'He must have heard about Rita,' Jenny said in a low voice, casting a scowl in Richie's direction. 'Even if he had nothing to do with it, how can he be so heartless? He knew her.'

Edwin studied the man over the rim of his cup. 'We have to be careful,' he said. 'We don't know anything for sure.' He threw an apologetic look at Thea. 'We already know how unfair it is to make false accusations.'

Thea grimaced. 'I know you're right. I mean, those months when no one would speak to me were miserable, so I'm the last person who should be accusing anyone of anything without concrete proof. But Richie's a nasty piece of work. Whether or not he was involved in Rita's death, the way he treated Lily proves that.'

'I know,' Edwin said. 'All I'm saying is that we shouldn't throw accusations around. But I'm jolly well going to make sure the police find out where he was last night.'

'Me too,' Jenny said.

Although Edwin told himself the glint of fire in her expression was solely due to her determination to see justice for Rita, he couldn't seem to stop his thoughts drifting to the way she had looked at him before their kiss. Every time he looked at her, his stomach gave a swoop of desire, yet for Mina's sake he had to control his wayward emotions. Especially when Jenny herself had told him it could never happen again. He forced himself to concentrate on the best way to convince the police to take their concerns over Rita's death seriously.

But when Inspector Farley arrived to take their statements, it was clear he had already drawn his own conclusions about Rita's death.

'She was seen drinking heavily at the White Horse last night,' he told Edwin when he led him into the briefing hut, which had been set aside for the inspector to take the statements of anyone who had seen Rita the night before. 'The landlady told me she had drunk more than usual, and she was last seen leaving the pub alone. The police surgeon tells me she died of suffocation. You say she was lying face down when you found her?'

'Yes, but—'

'Then it looks like she fell down insensible from drink, and smothered herself, lying with her mouth and nose pressed into the bank.'

How drunk would you have to be for that to happen? Edwin wondered, but said nothing, for the police must have been given expert medical advice. All he could do was give his statement and stress the underlying violence he had sensed in Richie's actions. At the end, Farley told him the inquest would be on Monday and he would be required to appear as a witness, together with Fitz, Jenny and Thea.

When he got together with the others afterwards, they all reported the same dissatisfaction.

'I honestly thought he was about to tell me not to worry my pretty little head about it,' Thea said. 'He told me to leave it to the professionals and I had to restrain myself from asking who they were.'

'You know what I think we should do?' Jenny's face was set in determined lines. 'We should go to the White Horse and ask the landlady about it.'

'I'm game,' Thea said. 'I definitely think there's something fishy going on.'

'Good.' Jenny looked from Edwin to Fitz. 'What about you two?'

Edwin shrugged. 'I don't know what else we can find that the landlady won't have told the police, but there's no harm in trying.' And considering one suspicious death had happened locally, he wasn't about to let either Jenny or Thea walk around the lanes unescorted.

'That makes four of us, then,' Fitz said.

'Good,' Thea said. 'But I think we should leave Pearl out of it if we can. I don't want to worry her.'

Jenny raised her brows. 'You've changed your tune. This from the person who got annoyed every time Pearl tried to interfere in your life!'

'I'm not interfering. Just protecting her.' Then Thea chuckled. 'Which is exactly what Pearl would say about me, I know.'

Edwin couldn't take his eyes off Jenny as the two friends laughed together. Only last night he and Jenny had kissed, yet

184

now she seemed completely unselfconscious in his presence. Maybe the kiss really had meant nothing to her. Maybe Edwin's feelings were one-sided.

And that's when it hit him that he didn't want his feelings to be one-sided. How selfish was that, when he was engaged to Mina? Yet why was he still with Mina? He wasn't in love with her any more; he had to be honest with himself. He was clinging to the engagement because he felt protective of her. But was that really being fair to her? Wasn't she entitled to be free to choose a man who loved her as much as she deserved? Was it really helping her to go through with an engagement when he was in love with another woman? Even if Jenny didn't love him, he shouldn't go on deceiving Mina.

He would have to tell her, but he also couldn't abandon her if she didn't want to break off the engagement. Since her brother had died, she had no one else in her life, and if she wanted to stay with him he would marry her. It was the least he could do.

–

The White Horse was surprisingly quiet when the four friends arrived later that afternoon, and those who were there still appeared to be recovering from the excesses of the night before. Edwin had wondered how they would introduce Rita into the conversation with Norah Brumby, the landlady, but Norah herself gave them the opening they needed.

'It's a bit quiet here today,' she said as she pulled Edwin's pint. 'The villagers are in shock. I don't know if you heard, but a woman was found dead last night.'

'We know,' Edwin said, handing over a shilling. 'We're still in shock ourselves. We were the ones who found her.'

'You poor things. That must have been awful.'

'It was,' Jenny replied. 'We couldn't imagine how she had ended up there all alone.'

Norah shook her head. 'It's terribly sad. That Inspector Farley was in here earlier, wanting to know all about her.'

'He was asking us, too,' Jenny said, 'but we couldn't really tell him anything. We've seen her here a few times, but we didn't know her at all.'

This turned out to be a clever comment, because Norah immediately took it as a request to tell them everything she knew. 'I knew her quite well. She lives here in the village.' She shut her eyes briefly. '*Lived*. It hasn't really sunk in yet. It's a sad story, though. Before the war she had got herself a good job in Lincoln as a secretary, and she moved into lodgings in the city. But not long after the war started her mother was taken ill – tuberculosis – and Rita moved back home to take care of her. Her father died some years ago and both her brothers joined the army and have been serving overseas, so poor old Rita was having to work all day and then dash home and do all the cooking and cleaning. She couldn't afford to give up her job because her mother was on a tiny pension, so they needed Rita's wage. Ironically, her mother's much better now, but I've watched Rita go from a happy young woman, full of the joys of life, to a ghost of her former self. She's… she *was* always exhausted. A kind neighbour would look after her mother one night a week just so she could take a break.'

'Oh.' Jenny looked horrified. 'So that's when she would come here, I suppose.'

Norah nodded. 'Poor girl. She was often so tired she would fall asleep, and I would have to wake her up and send her home.'

Edwin could almost see Jenny's mind working, and wondered if she was thinking the same thing he was. If Rita had been so busy all the time, how could she have got involved with Richie?

'That's so sad,' Jenny said. 'And now her mother must be all alone too.'

Norah nodded. 'She's been much better these past few months, and hasn't needed Rita to be on hand all the time. Curiously, Rita's been looking even more tired. I did wonder if she was ill. Maybe that's how she died. Could be she was taken ill after the celebrations.'

Jenny couldn't get Rita's fate out of her head in the days that followed. She, along with Edwin, Thea and Fitz, was called to attend the inquest as a witness a few days later, and so she dressed in her smartest uniform and took the bus into Lincoln with her friends. To her surprise, Pearl was already in the room, notebook in hand, when they walked into the coroner's court.

'You can't expect me to stay away when you're all involved,' she said in answer to Thea's enquiry, as they sat down. 'Anyway, a mysterious death on our doorstep is too good a story to miss.'

Jenny supposed she shouldn't be surprised, although she thought that if Pearl had actually seen the body she might not have been in such a hurry to learn more.

'I see there's a jury,' Pearl said, nodding to where they sat. 'That means the coroner must think there's at least a chance Rita's death wasn't by natural causes.'

Jenny regarded the jury with interest. While she had read widely, she didn't know much about legal proceedings. 'So, what is their role?'

'I think they have to return a verdict on whether the death was, for example, suicide, manslaughter, murder or death by misadventure. I've read up reports on other inquests and that seems to be what happens. Interesting, isn't it?'

'Maybe for you,' Thea muttered. 'I'm not looking forward to giving evidence. I've been trying to forget how it felt, the moment we realised Rita was dead, and now I'm going to have to go through every detail.'

Jenny nodded. She was feeling the same way.

As it turned out, however, their witness statements were easier than she'd feared. As they had found the body, they were called upon near the start. The coroner was a kind-looking man in his early sixties and he guided Jenny through her statement, asking questions that required only brief factual answers. Under his guidance she found the experience less of an ordeal than she'd feared, and she was soon back in her seat, pressing her sweaty palms on her skirt, watching as Edwin rose to take his turn.

Thea patted her arm. 'You did well,' she whispered.

As Thea had also given her evidence, they were now able to sit back and take more interest.

Edwin was taken through the same questions as the others – what time they had found Rita's body, the precise location and how the body had been lying.

'She was lying in the ditch,' Edwin said in response to this latest question. 'She was face down, with her head out of the ditch, resting against the bank. I had no idea she was dead, but as soon as I turned her over and saw her eyes—' He swallowed, and Jenny knew he was remembering, as she was, those wide, staring eyes and the way the head had flopped, unresisting, against the bank. Edwin appeared to recover himself. 'Well, I knew she was dead.'

'You turned her?' the coroner asked.

'Yes.'

'Did you notice if the body was cold or stiff?'

'It wasn't stiff. I stepped back as soon as I realised she was dead, and didn't touch her again, so I didn't notice how cold she was.'

After a few more questions covering whether anyone else had touched the body after that and in the time that elapsed before the police arrived, Edwin was also dismissed.

It was Norah Brumby's turn next, and she gave a statement that was much the same as the information Jenny and her friends had gleaned on their visit to the White Horse. Rita had arrived at the White Horse at seven in the evening on Thursday 8 May. Although she had come with friends, the friends had soon left, stating their intention to join the celebrations in Lincoln. Rita had refused to go, saying she didn't want to leave her mother that long.

At that point in Norah's statement, a frail-looking woman in her late fifties or sixties caught Jenny's eye. She was sitting in the row in front, sobbing into her handkerchief. Although her hair was streaked with silver, Jenny could tell it had been a vivid shade of copper in her younger days, and she guessed this was Rita's mother. Her heart went out to the woman who had survived a long, difficult illness only to lose her daughter just when she was able to grant her more freedom.

'Did Miss Fox leave soon after?' the coroner asked, drawing Jenny's attention back to Norah.

'No, she stayed at her table. I got the impression she was waiting for someone, because she kept looking at her watch.'

'And what was her general appearance? Did she look ill? Had she been drinking heavily?'

'I thought she looked rather tired but agitated. She did drink more than usual.'

'More than usual? So she was a regular at your establishment?'

Jenny bristled on Rita's behalf, not happy with the unspoken disapproval in the coroner's tone. She couldn't help but wonder what his opinion would be of her, considering she too often socialised at the pub.

Norah seemed to feel the same way as Jenny. 'She came once a week. Her other evenings have, until very recently, been spent taking care of her mother. And when I say she drank more than usual, I mean she had three gin and tonics, spread over the evening, rather than her usual one. It was the VE Day celebrations and she was more restrained than most of my customers that evening.'

'I see. And what time did she leave?'

'I didn't see precisely when she left. We were very busy that night, and I was run off my feet. But I do remember that when we turned on the radio at nine to hear the king's speech she had gone.'

'Can you recall the time you last saw her?'

Norah's brow wrinkled. 'I think it must have been at about half past eight.' Her brow cleared. 'Yes, she came to the bar to order her third drink and I remember someone asking how long before we needed to turn on the radio. I looked at the clock and saw we still had half an hour to go.'

The coroner nodded. 'So she left some time between half past eight and nine. Did you see her with anyone else after her friends left?'

'No.'

The friends Rita had been with that night were also called upon to describe Rita's movements and her general state of mind, although they had nothing to say that hadn't been covered by Norah.

When it was time for the medical evidence, Jenny wished she could leave, but it wouldn't have been possible to leave the room without creating a disturbance, so she was forced to listen to the distasteful findings from the post-mortem. In a matter-of-fact voice that somehow made it worse, the pathologist described the stomach contents, concluding that Rita had been drinking on an empty stomach. After describing the progression of rigor mortis, he concluded that the victim had died no more than an hour before she had been found. At this point Jenny was able to drag her thoughts from the horrors of a post-mortem and, recalling that it had been half past ten when they had stumbled upon the body, calculated that Rita had died no earlier than half past nine.

'Have you ascertained a cause of death?' the coroner asked once these facts had been noted.

'I have. I found mud and grass in the victim's nose, mouth and throat and also observed slight frothing around the mouth and nose and petechiae in the eyes. This led me to conclude that she collapsed as a combined result of drink and exhaustion and, having fallen face down in soft mud, suffocated.'

'Is there any sign of foul play?'

'I didn't find any evidence to suggest one way or the other.'

Next, Rita's doctor was called upon to give evidence. Looking around the room as Dr Hendon outlined his recent treatment of her for stress and exhaustion, saying he had at one time prescribed Benzedrine to help her cope with her work-load, Jenny could tell that people were forming the conclusion that Rita had brought her death upon herself, drinking too much when she was already exhausted.

Sure enough, once the coroner had summed up the evidence and it was time for the jury to reach their conclusion they returned a verdict of death by misadventure.

'I can't believe no one questioned why Rita was found outside the village when she was supposed to be so tired,' Jenny said once they had left the coroner's court and were out in the bright sunshine. 'Why didn't she go straight home?'

Pearl nodded. 'I agree. It does seem strange. Also, if you consider that the latest time she could have left the pub was nine, and it's only about a ten-minute walk from there to the place she was found, what was she doing in between times?'

'Not forgetting that Norah clearly didn't think she had drunk enough to collapse in a ditch,' Thea put in. 'The whole thing seems so suspicious, I don't understand why no one else thinks so.' She glanced at her watch. 'I'm starving. Let's go to the Bishop's Pal.' Jenny saw her cast a glance at Pearl and knew she was reluctant to discuss the case with her sister. 'Are you sure you shouldn't go back to the office, Pearl?'

Pearl's eyes narrowed. 'Don't you dare try leaving me out. I'm not an invalid, you know. Honestly, can you imagine what it's like to have people thinking they can express their opinion on what you're eating or doing or wearing, every day?'

'I've got a pretty good idea,' Thea said with a wry smile.

Pearl obviously realised the irony, for she grinned. 'Yes, I know I'm getting a taste of my own medicine, but it's no excuse to leave me out.'

'Fine. Come along if you insist, but I don't want to hear Greg complaining because I got you involved.'

–

'The thing is,' Pearl said once they had discussed the case from all angles, 'even though there are questions to be answered, I don't see what we can do about it. We don't know her friends or her mother, so it would look odd if we approached them.'

'I don't see why,' Thea argued. 'Rita's death is the talk of the village. Norah was practically falling over herself to tell us what she knew.'

'That's true,' Jenny said. 'There's nothing stopping us just getting into conversation with people and seeing what they know. We're not the police – we don't have to interview them.'

'I suppose you've got a point.' Pearl consulted her ever-present notebook. 'So the people we need to speak to are Rita's mother, her friends and anyone who might have seen her in the pub that evening.'

'And Richie Evans,' Jenny put in. 'I want to know what they were arguing about.'

Pearl put down her book and frowned. 'Be careful, Jenny. Just because you don't like the man, it doesn't make him a killer. You could get into trouble if you accuse him without evidence.'

'I'm not going to be that stupid,' Jenny retorted. 'But I do think it suspicious that Rita seemed to know something to his disadvantage, and only a few days after she threatens to tell others she's found dead. So I'm not going to ask him right out if he had anything to do with her death, but I do think we should try and find out where he was that night.'

'You're right. I suppose the first people to ask would be any of his friends. Who does he go around with?'

Jenny thought about it. 'His crew, mostly.'

Thea leaned across the table, grinning. 'Isn't it lucky that one of us already has a friend on his crew?'

'Who?' Then, with a sinking feeling, Jenny realised who she meant. 'Wait. You're not thinking about Ben Newton, are you?'

'I certainly am.'

'But I can't speak to him.'

'Why not? I'm not asking you to go on a date.'

'But he'll think I want to go out with him again.' She turned to Pearl. 'Make her see sense. It took him ages to accept I didn't want to see him again.'

Pearl shrugged, her lips twitching. 'I've spent most of my life trying and failing to make Thea see sense. And you've got to admit she's got a point. Ben likes you. None of us know any of Richie's other friends so, if you're serious about finding out where he was that night, he's the logical person to approach.'

Edwin, who had remained silent until then, frowned. 'We can't force Jenny to speak to this Ben alone. Not if she doesn't like him.'

It gave Jenny a rush of pleasure to know Edwin was on her side. And was it possible that he was jealous? Perhaps the VE Day kiss had meant more to him than she had realised. She had hoped he would speak up after that, but when he had said nothing she had come to the conclusion that whatever his feelings he wasn't going to end his engagement with Mina. Therefore she had done her best to appear unconcerned around him, not wanting him to see how much she loved him. She didn't want his pity. Hope could be a painful thing. Every time she thought she had her feelings under control, Edwin would do or say something to make her hope that this time he would speak up, this time he would tell her he was going to break up with Mina. But he never did, and if she was to remain sane she had to get it through to her aching heart that they would never be more than friends.

All this flashed through her mind at the same time as she noticed Thea pat Edwin on the arm. 'Of course Jenny shouldn't speak to Ben alone. Perhaps you could go with her? We wouldn't want Ben to pester her for another date, would we?'

Thea looked smug and totally oblivious to Jenny's glare.

'I could do that.' Edwin turned to Jenny. 'If you're happy with that?'

'I… yes, all right. Where will we find him?'

'Probably in the Piebald Pony. No one's flying anywhere today, so everyone will probably be there.'

Jenny looked at the others. 'What are you all going to do?'

Pearl looked apologetic. 'I'm feeling quite tired and uncomfortable. I don't think I can face sitting around in the pub all evening.'

'Of course not.' Thea looked concerned. 'You and Greg should sit this one out. But Fitz and I can come to the pub.' She glanced at her fiancé. 'We could look for Rita's friends and see if there's anything new they can tell us.'

Jenny felt better knowing that at least she would have friends to hand if she found Ben at the pub. 'Who else should we try speaking to?'

'Her mother,' Pearl replied promptly. 'She's the one who's spent the most time with Rita. She's bound to know something that could help.'

Thea frowned. 'She won't be at the pub. But maybe someone there will know her and will be able to introduce us or something. I'll ask around.'

And so they drained their teacups with a fresh sense of purpose, although Jenny still quailed at the prospect of having to speak with Ben again.

When they had finished they headed down the hill, making for the bus station. Halfway down Steep Hill, Jenny noticed a tall, elegant woman in WAAF uniform trudging up the way. Her head was lowered so Jenny couldn't see her face, but something about her looked familiar. It was only when they were nearly level that the woman happened to look up. Jenny stopped dead. It was Mina.

Chapter Nineteen

At first Edwin couldn't work out why Jenny had stopped. Then he saw Mina and he felt as though the bars of a cage had closed around him.

'Mina!' he said. 'I didn't know you were coming.' Why was she here? He could only think of one reason. Now the war in Europe was over, was she going to suggest naming a date for the wedding?

She smiled at him, although he could sense tension behind the smile. 'I couldn't get away for VE Day, but I wanted to celebrate with you as soon as I could.'

VE Day. Edwin couldn't help darting a glance at Jenny, and he felt heat rise above his collar as he remembered the kiss.

'It's good to see you,' he said, hating himself for the lie. 'Have you just arrived? Where are you staying?'

'I've come straight from the station. I thought I'd find a guesthouse before heading to Fenthorpe.'

'How long are you staying?' He was painfully aware that this was hardly the way to greet his fiancée, but he was too taken aback, too aware of Jenny at his side, to do anything more than ask the kind of questions you would usually ask a casual acquaintance.

'Only a couple of days. I got a forty-eight-hour pass.' Mina, too, seemed stiff and awkward. Nothing like her usual self.

It was Jenny who stepped in to relieve the awkwardness. She gave Mina a quick hug, then said, 'It's lovely to see you again. Why don't you try getting a room at the White Horse? We were about to go back to Fenthorpe, so we could take you there.'

Mina agreed, although she seemed oddly reluctant, and so they trooped to the railway station, which held the nearest telephone box, and rang the White Horse. There was a room available, so Mina collected her case from the left luggage office and accompanied them to the bus stop.

'I'm glad I ran into you,' she said when they had scrambled on the bus and managed to claim the back seat. 'How on earth did you all manage to get a day off together?'

Edwin, who found himself wedged between Mina and Jenny, explained about the inquest. All the while he was aware of Jenny's leg pressed against his, and the only thought running through his head was that he was going to have to tell Mina what had happened as soon as he could get her alone.

'How shocking!' Mina wove her arm through Edwin's and gave it a squeeze. 'I can't believe something so awful could happen here of all places. Fenthorpe is so peaceful.'

'When our boys aren't flying Lancasters overhead,' Thea put in.

'Well, yes, but the village itself struck me as being very quiet. And for it to happen on VE Day of all days. I'm sorry you had to deal with that. So what was the verdict at the inquest?'

'They said it was death by misadventure,' Edwin told her.

His voice must have given away his opinion, for she frowned at him. 'But you don't agree.' It was a statement, not a question.

Edwin hesitated, aware of the other passengers on the bus. 'I can see why they would reach that verdict,' he said carefully. 'But I'll tell you all about it later.'

Evidently Mina picked up on his caution, for she nodded and changed the subject, describing how she had celebrated VE Day in Bletchley. Edwin only listened with half his mind. The other half was taken up with worrying about how to tell her about his own VE Day experience.

When the bus arrived in the village, Jenny and Thea got out with Edwin and Mina, leaving Fitz, Greg and Pearl to carry on to Fenthorpe Hall. Fitz promised to meet them at the pub later, but Greg said he would stay with Pearl, who was looking tired. Jenny and Thea set out for RAF Fenthorpe, while Edwin picked up Mina's case and went with her to the White Horse.

Knowing he couldn't put off the painful moment any longer, he said, 'We've got to talk,' only to stare at Mina in surprise when she said the same thing at the same time.

'Mina,' he said, trying again, knowing he had to make his confession before she made any mention of wedding dates. 'There's something I need to tell you.'

'Maybe, but I really need to go first.' Her expression was so serious that Edwin could only nod. 'I can't marry you, Ed.'

'What? Why not?' This wasn't at all what he had expected. To his dismay he saw tears welling in her eyes. All he could think was that someone had already written and told her about him kissing Jenny, but who would do something so mean? He waited while Mina dabbed away her tears.

'I do love you, Ed, and I know you love me in your own way, but you're not *in* love with me.'

'Why would you think that?' He had always felt protective of her and he couldn't bear to see her distress, no matter how accurate her statement was.

Mina sighed. 'Because when I see you with Jenny, I see a man in love. The way you look at her is how I always wanted you to look at me.'

'Mina, I—'

But she shook her head, silencing him. 'I came here to say this, so please let me finish before I lose my courage. I've thought about this a lot since my last visit and it hasn't been easy, even though I know I've made the right decision. Last time I came because I was worried about you. I knew you were weighed down by some awful burden, yet you wouldn't tell me about it. The thing is, I told Jenny about my worries and asked her to try and find out what was wrong. And when she wrote to me after your Forest of Dean trip, she said you had confided in her.' Mina flung out her hand to stop his protest. 'Oh, don't

197

worry. She didn't break your confidence. But she knew I was worried and she wanted to let me know you were going to be all right. I've got nothing to blame her for, but it made me see that you have a connection with Jenny that you don't have with me. The relationship we have… it's a deep friendship and I never want to lose that, but we're not in love with each other.'

Even though it was something he had, deep in his heart, known to be true, it hurt more than he could have expected.

He bowed his head. 'I… you might be right, but I don't know if I'm ready to let you go.'

'I don't know if I'm ready, either. But I have to try, because I don't think either of us could ever be truly happy if we married. We could be happy on the surface, I'm sure, but we wouldn't be giving our souls what they need. *Your* soul will only be truly happy with Jenny.'

'And what about you, Mina? What would make you happy, deep down?'

She shook her head. 'I don't know. But lately I've been thinking that maybe the adventure of finding that out is what I need. I don't know if that makes sense. Anyway, what did you want to say to me?'

Edwin drew a deep breath. 'It's something that might make ending it easier for you.' Although she had given him an excuse not to tell her, it felt wrong to keep it secret. After all, this was something he had done when they were still engaged and therefore it was a wrong he had done to her. 'I honestly don't know how it happened but I kissed Jenny at the VE Day celebrations. I'm sorry.'

She pressed her lips together although not fast enough to conceal the grimace of pain. Edwin ached to comfort her, to pull her into his arms and beg her forgiveness. It was only the knowledge that Mina was right that held him back.

'I'm sorry,' he repeated. 'You're right, though. For so long I wanted to make up for all you had lost and I didn't see how unfair I was being to you. You deserve someone who loves you with their whole heart, and now I know that could never be me.' She deserved someone who loved her as much as he loved Jenny.

Mina squared her shoulders and raised her chin, giving him a determined smile. 'Are you and Jenny together now?'

'No. We found Rita's body soon after, and that pushed everything out of my head. Anyway, I think she's been avoiding me since then.' And when they had been together, she had acted as though nothing had happened, which hurt.

They had reached the White Horse by this point, and it was a relief to get off the subject of Jenny. He had come dangerously close to asking Mina relationship advice, which would have been in bad taste considering the circumstances.

He opened the door for her. 'Let's get you settled.'

It was only when Mina had been given her room key and Edwin was about to leave that he remembered his promise to go to the pub with Jenny that evening. On reflection, perhaps it would have been best if Mina had stayed in Lincoln.

'I ought to warn you that most of us will be back here tonight,' he said. Then, lowering his voice so no one else in the pub could overhear, he added, 'We're going to ask around about Rita.'

Mina's answering smile was a shade too bright. 'Then I'll see you later. You never know what I might find out for you. People might be more willing to speak to a stranger.'

'Is something the matter?' Jenny asked Edwin later. They were walking down the high street to the pub, Edwin and Fitz having met Jenny and Thea outside the Waafery entrance. Thea and Fitz had walked ahead, involved in an animated discussion, leaving Jenny and Edwin to walk together. Edwin had seemed distracted for the entire time and had barely said two words.

'No. Well, yes.' Edwin stopped and faced Jenny. Or, rather, he appeared to be looking at someone just past her left shoulder, because he didn't seem able to meet her gaze. 'Mina and I... we're no longer engaged.'

'Oh, I'm sorry.' She could only pray that, as Edwin still wasn't looking directly at her, he couldn't sense her blaze of elation. 'What happened?'

But he only shuffled his feet and muttered something about 'growing apart' and it being 'for the best'.

She couldn't think of anything to say. Well, she could, but nothing that would convey sympathy. 'I'm sorry,' she said again. Then a thought struck. 'Will Mina be in the snug this evening?'

'Yes. She wanted to help.'

'Help?' Jenny could only stare at him blankly for a moment, the purpose of their visit completely absent from her thoughts. Then, gradually, it returned. 'Oh, you mean speaking to Rita's friends?'

Edwin nodded and started walking again, but said nothing. Jenny paced beside him, unable to think too much about their plan in the wake of this momentous news. Had Edwin confessed to Mina about their kiss? Was that why they had broken up? If so, did that mean he was going to ask her out?

An itch of anticipation tingled at the back of her neck, but she tried to ignore it and reminded herself that, whatever their reasons, if Edwin and Mina had broken up they must be hurting.

She grabbed his arm, forcing him to look at her. 'I don't mind if you'd rather not come tonight. I'd understand if it's too awkward.'

Edwin straightened his back, shaking his head. 'I'll be fine.' Then he gave the ghost of a smile. 'But thank you for your concern. Anyway, I promised I wouldn't leave you to face Ben Newton alone.'

Was that the only reason he was here – just because he had promised? Or did the thought of her seeing Ben make him jealous? Her thoughts flew to the kiss and she relived the glorious feeling of being folded in his arms. Would she soon know it again? After all, there was nothing standing between them now. No reason for them not to be together. Although she felt for Mina, her heart sang and refused to be quelled.

Ben was in the snug, gazing morosely into his pint. He was sitting alone at a corner table, and so, once Jenny had bought herself a ginger beer, she approached him. 'Mind if we sit here?'

He gave her a wide smile that made her skin crawl. 'Come to your senses at last, have you? Well, you're welcome to join me. Richie was supposed to be here but I can't think where he's got to.'

Jenny glanced around, alarm dousing the thrill awakened by Edwin's announcement. Much to her relief, she could see no sign of Richie. 'I'm sure he'll turn up soon,' she said, very much hoping she was wrong. Oddly enough, although she had expected most of RAF Fenthorpe's off-duty personnel to be at the White Horse, she hadn't considered that Richie might be there. She could only pray for his continued absence, because making enquiries about Rita's death would be difficult if their main suspect was present.

'It's been a while since I've seen you,' Ben said, and Jenny shrank inwardly at his evident admiration. She had to wrestle with her conscience, telling herself that it was important to discover Richie's whereabouts on VE Day. Because if there was a possibility that he murdered Rita then she was justified in using her acquaintance with Ben.

Thankfully Edwin arrived at that point, and sat down beside Jenny in a manner that seemed to suggest they were together. Was that what he really wanted or was he simply protecting her? She wished she knew.

It was a struggle to drag her mind away from Edwin and she had to give herself a stern reminder that she owed it to Rita to find the truth. 'I've been too busy to go out much,' she said, seeing her opening. 'Though I did go into Lincoln for the celebrations, of course. Were you there?'

Ben grinned. 'I was. I'm not going to forget that night in a hurry.'

'I don't remember seeing you,' Edwin put in. 'I was looking out for people from Fenthorpe, but it was hard to pick out anyone in all the crush. I thought I spotted Richie Evans at one point, but it was hard to be sure.'

Ben shrugged. 'I couldn't tell you if it was him. I haven't seen him much recently when we've been off duty. But I got dragged into a dance on the high street and I didn't leave until the last transport back. It was so crowded I was worried I might have to walk. What about you – did you have trouble getting back?'

'Not really. We left after the bonfire was lit.' Jenny felt heat flood into her face as she had another flash of memory. It seemed as though the image was permanently etched onto the back of her eyelids, and she only had to blink to relive the kiss. 'We walked back from the common.'

Ben's gaze sharpened. 'That's right. You're the ones who found that body, aren't you? What was it like?'

'Horrible.' Jenny couldn't prevent a shudder.

'It's all anyone's been able to talk about.' Ben leaned forward. 'What do you think happened to her?'

Jenny saw with an inward sigh that getting Ben to talk wasn't going to be the problem, but she should have predicted the ghoulish interest in a dead woman who, after all, no one on the base seemed to have known. Apart from Richie, of course.

'We had to go to the inquest earlier today. The verdict was death by misadventure.'

'Oh.' Before Jenny could interpret the odd expression that flickered across Ben's face, he raised his glass, hiding it from view. By the time he put his drink down his expression was one of mild curiosity.

A group of WAAFs just behind him suddenly shrieked with laughter, giving Jenny the excuse to lean forward and appear to be watching them while actually studying Ben's face. What was it she had seen before – relief? He was a friend of Richie's, after all. Did he suspect something?

Ben took another sip, then commented, 'It's awful to think that someone I've seen around here should be dead. A civilian, I mean.'

Jenny knew what he meant. As harsh as it sounded, the RAF personnel had hardened themselves to deaths among the crews. Not that they weren't saddened by the losses, but that they weren't shocked by it and had learned not to dwell too deeply on those who hadn't returned from a mission. It was the only way they could carry on. But for a villager to die unexpectedly was hard to deal with.

'Did you know her?' She did her best not to sound overly interested in his reply.

'I've seen her a few times. She seemed to know Richie.'

Jenny was aware of Edwin sitting up beside her, and she felt a prickle of excitement. 'Oh?' she said, hoping she wasn't overdoing her casual air. 'Were they close?'

'Not particularly. At least, I don't think so.' Ben's forehead wrinkled. 'I could never understand it, really. They never seemed particularly happy around each other, but I would often see them together.'

'That's odd,' Jenny said. 'At the inquest we heard that she was caring for her mother and didn't have much time for socialising, bar a visit here once a week when her neighbour would take over for a few hours.'

'That would explain why she always looked so tired. I could never really work out what Richie saw in her, to be honest.'

'You thought they were having an affair?'

'That's what I thought at first, and I had words with him because he was seeing Lily at that time, and I thought she was a nice girl. Deserved better.'

'She certainly did,' Jenny said with feeling.

Ben looked embarrassed. 'I had no idea he was married. I wanted to wring his neck when I found out.'

There was a brief pause, and Jenny contemplated the satisfaction it would give her to see someone wring Richie's neck.

'You said you thought they were having an affair at first,' Edwin prompted. 'Did you change your mind?'

'Yes, once I realised I'd only ever seen them together here in the pub. I never saw them leave together or anything. And, as I said, they never seemed particularly happy to see each other.'

Jenny thought of the encounter she had witnessed outside the pub, which fitted with Ben's description. 'Odd that they would keep meeting up if they didn't even like each other.'

Ben shrugged. 'I didn't really think about it. It was Richie's problem, not mine.' He paused, frowning at Jenny and Edwin over the rim of his glass. 'What's it to do with you, anyway?'

'Nothing,' Jenny hurried to say. 'We were just making conversation.'

'Yeah, well, better not let Richie know I was talking about him. He can get nasty when he's crossed.' Ben drained his glass, rose and pointed to the doorway. 'Speak of the devil, there he is. Be seeing you.' He leered at Jenny. 'Let me know when you come to your senses, and we can go dancing.'

Jenny shuddered and watched him head into the public bar with an arm slung round Richie's shoulders. 'I can safely say we'll never go dancing. I don't know how he can still be friends with Richie when he knows what happened to Lily.'

If Edwin had an answer he didn't get a chance to give it, for Thea and Fitz arrived at the table. 'How did you get on with Ben?' Thea asked, taking his vacant seat.

'I don't think we got much useful information. He couldn't even tell us where Richie was on Thursday night.' Jenny summed up what little they had gleaned, concluding with, 'It doesn't sound like Richie and Rita were having an affair, just that they met here a few times.'

'We might be able to help with that,' Thea said. 'Fitz and I were just talking to Rita's friends.'

'What did they say?'

'It was a bit frustrating at first, because they said they didn't know Rita all that well any more. They used to go to school together but drifted apart when her mother got ill.'

'How does that help?'

'Patience! I'm coming to that. They said they still used to see her here occasionally and, since her mother's health had improved, she agreed to join them here for VE Day.'

'But we already know all that from the inquest.' Jenny was starting to get impatient.

'Ah, but there's more. Dora and Wendy – those are the friends' names – have been ignored by the police and are mighty aggrieved no one seems to want to hear their tale.'

'Until we turned up,' Fitz observed. 'They were only too flattered by our interest and were falling over themselves to tell us everything they knew.'

'Go on then. What else did they have to say?'

'Well' – Thea settled herself more comfortably – 'would it interest you to know that although one of the reasons Rita gave for not going with Dora and Wendy to Lincoln was that she was tired and needed to get back to her mother—?'

'As they said at the inquest,' Fitz put in.

Jenny rolled her eyes but said nothing. They were deliberately provoking her, she was sure.

Thea grinned and nudged her fiancé. 'Shall we tell her before she explodes?'

'I think we ought to.'

'Preferably before *I* explode,' Edwin muttered.

'Fine.' Thea propped her elbows on the table, leaning so far forward she was in danger of slipping off her chair. 'Besides the reason Norah gave, Rita's friends also said she had expected to meet a man and didn't want to miss him.'

'Who?' Jenny had to restrain herself from reaching across the table and shaking her friend. Surely now she was going to hear something that would break the case wide open, as they said in detective novels.

'Ah, well, Rita didn't name him, but as they were leaving they passed Richie and a friend of his in the doorway, and they noticed Rita making their way towards him.'

'Why didn't they mention this as the inquest?'

Thea rolled her eyes. 'I asked them that. They said the police had got it into their heads that Rita was a loose woman and they weren't going to give them any more ammunition.'

'But—' Jenny closed her mouth. It was pointless venting her frustration when Fitz and Thea clearly felt the same way about Rita's friends withholding evidence. Besides, they had finally been persuaded to reveal the truth. 'So she *did* meet Richie that night.' Jenny gazed at her friends in triumph. 'We should tell the police.'

Chapter Twenty

Although Jenny's head was buzzing with this new information, it never quite managed to drive out Edwin's revelation about the end of his engagement. Throughout the evening, she was constantly aware of Edwin's presence beside her; she could swear she felt the heat from his body despite the wide gap between them. So when Mina appeared, looking subdued, Jenny felt a surge of guilt at her elation. She had known all along that it was a mistake to be Mina's friend, yet she couldn't help herself because it was impossible not to like her.

Seeing Mina head to the bar, Jenny muttered something to the others about getting another drink and joined her. Mina was so absorbed in her thoughts that she didn't appear to notice her until Jenny tapped her shoulder.

Mina jumped, then relaxed when she saw who it was. 'You nearly gave me a heart attack.'

'Sorry. I just wanted to know how you were.' She hesitated, then plunged on. 'Edwin told me you'd broken up.'

Mina nodded, pressing her lips together. Finally she managed a weak smile. 'I'll be fine.' She glanced across the snug to where Edwin was sitting and then back at Jenny. 'Actually, I'm not sure I can face the others right now. Have you got a minute?' She gave a nod of the head towards a table that had just become vacant.

'Of course.' Jenny followed Mina to the table on the other side of the snug, her stomach knotting in trepidation, knowing she was hardly the best person to offer comfort when she was pining after Edwin herself.

Mina got to the point straight away. 'I'm leaving tomorrow.'

'But I thought you had a forty-eight-hour pass?'

'I do, but there's nothing to stay for. I've said what I came to say, and it would only prolong the pain if I stayed any longer.'

'*You've* said? So it was you who broke the engagement?'

Mina looked surprised. 'Yes, why, what did Ed say?'

Jenny tried to remember Edwin's exact words. 'Now I come to think of it, he didn't say who had done the ending. I just assumed...' She tailed off. Assumed that Edwin had told Mina about their kiss and broken off the engagement because he wanted to be with Jenny. She felt deflated, drained of all elation.

'He did tell me that he'd kissed you,' Mina said gently, almost as if she could read Jenny's mind.

'I'm not even sure if he kissed me or if I started it,' Jenny felt compelled to admit. 'If that's why you broke up with him, maybe—'

'No.' Mina's voice was firm. 'It's something I've been thinking about for a while. I'm not saying it was an easy decision, but it was the right one.' She sighed. 'And when you wrote and told me he'd finally confided in you, it made up my mind.' Mina looked Jenny squarely in the eyes. 'I know how you feel about each other.'

Jenny squirmed. To her shame, her first impulse was to beg to know how Edwin really did feel about her. What had he said when he'd confessed to their kiss? Thankfully her better instincts took control and reminded her of how hurtful this must be to Mina, despite her admission that she'd been the one to finish things.

'I'm sorry,' she said finally. 'I didn't even know you and he were engaged until he told me earlier this year. I would never have let myself get so close if I'd known.'

'I know. I don't blame you. The thing is, as I told him earlier, although I do love him I've worked out that I'm not in love with him.' Mina looked away for a moment, and Jenny was sure she was blinking back tears. When she turned back she gave a wry smile. 'Sorry. I thought I was ready to talk about this without crying. It's all right, I know I'll be fine,' she said in response to Jenny's sympathetic murmur, 'but it's hard to let go. He's been such a big part of my life.'

Jenny could only gaze at her, unable to think of anything helpful to say, not when she couldn't say in all honesty that she was sorry Mina and Edwin were no longer together.

Eventually Mina was able to continue. 'When I met Ed, I was looking for a family and looking back I can see I latched on to him, desperate for someone to fill the void in my life. I thought…' She paused, fiddling with a ring dangling from a chain round her neck. Intercepting Jenny's gaze, Mina grimaced. 'Yes, it's my engagement ring. I'll have to give it back before he leaves tonight.'

'I can do it if you'd prefer not to.'

Mina shook her head. 'I'm the one who ended it. I need to be grown up about it and return it in person. But thank you for the offer.' She sighed and returned to the point she had been making before Jenny had diverted her train of thought. 'I thought I was in love with him but I was wrong. In my loneliness I mistook friendship for love. I'm not even convinced that Ed was ever in love with me. I think he wanted to protect and support me and thought marriage was the way to do it.'

'What are you going to do now?'

Mina squared her shoulders. 'I've thought about nothing else since I said goodbye to Ed a few hours ago. What I really need to do is learn to stand on my own two feet. At first I found it daunting, but now I'm starting to get excited about it.'

Jenny looked at her, wondering if she really meant that or if she was simply trying to hide her fear. But Mina looked determined rather than afraid and Jenny was glad to see a sparkle in her eyes.

'Have you got good friends back in Bletchley? I don't like to think of you with no one to turn to.' Mina had never mentioned any particular friends in her letters.

'Not really, but that's my fault. I was so buried in my work that I never really felt the need to socialise much. That's all going to change now, though. I'm going to make an effort to make friends with the girls I work with. Of course, I've no idea how my work is going to change now the war in Europe is over. But when the WAAF no longer needs me I'm going to return to Cambridge and see if they'll take me on as a postgraduate. I want to get my doctorate and then who knows? I'm looking forward to being independent. It's going to be an adventure.'

Jenny smiled at her, glad to see Mina was taking it so well. 'I wish I hadn't kissed him though,' she confessed. 'I still feel awful. The last thing I wanted to do was hurt you.'

Mina shook her head. 'You didn't. In my heart, I've known for a long time how he feels about you.'

Jenny squirmed. Even though Mina had been the one to end the relationship, she still didn't feel right discussing a possible relationship with her very recent ex-fiancé. She just wished she could be as sure as Mina about the strength of Edwin's feelings.

–

Mina didn't stay long in the snug after that. She had a brief word in private with Edwin, and Jenny guessed she was letting him know she would be leaving the next day. When Edwin returned to the table, he was tucking something away in his pocket; the engagement ring, she was sure.

'I think we've spoken to everyone we can,' Jenny said, anxious to leave so she could talk things through with Thea.

'Except Rita's mother,' Thea said.

'The poor woman's hardly likely to be here, though, is she?'

'No but Dora said she's a friend of Mrs Nugent who runs the Honeysuckle Tea Rooms on the high street. Apparently Mrs Nugent has persuaded her to go there every morning at eleven so she can have a bit of company. There's nothing to stop us popping in at the same time.'

'I don't know how comfortable I feel about questioning her when she's just lost her daughter.'

Thea frowned. 'Jenny, it's clear the police aren't looking into this, and even though we know Rita met Richie the night she died, that doesn't prove anything. We can tell the police but I don't know if they're going to take it seriously. Yet if Richie did kill her, it looks for now like he's going to get away scot-free. Are you comfortable with *that*?'

'No, of course not.'

Accordingly, Jenny and Thea agreed to visit the Honey-suckle Tea Rooms on the next morning they were free together. As it happened, that wouldn't be until Friday, which was also the day after Rita's funeral. Thinking it unlikely that Mrs Fox would be going out before the funeral, they decided this was probably the earliest they would be able to speak to her anyway.

–

'Are you going to tell me what you and Mina were talking about?' Thea asked the moment they were alone and walking down the lane to the Waafery.

Jenny had sensed Thea's curiosity when she had returned to the others, and had been prepared for the question. 'If you must know, Mina wanted to tell me she knew how I feel about Edwin.'

'What! I hope she didn't threaten you.'

'Relax, she also said she was the one who broke their engagement.'

'Wait.' Thea grabbed Jenny's arm, dragging her to a stop. 'Has something gone wrong with my ears or did you just say that Mina and Edwin are no longer engaged?'

'Your ears are fine.'

Thea studied Jenny for a long moment, then shook her head. 'I don't understand you. If I was in your shoes, I'd be dragging Edwin off to the nearest dance and smooching the night away. You're single and he's single and it's blindingly obvious you're crazy about each other. Why aren't you going after him? For that matter, why don't you look happier?'

Jenny sighed and started walking again. 'To tell you the truth, I've been asking myself the same thing, but it's complicated.'

'I don't see the problem.'

'What if I told you Edwin and I kissed at the bonfire?'

Thea's answering shriek sent a flock of sparrows shooting out of the nearby hedgerow in a whir of wings. 'Why didn't you tell me?'

'Why do you think? To start with, we found Rita not long after, and it seemed plain wrong to talk about kisses after that. And then Edwin seemed to want to carry on as though nothing had happened and I was hurt and didn't know what to think.'

Thea flung an arm around her shoulder. 'I thought you'd been quiet recently, but I put it down to the shock over Rita.'

They walked on a while in silence; Jenny let the sleepy peace of the evening fold around her. The disgruntled sparrows returned to their roosts and as their shrill song gradually faded, leaving no sound but the rustle of leaves and the gentle coo of a distant wood pigeon, some of the knots in her stomach unwound.

'Why don't you tell me about it? The kiss, I mean,' Thea said eventually.

Jenny didn't answer straight away; just remembering that moment brought back so many conflicting emotions, it was hard to describe what had happened in any coherent way. Maybe that was why Edwin hadn't spoken about it either.

'It was… a blur,' she said in the end. 'I honestly don't know how it happened. We were watching the fire being lit and I had this vivid flash, a moment of clarity'

Thea nodded in understanding. 'That you wanted to snog his face off.'

Jenny rolled her eyes. 'No. That I wanted to be a journalist.' The several churning emotions she had experienced since that moment had thrust it from her mind but now she felt it again as vividly as the first time, and she knew she wouldn't forget again as she explained the reasoning behind her decision.

'You know, there are times I really don't understand you.'

'If it makes you feel better, I'd just told Edwin what I'd thought and the next moment we were kissing.'

'That's more like it. How was it?'

'Wonderful. Amazing.' For all her wide reading, an adequate description failed to materialise. 'It just felt so right, you know?'

Thea nodded, smiling the dreamy smile that told Jenny she was thinking about Fitz. 'And then what? You must have spoken about it. You don't get into a passionate clinch one moment and then carry on as though nothing's happened.'

Jenny kicked a pebble, sending it skittering down the road. 'But that's pretty much what we have done. Someone bumped into us and it sort of brought us back to reality. I apologised and said it should never have happened. Because of Mina, you know. And Edwin said something about it being in the heat of the moment and we mustn't let it spoil our friendship.'

'And that's it? You haven't mentioned it since?'

'Not a word.' And now all the frustrations and dashed hopes of the past few days seemed to crash down upon her. 'And you know what the worst of it is? Just before we got to the pub earlier, he told me he and Mina had split up. And I thought, this is it. This is the moment he tells me he loves me, and we can finally be together. But he didn't say a word. I don't understand. Why couldn't he tell me? Even Mina said she could tell he was in love with me, so what's stopping him?'

Thea's face creased with sympathy. 'I don't know. Maybe he needs more time. After all, Mina is still here. Perhaps he thought it would be rubbing salt in the wound if she saw the two of you together.'

'Maybe.' Jenny drew a deep breath. 'Anyway, there's not much I can do at the moment. I feel I've been enough of a fool over him, what with the mistletoe incident and now this. I'm going to wait for him to make the next move. If he ever does,' she concluded glumly.

Chapter Twenty-One

Jenny was kept too busy over the next few days to brood over-much. Although the Lancaster crews were no longer needed to drop bombs, they were assigned to carry more supplies to the troops in Europe, and accurate forecasts were just as important for peaceful missions as they had been for bombing missions. Jenny didn't mind the hard work, and at least the lengthening days and sunshine made the trips around the base to the weather instruments a pleasant experience. She only saw Edwin when he came to the Met Office, so even if he did want to declare his feelings, in front of the other staff he wasn't able to do so.

On Friday, she went with Thea into Fenthorpe as agreed, in search of Rita's mother.

'I hope she's there,' Jenny said as they approached the Honey-suckle Tea Rooms, 'although I've no idea what to say.'

'We'll have to play it by ear.' Thea grasped the door handle. 'Ready?'

At Jenny's nod, Thea pushed open the door, and the sweet scent of baking wafted out, enticing them inside. The popular tables were the ones near the large bay window, where customers could gaze out at the shoppers strolling up the high street. These tables were all full, and Jenny scanned them, disappointed when she didn't see Mrs Fox right away. However, when she turned her attention to the few tables situated further back, she saw the frail woman who had been at the inquest. She was sitting alone at a small table tucked right in the corner.

Jenny nudged Thea. 'That has to be her.'

Thea nodded, and they took a table just in front of Rita's mother. On their way into the village they had discussed asking Mrs Fox if they could sit with her, but, as she occupied a small table that could only seat two, this was out of the question.

'What should we do?' Jenny asked in a low voice.

Thea didn't get a chance to answer, however, for the waitress had already appeared beside their table, order pad in hand. 'What can I get you ladies?' she asked. 'We do a ten per cent discount for servicewomen.'

They both ordered tea and, tempted by the delicious aroma, carrot cake. Instead of returning straight to the kitchen, the waitress went to the table behind. 'Can I get you anything else, dear?' she asked. 'On the house. It's the least I can do after the day you had yesterday.'

This put an idea in Jenny's head and, once the waitress had taken Mrs Fox's order and departed, she turned to the table behind. 'I don't mean to bother you,' she said, 'but I didn't get a chance to speak to you after the inquest and I wanted to offer you my condolences.'

'Thank you. I—' The woman broke off, pressing a hand to her quivering mouth. She pulled out a handkerchief.

'I'm so sorry,' Jenny cried as Mrs Fox dabbed her eyes. 'I didn't mean to make things worse.'

'You haven't, dear.' Mrs Fox's voice was husky to begin with, but strengthened as she went on. 'Nothing can make this worse, and it's very kind of you to offer your sympathies. Most people seem too embarrassed to speak to me, but I do so want to talk.'

'You'd be very welcome to join us,' Jenny offered.

The woman hesitated, then said, 'Thank you. I'd like that.' She gathered her belongings and took the seat next to Jenny. Once she had arranged her bag and coat on the back of her chair, she peered at Jenny through reddened eyes. 'I remember you. You're one of the ones who found my Rita.' Her lips quivered, although there were no fresh tears.

'That's right. I'm Jenny and this is Thea. We're both from RAF Fenthorpe. We'd seen your daughter in the village a few times, and we were terribly sad to find her as we did.'

Looking at the broken woman, Jenny knew that there was no way she would be able to press for information she was unwilling to give. However desperate she and Thea were to find the truth, Mrs Fox's needs had to come first and she would take her cue from her. When she exchanged a brief glance with Thea, she could see from her friend's expression that she felt the same way.

Mrs Fox put her handkerchief back in her bag and gave a weak smile. 'You're very kind. It's good to meet you. It's not much, but it does help to know she wasn't lying there alone for long, so thank you for all you did.'

Thea reached across the table and squeezed Mrs Fox's hand. 'I just wish we could have done more.'

The waitress arrived with their tea. 'It's nice to see you with some company,' she said to Mrs Fox. 'Shall I bring your order to this table?'

'Yes, please do,' Jenny said when Mrs Fox looked unsure.

'It *is* lovely to have company,' Mrs Fox remarked when they were all furnished with tea and cakes. 'I've been ill for some time, you see, and I haven't been able to go out and meet my friends as I used to. And now, just when I'm feeling better and was looking forward to going out and about more, this happens. I'm so sad for Rita. She gave up meeting her friends so she could look after me and then, just when I was well enough to let her live her own life again, she lost it.'

It seemed Mrs Fox was taking comfort in talking, so Jenny let her speak, confining herself to the occasional sympathetic murmur. Although she was longing to know if Rita had told her anything about Richie, she held her tongue.

Eventually, after a long description of her sons, who were both stationed abroad, and her worries about whether they had heard the news yet, she said, 'At least my neighbour, Mrs

Hughes, has been very kind. She used to sit with me once a week to let Rita go out. I know she used to enjoy meeting some of the fellows from RAF Fenthorpe.' She gave a sad smile. 'She was young like the two of you, and I know she missed socialising when all her other friends had young men on the station. But she was a good girl. She was never out too late and when she came home she would amuse me by telling stories about what they were all getting up to. I know some of the villagers complained about the noise, but I never minded. When you think what they had to do, it was only right that they could let off steam from time to time.'

'I think the villagers have been very understanding for the most part,' Jenny said. 'We have rather taken over the place.'

'Better that than having the place deserted because the men are all elsewhere. And the shopkeepers all say you've kept them in business, what with the difficulties over rationing. They'll all suffer when RAF Fenthorpe closes down.' Mrs Fox expounded on the various businesses that had prospered with the proximity of the RAF station. Jenny let her talk, with the sinking feeling that she knew nothing that would cast light on who might have killed her daughter. Although Rita had seemed increasingly troubled when Jenny had seen her, it was clear she had done her best to hide her agitation from her mother.

'Oh, my goodness,' Mrs Fox exclaimed a short while later. 'Will you look at the time! And there was me wanting to get to the chemist before he closes for lunch.' Her head drooped. 'I must dash,' she said, looking utterly unable to do anything so energetic. 'I have a prescription to collect.' She glanced at her watch again. 'Oh dear, I don't think I'm going to get there in time. He's right the other end of the high street.'

'Why don't you stay here and let me fetch it?' Jenny asked, rising. 'Is there anything else you need?'

'Oh, would you do that? You're so kind. There are a few things I need, none of them rationed, so it shouldn't be too much trouble.'

She produced a list and handed Jenny some money, and Jenny hurried away to complete her errand before all the shops closed for lunch. There was a small queue at the chemist, and Jenny got out the money in advance to save time. Glancing at the ten-shilling note Mrs Fox had given her, she saw it had a message scribbled in pencil: *Buy yourself something nice. Rita x.* Jenny gave a little shiver, thinking it could be the last message Rita had ever written to her mother. Had Mrs Fox even seen it? There was no way she could spend it, so she scrabbled in her purse for loose change instead and tucked the note away.

She managed to complete all Mrs Fox's errands before the shops closed, and was soon back in the Honeysuckle Tea Rooms handing over Mrs Fox's prescription, together with the other goods and her change.

'You're really too kind,' Mrs Fox said, fumbling with her purse. 'You must let me give you something for your trouble.'

Jenny was horrified. 'No, really, it was no trouble at all. Besides, you were doing me a favour. My purse was getting weighted down with small change and I was able to spend that instead of the note you gave me.' She pulled it out of her purse. 'I thought you might like it back, actually. Rita had written a little message on it for you.' She showed it to Mrs Fox.

Tears welled in the woman's eyes. 'Oh, no. To be honest, I was glad to be rid of it. It's the last of the money Rita gave me before she went out that night. "Just in case I'm not up before you go to the shops tomorrow," she told me. "I want you to buy yourself a nice treat for VE Day." Well, I've barely been able to look at it since then. I can't see it without remembering that the last thing she said was, "Don't wait up. I'll be staying until closing time." Oh dear.' For fresh tears were pouring down her cheeks and her handkerchief was already drenched.

'Here,' said Thea, handing over hers. 'It's clean.'

Jenny and Thea hovered anxiously while the bereaved mother mopped the tears from her face. It was a relief when the waitress arrived.

'You poor thing,' she said to Mrs Fox. 'Mrs Davis is taking over from me for half an hour. Why don't I see you home?'

Mrs Fox agreed and so, after expressing their sympathy once again, Jenny and Thea made their escape.

'I feel awful,' Jenny said. 'And we're no further along. I don't think we found anything useful, and I just feel like we made Mrs Fox relive her last day with Rita for nothing.'

Thea shook her head. 'We might not have learned anything useful, but I think it did her good to talk.'

'I hope you're right. I suppose I was hoping she would say something that would explain what Rita was doing on the other side of the village, and who she was with, but from what she said it sounds like she'd intended coming straight home from the pub.'

'Then we did find something out,' Thea said. 'Rita didn't intend going further than the pub, so something must have happened to change her mind. All we have to do is find out what that was.'

'You make it sound so easy.'

'It is. We just haven't spoken to the right people yet. I think this calls for another night at the pub.' Thea shot Jenny a grin. 'And we can ask the lads to come with us. I'm sure you won't object to spending the evening with Edwin now he's single.'

Edwin only listened with half a mind to Thea's description of the meeting with Rita's mother. The rest of his attention was firmly on Jenny. They were in their usual corner table in the snug, yet instead of sitting beside him as she usually did, she sat between Pearl and Thea and seemed to be avoiding his gaze. He guessed it was because he had resolutely avoided confessing his feelings even though he was now free to do so. He was sure she couldn't understand it. He wished he understood it himself. What was holding him back now he was free to tell Jenny exactly how he felt? It must be Rita's death, he thought. It didn't feel right to pursue his own happiness with that dreadful event hanging over them like a pall. Maybe in another week or so he would feel differently.

With a start he realised Thea was still talking and he had hardly taken in a word she'd said. Giving himself a mental shake, he gave her his full attention.

'Mrs Fox said Rita had intended coming straight home from the pub after it closed,' she was saying, 'yet Norah said she left before the king's speech. We need to see if anyone saw her go and who with, especially if it happened to be Richie. Her friends said that she met him, but they didn't know if she was still with him when she left.'

Pearl frowned. 'But who else can we ask?'

'Why don't we ask Richie?' Edwin said with a nod towards the door. For the man himself had just walked in, accompanied by Ben and a group of gunners.

Jenny spoke up for the first time since she had arrived with Thea. 'What do you suggest asking him – why he killed Rita? Anyway, I don't think I could approach him after the way he treated Lily. I'd be too tempted to slap him.'

'Me too,' Thea said with a grimace.

'I'll speak to him if no one else wants to,' Edwin said. 'I don't think we can accuse him without giving him a chance to put his side of the story.'

'He's an obnoxious reptile, I know that much.' Thea clutched her glass so tightly her knuckles were white, and Edwin half expected it to shatter. 'He's a two-timing bastard.'

'Yes, but that doesn't make him a murderer. Anyway, we know he was here that night, so if he finds out we've been asking around he might wonder why we didn't ask him.'

Edwin drained his glass and went to the bar, timing his move so he got there at the same time as Richie. There was a queue, which suited his purpose. Seeing Richie lean against the bar looking bored, he put down his empty glass and propped his elbow on the counter, taking care to avoid a puddle of beer that Norah, in her haste to serve all her customers, had overlooked.

'Busy night,' he observed. 'I was in here the other evening and it was so empty you'd have thought there was still a war on. I suppose not many of the villagers felt like celebrating after what happened.'

'To Rita Fox, you mean?' Richie replied. Although Edwin had made his own remark as a way to introducing the subject, he was surprised to hear Richie name her so easily. 'Yeah, that was a bit of a shock.' He frowned at Edwin. 'Weren't you one of the ones who found her?'

Edwin nodded. 'Shock doesn't begin to describe it,' he said.

Richie seemed only too keen to talk even without the aid of a pint of beer. 'What I can't understand is what she was doing all that way out of the village. I saw her that evening and she said she was too tired to go into Lincoln with the rest of us and she wanted to go straight home. So when I heard she'd been found not far from RAF Fenthorpe I couldn't understand it.'

Was he trying to maintain his innocence by acting as surprised as the others? Edwin hadn't expected it to be this easy to get Richie to mention the subject.

'We thought that was strange too,' he said, deciding to be frank. 'How did she seem when you saw her?'

Edwin had to struggle to hide his suspicion when Richie looked decidedly shifty. 'Well, she was tired, you know.'

'Is that all? I'm surprised to hear you were with her that night after the run-in I witnessed between you and her a while back.'

The skin above Richie's collar turned beetroot red, and Edwin regretted mentioning that encounter. 'That was just a misunderstanding,' he said. 'I sorted it out and she was fine after that.'

'I'm glad to hear it,' Edwin replied. 'It might look awkward for you if the police were to find out you'd been seen close to blows with her not long before she was found dead.'

'Are you threatening me?'

'Not at all.'

'Good. Because anyway, I read in the papers that Rita died after half past nine, and I was already in Lincoln by then. So if you try pinning anything on me, *sir*, you're going to look stupid.'

It was a relief that Norah finished with a customer just then and called, 'Who's next?'

After shooting a malicious glance at Edwin, Richie said, 'Me,' and gave his order.

'Everything all right?' Greg asked when he returned to the table a couple of minutes later with his pint. 'For a moment I thought Richie was going to deck you.'

'Let's just say he got rather defensive when I reminded him that I'd seen him arguing with Rita a short while before her death.' He summarised their conversation, ending with, 'But if he really did go into Lincoln when he said he did, he couldn't have been the murderer. If it was murder. Maybe Rita really did go for a walk to clear her head.'

'But why would she have walked out of the village?' Jenny asked. 'She could have strolled around the high street for that. And everyone says she was tired, so heading all the way out there just seems insane.'

This led to the friends considering various explanations for why Rita had left Fenthorpe, none of which seemed likely.

'We seem to be going round in circles,' Fitz said eventually. 'Why don't we give it a rest for now and come at it fresh another day?'

The others agreed, although in Jenny's case it seemed to be with reluctance. They turned the conversation to Pearl's plans for her final edition of the *Bombshell*.

'I do hope you will all continue to contribute,' Pearl said. 'The RAF don't want to second anyone else to be editor, but Grandpa has promised to keep it going for now. And he was impressed with your article about Operation Manna,' she said to Edwin. 'He wants to use it in the *Lincolnshire Bugle*.'

The reminder of Operation Manna gave him a warm glow and, while he couldn't forget Rita's death and the puzzle surrounding it, he could at least push it to the back of his mind and talk about happier things for the rest of the evening. When it was time to leave, he gathered up their empty glasses and returned them to the bar. A woman he vaguely recognised as one of Rita's friends was also returning her glass. He was surprised when, instead of returning to her table, she hovered as though she wanted to speak to him. 'Can I help you?' he asked finally.

'I couldn't help overhearing what you were saying to Richie earlier,' she said.

'Oh, well, please don't spread it around. I wouldn't want to start any rumours.'

'Don't worry. But I wanted to say that we all thought it was odd about Rita ending up where she did. She really was tired, and she said she wanted to go straight home. Something must have happened to make her go all that way out of the village.'

'Any idea what?' Edwin, who had convinced himself he would leave the matter alone from now on, found himself burning with curiosity.

However, the girl shook her head. 'If I knew, I would have told the police. I was that upset about them implying Rita had been up to no good. She was a good girl, and she would never have got mixed up with Richie and buying them pills if she hadn't been so exhausted all the time.'

Richie felt the hairs on the back of his neck tingle. 'I beg your pardon. What pills?'

The girl clapped a hand over her mouth, looking horrified. 'I thought you knew! I thought that's why you were cross with him.'

'You'd better tell me all about it.'

'Not here. Not where we can be overheard. I don't want this to get back to Mrs Fox. It would break her heart.'

'Fine. We'll go outside. Hang on.' He dashed back to the others and told them he would catch them up, then took the girl out to sit on a bench in front of the church. 'Right. No one can hear us now. Why don't you tell me what this is all about. What's your name?'

The girl drew a deep breath. 'Wendy.'

'And what's this about pills?'

'Well, I don't know where Richie got them from, but he would sometimes have these pills that he would sell. He told us they were for busy women to help them stay alert for longer and they were also good for the figure.' She wrinkled her nose. 'I never took any, but a few of the other girls did.'

'And Rita took them?' Edwin could hardly believe what he was hearing. It sounded as though Richie had been selling the Benzedrine pills that were routinely supplied to the aircrews.

Wendy nodded her head. 'Please don't think badly of her. She was worked to the bone, what with her job and taking care of her mother and then the ARP duty on top of that.'

'I don't. She was doing what was necessary to see her through a hard time.' He thought for a moment. 'Look, I might have to tell the police, but I'll keep your name out of it if I can.'

'Oh, I don't mind telling the police. I would have told them before, only they already seemed to have made up their minds that Rita was a bad sort, and didn't seem interested in listening to anything I had to say.'

Edwin nodded, remembering the opinions of the police who had attended the scene when he and his friends had found the body. 'Well, thank you for telling me. These pills, by the way, do you know what they were called?'

Wendy shrugged. 'I don't know their proper name. He called them "wakey-wakey pills".'

When Edwin caught up with the others his head was spinning. 'Listen to this,' he said, and repeated what Wendy had told him. 'Richie must have been hoarding Benzedrine pills and selling them on,' he concluded. 'This makes sense of the times we saw Rita. She was finding it hard to function without them and was getting desperate for more. I expect Richie never had a regular supply because it would depend on him flying a mission and then managing to purloin the pills from those of his crew who didn't actually take theirs. And with the longer missions we were flying towards the end, it's likely that more crew members were using them.'

'And recently we've only been flying short hops into the Netherlands or Belgium,' Fitz said, 'and we haven't been supplied with pills for those trips.'

'If Rita was taking Benzedrine regularly, what would it do to her?' Jenny asked.

Edwin shrugged. 'No idea. I've only taken the stuff once and that was enough for me. I couldn't sleep for hours after I got back and hated how it made me feel.'

'Same here,' Greg said. 'I stuck with the caffeine pills after that.' For they were also supplied with those and advised to save the Benzedrine for emergencies.

'But aren't all the pills collected when you get back?' Jenny asked. 'How could he end up with a regular supply?'

Edwin had thought this through while catching up with his friends. 'It wouldn't be too difficult. All he would have to do was say that he had taken his. And as a gunner, he would have to spend most of each flight staring out into the darkness with nothing to see or do. Gunners take Benzedrine to help them maintain concentration at all times, so it would be believable for him to always be taking his and no one would question him for not returning it. He could easily have collected pills from others in the crew, offering to give them back but hoarding them in reality. And there are tricks he could pull to get more pills before a mission, like saying he'd lost his and asking for more.'

By the time he had finished, the group had reached the junction where Jenny and Thea needed to go one way for the Waafery and everyone else the other for Fenthorpe Hall. They stood at the side of the road.

'So what do we do now?' Jenny asked. 'How does this relate to Rita's death?'

'Don't you remember the argument we saw between Richie and Rita?' Edwin asked. 'Knowing about the pills makes sense of it. I reckon Richie had run out of pills and Rita was threatening to blackmail him if he didn't get her any more. She said she could tell the authorities what he'd been doing.'

'That does make sense,' Jenny said. 'So you're saying that Richie killed her to keep her quiet?'

'We can't know that for sure, but he's certainly got a motive.' Edwin looked at each of his friends in turn to be sure they understood the gravity of the situation. 'Remember, however bad this looks, this is only a theory, so for goodness' sake don't go blurting it out to all and sundry. I'll go to the police first thing tomorrow and tell them what we know.'

Chapter Twenty-Two

As it turned out, it was a few days before Jenny could meet with the others and hear how the police had responded to Edwin's tale. The crews were kept busy with more supply flights, and her duties were as frantic as ever, for the weather instruments needed reading and the charts had to be plotted whether or not there were flights from the station that day. What she couldn't understand was why she didn't see Edwin so often in the Met Office. If she didn't know better she would almost think he was avoiding her.

In the end the group didn't get together until the middle of the following week, for Deedee had found out it was Jenny's birthday.

'Deedee says the NAAFI is no place to celebrate,' Thea told her when they were in Hut Three together the day before Jenny's birthday. 'She's organising a party at the Gatehouse for everyone. And, yes, before you ask, "everyone" includes Edwin.' Thea frowned. 'What's that face for? Don't you want to see him?'

'I don't know if I can face it. It feels like he's avoiding me. Why would he do that?'

Thea dropped onto the bed beside Jenny and sighed. 'I don't know. I really can't make him out. He's plainly crazy about you, though, so take heart.'

'Easier said than done. It doesn't make sense. All the barriers between us have been removed, so why won't he make a move?'

'Maybe all the barriers haven't been removed.'

Jenny dropped the comb that she'd been using and twisted to look at Thea. 'What do you mean?'

'All the barriers that you know of have been removed but maybe there's something else that you don't know about. You should try talking to him, because he's the only one who can explain.'

And so the next day Jenny and Thea, who had both got late passes, headed for the Gatehouse once their watches were over. Jenny's mind was less on her birthday and far more on whether she should take Thea's advice. If she did, what on earth would she say?

'Happy birthday, Jenny! Many happy returns.' Jenny had hardly stepped into the hall before Deedee pulled her into an enthusiastic hug. 'The others are already here, so come on through.'

Jenny stepped into the living room and was immediately greeted by cheers. Greg and Fitz had even managed to get hold of some party blowers, which added to the din.

'Happy birthday, Jenny!' Pearl greeted her with a hug, only slightly hampered by her bump, and produced a daisy chain, which she ceremonially placed on Jenny's head. 'Freshly picked from the lawn,' she said. 'I wanted a paper crown at first, but Deedee had just taken all the used papers to the salvage, so I had to improvise.'

'This is far nicer.' Jenny patted the circlet to make sure it wouldn't slip off. 'I wasn't expecting so much fuss, though.'

'But this is your first peacetime birthday in years. We have to celebrate properly. And besides' – Pearl suddenly looked glum – 'I might be in Australia before your next one.'

'Why – have you heard anything?'

'No but I suppose I've got change on my mind, what with the baby coming, Deedee getting married, Thea getting engaged and the war ending.'

Jenny supposed it must be a lot to get used to for someone who liked security. 'Well, if I'm being selfish, I hope you won't leave any time soon. I want the chance to get to know Pearl or Greg junior.'

'Oh, you will, whatever happens. I'm going to bombard you all with so many photos, you'll have to move into bigger quarters just to fit them all in.'

Jenny enjoyed every moment of her party. Mrs Stockwell had performed her usual magic with the food and produced a spread that Jenny thought could rival anything eaten in Buckingham Palace. At the end there was a magnificent fruit cake with a single candle burning in the centre.

'We didn't give you twenty-two candles because we didn't want to embarrass you by displaying how young and callow you are compared to the rest of us,' Thea told her, laughing.

Once the candle had been blown out and the cake eaten, it was time for the gift-giving.

'I really didn't expect anything. This is too much,' Jenny said, regarding the pile of presents that had magically appeared by her side with considerable embarrassment.

'Shut up and open them!' Thea cried. 'I want to see what you've got.'

Jenny picked up the first present, wrapped somewhat haphazardly in newspaper. She was beginning to see why there hadn't been any left for a paper crown. 'Let me guess. This is from you?'

Thea scowled. 'I didn't have time to wrap it properly. I had to sneak into the kitchen and do it any old how while Pearl distracted you with your daisy chain.'

'I'm sure I'll love it, whatever it is.' She made short work of the paper and found a new Yardley Natural Rose lipstick and some mascara nestled inside. 'Thank you! I've run out but I couldn't find new ones anywhere.'

'I persuaded Deedee to get them for me,' Thea told her. 'I said if she didn't, I'd tell Grandpa all about the time she stormed into school and told off my English teacher for marking down an essay.'

'I already knew,' Thomas said, his arm firmly around his new wife. 'There are no secrets between us any more. And I could scarcely believe some of the things she told me about you, Thea.'

The rest of Jenny's presents were a mixture of things it was hard to get hold of during the war, including some nylons from Deedee, who said she had persuaded Thomas to get them from his American contacts. Jenny tried and failed to imagine the dignified Thomas asking for nylon stockings. There were also books, and the last present Jenny opened was from Edwin. It was a large, flat package.

'I can tell it's a book,' she said, her anticipation rising, 'so I already know I'm going to love it.' It turned out to be an atlas of the night sky. Jenny turned the pages, breathing in the wonderful new book scent, delighted at the detailed diagrams showing which constellations were visible in each month and where to find them in the sky. Each picture was accompanied by informative text about the stars making up each constellation. 'Thank you. This is wonderful.' Jenny hesitated, wanting to hug him but feeling suddenly self-conscious. 'It's almost as good as having you with me to explain everything.'

'You seemed to be so interested, I thought you'd like this for when I'm not around,' he told her.

Jenny felt as though she had been slapped in the face. It sounded as though he wasn't expecting to be with her for much longer. She blinked back tears, hoping people would think they were from happiness at her gift.

'I love it. But I'd still prefer to have you to tell me about them.' It was the only thing she could say with the others present, but she hoped he had got the message.

Once the dishes were cleared away and Jenny had put all the paper into the salvage basket, everyone sat back at the table to play rummy. Jenny was glad they had chosen a game that didn't take much concentration because she didn't feel up to much after Edwin's remark. Had he meant that he didn't intend to be in her life for much longer, or had he simply been saying Jenny could refer to the book at those times he wasn't around? Maybe she had been mistaken? She could only hope that was the case. The way Edwin had taken her seriously concerning Rita's death had gone a long way to reassuring her that he didn't consider her beneath him due to her lack of education. But now there was no longer anything standing between them, her old fears were starting to return.

'Your turn, Jenny.' Thea's prompt brought Jenny's attention back to the game with a jolt.

'Sorry.' She put a random card on the discard pile and picked up a replacement.

Thea, whose turn it was now, seized upon the discarded card with glee and after some thought selected a card to throw away. 'At the risk of spoiling the mood, did you get a chance to speak to the police yet, Edwin?'

'I did, but I could tell they weren't interested.' Edwin rearranged the cards in his hand, then pulled a face. 'Well, that's not exactly true. What the sergeant I spoke to actually said was that there's no direct evidence to prove Richie or anyone else was with Rita that night and no medical evidence to prove she was murdered. She might well have been buying Benzedrine from Richie, but apparently there's more of that going on than we might think. And an argument we witnessed some nights before her death still isn't enough to prove he had a hand in her death.' He sighed. 'I suppose he has a point. We mustn't forget murder is a hanging offence. Are we really convinced enough of Richie's guilt to accuse him when we could end up getting a man hanged? I, for one, have had quite enough of dealing death.'

A silence hung over the table for a while after that. Jenny looked at Edwin, her heart twisting in sympathy. She knew he must be thinking of the man he had killed, and Greg and Fitz would be thinking of all the bombing missions they had flown.

Eventually she cleared her throat. 'You're right. I suppose I have let myself get carried away without considering the consequences. Anyway, if the police don't think there is enough evidence, there's nothing else we can really do.' After a moment's thought she added, 'And I need to think carefully about whether I want him to be guilty just because of the way he treated Lily.'

She was so mired in her thoughts that she jumped when Thea squeezed her arm. 'For what it's worth, I still think the death is suspicious,' she said. 'But we've done all we can. We've told the police everything we know, so now we can leave it to them with a clear conscience. I'll still keep my eyes and ears open though.'

'I suppose that's the best we can do,' Jenny said. 'I just feel like we're letting Rita down.'

Pearl shifted in her seat. 'I don't like to give up either but I don't think we should look at it like that. We've done all we can and now it's time to step back and reassess what we know. As Thea says, we can keep an open mind. Anyway, I'm not in any condition to take an active role but I'll happily lend an ear to anyone who wants to talk things over.'

Thea nodded. 'Maybe we should change the subject. This is getting very gloomy for a birthday party.' She frowned. 'How's Lily getting on, by the way?'

'Not too bad. She'll be leaving next month to go into a mother and baby home in Lincoln. She'll have to hand the baby over for adoption.'

Deedee shook her head. 'It's hard to believe her parents want nothing to do with her or the baby. A grandchild is something to be cherished. Still, if that's their attitude, I daresay the child will be better off with a family who can lavish it with all the love it wouldn't get from its grandparents.'

Jenny nodded. 'That's pretty much what Lily says. She wants the best for her baby, and she knows she's in no position to provide for it. It's going to be hard on her, though, to give it up.'

'We'll just have to be there for her,' Deedee said. 'And when she leaves the home, I'm sure Tom will be able to find her a job.' She nudged her husband. 'Won't you, Tom?'

'Oh, yes. Tell her to come and see me. I'm sure I'll be able to find something for her.'

'That's so kind. She's a good worker, so I know you won't regret it.'

And so even though Jenny's birthday had been overshadowed by Rita's death, she still managed to enjoy it.

–

The days went by and spring turned into summer. Lily bid a tearful goodbye to Jenny and went into the mother and baby home; Jenny passed on the message from Thomas and promised to keep in touch. As operations at RAF Fenthorpe were easing off, several WAAFs were being transferred elsewhere, and so Lily's departure didn't create as much comment as it might have done a few months earlier. Pearl, too, finished work, with a good deal of regret, and spent most of the time when Greg was on duty at the Gatehouse with Deedee. She had arranged to have the baby at the maternity hospital in Lincoln and, as limited fuel was now available again for civilian use, Thomas had his car fuelled and serviced and was ready to drive her there at a moment's notice.

Jenny was still busy and so, what with her work and the impending excitement of Pearl's new baby, she didn't have much time to brood either about Edwin or her inability to solve the mystery of Rita's death. However, every time she opened her purse she received a reminder, for she found herself unable to spend the ten-shilling note she'd had from Mrs Fox. Somehow, knowing it had been Rita's, she felt that if she let it go she would be letting go of the case, and she didn't feel ready to do that. In the end, to avoid spending it by mistake, she tucked the note inside the book she'd had from Edwin. It was irrational, she knew, and it wasn't as if she had so much money that she could easily afford to set aside ten whole shillings, yet she couldn't get rid of the niggling feeling that if she spent it she would be letting Rita down. Mrs Fox deserved answers about her daughter's death and, if the police were of the opinion that they had already resolved the case, that only left Jenny and her friends to make them reopen the case.

In the meantime, as Jenny had no idea where to turn next for answers, she decided to take Thea's advice. She would carry on with her day-to-day life while keeping her eyes and ears open for a fresh lead.

Chapter Twenty-Three

'I'm getting tired of seeing nothing but Fenthorpe and Lincoln,' Thea said one day in early August. 'I wish we could go further afield.'

Jenny and Thea both had the afternoon off, and, as the men weren't required to fly anywhere, they had all gathered at the Gatehouse. It was a beautiful day, so rather than sit inside they had gone for a stroll around the grounds of Fenthorpe Hall and then settled in the rose garden.

Edwin, sitting on the grass beside the bench where Pearl, Deedee and Thomas sat, was only half listening to the conversation. He found he couldn't tear his gaze from Jenny, who was sitting with Thea beside a brilliant crimson rose bush. Her head was tipped back, her eyes closed, and he could tell she was enjoying the warmth of the sun on her face and the scent of the roses. She stirred herself enough to reply to Thea's complaint. 'Where would we go? I don't fancy cycling far in this heat.'

'I don't know.' Thea batted aside a hovering wasp. 'It just seems a shame that we live not far from the Lincolnshire coast and I've never seen it. Well, except for the times I've been up on a training flight, but that doesn't count because I was thousands of feet in the air instead of standing on the beach with my feet in the water.'

'What I wouldn't give to have a paddle in the sea right now,' Pearl said. 'Feeling cool waves on my puffy feet would be sheer bliss.' Then she sighed. 'Not that I'm in any state to spend the day on a beach.' She patted her enormous bump.

'Not with the number of times a day you need the loo,' Thea told her with a grin.

Pearl shot her sister a glare. 'Thanks for reminding me.' She heaved herself to her feet. 'Now I've got to go again.' She waddled off in the direction of the Gatehouse.

'Even if Pearl can't go, it doesn't mean the rest of us couldn't have a day out,' Fitz remarked. 'I quite fancy a day at the seaside.'

'Count me out,' Greg said. 'I'd never forgive myself if Pearl went into labour and I wasn't there. You should go, though. My motorcycle's got a full tank and you're welcome to borrow it. There's more than enough petrol to get you and Thea to Skegness and back.'

'Oh, but that would mean only the two of us could go. What about the rest of you? You'd like a day out wouldn't you, Jenny?'

'I'd love to go on a day like today. I've hardly ever seen the sea.'

Edwin stared at her in amazement. 'But the Forest of Dean isn't far from the coast.'

Jenny shrugged. 'There used to be Sunday school outings to Barry when I was growing up, but my grandparents didn't often have the money to let me go.' Her face lit up. 'I did go along twice and they were the happiest days of my life. Grancher even gave me a shilling for pocket money when my granny wasn't looking.'

Edwin was filled with a sudden fierce determination that Jenny should have her day out by the sea. 'What's stopping us from going? There's a train to Skegness.'

Thea sat bolt upright, her eyes shining. 'We could get a forty-eight-hour pass. Just think of it – two whole days at the seaside!'

Two whole days away with Jenny. Edwin wasn't sure if that was a good idea but at the sight of Jenny's eager face he was forced to agree, albeit with serious misgivings. Recently he had managed to avoid spending time with her alone but, if they went with Thea and Fitz, it would be only natural for the couple to want to spend some time alone, meaning he and Jenny would be obliged to keep each other company. That would be uncomfortable to say the least. He knew she must be hurt and confused, wondering what was stopping them from being together now he and Mina were no longer engaged. The trouble was, he couldn't explain it to himself, let alone to Jenny. However, the others' enthusiasm for the plan was contagious and by the end of the evening he was looking forward to the trip. Maybe this time away would give him the space to sort out his confused feelings.

–

To make the most of their time away, they caught the train to Skegness the evening they finished duty. Even though it was midweek, there were a fair few other passengers clearly going on a short break. Several of them were in uniform but there were also mothers with young children and older couples, all of whom would not have had a trip to the seaside in years.

'What shall we do first?' Fitz asked when they got out of the train. 'Guesthouse or beach? If we want to see the sea this evening, we should go soon before it gets dark.'

'Let's drop our things at the guesthouse,' Jenny said. 'Then we can stay on the beach until it's time to eat.'

They had telephoned ahead and secured two rooms at a place near the seafront, so they followed the directions the landlady had given them over the phone and soon found themselves being welcomed by a cheerful woman.

'Good thing you didn't wait until next week,' she said, showing them up the stairs. 'The place is going to be packed for the August holiday, and about time too. It'll be wonderful to see holidaymakers in the town again.'

Edwin followed her into the room he would be sharing with Fitz and immediately crossed to the window. Judging from the exclamations of delight he could hear from the next room, he thought the girls must have done the same thing and were now looking out at the sea view.

'Makes a change to see it from ground level,' he said with a grin at Fitz.

No one wanted to remain indoors for long and, armed with suggestions of places to eat, they soon dashed out and made their way to the beach.

'Paddling first,' Jenny cried the moment her feet touched the sand, and without waiting to see what the others were doing she stripped off her shoes, socks and jacket and made a dash for the water. The others followed suit, but Edwin had only taken a couple of steps when Thea grabbed his arm and hauled him back.

'What do you think you're playing at?'

He stared at her, uncomprehending, and pointed at the waves. 'I was going to paddle.'

'Not that, you idiot. I mean with Jenny.'

He decided to brazen it out. 'I don't know what you mean.' The last thing he wanted to do was explain to this enraged wildcat when he scarcely understood himself.

Thea scowled. 'Then let me refresh your memory. All the time you're with Jenny, you gaze at her like a man in the desert seeing water for the first time. Only, inexplicably, you're engaged to someone else so you can't do anything about it. Then you kiss her on VE Day…'

He flinched. So Jenny had told her about that. 'That was just the heat of the moment.'

Thea snorted. 'The heat of three years of moments, more like. Anyway, not long after that you announce your engagement is over. Everyone, and I mean everyone, expected you to tell Jenny how you feel after that, but no. You carry on like nothing has happened yet still gaze at her from a distance like a lovelorn puppy, thinking no one will notice.'

'I don't!'

Thea didn't answer him but instead called to her fiancé, who was trotting down the beach towards the sea. 'Fitz, come here a moment.'

Fitz turned and ran back. 'What's up?'

Thea pointed at Edwin. 'Show Edwin how he looks when he's staring at Jenny.'

'Oh, that's easy.' Fitz arranged his expression into one of dreamy-eyed longing. If he'd been a cartoon character, love hearts would have been popping from his eyes.

Edwin was outraged. 'I do not look like that.'

'Oh yes you do,' Thea and Fitz chanted in unison. Then Thea turned to Fitz. 'Thanks. You can go back now and keep Jenny company. I don't want her to overhear what I've got to say to this idiot.'

Once Fitz was gone, Thea put her hands on her hips and glared at Edwin. 'I'm saying this as a friend because I like you and I know you'd be good for Jenny, but for goodness' sake please tell me what's stopping you from asking her out?'

Edwin raked his fingers through his hair, feeling like a cornered animal. 'It's hard to explain.'

'Try me!'

'I mean, it's hard to explain because I don't even understand it myself.'

Thea drew breath as though about to launch on a tirade, then closed her mouth and frowned. 'Wait. You're telling me *you* don't even know why you can't tell Jenny how you feel?'

Edwin nodded.

'But you love her?'

'Yes! I'm crazy about her.' The admission burst out without thought. He would never have made it without Thea backing him into a corner like this. He reflected that it was a good thing he hadn't been captured in Holland, because he would have folded under interrogation.

'Then why can't you tell her?'

He shrugged.

'Think! There has to be a reason.'

'All I know is that it has something to do with Mina.'

Thea's brow furrowed. 'Are you still in love with her?'

'No.' This was something he did know. 'I'm beginning to see I never was in love with her. But whenever I think I should tell Jenny my feelings, I think of Mina and I feel…' He tailed off, unable to put the feeling into words.

'Go on! What do you feel? You must know, deep down.'

Edwin gazed at his feet, which were sinking into the sand. He was painfully aware of a profound reluctance to look within and examine the workings of his mind, and without Thea's insistence he would have avoided it. But he wasn't being fair to Jenny, he'd known that for some time, and now it was his guilt that prodded him on.

Guilt. That was it. He met Thea's gaze. 'Guilty. I think of Mina and I feel guilty.'

'Good! I mean, not good that you feel guilty but good that you've worked out how you feel. Why guilty?'

But that was something that, try as he might, he couldn't understand. All he could do was shrug and extricate his feet from the sand, shaking off the sandflies that were nipping his ankles.

Finally, Thea sighed. 'Well, you've made a start. But you owe it to Jenny to tell her what's going on.'

'Haven't you been listening? I don't know what's going on or I would tell her.'

'You don't have to present her with a complete solution, you know.' Thea's stern expression faded, to be replaced with kindness and concern. 'She's not an examiner. She's a confused, hurt young woman who needs to be let in on your thought processes. If you need time she'll give you that. She *has* given you that, with a patience I could never show. But sooner or later you're going to lose her, if you don't at least try to explain what you're going through.'

She had a point, and the prospect of losing Jenny altogether made him feel giddy with loss. 'You're right. I'll find time to explain.'

'Good.' Thea slapped him on the shoulder. 'Now let's get in the sea before I get bitten to death by sandflies.'

Jenny shot them a curious look when they arrived, splashing into the cold water with yells of mingled shock and delight. 'Is everything all right?'

'Everything's fine,' Thea assured her. 'I just needed to ask Edwin if his compass was still working after I fixed it last week.'

If Jenny wondered why Thea couldn't have waited, she said nothing, and soon she'd imitated Thea and hitched her skirt up so she could wade deeper into the water. Although he kept a cautious eye on the waves so he wasn't engulfed by one larger than the rest, Edwin found his gaze kept drifting to Jenny. Specifically her legs, which were revealed to mid-thigh, long, lean and glowing with a light golden tan. He could only hope his face didn't resemble the ghastly lovesick expression Fitz had pulled. Thea was right, though. He'd been unfair, expecting Jenny to carry on as though nothing had happened. He would have spoken to her long ago if only there wasn't this strange block that he'd now identified as guilt. But guilt about what? How was he going to explain himself to Jenny when he still hadn't worked it all out? He was used to being the one with the knowledge, the one with all the answers, and he felt wrong-footed at being unable to understand what was really going on in his mind.

In the end he decided he needed a bit of time alone if he was going to work out what to say, so, declaring that his feet were cold, he left the others in the water and retired to the heap of discarded shoes, socks and jackets that they'd left at the top of the beach. He settled down on the sand and let the sun dry his legs. It really was a comfortable patch of sand they'd found. All around he could hear children squealing with excitement, the wash of the waves upon the shore, the wail of gulls overhead.

The sun was sinking towards the rooftops, yet it was still hot. He closed his eyes against the glare and felt the warmth creep into every muscle. His whole body slowly relaxed and his thoughts drifted, as ephemeral as the sparkles of sunlight upon the sea.

'We're going for fish and chips. Want some?'

Edwin awoke with a start to see Fitz sitting next to him, pulling on his socks. He sat up, his mind heavy and sluggish from sleep. Jenny and Thea were also sitting nearby, lacing their shoes. 'What?' Then his stomach rumbled, and he slowly pieced together what Fitz had said. 'Oh, yes please.' He fished in his pocket for money, but Thea stood and waved it away.

'Fitz and I will get them. Our treat.' She shot him a smug grin. 'You stay here and keep Jenny company.'

Great. So this was a set-up to get him and Jenny talking. The trouble was, he still hadn't worked out what to say; no inspiration had come to him in his sleep. He watched Fitz and Thea walk across the sand holding hands, knowing Thea would lose all patience if he didn't take this opportunity to clear the air with Jenny. Yet he couldn't help wishing she'd asked him to do something easier. Like unifying quantum mechanics and general relativity.

'I hope I wasn't snoring.' Great start, Edwin.

Jenny giggled. 'No. I'm sorry we woke you. You looked so peaceful, but Thea and Fitz were starving and said they couldn't wait.'

Seeing her obvious happiness eased his worries. This was why he had come to Skegness, after all, so that Jenny could have her trip to the seaside. Hanging on to the knowledge that he only wanted to make Jenny happy, he used it to force himself to talk.

'Actually, I'm glad to catch you alone for a while. There's something I need to say.'

Edwin looked so serious that Jenny felt her heart give a lurch. She'd seen Thea speaking to him earlier and knew her explanation about Edwin's compass was untrue. Despite her begging

Thea not to corner Edwin, she knew her friend had done just that. She could only wait, dry-mouthed, for him to continue.

Edwin, however, after announcing he wanted to talk, seemed unable to get any words out. He gazed at her, his brow furrowed, for a few seconds before looking down at the sand and prodding it, apparently with great concentration.

'What did you want to say?' she asked in the end, not wholly sure she wanted to know. Surely if it was anything that would make her happy, he wouldn't be displaying such reluctance.

'I… need to tell you about why I haven't said anything since… well, since VE Day.' His words were addressed to the sand.

Jenny decided to take the bull by the horns. 'About the liberation of Europe, or our kiss?'

Edwin looked up, startled, and in other circumstances she might have laughed, but right at that moment her throat felt so tight she could hardly draw breath.

'The kiss,' he said finally. 'It's not that I haven't thought about it, because I have, pretty much every waking minute, in fact.'

'Then why haven't you said anything?' To her horror she felt the beginnings of tears, and she blinked them away furiously. This was no time for crying. It was hard though because three months of bottled-up frustration and anticipation suddenly screamed to be heard. She drew several deep breaths.

'It's hard to explain because I don't understand it myself.' He gave a twisted smile. 'I thought I needed to wait until I did understand, but Thea—'

'You've been talking about it with Thea?' Her sense of betrayal was hypocritical, considering the number of times she had discussed Edwin with Thea and Pearl, but at least the sudden flare of anger helped keep her tears in check.

He held out his hands as though warding off a blow. 'More like Thea cornered me and threatened me with dire retribution if I didn't explain myself to you.'

Jenny subsided. 'I suppose that sounds exactly like the sort of thing she would do.'

'She also made me see that I've been shutting you out while I try and work things out alone when I should have included you.'

'She's right.' Jenny wasn't going to let him off that easily just because he was finally talking. 'What things are you trying to work out?'

Edwin seemed to notice for the first time the holes he was digging in the sand, and he brushed his hands before replying. Jenny waited, scarcely able to breathe, her chest felt so tight. 'There's this… block,' he said finally. 'I can't explain it better than that. But whenever I try telling you how I feel, it stops me. Thea helped me see it's guilt. Something to do with Mina, I think.'

Jenny, however, could only really focus on one part of his statement. 'But you do feel something?'

He nodded. 'Only I can't do anything about it until I resolve whatever is giving me this guilt. And I don't know how long it will take or if I'll ever get over it. That's why I didn't want to say anything before. I don't want to promise you something that might never happen. I might never be able to push past this block.'

Why didn't she feel reassured? 'If you do, promise you'll tell me?'

Edwin nodded.

Somehow she managed to smile and say, 'Then maybe I can wait.'

For how long, though? Did he expect her to put her whole life on hold while he worked out what he felt? Ever since he and Mina had split up, she had waited for him to confess his feelings for her, first in expectation, then in hope. Gradually that hope had waned, leaving her with nothing more than a wistful longing that she feared would remain unfulfilled.

Thea and Fitz arrived back at that point, saving her from having to say anything else. They were preceded by an appetising aroma wafting from the newspaper-wrapped packages in their arms. Jenny's stomach rumbled, reminding her that she hadn't eaten since midday.

'Fish and chips at the seaside has to be the best meal ever,' she said later, when all that remained were empty wrappings. She licked the last of the salt and vinegar-flavoured grease from her fingers.

'It is as long as the seagulls don't want a share.' Thea scrambled to her feet. 'I remember sitting on the pier at Llandudno, getting dive-bombed by gulls.'

'Pity the pier here is still closed.' Jenny cast a longing glance at the deserted structure that stretched out over the water. 'I've never been on one before.'

'We've got years ahead of us to make all the seaside trips and walk on all the piers we want, and that's why we're here to celebrate.' Thea tugged Jenny to her feet. 'Come on, I'm starting to get cold. Let's go and find the cinema.'

–

The next two days passed in a flash of sunshine, sea bathing and giggling in cafes. Jenny knew it was a trip that would stand out in her memory for years to come. They packed so much into each day that she never even got a moment to tell Thea what Edwin had told her. Being so happily occupied made it easier for Jenny to hide her disappointment over Edwin, which she was determined to do, not wanting to dampen Thea's high spirits. Her friend was, after all, eagerly anticipating her wedding, and at the rare times when the women had a moment alone Thea was full of her plans for the big day. Although the couple didn't have a firm date set, they were only awaiting confirmation of their requested leave.

It wasn't until they retired to their room on their last night that they spoke of Edwin. 'I never got a chance to ask how your talk with Edwin went,' Thea said, folding her bathing costume and towel into her case. They had to report back to Fenthorpe the next morning and so they would need to catch the first train back to Lincoln. 'I told him I was cross for keeping you dangling. Did he explain himself?'

Jenny had a split second to decide whether she could keep up her pretence any longer, and her need to confide in her friend overcame her unwillingness to spoil their last evening. 'Not really. He tried, but all he really ended up doing was ask me to keep on waiting.' She explained what Edwin had said. 'He's been through so much,' she concluded, 'that I have to give him the benefit of the doubt.'

Thea nodded. 'I don't think anyone who didn't serve in the bomber crews can ever truly understand the strain that sort of thing can put on your mind.'

'Exactly. That's why I don't want to put him under any pressure. The trouble is, there's a part of me that wonders if he's trying to let me down gently. We're from such different worlds that I can't help thinking he'd be happier with Mina or someone like her.'

'Don't you ever let me hear you say that again!' Thea's vehemence took Jenny aback. 'Edwin's seen where you come from. Did he ever give a sign that he thought you were beneath him?'

'Well, no, but—'

'Or make you feel inferior because you don't have a degree?'

'Of course not! He's always encouraged me to learn new things but never in a patronising way.'

'Then what do you mean by saying he'd be happier with someone like Mina?'

Jenny was unable to answer. Long after they had gone to bed, and Thea's deep, even breathing revealed she had fallen asleep, Jenny couldn't get her friend's question out of her head. Somehow the way Thea had put her questions had turned Jenny's thinking on its head. Of course Edwin didn't look down on her. His open-hearted friendship, despite their different backgrounds, had been one of the reasons why Jenny had warmed to him so quickly. He valued her for who she was and encouraged her in her pursuit of knowledge because he could see that was what she wanted, not because he couldn't accept her unless she improved.

It was her jealousy of Mina that had caused her to question her worth. She could see that now.

Her head and heart full, she crept out of bed and peered through the curtains. There in the dark sky hung a crescent moon. Instantly she remembered what Edwin had told her about earthshine, but, no matter how hard she stared, she couldn't make out more of the moon than the illuminated crescent, probably due to the street lights. She had never felt further from Edwin than she did at that moment. It was as if the magic she had felt when he had explained the phenomenon had dissipated. Had his love for her faded too? If so, perhaps it was time she took the advice Thea had given her months ago and looked for love elsewhere.

Yet Edwin hadn't said he didn't love her, only that he needed time to work out his confused feelings, and if anyone deserved time after all they had been through, it was him. Especially as she had only just begun to understand that her sense of not being good enough for him had all been in her own head.

She stood at the window, thinking over everything he had told her, while the moon arced overhead.

–

'I've decided to give Edwin the time he's asked for,' she told Thea when she leapt out of bed the next morning. 'He's been nothing but kind, generous and patient with me, and he deserves the same in return.'

'If it helps, I think you'd regret it if you didn't,' Thea replied as she buttoned up her shirt. 'Hopefully he'll get there sooner rather than later, though, because I don't know how much longer we'll all be together.'

This was a worrying thought, and a fear Jenny had had in the back of her mind for some time. Already personnel were being transferred. She didn't think she would be demobbed any time soon, even though matters also seemed to be coming to a head in the war against Japan. There were plenty of WAAFs who had joined the service before her, and it had already been explained that the women who had been serving for longest would be the first ones to be released. However, Thea had joined very early on in the war, and so it seemed inevitable that, once the WAAF started releasing their women back into civilian life, Thea would be among the first to go. Jenny didn't like to think about life in Fenthorpe without her friend. Although she got on well with the others in her hut and in the Met Office, there was no one else on the base who she felt able to confide in. She had to comfort herself with the thought that Thea probably wouldn't move far while Pearl and Deedee were nearby.

'Have you decided what you're going to do when you leave the WAAF?' she asked. 'It might be difficult to find a job if Fitz is going to be moved around a lot.'

'Actually Section Officer Blatchford suggested I might want to stay on too.' Thea, who had finished dressing, picked up her pyjamas and stuffed them in her case. 'She thought arrangements could be made for us to be posted together, or at least near enough for us to be billeted in the same place.'

'That sounds exciting.' Jenny wondered if she would be able to do the same. 'Where do you think you'll be sent?'

'Most likely Germany to start with. There's a lot of work to do.'

Jenny thought of the flash of inspiration she'd had on VE Day. The kiss had overshadowed it, yet she had never completely forgotten. 'I wish I had more experience with the sort of journalism I want to do. Writing "Day in the Life" articles for the *Bombshell* isn't really the same.'

'No, but it's a good start. Pearl and Grandpa were really impressed with your VE Day article. You should talk to them, especially Grandpa. He's bound to have good advice.'

'You don't think he'll laugh at me? I'm worried he'll think I'm being too ambitious, considering I don't have any qualific-ations.'

'But look at all the experience you've had in the WAAF, not to mention the years of writing for the *Bombshell*. You've seen more life than anyone fresh out of school, and for a writer that has to give you an edge, better than any number of passes with distinction.'

This was a perspective that hadn't occurred to Jenny, and her sense of inferiority eased. For years her lack of qualifications had been like an unmovable boulder blocking her road to the future and only now did she begin to hope that her life experiences were just as important as exam results, if not more so.

'You're right. I'll make an effort to speak to him about it.' The fact that Thea had heard her out and been nothing but encouraging gave her the courage to think that Thomas, too, would take her seriously.

All in all, Jenny was feeling much happier about her life outside the WAAF by the end of the holiday. The only cloud on the horizon was Edwin's inability to speak of his feelings.

Chapter Twenty-Four

Edwin felt more at peace with himself when he returned to duty. Thea had been right to force him to speak to Jenny and, even though he felt he hadn't explained himself very well, Jenny had seemed to accept his reasoning. If only he could accept it himself. What was causing this surge in guilt every time he tried to tell Jenny how he felt? He and his crew were kept busy with more supply runs to the Continent, but as often as he could he tried to make time to examine his thoughts and work out the root cause of his mental block.

Only two days after they returned from Skegness, the news swept through the camp that the Americans had dropped an atomic bomb on Hiroshima in Japan. Edwin was appalled at the destruction caused by one single bomb. He also felt anger that this seemed to be the only way to bring about peace. Surely the Japanese had to surrender now. Yet still they clung on, and a second atomic bomb was detonated over Nagasaki. After that the Japanese leaders bowed to the inevitable and finally announced their surrender on the fifteenth of August.

This time, instead of the wild celebrations in Lincoln, the friends gathered for a simple meal at the Gatehouse to mark the final end of the war.

'It feels like the world went mad for six years, and I've still no idea how we're going to get back to normal,' Pearl said when they had polished off the last of the chicken salad. Then she put her hand on her bump and winced.

Greg was instantly at her side. 'What's wrong?'

'Nothing. Just a random pain. Same as all the other times you've asked me.' She leaned forward in her chair. 'My back's aching, though. Help me up. I need to walk around for a bit.'

The pair made their slow way through the open French windows and out into the garden.

Edwin noticed Thea's gaze follow them and had to smile at the way she had taken over the role of concerned sister after years of struggling to break free from Pearl's interference. Something niggled at the back of his mind, but when he tried to focus on what it was trying to tell him it eluded him.

They all made short work of clearing the table and then washing up, ignoring Mrs Stockwell's protests, and once they had finished, seeing Pearl and Greg had not yet returned, they followed them out. There was no sign of the couple in the Gatehouse's small garden, so they strolled out of the gate and took the path to the rose garden.

When Edwin walked through the gap in the tall yew hedge, he saw Greg and Pearl among the roses, walking their way. Greg had his arm round Pearl and looked worried, but only when Pearl suddenly stopped and pressed her hands to her bump, bending over, did the reason for the worry dawn on Edwin. A moment later, Pearl seemed to recover and the pair carried on.

'Looks like the baby's on the way,' Greg called when he looked up and saw them.

Immediately Thea and Deedee clustered around Pearl until she cried, 'Stop, both of you! I'm not ill, but I don't want to give birth out here either.'

Thomas stepped forward and took Pearl's free arm. 'Let's get you to the car. I'll drive you to the hospital.'

'I'll come too,' Thea and Deedee said simultaneously.

However, Greg shook his head. 'The maternity hospital already said they couldn't handle a lot of relatives in the waiting room and they'd prefer it if it was just me there. Anyway, it will probably be hours yet.'

'It better not be,' Pearl muttered darkly.

'I promise to call as soon as I have news,' Greg said with a grin.

The expectant parents made their way with Thomas slowly round the house to the garage. Everyone gathered to wave them off, then retired to the living room to wait.

An hour later, Thomas arrived back. Thea and Deedee leapt up the moment he walked through the door and fired so many rapid questions that he was forced to throw up his hands to stop them.

'Pearl's fine,' he said, 'but they say she's only in the early stages of labour, so we could be waiting for hours yet. It's a good thing no one else came because they were quite firm about not allowing many people to clutter up their waiting rooms.'

Deedee nodded. 'I was in labour for two days with Clara and she was in labour for almost as long with Pearl.'

'Two days!' Thea looked horrified. 'But Jenny and I have to be back in the Waafery by midnight.'

'Well, of course I'll phone the hospital and tell them that Pearl has to have the baby by then or her sister will be most put out,' Deedee said.

'I know I'm being silly but I can't help it. I don't like to think of Pearl going through this without me being there.'

'She'll be fine,' Deedee said. 'Childbirth isn't an illness. Women have been doing it for as long as humans have been around.'

'I know but I can't help worrying. She is my sister after all. And she's old to be a mother for the first time.'

Something about Thea's worry for her sibling struck a chord with Edwin, although it took a moment to work out what it was. Then he had it. It was just like Mina's concern for her brother. She had been very protective of him, quite natural considering that he was all the family she had left. She had been so happy when Edwin had taken him under his wing.

252

And then the guilt hit him. Daniel had hero-worshipped Edwin, to the extent that he had joined the RAF and volunteered as bomber crew. And Edwin had encouraged him! That was why he felt so guilty when he thought of Mina. Not because she had seen he hadn't loved her enough to marry, but because he felt responsible for her loss. He had always felt protective of her, but this explained why his protectiveness had only increased over time instead of easing off once she had joined the WAAF and proved that she was perfectly capable of looking after herself.

Was this why he felt unable to tell Jenny he loved her? Although he had promised to tell her if anything changed, he decided not to say anything yet. He needed time to think things through and work out what this really meant.

The group started a desultory game of cards after that, but no one really concentrated and it dragged on with no winner. After what seemed like an endless evening, at nine Greg telephoned. Deedee took the call, and everyone else hovered in the study doorway, trying and failing to work out what was happening from Deedee's end of the conversation. As far as Edwin could make out there was no sound of either great joy or worry, and so he concluded that the baby had not yet made an appearance but Pearl was still doing well.

Deedee confirmed this when she emerged. 'Pearl's fine but no sign of the baby yet. It'll probably be tomorrow before there's any news. I don't care what the hospital is saying, I'm going to sit with Greg.'

'I'll come too,' Thea said.

'No you won't. I've got a message from Pearl. She says to make sure you get back to the Waafery on time because she doesn't want the baby's aunt to be on jankers for the first week of its life.'

Thea gave a reluctant laugh. 'She's even trying to organise me from her hospital bed. I hope the baby comes soon so she's got a child of her own to manage. Maybe she'll leave me alone then.' But there was none of the irritation towards her sister that Thea had displayed when Edwin had first known her.

'Seriously,' Deedee said, 'You two girls should go back to the Waafery and get some rest. You're both on duty tomorrow, so you need to get a good night's sleep.'

'Fat chance of that,' Thea muttered, but she agreed to let Thomas drop her off at the Waafery gate on his way to taking Deedee to the hospital.

Edwin and Fitz headed back to Fenthorpe Hall at the same time as the others left. Despite his concern for Pearl, he found his thoughts continually returning to his revelation regarding Mina and her brother. What did it mean? He could only hope that he could work it out soon because he didn't want to keep Jenny waiting. Still, she had said she understood when he had spoken to her at Skegness and he didn't want to say anything until he was sure he wasn't making a mistake. He had done that with Mina and ended up hurting them both. Whatever happened, he didn't want Jenny getting hurt.

'Any news?' Jenny sat at Thea's table in the NAAFI and poured her lemonade into a glass. 'On second thoughts, don't bother. I can tell you haven't heard. You'd be on your way to the hospital if you had.'

Thea chuckled. 'No, nothing. I rang the hospital when I got off duty and was told she was making good progress. The nurse made it sound as though Pearl was sitting an exam instead of in labour.'

'I'm surprised to see you off duty so soon.' Thea frequently worked beyond her scheduled hours, even when there was no flying on, as was the case today.

'My sergeant sent me packing half an hour early after I got an altimeter mixed up with an artificial horizon. Told me not to come back until I could concentrate.'

Jenny toyed with the idea of commenting on the lines of Thea getting a month off, but decided her friend was probably not in the mood to be teased. She completely understood; she was worried about Pearl too.

Instead, she asked, 'Should we go to the Gatehouse or the hospital?'

'The hospital,' Thea said firmly. 'I don't care if they don't encourage visitors. That's where I'm going and I won't budge until the baby arrives.'

Jenny didn't bother trying to argue, just drained her lemonade and rose. 'We'd better get going then.'

Two bus journeys later, they trooped into the hospital waiting room and saw that Greg, Deedee and Thomas were already there. All three were dishevelled, and Greg's uniform looked like it hadn't seen an iron in a week.

'I was wondering when you were going to show up,' Deedee said. 'The staff have given up trying to send me away.'

'How's she getting on?' Thea asked.

'She's doing "as well as can be expected", whatever that means,' Greg answered. Jenny gazed at him in concern. She had seen him after harrowing missions looking in a better state than he did now. His hair was tousled as though he had repeatedly run his hands through it and there were dark rings round his eyes. His jaw was covered in stubble, and she guessed he had been up all night.

He looked as though he was going to say more, but then a nurse appeared and beckoned to him. Everyone sprang to their feet.

'Flying Officer Tallis?' the nurse said. 'Come this way, please.' She looked almost as tired as Greg but she was smiling.

Greg dashed after her and disappeared into a room a short way down the corridor.

Deedee clung to Thomas's hand. 'What does that mean? Do you think the baby's arrived?'

Thomas pulled her close. 'Relax. I'm sure everything's fine. The nurse wouldn't have been smiling like that if anything was wrong. Greg won't keep us waiting any longer than necessary.'

No one spoke after that and they all kept their gazes fixed on the door that had closed behind Greg. When it opened, everyone sprang to their feet again. The same nurse emerged and, when she saw them already watching her, she beckoned.

'There's someone who would like to meet you,' she told them in a low voice and then stepped back from the door. Her place was taken by Greg, who carried a tiny bundle in his arms, wrapped in a blanket. Jenny was stunned by the transformation that had overwhelmed him in the short time since he had gone into the room. The lines of exhaustion had magically disappeared and a beaming smile split his face from ear to ear.

When he spoke it was in a hushed voice, so Jenny, who had let the others stand in front of her, had to strain to hear what he said. 'This is our brand-new daughter. Isn't she perfect?'

Deedee and Thea were already leaning over the bundle in his arms, uttering soft cries of delight. Now Thea looked up. 'A girl! How wonderful.'

Deedee chuckled. 'You're outnumbered, Greg.'

Greg just smiled, and now it occurred to Jenny that he didn't look delighted so much as concussed, as though he couldn't quite believe what was happening. 'I don't mind. If she turns out anything like Pearl, she'll be a force to reckon with.' Then he bent his head over his tiny daughter, rocking her gently. 'Won't you, little one? And you won't let a war stand in your way, either. Because you're our little peacetime baby, and we're going to make the world a wonderful place for you to live in.'

Jenny found herself blinking back tears, and silently renewed her vow to work hard so she could achieve her dream of being a journalist. She pulled herself up onto tiptoes and peered over Thea's shoulder to get a better look at the baby. And breathed a sigh of adoration when she saw a red, scrunched-up face amidst the blankets, one-minute curled fist just visible, poking out. The baby's eyes were closed and she appeared to be asleep. Jenny found she couldn't tear her gaze from the sight, and marvelled at each perfect feature rendered in miniature.

'Can we see Pearl?' Thea asked. 'How is she?'

'Not yet,' Greg replied. 'She's fine but tired. She fell asleep about five seconds after I saw her.'

'Has the baby got a name yet?' Jenny asked.

Greg shook his head. 'We thought of a couple but nothing seems to fit. I want to find the perfect one.'

'How about Alice?' Thea suggested.

Greg cocked his head to one side, appearing to consider this and obviously not noticing the mischief in Thea's voice. 'Alice. I like it. I'll suggest it to Pearl. Alice Tall—' He broke off, scowling at Thea. 'Alice Tallis. Very funny. Did it take you all night to come up with that?'

'Not all night. I spent half the night trying to think of a good name for a boy but I couldn't think of anything as good as Alice. It's such a relief you had a girl.'

Deedee put a firm hand on Thea's shoulder and steered her away. 'We'd better leave you to it. Preferably before you wring Thea's neck.'

Chapter Twenty-Five

With all the excitement over the new baby, Jenny's worries were pushed to the back of her mind. Over the next two weeks, her free time was spent cooing over the baby, first at the hospital and then, once Pearl and the baby were released, at the Gatehouse. Deedee and Thomas proved to be doting great-grandparents, and Jenny took great joy in Thomas's happiness at seeing his great-granddaughter when he had never met his daughter and had only recently got to know Pearl and Thea.

'I don't want to miss a moment of this little one's life,' he said happily on Pearl's first evening back at the Gatehouse. Then his face fell. 'Well, until you all go to Australia.'

Jenny's heart gave a lurch. She had been trying not to think too much about Pearl and Greg leaving for Australia. While she knew she was being selfish, she couldn't help hoping it would be a long time before ships became available to transport the Australian servicemen and their families.

'We don't know anything about it yet,' Pearl assured everyone. 'So let's make the most of the time we've got.'

Jenny could see Thea was looking distressed, so she said the first thing that came to mind as a distraction. 'Have you thought of a name yet? At this rate we'll still be calling her "baby" and "little one" when she turns eighteen.'

'As a matter of fact, we have,' Pearl said. 'Everyone, this is Rose Clara Tallis.' She grinned. 'Greg and I took her for a walk in the rose garden this afternoon and we were inspired.'

'I think it's the perfect name,' Thea said. She was holding the baby at that point, and she stroked her cheek with a gentle finger. 'What do you think, little Rosie?'

Rose gripped the finger and stared at her aunt with solemn blue eyes. Thea laughed. 'I think she approves. What about you, Deedee?'

Deedee had been dabbing her eyes with a handkerchief, which she now hastily put away. 'I couldn't think of a better name,' she said, her voice suspiciously hoarse. Jenny remembered then that Pearl and Thea's mother had been called Clara.

'Actually, I've got some news too,' Thea said. 'Fitz and I have booked our wedding.' She looked at Pearl. 'We wanted to be married while we're still all together.'

Pearl beamed. 'That's wonderful! When?'

'The twenty-ninth of September. At All Saints in Fenthorpe. It's going to be very small, just family and no fuss, but we'd love the two of you to be bridesmaids.'

And for a while, in the happy discussion that followed, Jenny forgot her dismay at the thought of being separated from her friends.

As Pearl recommended, in the days that followed Jenny did her best not to worry too much about how she was going to cope when Pearl, Greg and Rose left but tried to enjoy the time that still remained with them all together. However, one day in early September, when they were proudly pushing Rose in her pram through Fenthorpe, she saw Mrs Fox. Just like every other woman they had passed that day, she stopped to admire the baby. Seeing her give a wistful smile, Jenny knew she must be thinking of her own daughter and mourning the fact that she would never see Rita's children.

When she and Thea returned to their hut that evening, she burst out, 'I wish we could find out the truth about Rita's death. Every time I see Richie's smug face I want to punch him, because I'm sure he was responsible.'

'I feel the same way,' Thea said, 'but you must be careful. Granted, Richie's a nasty piece of work, but that doesn't make him a killer.' She gave a wry smile. 'I can't believe I'm cautioning you to be careful.'

'That's because you're about to get married, so you're all grown up.' Jenny could only pray that her comment hadn't revealed her own dissatisfaction with her life. It was hard to see her best friends happily planning their futures when she herself felt she was no further forward.

'Says the woman who's going to change the world,' Thea said. 'If anyone's grown up, it's you. I can't believe how far you've come. That reminds me – did you speak to Thomas?'

'Yes, I meant to tell you. I saw him yesterday. What with the excitement surrounding the baby, I forgot until now.'

'And?' Thea, who had picked up her sponge bag and had been about to head to the ablutions block, dropped it on the bed and gazed at Jenny expectantly.

'It went better than I'd thought it would, actually. He was very encouraging. He knows I want to get some qualifications, and he suggested that I could do evening classes. In the meantime he said that he would be happy to employ me when I eventually leave the WAAF if I wanted to stay in Lincoln. And if I move elsewhere, he said he'd be more than happy to recommend me to one of his contacts elsewhere in the country.'

'I'm so glad,' Thea cried. 'I told you he would come up trumps.'

'Yes, well, he also made a suggestion that's got me quaking in my shoes. He said there was nothing stopping me from getting a degree if I put my mind to my studies. He said I'd probably educated myself to Higher School Certificate standard on several subjects already so it would be worth seeing if I could take some formal exams and try to get into university.'

'I can see it now,' Thea said, 'you dressed up in robes and a mortarboard, getting your degree.'

'It would be a dream come true,' Jenny said.

She pulled a book down from her little library, and a ten-shilling note fluttered out. For a moment she couldn't work out what it was doing there, then she remembered it was the note she'd had from Mrs Fox. Something dawned on her, something that had been niggling at the back of her mind ever since Rita's mother had told her about the money.

'I've just remembered something,' she said.

'What's that?' Thea asked absently, picking up her towel.

'The money Mrs Fox gave me a while back. She said it was the last of the notes Rita had given her that day. Don't you think it strange she had that much money on her?'

Thea nodded slowly. 'I suppose it is strange considering she can't have had much money to spare.'

'Well, then I remembered what Rita had been saying when I overheard her that time. She said Richie would be sorry if she let slip what she knew.'

Thea went still. 'Are you saying she blackmailed him? Be careful, Jenny. It's hardly going to make things any easier for Mrs Fox if it turns out Rita was blackmailing people.'

'I know. But it would explain how she had all that money.'

'But we still don't know anything for sure, and we can't prove anything. We're not any further forward.'

Jenny reluctantly agreed, then she collected her own wash things and followed Thea to the ablutions block.

–

The next day happened to be pay parade, and she was still mulling over the ten-shilling note, wondering if there was any way of linking the money to Richie. She was so lost in thought she jumped when the person standing next to her poked her in the ribs. 'They just called your name,' her neighbour whispered.

Feeling her face flaming, she marched forward to the pay table, saluted, and gave her name and the last three digits of her serial number. At the same time she held out her left hand to take her pay. Once she'd walked away she put away her money, idly noting that the serial numbers on the notes were consecutive; but of course that made sense if the money was issued centrally. She didn't think much about it at first but then, just as she reached the Watch Office, her thoughts drifted to the ten-shilling note she'd had from Mrs Fox and she stopped dead in the doorway.

'Mind what you're doing,' a WAAF said, pushing past.

'Sorry.' Jenny recollected herself and hurried to the Met Office, her head in a whirl.

She fidgeted so badly all the way through her shift that for the first time ever she earned herself a reprimand from the duty officer. She had never known a watch to pass so slowly; every time she looked at the clock she was amazed to see how little the hands had moved in the age since she had last looked. When she was finally relieved at the end of the watch she dashed to the NAAFI, where she had arranged to meet Thea prior to heading across to the Gatehouse.

'I've had an idea!' She waved her wages in Thea's face almost before her friend had had a chance to sit down.

'What – that you're going to give me all your pay from now on?'

'No, you dope. The serial numbers!'

Thea sighed. 'I've just spent hours fiddling around trying to get *J-Jackson*'s altimeter to unstick so it doesn't look like we're perched on the top of Mount Everest, and now I'm not in the mood for riddles. Please explain to me in simple language that Rose would understand, because that's all I can cope with.'

'I'll try, but I haven't got it all sorted out yet. Have you got your pay on you?'

Thea fished it out of her pocket and Jenny compared the notes to her own. 'Yes, look. You're before me in the alphabet, and the serial numbers on your notes are consecutive but lower than mine.'

'Are you going to explain what you mean before I die of old age?'

Jenny drew in a deep breath. 'We think the money Rita gave to her mother was from the money she got from Richie, right?'

'Yes, but I don't see—'

'The Accounts Section must keep pay ledgers, and you know what a stickler the RAF is for recording everything. If the money issued at each pay parade consists of notes of consecutive serial numbers, what's the betting the pay ledgers record the serial numbers? If we could take a look, we could check the records against the ten-shilling note Mrs Fox gave me. We might be able to track it to Richie's pay.'

'Jenny, be realistic. Even if the serial number does match with a note Richie was issued, it doesn't necessarily mean he gave it to her. He might have spent it in the pub and then it was given to Rita later in her change.'

'But it would be a start!' Jenny couldn't understand why Thea was being so reluctant, and put it down to tiredness. 'It would give us some connection between the money and Richie. Then we could take it to the police and surely they would investigate from there.'

'I suppose you're right. How do you propose to get a look at the ledgers?'

This was more difficult. Jenny didn't know any of the WAAFs who worked in admin, who might have access.

'I think we'll have to be completely open about it and just ask the officer in charge of the Accounts Section if we can see it.'

Thea chewed her lip, appearing to consider this. 'It might be easier if we ask Fitz or Greg to do it for us.' She hesitated before adding, 'Or Edwin.'

Jenny could see the sense in this, much as she would prefer it not to be true. Their officer friends would probably already be acquainted with the officer in question, considering they all lived in Fenthorpe Hall and shared the same mess. It would be easier for them to approach him in a casual way and ask it as a favour. 'Fine. We'll ask Fitz or Edwin this evening. Not Greg. He's already got too much on with Rose.'

Thea nodded and got up. 'I suppose we ought to head across now.'

They went and signed out at the gate, and were surprised to see Fitz and Edwin waiting on the other side.

'Change of plan,' Fitz said. 'Rose has been colicky all day and they've just got her to sleep. They're not up to visitors, so we've decided to go to the Piebald Pony instead. Fancy coming?'

'It sounds more appealing than a colicky baby,' Thea said, weaving her arm round Fitz's. 'Coming, Jenny?'

'Why not?' She fell into step with Edwin.

It was pleasant to be back in adult company, Edwin reflected as he put the glasses he was carrying down on their usual corner table. Now that baby Rose had arrived, it was funny how all their activities revolved around her. Edwin was as besotted as everyone else with the baby and was sorry she had not been well, yet he also couldn't help enjoying the freedom of being with his friends that evening. He had scarcely had a moment alone with Jenny since their seaside break. Granted, Fitz and Thea were also there, but they hardly counted as they had their arms around each other and were talking in low voices. From the soppy expression on Fitz's face, Edwin decided he had no desire to hear what they were saying. Thankfully, the racket Richie Evans, Ben Newton and their friends were making on the next table drowned out his friends' words.

Jenny squeezed into the seat beside Edwin. 'I'm glad we've got a chance to speak,' she said, 'because I wanted to ask a favour.'

'Anything,' Edwin promised.

She gave a wry smile. 'You might want to hear what it is before you make any promises.'

'Go on.' He was intrigued rather than wary.

Instead of speaking, Jenny pulled a ten-bob note from her pocket and handed it to him.

'What's this for? You don't have to pay me.'

'It's not payment. It's the exact note Mrs Fox gave me when I ran some errands for her. It was taken from a roll of money she was given by Rita on the night she died.' She paused and shot a glance at the rowdy men at the table next to them. Following her gaze, Edwin saw that, although Ben was leaning back in his chair looking bored, the others were all absorbed in listening to Richie. Evidently reassured by what she saw, she launched into her tale. 'Remember when we overheard Rita essentially threatening blackmail? Well, I think this is from the money she was given.'

Edwin listened with growing interest as she explained about the serial numbers and the message Rita had jotted on the note.

'So you see,' Jenny concluded, 'if we can take a look at the pay ledger, we can see if any of the serial numbers of the notes given to Richie match.'

Edwin had to admit he was impressed. 'I can't believe you kept the note all this time.'

'I probably wouldn't if it hadn't been for Rita's message. At first I kept it because I thought Mrs Fox might like to have it back, despite what she said, but then I hung on to it because it was a reminder to me not to give up until we'd found the truth.'

Edwin looked at her earnest face and knew this was one of the reasons he loved her – her determination to see justice done. He supposed it came from the same source as her drive to improve herself. She didn't just want a better life for herself but for everyone else too. Who else would have taken care of Lily and made sure she had a job to go to once her baby had been adopted?

'Of course I'll help,' he said. 'Flight Lieutenant Jarvis works in the Accounts Section and I know him fairly well. I'll see if I can persuade him.'

Jenny's blazing smile was all the thanks he needed. He took the ten-shilling note and tucked it safely into his pocket.

Later that evening, when it was time to leave, he noticed Ben murmur something to Richie and then glance at Jenny.

There was something about that look that made him uneasy and he remembered that Ben hadn't been engaged in conversation when Jenny had been explaining about Rita's money. He could only hope that he hadn't overheard and was now telling Richie. But no. If he had overheard then he would also have known that Jenny and Edwin considered Richie a murder suspect, and he didn't think Ben would want to protect someone like that. He was just getting jumpy and overprotective of Jenny.

However, his wariness made him hear sinister rustlings in the bushes after they left the street lights of Fenthorpe behind. Now they were into September, the nights were drawing in. Somehow the lights shining out from RAF Fenthorpe only seemed to make the shadows deeper. Edwin found himself shining his torch beam this way and that with every unexpected movement he heard in the overgrown verge. *Idiot*, he said to himself. *It's probably just rabbits.* Yet he couldn't relax. When they reached the junction where they would usually part company, he thought he caught a movement in the corner of his eye. With the hairs on the back of his neck standing up, he strained all his senses but could detect no more movement.

Even so, he said, 'We'll walk you to the gate this evening.' He tried turning it into a joke, embarrassed by his jumpiness. 'I'm sure Fitz and Thea won't mind a few extra minutes together.'

No one objected and so they carried on to the Waafery entrance together. Edwin remained alert throughout but heard nothing more sinister than an owl and the distant yelp of a fox. He really shouldn't let his imagination get carried away like that. Still, when he said goodbye to Jenny he promised to see Flight Lieutenant Jarvis at the earliest opportunity.

Jenny felt on edge the whole of the next day. In the morning the camp was busy with more flights taking supplies to the troops on the Continent. Jenny went about her work, wondering if Edwin had had a chance to speak to the pay officer, and when he came into the Met Office to get the latest weather report she shot him an enquiring glance.

'Sorry,' he muttered. 'Thea needed my help to test the air position indicator. I haven't had time for anything else. I'll have to see the pay officer when I get back.'

The trouble was, now that she had come up with the plan she wanted everything to be resolved as soon as possible. She toyed with the idea of visiting the accounts office herself, but had to abandon the idea when she was asked to cover the night watch for a WAAF who had gone down with a stomach bug. Instead she snatched what sleep she could in the afternoon, and rose when the sky was gaudy with a sunset in all hues from gold to purple.

Night duty hadn't been so bad at midsummer, when the skies remained light for most of the night, but now they were on the cusp of autumn it meant going out in the dark to take the readings. The first couple of trips weren't too bad, because there were still plenty of lights shining out of the windows and, with the end of the blackout, outside lighting had been set up around the paths. However, as the night went on the office lights blinked out one by one, leaving Jenny with only the illumination around the paths and that of her own torch. Still, she had done this countless times before, so she wasn't too bothered, and at least now she was able to carry a more powerful torch.

She had been fidgety all evening, frustrated that she wouldn't have a chance to see Edwin. Had he found time to speak to the pay officer and, if so, what had he found? She was itching to find out. By nine thirty, when she was on her way out to take the next set of observations, she even considered making a quick detour to the telephone box so she could call him.

She switched on her torch and turned off the lit main path and down the track leading to the Stevenson screen. She had just opened the door and was shining her light on the instruments within when a shadowy shape stepped out from behind her. She jumped violently, letting out a squeak of fright.

'Hello, Jenny.'

It was Ben. Jenny clapped a hand to her chest, feeling the violent pounding of her heart gradually ease. 'Ben! You made me jump a mile. What are you doing here?'

'I came to see you. I heard you were on duty tonight.'

There was a slight edge to his voice that made her uneasy. She held up her torch to illuminate his face, and shivered a little at the menacing appearance of a pale face against a dark background.

'That's nice, but I don't really have time to speak. Perhaps we could meet tomorrow?'

'No. We'll speak now. Give me that ten-shilling note.'

'What? Why should I give you any money? You earn more than me.' Jenny couldn't make sense of the situation. He couldn't possibly know about Rita's money, could he?

'I'm not talking about just any money. I want the note you got from Mrs Fox.'

Steely fingers closed around her upper arm in a bruising grip, and she cried out in shock, dropping her torch. Instantly a hand closed round her mouth and she felt herself being pulled back against his chest. She struggled to break free and bit down on the fleshy part of his thumb, but all she got in return was a slap round the face that shocked her into silence. By the time she had recovered her wits to attempt a scream, the hand had pressed across her mouth and nose again, this time clamping her jaw shut.

A voice hissed in her ear. 'Shut up, you bitch. Just give me the money and I'll let you go.' He felt in her pockets, flinging out pencils, her handkerchief and her treasured birthday lipstick with a cry of disgust.

Jenny, confused at the suddenness of the attack, tried to kick his shins, but he was holding her so close she couldn't get a good angle.

'Where is it?' Ben demanded, giving her a shake. Tears of shock and confusion splashed down her cheeks, and he gave an exclamation of disgust. 'Don't pretend you don't know what

I'm talking about. I saw you put it in your pocket last night, so where is it?'

How she was supposed to answer with his hand smothering her, she had no idea. Shock was turning into real fear now. Just forcing breath in and out of her lungs was taking her whole concentration. She was overwhelmed by the mingled salty, cheesy smell of his hand, and her senses swam.

As if from a great distance she heard him curse. 'If I remove my hand, will you promise not to scream?'

She would promise anything if it meant getting a breath of clean air. She nodded.

Ben's hand moved from her mouth only to rest lightly around her throat in a gesture of warning, but she was too busy gulping in fresh air to try fighting him off or shouting.

Ben spoke again. 'Where is it?'

'I don't have it. Why are you doing this to me?'

'Why?' He gave a bitter laugh that sent shivers down her spine. 'I heard you discussing it with your precious boyfriend last night, that's why.'

'But it was Richie—'

'Richie? He hasn't got the brains to do anything other than what I tell him. I was the one with the sense to keep quiet and pay off that Rita woman when she started to make a fuss.' He snorted. 'Only then she thought she'd be clever and try it on with Richie too, so I had to shut her up.'

Shards of ice pierced her chest and once more she was struggling to draw breath. This time it was from sheer panic. Ben was the murderer! And now she was at his mercy.

'I'm going to ask you one last time. Where is that note?'

Knowing this was her last chance, she managed to raise her leg and rake her heel down Ben's shin, stamping on his foot for good measure. He howled, loosening his grip just enough for her to tear herself free. She sprang forward, yelling for help, only to step on her torch. It rolled under her foot, turning her ankle. She crashed to the ground, and then Ben was on top of her, his knee in her back, forcing her face into a soft patch of mud.

'I'll show you what I did to that bitch Rita.' He pressed harder.

She struggled for breath but the combination of grass and soft earth filled her mouth and nose with every inhale, sealing out the air. Ben's voice faded and her vision turned grey.

Chapter Twenty-Six

What with flying supplies that morning, Edwin had been too busy plotting routes and checking the forecast for the predicted wind speeds to find Flight Lieutenant Jarvis. Then, thanks to a problem with *J-Jackson*'s port inner engine, they had needed to land at an airfield in Belgium while the flight engineer made hasty repairs, helped by some of the ground crew. By the time they got back to RAF Fenthorpe, the man had already gone off duty and was no longer at the base. By now Rita's ten-bob note was burning a hole in his pocket and he was anxious for some answers.

Edwin finally ran into Jarvis in the anteroom at Fenthorpe Hall. 'Evening, Jarvis,' he said, dropping into a nearby armchair. Having had the whole day to figure out his approach, he'd toyed with the idea of claiming he needed the information for a bet, but in the end opted to tell the truth. 'I wonder if you could do me a favour?' he asked once they had got the initial pleasantries out of the way.

'I'll try,' Jarvis replied. 'What do you need?'

Edwin poured out his tale, knowing how ridiculous it sounded but hoping Jarvis wouldn't dismiss him out of hand.

When he had finished, Jarvis said, 'Let me get this straight. You want me to go through the pay ledger to compare the serial numbers with the number on the ten-bob note your friend gave you?'

Edwin nodded. 'It's a long shot, I know, but if there's any chance this ties into Rita Fox's death, I have to look into it.'

Jarvis looked thoughtful. 'That was a bad business. And right outside the station, too.' He rose. 'Come on, then. No time like the present.'

Edwin stood, confused. 'You want to go back to your office now? There's no real hurry, you know.'

'But I'll be busy all day and won't have a chance to go through my books until the evening. Far better to do it now.' He glanced at the clock. 'There's a transport leaving for the station in five minutes, so if we can hop on that we'll have the job done in no time.'

Edwin couldn't argue with him, especially as Jarvis was doing him a favour. Mentally saying goodbye to the quiet evening spent with his science journals, he followed Jarvis outside.

The admin block at RAF Fenthorpe was in darkness when they arrived. Jarvis went in and unlocked his office door, flicking the light switch as he did so, and Edwin blinked at the sudden blaze of light.

Jarvis opened a filing cabinet. 'Right. What date do you think Evans would have received the note?'

Edwin thought about it. 'Rita gave it to her mother on VE Day, so it would be before then.'

Jarvis pulled out a ledger and went to sit at his desk. He leafed through a few pages, then leaned close to inspect the handwritten entries.

'Here are the records for that time. We had a pay parade the week before VE Day.' He leafed through a few more pages, muttering to himself. 'Let me see... let me see.' Edwin took a seat on the other side of the desk, squinting at the upside-down writing, trying to read it as Jarvis ran his finger down the list of names. The ticking of the clock marked out the seconds as each one slipped by. Tired out from his busy day, he found himself nodding off and was startled awake by Jarvis stabbing his finger at the page, announcing, 'Here's the serial numbers of the banknotes we were issued. What's the number on the note you got from your friend?'

Edwin read it out, and Jarvis scowled. 'It's from this batch all right. I was hoping you were mistaken. I don't like to think one of our lot was involved in that business.'

Edwin sat up, his tiredness gone. 'Can you work out who the note was issued to?'

'Give me a moment. We don't list which notes are given to each person but, as they're issued in numerical order, I can work it out.' He bent over the book, checking names and jotting numbers on a scrap of paper. Finally, he announced, 'I've got it!'

'Well? Was it Richie Evans?'

'No. Sergeant Benjamin Newton.'

Edwin's blood turned to ice. And he had thought Ben might have overheard him talking to Jenny last night. Not to mention the figure shadowing them that had only disappeared when Edwin had declared he would accompany the women to the gate.

He swore and dashed for the door.

Jarvis called out after him, 'Where are you going?'

'To warn Jenny. She's on night watch tonight.'

'What should I do?'

'Call the police. They need to be told.'

Please let her be safely inside! The Watch Office, where the Met Office was housed, stood at the far side of the cluster of buildings, its squat, square outline a black silhouette just visible against the night sky. Until now, Edwin had never registered just how far it was between the admin block and the Watch Office, but now, as he raced across the paths, gravel crunching beneath his feet, it seemed endless. At last he reached the door and opened it with such force that it slammed against the wall. He tore down the corridor and threw himself into the Met Office, but his heart sank when he saw that there was no sign of Jenny, just a flight lieutenant fiddling with the teleprinter.

'Where's Jenny?' Edwin demanded.

The man's eyebrows shot towards his hairline. 'What the devil are you doing here?'

'She might be in danger. Where is she?'

'Who?'

Edwin had to resist the urge to throttle him. 'Jenny. Jenny Hazleton.'

'She must be out taking the latest observations.'

In the dark. Alone. Edwin had already run outside before he realised he wasn't sure where the various weather instruments were located. He slapped his forehead. *Think! She must have told you.*

Then he remembered. The roof! She had definitely said something before about enjoying the view from the roof. He pelted round the building until he came to the staircase running up the outside. The steel treads rang as he bounded up them two at a time. Gasping for breath, he reached the top and shone his torch beam around. The roof was deserted.

Then a cry, abruptly broken off, sent him to the railing. He peered out, his eyes straining to pierce the darkness, staring in the direction from which the cry had come. Was it his imagination, or was there movement about fifty yards from the tower's base? Then he heard another cry, and he didn't wait any more but flew down the steps and ran full pelt into the darkness. As he got closer to the spot where he had seen the dark shapes, he could make out a voice. A male voice, distorted in anger. His lungs were bursting by this time but he couldn't allow himself to stop. The man was bent over a figure on the ground, pressing it down. Now he could see the figure on the ground was smaller, slighter. A woman. She was struggling but making no sound.

Then he saw that the man was forcing her face into the mud and he didn't think. He raised the arm holding his torch and brought it slamming down upon the attacker's head. The man gave a grunt and pitched forward, then lay still.

Edwin, panting, dragged the man's limp body off the woman and then turned her over. Immediately she drew a deep, rasping breath, sobbing and coughing. Now Edwin could see that it was, indeed, Jenny. He flung himself onto his knees beside her and eased her into a sitting position. She slumped forward, folding her arms across her knees, still alternately gasping and coughing.

He put a supporting arm around her shoulders. 'You're safe now, Jenny. I'm here. I won't let him hurt you again.' He hardly knew what he was saying, but he needed to reassure her after the terrifying experience she had been through.

He gave her time to regain her breath, rubbing her shoulders and murmuring soothing words that probably didn't make sense, but he needed to let her know she was safe. While he waited for her to recover, he shone his torch at the man and wasn't at all surprised to see it was Ben. He spared just enough attention to check his pulse and ensure he was breathing before returning to Jenny.

She raised her head from her knees and stared up at him. 'It was Ben!'

'I know. He had us both fooled.'

She coughed again, then scrubbed her hand over her mouth. 'He killed Rita.' Her face crumpled. 'He wanted to kill me.'

Edwin held her gently, letting her cry. He couldn't tell how badly she was hurt, but she must be in shock at the very least, and he felt helpless. He knew he ought to get her inside but he didn't want to leave Ben unattended. There was no way he was going to let him get away with what he had done.

He had just decided that Jenny's needs came first and was about to help her to her feet when he heard a shout. He sat up straight, listening. It came again – a voice calling his name.

'Over here!' He stood up, waving his torch, and was rewarded by the sight of three figures approaching. He called again, then sat back beside Jenny, whose sobs were slowly subsiding.

When the men got closer he saw it was Jarvis accompanied by three members of the RAF police.

'Sergeant Newton needs to be turned in to the civilian police,' he said. 'He killed Rita Fox, and he also tried to kill

275

Jenny. He should probably have some medical attention,' he added as an afterthought.

–

An hour later, he left the room where they had interviewed Richie and hurried to sick quarters, anxious to know how Jenny was faring. He met the MO emerging from a side room. 'I thought you'd be along. You can see her for five minutes. No more.'

'Is she all right?'

'No lasting injuries, thankfully, although we're treating her for shock, and she'll be bruised and sore for a while.'

Jenny was sitting up in bed, wearing a hospital gown. All the grime and blood had been cleaned from her face, and he drew a sharp breath at the bruising around her mouth and nose that was now revealed in the harsh electric light.

She smiled, then winced, the action having evidently pulled her cut lip. 'I look a sight, don't I?' Her voice was rather hoarse; Edwin poured her a glass of water from the jug by her bedside.

She took a sip and when she spoke again her voice was stronger. 'You always seem to know what I need. You're the eppy tome of a gentleman.'

It only took him a moment to work out what she meant. 'Is it gentlemanly to point out it's pronounced epitome?'

She pulled a face. 'It is, because at least you're stopping me making the same mistake twice. I wish I didn't keep getting words wrong, though.'

'If it makes you feel any better, I thought caveat was pronounced cave-at until I used it in a university debate. Needless to say, I lost.' He perched on the end of her bed. 'Anyway, I'm relieved to see you smiling. For an awful moment I thought I was too late.' He shuddered, unable to dispel the sight of Ben Newton savagely pressing Jenny's face into the ground.

The feel of Jenny's fingers squeezing his hand recalled him to the present. 'But you weren't and that's all that matters. I can't thank you enough for saving me. How did you know I needed help?'

'That was Jarvis's doing,' he told her, perching on the end of her bed. 'He insisted we look up the serial numbers tonight. I nearly had a heart attack when I saw that ten-shilling note had been Ben's. I knew I had to warn you. When I went to the Met Office and heard you were out on your own, I was frantic.'

It was Jenny's turn to shudder. 'I thought I was going to die, and then you came from nowhere and saved me.' A pause, and then, 'What's happening with Ben?'

'He's been arrested for your attempted murder and Rita's murder. They've arrested Richie too. It all came out when they questioned Richie. Apparently the two of them had been selling the Benzedrine and caffeine pills crews were given on missions. Richie says it was all Ben's idea, and I think I believe him. Poor Rita got involved because she was so desperately tired all the time, she jumped at the chance when Richie offered to sell her pills to pep her up. Then when ops tailed off before VE Day, they couldn't get hold of pills any more, and Rita got desperate.'

'Poor Rita,' Jenny said. 'No wonder she looked so awful when we saw her at the dance.'

Edwin nodded. 'Richie said that when Rita threatened to tell the police, he'd wanted to call her bluff, not believing she really meant to go through with it. But Ben wasn't convinced and he paid her off.'

'Then why did he kill her?'

Edwin took off his cap and raked his fingers through his hair, remembering Richie's terrified face. He had practically fallen over himself to confess, plainly fearing he would face murder charges along with Ben if he didn't reveal all.

'It was Ben that Rita had arranged to meet at the pub that night, not Richie. But Richie was with him.'

Realisation dawned on Jenny's face. 'Of course. I remember now that Rita's friends said they had seen Rita approach Richie and another chap. I never questioned that it was Richie she wanted to see.'

'Nor me. But apparently she asked again for Benzedrine and got desperate when Ben said their supplies had dried up. Then Ben said he thought he knew where he could get some if she came with him. Richie saw them leave, and after Rita was found dead he knew Ben must have killed her, afraid she would give them away.'

Jenny looked horrified. 'So he lured her out alone by pretending he could get hold of more pills?' She shuddered. 'Poor Rita.'

Edwin simply nodded, still shaken at how close Jenny had come to the same fate.

'Where's Ben now?' Jenny asked, looking around as though she expected him to walk through the door at any moment.

'Relax,' he said. 'He's in hospital in Lincoln because I knocked him out cold.' He was taken aback at the satisfaction he felt at saying that. For someone who had agonised over the killing of the German soldier, he was surprised at how little regret he felt over his treatment of Ben.

'Good.' Then Jenny studied him, narrowing her eyes. 'Please tell me you don't feel guilty. Because he would have killed me if you hadn't stopped him.'

However, before he could reassure her that he had no regrets, the door opened and the MO stuck his head inside. 'Your five minutes are over,' he said.

'Wait,' Jenny said. 'There's one more thing I have to say.'

The MO gave a reluctant nod and withdrew.

Jenny drew a deep breath. 'I just want you to know how grateful I am for what you did. Your quick thinking saved my life.' She paused. 'And it probably saved both yours and Greg's life back in Holland. Promise me you'll remember that.'

Edwin opened his mouth to reply but stopped when Jenny gave a huge yawn. Instead he stooped and kissed her cheek. 'I promise,' he said. 'Now go to sleep and I'll see you tomorrow.'

His last sight of her before he closed the door was of her lifting her hand to her cheek, looking dazed.

As he headed off to the gate, he wondered if he could finally lay his ghosts to rest and tell Jenny how he felt. Only time would tell.

Chapter Twenty-Seven

'Are you sure you're all right?' Pearl asked Jenny for about the hundredth time.

Before she answered Jenny shook her hair over her shoulder, trying to keep it away from Rose's eager fingers. 'I'm fine. A little stiff and bruised, that's all. And I was bored out of my mind in sick quarters.'

The MO had insisted she remain there for the whole of the day following the attack, and Jenny had not minded too much. She hadn't felt up to answering the barrage of questions that were sure to come her way the moment she returned to her hut in the Waafery. It had been bad enough reliving the experience when the police had arrived to take her statement and again when Thea had burst into the room, white-faced, demanding to know what had happened. Still, Thea had proved a great help for she had persuaded the MO to release her the next day, saying Thomas and Deedee had invited her to spend the day there. Five minutes after she had been settled in the most comfortable armchair, Pearl had arrived with Rose, and playing with the baby had helped dispel the bad memories.

Surprisingly, she also found that it had helped to describe what had happened to Pearl and Deedee. She had spent most of her day in sick quarters alone, for Thea had been on duty and the men had been flying another supply mission. Having nothing but the book that Thea had dropped in did little to distract her and she had relived the attack over and over. However, when she had spoken of it, it seemed to release the nightmare from her mind.

Finally, when Deedee disappeared into the kitchen to see about lunch, Jenny asked, 'Do you know if Greg or' – she hesitated, then took the plunge – 'or Edwin will be round later?'

'I don't know. Greg telephoned earlier to say they were flying again today, so it certainly won't be before the evening. Why?' Pearl gave her an arch smile. 'Were you hoping to give Edwin a special hero's thank-you?'

'Well, yes, but I really just wanted to make sure he was all right. Everyone's asking me how I feel but he put Ben in hospital, and I'm worried how he'll react after—' She closed her mouth, appalled that she'd nearly let slip about Edwin's horror of shooting the German soldier.

'Don't worry, I know what happened in Holland,' Pearl assured her. 'Greg told me he'd shot a soldier and, although he didn't go into Edwin's reaction, I can see that it affected him deeply.'

Jenny released her breath. 'He told me more about it when we were in the Forest of Dean.' She picked her way carefully, not wanting to break a confidence. 'I thought he was getting over it, but in that case why hasn't he told me how he feels? He's not with Mina any more and, at the risk of sounding bigheaded, I'm sure he loves me.'

'You don't sound big-headed. I don't know what's stopping him either, but I can tell he does love you.'

Jenny sighed. 'It used to make me feel better to hear you or Thea say that, but now I think what's the point? It doesn't make any difference if he loves me if he won't do anything about it. And I'm starting to worry that one or the other of us will get transferred or demobbed before anything changes. If that happens, we might never see one another again.'

'Well, whatever happens, you're going to see him on Saturday.'

'Why?' Then Jenny clapped her hand to her mouth. 'Thea's wedding! I didn't forget, honestly. It's just—'

'So much has happened,' Pearl finished for her. 'It's completely understandable. Anyway, perhaps it will be best if you don't see much of Edwin until then. It will give you a chance to work out what to say.'

'What *I'm* going to say?' Jenny looked at her friend in surprise.

'Yes, why not? You want to know one way or the other, don't you?'

Jenny wanted to ask what she was supposed to say to Edwin but at that moment Rose squirmed in her arms, screwed up her tiny face and started to wail.

'I think she wants a feed.' Pearl sniffed and pulled a face. 'And probably a change.' She took the baby from Jenny and disappeared up to Deedee's bedroom, leaving Jenny alone with her thoughts.

Should she speak to Edwin? She still hadn't entirely got over the embarrassment of the last time she had tried to make the first move. Yet the VE Day kiss had left her in no doubt of his deep attraction to her and since then she had waited and waited for him to speak. And now time was running out, for she was sure it couldn't be long before they were separated. So why was she hesitating?

Because you're not good enough for him. The voice in her mind had been silent for a while but now it was back. She knew why. Edwin would be returning to Cambridge as soon as he was demobbed, returning to one of the most prestigious places of learning. Jenny hadn't even got her school certificate.

She was still swamped in these unhappy thoughts when Thea burst in, carrying a huge flat box.

'Look what I got!' She lifted the lid to reveal a froth of creamy lace.

'You got a wedding dress!' Jenny gasped. 'I thought you were going to get married in your uniform.' They'd had a long conversation about it the day Thea had announced the date.

'I know but I was walking through Lincoln earlier and I found my feet taking me to Miss Honeycroft's house.' Miss Honeycroft hired out wedding dresses to brides who were struggling to find a gown in these times of strict rationing. 'And I thought why not pop in to see if she has a dress? I thought she would laugh and send me away when I told her how soon I needed it, but she was so kind. And guess what? Remember the flapper dress I loved when we were choosing Pearl's gown? Well, it's available and it fits perfectly. There's a matching veil and shoes and now I can't believe I ever thought I'd be happy marrying in my dowdy old uniform.'

It was Thea's joy and excitement that decided Jenny. One day soon, she would like to be anticipating her wedding to Edwin with the same eagerness, and that wasn't going to happen unless one of them made the first move. So what if she'd been humiliated the first time she had tried to show him how she felt? Wasn't it worth the risk to experience the same happiness as Thea?

She only belatedly noticed that Thea had stopped speaking and was regarding her with a grin.

'You're thinking about Edwin, aren't you?' Thea said. 'Have you decided to take matters into your own hands?'

'I have. I've given up worrying about him rejecting me again. It doesn't matter that I'm not good enough for him, the next time I see him I'm going to let him know I can't wait any longer.'

'Good for you!' Then Thea frowned. 'Wait. What do you mean you're not good enough for him? That's not true!'

'But look at Mina. She's the most intelligent woman I know – she was at Cambridge and now she's at Bletchley. I can never compare to her.'

'You're wrong. She's not the most intelligent woman you know, because *you* are.'

'Don't be daft. I never even took my school cert.'

'All that means is that you grew up without the same advantages in life as Mina. But look at you. You didn't take the school cert but you've taught yourself to a much higher level through your own effort. You know more than I do, and I took

283

the Higher School Certificate. If you'd have been able to stay on at school, you'd have passed that with flying colours and Cambridge would have been begging you to study there. Why do you think Edwin always came to you for a forecast? Because he knew you were the most intelligent person in the Met Office and he didn't care you hadn't finished school. Anyway, he didn't love Mina, but he loves you.'

Jenny didn't get a chance to reply, for both Deedee and Pearl arrived back in the room and were demanding to see Thea's dress. As they exclaimed with delight over the beautiful Twenties-style gown, Jenny was relived to find herself out of the limelight with a moment to think. It was funny how a different viewpoint could change your perspective. She had been so wrapped up in her lack of formal qualifications that she hadn't appreciated the value others placed on her sheer determination to educate herself. And Thea was right – Edwin had always sought out her opinion on the weather forecast. Although she had thought it was just an excuse to see her, now she realised that he wouldn't have depended on her forecast if he didn't have faith in her intelligence. There had been too much at stake for that.

So the only question that remained was would she find the courage to risk her pride and heart one more time?

–

'How are you feeling now?' Edwin asked when Jenny took his arm and marched down the aisle to the organist's enthusiastic rendition of the wedding march. While she hadn't forgotten Pearl's advice to avoid Edwin, she'd decided she couldn't bear it. Annoyingly, though, their respective duties had kept them apart over the past few days, meaning the brief conversation in sick quarters was the last time they'd met until today.

'I'm fine, honestly.' Jenny kept her eyes fixed on Thea's back, although she was acutely aware of Edwin's nearness. She could swear her hand tingled where it touched his arm. Thea and

Fitz took their time, smiling and waving at friends and family as they passed. Although she couldn't see their expressions, she knew they would be bathed in the same joyous radiance they'd displayed throughout the service. It was a contagious delight that she could see reflected back from everyone in the congregation. Jenny couldn't help wishing she and Edwin were in their place and it was they who had just been married and were about to set out on a honeymoon to the Lake District. Still, if she stuck to her resolution, that might soon be the case.

She drew a deep breath. 'I'd like to talk to you when we can find a moment.' There. She'd done it. She couldn't chicken out now.

'We could talk while the photographer is working.'

Jenny glanced at Edwin in surprise, having expected him to say they should wait until they got to the Gatehouse. Could it be he was as eager to talk as her?

Edwin made good on his promise and led her a little way from the group crowded around the church door. He gazed at her, his expression serious. 'I wanted to speak to you, too, actually.'

'Let me go first.' Jenny was breathless with anxiety. What if he was going to say they shouldn't see each other any more? She wanted, *needed* to leave him in no doubt of her feelings so that, if this was the last they were going to see of one another, she would have the bleak comfort of knowing she had done everything in her power to bring them together. When he nodded, she blurted out the speech she had been mentally rehearsing ever since her day at the Gatehouse. 'I want you to know how much I' – she gulped – 'I love you, Edwin.' When working out the speech, she had opted to get the most difficult and important fact out at the beginning in case she forgot the rest of her lines in her panic. Edwin opened his mouth, but she ploughed on. 'You're the sweetest, most gentle man I know and also the most intelligent, and I love how you've never teased me for my lack of education but have encouraged me to keep reading and learning.'

285

'I—'

'I haven't finished yet. I've also seen how you struggled after you had to kill that soldier, but that only makes me love you all the more, because it shows that you never let your heart be hardened by the horrors you faced.' She was running out of breath now but she managed to gasp, 'And I'll always be grateful that you punched Ben's lights out.'

Her words had run out and all she could do was stand and stare at Edwin, waiting for his response. He was silent for so long that her heart sank like a lead weight.

When he did finally speak, his voice was a croak. 'Oh, Jenny, what did I do to deserve you? I love you.'

He pulled her close and kissed her. Her heart pounding in her ears, she kissed him back with enthusiasm, not caring that everyone could see. Her heart, which had been a dead weight only moments before now soared, light as a feather. He loved her!

When he broke the kiss, he wrapped his arms round her, and she happily nestled her head in the crook of his shoulder.

'I've been such an idiot,' Edwin said. 'I've loved you for about as long as I've known you, but I thought I didn't deserve you.'

Jenny looked at him, startled. 'I thought I didn't deserve you! I thought you'd look down on me because of my lack of education.'

'Just because you didn't stay on at school, it doesn't mean you lack education. You're one of the most learned women I know, and the fact that you're almost entirely self-taught makes you all the more extraordinary.' His gaze bored into hers, setting her insides all aflutter, and the last shred of doubt detached itself from her thoughts and drifted away. 'But I, on the other hand, felt so weighed down with guilt, and that's what was holding me back.'

'Guilt about the soldier?'

'Partly, but I've only recently realised there was a deeper guilt and it was all to do with Mina.'

Jealousy spiked her heart, and she had to remind herself that he had chosen her above Mina. 'Can you explain without breaking any confidence?'

He nodded, pulling her close again. 'I need to explain because I need you to be perfectly clear what an idiot I am before you answer my next question.'

'What question?'

'All in good time. You've had your say, now let me say my piece.'

Jenny was all in favour of staying enfolded in his embrace for as long as possible, so she didn't mind listening at all. She simply kissed his cheek, enjoying the faint scrape of stubble against her lips, then said, 'Go on, then.'

'I think I told you Mina was orphaned, and when I first knew her she had no family apart from a younger brother, Daniel. She was about as protective of him as Pearl is of Thea.'

Jenny gave a wry smile. 'I get the picture.'

'I got on well with him, and he' – Edwin cleared his throat, looking embarrassed – 'well, he hero-worshipped me. He turned eighteen in the second year of the war and he wanted to join the RAF to be like me. And I encouraged him. What I hadn't known is that he intended to volunteer as aircrew.'

'Oh no,' Jenny breathed, feeling a twist of sympathy. She could already see where his story was leading, because Mina had already told her this part. 'He was killed. And you blamed yourself?'

Edwin swallowed, his mouth tight. When he spoke, his voice sounded strained. 'He was a good mechanic. When he said he wanted to join the RAF, I imagined he would end up working with the ground crews. I never dreamed he wanted to fly with the bomber crews. I would never—' His voice cracked.

Jenny wished there was something she could say to ease his pain, but all she could do was hug him tighter and wait until he was ready to speak again.

'I can see now that his death made me feel more responsible for Mina. That's when I asked her to marry me. I thought a lot

287

of Mina but never really as more than a close friend. But she was lost and said yes, and that's why I could never break it off with her, even after I met you and realised I didn't love her. And I've carried that guilt with me for years. And then after Holland I felt tainted. I couldn't have put it into words at the time but that's why I couldn't tell you how I felt, even after Mina and I broke up. I felt, to use a Victorian phrase, unworthy of you.'

'I can't bear to hear you say that,' she cried. 'Every day I count myself lucky to know such a wonderful man who makes my heart sing.'

He pulled back a little so he could look into her eyes. 'Do you really mean that?'

'Of course I do.'

'Then can I ask you a question?'

Her heart thudded. She was suddenly sure she knew what he wanted to ask, and her chest felt so tight she couldn't draw the breath to speak, so she nodded and prayed she would hear the question above the swish of blood in her ears.

He took both her hands and lowered himself onto one knee. 'Jenny, will you marry me?'

She nodded, tears splashing down her face, then pulled him to his feet and kissed him.

She only pulled away when she became aware of a voice calling her name. Then the exasperated photographer yelled, 'Bridesmaids and best man!'

She giggled. 'I think they've been calling for a while.'

They went to join Thea and Fitz, where they were forced to separate. Jenny joined Pearl beside Thea and Edwin took his place beside Fitz.

'Finally,' the photographer said. He disappeared behind his camera for a while before emerging to say, 'Best man, perhaps you could wipe off the lipstick before I take the picture.'

Jenny felt her face flaming. Thea squeezed her hand. 'I'm really happy for you.'

Jenny beamed back at her. 'I'm happy for me, too.'

The celebrations at the Gatehouse went on until after dark, but eventually it was time for the bride and groom to leave for the train station. Once Thea and Fitz had hugged and kissed everyone goodbye, they all went outside to wave them off as Thomas drove them away.

'Things have a way of working out, don't they?' she said to Pearl when the car had disappeared into the darkness. She pretended not to notice the tears welling in Pearl's eyes. 'I'd started to think Edwin and I were never going to get together, and now look at us. And neither you nor Thea have had smooth rides through romance. But it all worked out in the end.'

'True,' Pearl said, 'although I doubt I could have got through the worst of it without Thea, Deedee and you. What I have with Greg, well, it's the best thing that's ever happened to me. But you and Thea and Deedee, and now Grandpa, you're all the best things that have happened to me too. What I'm trying to say is cherish every moment you have with Edwin but cherish your friends and family too. Because there's all sorts of love in this world, and it's all equally important.'

'You're right. I'm the luckiest person in the world to have you all in my life. And now little Rosie, too,' she added with a glance at the baby in Greg's arms. 'I know we'll all be going our separate ways soon, but I promise to write to you all as often as I can. I can't wait to hear about your adventures in Australia, and Thea and Fitz, wherever they end up being posted. I'm going to miss you all horribly but we'll never stop being friends.'

Edwin joined them and took her hand. She smiled at him. 'I was just saying how much I was going to miss everyone when they're gone.'

'I will too, but we'll get together again and when we do, think of the fun we'll have.'

Jenny flung her free arm around Pearl's shoulders. 'We will. But we're still all together now and, as Pearl says, I'm going to cherish every moment.'

She glanced up and saw the moon climbing into view above the treetops, a slender silvery crescent against the heavens. Yet more than the crescent was visible; she could also see the remainder of the disc, dimly illuminated by earthshine. Edwin squeezed her hand, letting her know he had also seen it. She leaned against him and now she looked at the moon through a haze of happy tears, secure in the knowledge that, however scattered her group of friends became, she would always have Edwin by her side.

Author's Note

Staying awake and alert throughout a bombing mission was a problem acknowledged by the RAF early in the war, and in November 1942 Benzedrine, the brand name of amphetamine sulphate, was approved for use by aircrews. However, although it is a powerful drug, I couldn't find any records of how (or even if) its use was monitored. In the memoirs and oral histories that had any reference to Benzedrine, the men simply mention being handed 'wakey-wakey pills' to take if needed. All very frustrating for a novelist, who needs specific details! I'm not saying that there aren't any records with the relevant information, just that I wasn't able to locate them. However, it was this lack of information that led me to dream up the drug-dealing and murder plot strand, and I must stress that it was entirely from my imagination.

Having said that, one part of the drug/murder strand was not a weird flight of my imagination. In February 1942 Leading Aircraftman Gordon Cummins committed a series of attacks on women in London, murdering four of them and earning the nickname of the Blackout Killer. One of the pieces of evidence that led the police to identify and arrest him was two pound notes he had given to one of his victims. These notes were new, and the police were able to use the serial numbers to trace them to Cummins, who had been given those notes in his pay on the same day as the attack. When I read about that a couple of years ago I knew I wanted to use it in a book, and I finally found a home for it here.

Acknowledgements

It's hard to believe I've reached the end of another series! I couldn't have got this far without all the encouragement I've had from my wonderful readers, so a special thank-you to everyone who has taken the time to leave a review or comment on social media. Your lovely words have spurred me on.

One aspect of Jenny's story that I had a lot of fun with is her quirk of mispronouncing words that she's encountered in books but not heard said aloud. I've no idea what the correct term for this is but I call them 'Jennyisms'. By the time I started writing *High Hopes for the Bomber Girls* I was running out of inspiration for more Jennyisms, and so I went online and asked the members of the Saga Sisters Facebook group. They rose to the challenge admirably, and I ended up using two from the resulting list: gazebo and epitome. Thank you to Susan Etty Winwood for your brilliant suggestions!

The cottage in the Forest of Dean where Jenny grew up was inspired by my great-grandparents' smallholding in the Forest of Dean. The cottage was gone long before I was born but thanks to a cousin, John Williams, I have an account that brings it to life. He wrote a memoir for the family, describing in vivid detail his childhood growing up on his grandparents' (my great-grandparents') smallholding in the 1930s. It's a beautiful account, complete with gorgeous sketches of the chickens in the yard and the range my great-grandmother used for cooking. I couldn't have written the Forest of Dean scenes without it, so a huge thank-you to John for helping me connect with the forester side of my family.

To my wonderful editor, Emily Bedford, and the whole team at Canelo, thank you for all the hard work that goes into making each book the best it can be. And, last but not least, many thanks to my amazing agent Lina Langlee for believing in me and giving me the support and encouragement to keep writing.